A
MOST RELENTLESS
GENTLEMAN

ALSO BY ELIZABETH COLE

Keep Me Close
Reach For Me

Honor & Roses
Choose the Sky
Raven's Rise
Peregrine's Call

A Heartless Design
A Reckless Soul
A Shameless Angel
The Lady Dauntless
Beneath Sleepless Stars
A Mad and Mindless Night

Regency Rhapsody: The Complete Collection

A MOST RELENTLESS GENTLEMAN

ELIZABETH COLE

SKYSPARK BOOKS

PHILADELPHIA, PENNSYLVANIA

SkySpark Books
Philadelphia, Pennsylvania
skysparkbooks.com
inquiry@skysparkbooks.com

Publisher's Note: This is a work of fiction. Names, characters, places, and incidents are a product of the author's imagination. Locales and public names are sometimes used for atmospheric purposes. Any resemblance to actual people, living or dead, or to businesses, companies, events, institutions, or locales is completely coincidental.

Ordering Information:
Quantity sales. Special discounts are available on quantity purchases by corporations, associations, and others. For details, contact the "Special Sales Department" at the address above.

A MOST RELENTLESS GENTLEMAN / Cole, Elizabeth. – 1st ed.
ISBN-13: 978-1-942316-35-0

♊

Summer 1811

IN ONE OF THE MORE exclusive neighborhoods of London, innovative gaslights illuminated major streets, while Charleys and private guards patrolled from the hour of nine in the evening until two in the morning. Many households kept dogs to sound the alarm should an intruder attempt to scale the walls or even pick a lock to gain entry into one of the many large and gracious homes.

Petty thieves spoke greedily of the treasures within— silver, jewelry, tea leaves, fine clothes, possibly a horse from the mews. But few dared to actually rob any of the grand edifices sitting among the emerald-green walled gardens. It was too dangerous, too likely to end in a gaol or the gallows, or passage to Australia courtesy of King George…never to return to English soil.

Those homes were safe from the ordinary criminal armies of London's underground.

They were not safe from the Black Mask.

Whatever else he was, the Black Mask was not ordinary. On that, everyone agreed. They also agreed he wore black clothing head to toe, wore black leather boots that allowed him to climb like a cat and run like a deer, and sported a black mask that covered half his face.

From the victims of his robberies, to the Charleys who tried to chase him through the streets, to the ladies who seemed to consider him a figure of romance rather than rapaciousness—like the elegant highwaymen of the previous century—everyone agreed that he was extraordinary.

He could slip through solid brick walls like a ghost.

He could charm the most vicious guard dogs into lolling pups.

He could open any lock, slide any bolt, find any hidden cache.

He could rob any house in London.

He could steal the silver from under a butler's nose, or a lady's heart from under her husband's watchful eye.

Oh, the stories were incredible.

As in unbelievable.

Who would believe that a woman might interrupt the Black Mask in the middle of a robbery, and not only fail to alert the authorities, but also fail to remember anything about him...other than that he was a dashing, handsome figure with the cheek of a street urchin and the manners of a gentleman?

Whether kitchen maid or lady of the house, they all said he was unfailingly polite, apologizing for his theft even as he bundled up his stolen goods. He bowed and kissed their hands and then melted into the darkness of the night. Naturally, it took the ladies quite a while to recover, and by the time the alarm was raised, the Black Mask was long gone.

And in most cases he wasn't seen at all, and the robbery wasn't discovered until morning...when the trail was stone cold.

The Black Mask had been a figure of legend for years now. Five years? Surely. Ten? Perhaps. Long enough to frustrate the justices of the peace and excite the ladies of the *ton*, who often harbored a secret wish for the daring thief to rob their home. What were a few jewels compared to an experience such as that?

The man behind the mask counted on such attitudes. He cultivated the image to make his work easier in case he should be caught midadventure.

He was midadventure now, in fact. It was his second robbery of the evening.

After placating the dogs of his chosen house with laudanum-spiked beef, it had been the work of a moment to locate a particular window on the upper floor and clamber up the trellis next to the massive chimney. The lovely late spring air inspired the maids to leave the windows ajar, and he didn't even need to pull out the leather roll of special tools to pry open the latches.

Over the sill and inside! A house cat made an unexpected, inquisitive meow, but was soon turned to the thief's cause with a few scratches behind the ears and a couple of sincere compliments.

"Who's a handsome fellow?" the thief murmured in a tone that spoke of mutual respect for a creature of the night. "You rule this roost, do you? Well, I'll be gone shortly."

The cat, a well-fed specimen with tabby stripes, considered this news and responded by tilting its head upward.

The thief understood this to be an invitation for more affection, and dutifully scratched the exposed chin. After a moment, the cat stretched and sauntered off, utterly unconcerned with what this new person was up to.

The thief stood again, listened for any sounds, heard nothing alarming, and proceeded to open the hallway door and slip down the darkened passage to the room he wanted.

That room appeared to be a bedroom, for there was a tall four-poster bed at one end, the curtains pleated and pressed, the bedclothes evidently ready for a guest.

But this was not chiefly a bedroom—it was a store-room for secrets. The thief moved to the far corner, where a reading chair sat by the cold fireplace, a rug laid below. He lifted the chair to the side, and rolled the rug up, all without a sound.

The floor appeared to be plain wooden boards, but the cut of two of them was suspiciously short. He felt around for a catch, and finally slid his fingers under what seemed to be a loose knot.

The trapdoor opened to reveal a shallow space containing a metal box. It was locked, but the Black Mask pulled out his tools: an oiled cloth to prevent squeaking or to finesse a jammed mechanism, several slender metal picks with a variety of chiseled tips—almost like keys but not quite—and a hammer in the event the picks failed.

Defeating a lock can take time, more so when one is compelled to work in very bad lighting and with one ear cocked for noises in the corridor. The thief worked patiently, without any sign of frustration, trusting that his experience and the training he'd received would come through.

And so it did, when the lock popped open with a little clink. The sound was echoed by a meow from the cat, who'd returned to oversee the proceedings.

He put his tools away before opening the box. Then he began to sort through the few but extremely interesting contents, assessing each item for its value. Not to him personally, though he confessed to a certain awe at the dramatic potential of what he held in his hands, but rather for his superiors.

He knew he'd found the right piece before he really got a good look at it. But a long, considered scan in the dim moonlight made him sigh in relief. Yes, this was it. He looked at it an inordinately long time. If he were being observed by anyone at this moment (other than the cat), the observer would expect him to snatch the item and stuff it into his pack, leaving the box open on the floor, the rest of the contents disturbed and scattered.

Instead, he replaced the item exactly as he'd found it. He closed the box, reversed his previous moves to relock it, and replaced it in the hidden compartment. The rug was unrolled once more, the chair put back in its spot.

Soundlessly, the thief slipped across the hallway and to the room he'd entered first. He climbed out the window, and went hand over hand just far enough to enable a safe jump to the soft green lawn below, where he offered a silent prayer of thanks to whomever invented the trellis.

He sprinted across the lawn to the safety of a massive lilac bush, where he was met by a man of perhaps thirty years of age, who wore an expression of wariness. Wordlessly, they both ran, using darkness as cover, until they reached a narrow, unpleasantly fragrant alley a good distance away from the house.

"All right," the thief declared. "That's far enough. Any pursuit?"

The wary-eyed man checked. "Not a hint." He sighed and laid a pack on the ground, pulling out various items. "Time to transform."

"Past time," the thief agreed, beginning to undress as casually if he were in his own bedchamber.

"Got what you came for, sir?" the slim figure asked, taking the black silk mask and the black shirt in one arm while handing over a far more colorful item of clothing with the other hand, in the perfect attitude of a gentleman's valet—which he in fact was.

"Yes, indeed. The final piece of evidence to prove Peyton a traitor to the crown."

His companion sighed in relief. "Good. And with the jewels you nipped from the Bailey house earlier, everyone will assume the Black Mask spent his whole evening on the other side of the city. We're covered. What's next, then, my lord?"

The transformation from black-clad criminal to high-born lord took place before the valet's eyes, and yet it seemed a little bit like magic. In the space of a few moments, the Black Mask became Lord Cameron Perry, Viscount Deverall. Who would ever dream that the resourceful, relentless thief was also the dandyish, dissolute lord? No one, ever. That was Cameron's shield, and it worked perfectly. Not just one mask, but two. Cameron protected himself and what he cared about behind multiple layers of deception.

"What's next, Quinn," he said, putting on the finishing touch of Deverall's playboy appearance with a perfectly tied white cravat, "is that I pass this information to the Zodiac, then sleep for ten solid hours, then go to my second favorite club and play cards like I mean to lose my fortune."

Quinn nodded as if all this were perfectly normal to hear. "Will you be wanting supper at any point, sir?"

Cameron nodded. "After the visit to the Zodiac and before the nap."

"Very good, sir. Carriage is this way, if you please. You look like yourself again, but Lord Deverall wouldn't be caught dead in this alley."

"Right you are, Quinn. Lead the way."

♊

ONE CLANDESTINE MEETING, ONE MEAL, several drinks, and several hours later, Cameron sat in his second favorite club and laid his final card upon the table. "Five of clubs. Which gives me a straight flush."

The reactions of the other men around the table ranged from disgust, as Lord Moreland drained the last of his brandy and slammed the glass down, to resignation, as Sir Lucas Smart offered him a wry grin, to barely contained rage, as Lord Barriton's brow wrinkled up like an offended bulldog's. Cameron remembered their names because he remembered everything, but really, it did not matter who he played, and he did not care in the least how these particular men felt about the game.

Barriton said, "Holding us all to the table with a five of clubs? Outrageous!"

"No one forced you to continue to raise the stakes, my lord," Cameron pointed out. "Sir Lucas folded."

"I know when I'm up against the wall," Lucas said, watching his moderate stakes get swept away into Cameron's growing pile. "Nicely played, Deverall. Lady Luck is with you tonight."

Cameron nodded. The last six rounds had gone his way.

"Another round," Moreland declared, slurring his

words. "Must give me a chance to make back what I've lost!"

Smart glanced sidelong at the drunken lord, obviously thinking that playing cards with a man who could barely *read* the cards was no longer sporting. But one did not oppose Lord Moreland in anything, particularly when one was a mere baronet. He looked to Cameron for aid.

Cameron was a viscount…but he was also winning. A moral dilemma, he thought wryly as Lucas gathered the cards and slowly began to reshuffle. Should Cameron do as he was expected to do and continue to press his luck, or graciously bow out to preserve Moreland's dignity?

Before he could state a preference, one of the club's servants stepped up to him, bearing a single letter on a silver tray.

"Message for you, my lord," the servant murmured. "From your wife."

Though the man spoke at below normal volume, everyone in that room of the club seemed to hear him, and everyone looked at Cameron without seeming to look, because the state of affairs between Lord Deverall and his wife was…less than ideal.

Cameron took the letter without looking at the servant, because he knew he'd see the barely hidden smirk on the man's face.

His breath quickened as he read his name written in her lovely, flowing script. *Lord Deverall, Whitby's, St James Street.* What did Genevieve want from him?

He flipped the letter over, and saw the purple wax seal stamped with an impression of a Greek muse, an intaglio of what he knew was her own family ring. He slid his finger into the fold and broke the seal.

The message was brief. *My lord, an important matter has arisen and I would appreciate it if you could meet with me at your earliest convenience. Genevieve.*

No Lady Cameron, which was the name she ought to be using now. And what the hell was this important matter? That could mean anything. What was so vital as to break a three-year silence?

Someone's dying.

It was his first thought, and a chilling one, because if it was so dire as to force Gen to reach out to him, she must be in a state.

And yet, *I would appreciate it if you could meet with me* was hardly begging for help. Not that Genevieve was the begging type. No, she didn't go in for pleading or compromise. She simply judged and then consequently carried out that judgment like an avenging angel.

But now he held this letter.

"Deverall?"

"Hmmm?" He looked up to Lucas, who brandished the deck of cards.

"Another round?"

Cameron looked at the cards, at his winnings, at the letter. He stood up, nearly upending his chair in the process. "I'm afraid not, gentlemen. Duty calls."

Lord Barriton grunted. "First time you've ever answered."

The statement was quiet enough that Cameron didn't have to acknowledge it. And indeed, Lord Deverall ought to reply with only a laugh or a casually witty phrase that confirmed what everyone here already thought of him— Deverall, Devil-Take-It-All.

But for some reason, he did not do so this time. Instead, he faced Barriton. "What was that, my lord?"

Barriton's brow furrowed at this unexpected resistance. He had to think of something to say, which took him a moment.

But he was a lord, and rose to the occasion. "Don't play righteous, Deverall. You've avoided duty at every turn. You've got a duty to your family to get an heir, but you've spent the whole of your marriage avoiding your home and wife, leaving her to her own devices, which is not a natural state for any lady of quality. Yet there she is, riding around in the worst slums of London, and everyone knows it."

"On missions of charity, for which she is praised by many," Lucas interjected, looking rather scandalized that the good name of Lady Cameron had got dragged into this unpleasant discussion. "Let us leave her out of it."

"Hmmm, right enough," Barriton conceded. "Not her fault no one's around to take her in hand. When was the last time you even saw your wife, Deverall?"

"Oh, we sometimes meet at the same parties, you know," Cameron said carelessly. And when that happened, she inevitably left after casting a scathing look at the hostess, who would pretend it was all a mortifying mistake. But the truth was that people *liked* to have Deverall at their parties—it was a measure of success when he chose to attend. There was always room for a dashing lord who was up for some fun.

Barriton harrumphed. "That's the problem with young ladies and their marriages nowadays. They get their heads turned by charm of manner instead of sensibly selecting husbands for breeding and good character."

"Are you impugning my breeding or my character?" Cameron asked Barriton in a low voice, one quite out of the ordinary for him. *Cam, what the hell are you doing? Just leave.*

"I don't impugn," the older lord said without moving a step back. "I make a statement of fact. Every time you have a chance to do as you ought, instead you do as you like. Do you deny it?"

Yes, I deny it! Cameron wanted to howl. But Devil-Take-It-All would never show so much spine. He took a breath and forced himself to relax. He had to play the part. The right words came to him: "I don't deny myself much of anything, old boy."

He even chuckled. There it was. The persona of Deverall slid back over him like a mask. Still, it was time to get the hell out of the club before he slipped up again. He swept his winnings into the various pockets of his coat, and bowed with a theatrical flourish. "I must be off, but don't fear, I'll keep your money in very good hands… mine."

"Go to hell, Deverall," Moreland muttered, now with a fresh glass of brandy in his paw. He was a sore loser.

"My ultimate destination, but not my immediate one."

With that, Cam left the room, descended the stairs, and strolled to the main doors. He wished he could avoid the club altogether. The gentlemen he played cards with were interchangeable, and only rarely did he think of any of them when he wasn't actively engaged in a round. He breathed in the fresh air outside, grateful to leave the club behind.

One of the ubiquitous footmen dashed forward to hail a carriage for him, and soon Cameron was ensconced in a bouncing, rickety cab as the driver plowed through the streets of London. It was evening again—how long had he been playing cards? It was about dinnertime for the fashionable set, of which Lord Deverall was definitely a member. He was *very* fashionable, in fact. He tugged at his fashionable dark blue jacket and brushed a speck of dust off his fashionable leather shoes.

The Season was nearly over. Summer was about to begin her reign over the city, though the warm air had not yet brought out the terrible stench of the Thames that would emerge in a few weeks. Now it was actually pleasant, the air soft and the evening light of the sky filtering through newly leafy trees.

As he got closer to his destination, Cameron opened the letter again. Three years of nothing, and now this. In the solitude of the carriage, he allowed himself to speculate. Was it possible Genevieve was as sick of this separation as he was? Or was her family applying some pressure to live up to expectations? Perhaps they also disliked her crusading in the slums. Cam was aware that Genevieve had always been soft-hearted, but since she became Lady Cameron, she'd grown quite active in charity circles, a sort of cyclone of good works in the city. He followed news of her activities, though he never hinted of it publicly.

The carriage clattered to a halt in front of a familiar house with a golden glow seeping from all the windows. As he strode up the walk, he heard the faint sounds of laughter and talk. Gen was entertaining, a dinner party of some sort. He was vaguely annoyed at the idea of her happily toasting guests after she penned a letter implying that the sky was falling.

He knocked once, also annoyed by that. A man shouldn't have to knock on his own front door.

The door opened. The mouth of the maid also opened as she stared at him in shock.

Cameron stepped inside. "Where is my wife?"

"In the dining room…my lord," the maid squeaked out. "Shall I…shall I announce you?"

"Who else is in the dining room?"

"The whole board of the Society for the Improvement of Friendless Children, my lord. And their spouses."

Cameron curled a lip in disdain. "Ugh. Just tell her

I'm waiting in her study." He pointed to what he hoped was the correct door, and he also got annoyed about that. A man should never have to guess which room was which in his own home.

The maid nodded, finally regaining her composure. "Yes, my lord."

Cameron showed himself into the study. The room's windows were all open, letting in the evening breeze. A low fire burned in the fireplace, and several candles were lit. He looked at the expansive walnut desk, the surface covered with documents and ledgers. On the wall hung several framed charcoal drawings of no artistic merit. *Children could have done better*, he thought, before realizing that children probably were the artists and these were gifts to their greatest patron.

He leaned toward one, a crude rendering of Genevieve herself. Despite the rough medium and the scant talent of the creator, something of Genevieve was in that drawing. The remarkable height, the dark hair, the direct gaze of the avenging angel.

"What are you doing here?"

At the sound of the voice, Cameron turned to the door, where the real Genevieve stood. The drawing faded into nothing. There she was. Tall, slender, with the dark hair curled and pinned atop her head with only a silk ribbon as an adornment—she needed no other. He took in the rest of her in a glance, and then had to do more than glance, because her gown demanded it. It was a cloud of pink silk or gauze or something else utterly inappropriate for public wear. The neckline of the gown dipped enticingly low, treating him to an expanse of soft skin that no one but him should ever see.

And yet. Here she was, evidently thinking she looked perfectly acceptable to appear before the gaze of the entire board of the Society for the Improvement of Friend-less Breasts.

"I asked you a question, my lord." Genevieve crossed her arms. He saw her left hand as she wrapped it around her elbow. No ring. He added another item to the list of things that were annoying him, along with the fact that his breeches were suddenly a little too tight.

Cameron had to say something.

"Genevieve."

He probably should have said something wittier than that.

She narrowed her eyes. "Why. Are. You. *Here*?"

♊

GENEVIEVE, LADY CAMERON, VISCOUNTESS Deverall, Angel of Orphans, wanted to throw her husband out the window, a course of action she did not pursue only because the room was on the ground floor, and therefore the move would accomplish so little.

"Why are you here, Cameron?" she repeated, since he was just staring at her like she'd sprouted wings.

He held up a letter. "Because you asked me."

She rolled her eyes. Of course. After years of silence, she sent one measly note, and he chose to respond immediately. "But why tonight? I thought you'd write back and make an appointment."

"I'm your husband, not your man of business. I don't need an appointment. What's wrong?"

"What do you mean?" She tried not to notice just how perfect he looked. Cameron had always been so breathtaking. Genevieve had fallen for him within the first few days of their courtship, though she'd played the game reasonably well until he proposed. If only she'd been more careful! Those lovely blue eyes that were looking at her now, with the same tenderness he pretended early on.

"The letter said a matter of importance had arisen," Cameron said. "So tell me what it is. I trust your family is well?"

Ah, those eyes. That expression of concern, the sincerity in his voice. That wonderfully low, smooth voice. She fought off a little shiver when she thought of his voice so close to her ear, as it had been when she told him how happy she'd be to become his wife.

"Yes, everyone is in good health," she said. "Even Roger, as of last month." That had been the date of his most recent letter, postmarked from Florence. Her older brother had developed a passion for the great cities of the Continent, and was currently in Italy, taking in all the masterpieces of the *quattrocento*.

"And my family?" he asked.

"Your family is also doing well," she said. "Do you not speak to them?"

"Not more than I have to. I think they like you better as a daughter than they like me as a son."

Gen sighed in frustration. "If you behaved with a bit more propriety… Oh, what does it matter? Let's attend to this business, and then you can go."

"Go? Out of my own house, you mean?" He stepped toward her, his form eclipsing her own considerable height. "Or did you forget that this is my house, Genevieve?"

How could she possibly forget? "I know who the owner is, my lord, but I also know that we had an agreement." She lived here, he didn't.

"There was no agreement," he said. "You made a pronouncement, and then ran out of the room. I agreed to nothing."

"Then why did you move out?"

"To give you a little time to calm down!"

"A little time?" She gaped at him. "It's been three years!"

"Judging by your reception, perhaps I should have waited longer."

"Go to the devil." Genevieve spun around, furious

with herself for letting Cameron get to her. After what he'd done...

Then Gen rubbed her temples, recovered her wits, and walked over to the desk. "Never mind. I need you to sign this," she said, pointing to the paper on the desk.

He picked it up and read it with far more attention than she expected. "This involves what...property? What property?"

"Greyslake," she ground out. "Just sign the paper, please." One of the deeply vexing things about her situation was that she was a wife, and therefore had little control over the finances or properties that were rightfully hers. Greyslake Manor was a fairly modest estate, one that she loved from childhood. But she needed money now to continue her charity work. So Greyslake would have to be sacrificed. Beautiful Greyslake, with its lofty evergreens and little waterfall.

Cameron surveyed her for a very long moment. "You want to sell Greyslake?"

"That's my intent, yes. But it requires your approval."

He picked up the pen, and inwardly she sighed in relief. He dipped it in the ink...and then threw it like a dart toward the fireplace. It caught in the flames, and the acrid smell of burning feathers stung the air.

"What are you doing?" she demanded.

He took a deep breath, then said, "You maintain an icy silence for three years, and then ask me to sign away property without telling me a thing about what you're doing? Think again, Genevieve. I'm not signing a single paper without full disclosure."

Suddenly Cameron cared about her activities? "I need the money, and this is the only way to get it."

"What do you need money for? Why not ask those guests in the dining room to get up the scratch? After all, they should pay something for what they're receiving from you."

"What?" Gen asked blankly.

He let his gaze drop from her face to her chest. "The display you're putting on with…whatever you're supposed to be wearing."

Oh, he did *not* just raise that subject. Gen glared at him. "It's what's commonly known as an evening gown. You may recognize it as the article of clothing you rip off your mistress when you bed her."

"Don't give me ideas," he warned. "And you need to cover up before you go back into that dining room. You look scandalous."

"Of the two of us, *I'm* not the one who can be described as scandalous, my lord." Genevieve clenched her hand around the fan dangling from her wrist, willing herself to remain steady. "How dare you tell me how to dress or how to behave. After what you did, you have exactly no moral high ground left. Your moral high ground is a swamp."

"What did I do?" he asked.

The last of Genevieve's patience went up in smoke. She pointed at him with the fan. "Don't pretend you don't remember! It happened one room away from here. Everyone saw you with your tawdry mistress, her clothes half off…in our *home.*" It was quite expected for gentlemen to have mistresses, a fact Gen was well aware of. But a certain amount of discretion was expected. For Cameron to disregard that was the ultimate insult to Genevieve.

His jaw twitched, and she braced herself for an outburst. But then he just said, in a maddeningly measured way, "For the last time, it wasn't what it looked like."

"Oh?" She blinked innocently, then snapped, "Well, too bad! Because what it *looked* like was all that mattered.

Because what it looked like was what the whole *ton* was gossiping about for the next month and a half. And what it looked like was that you humiliated me, your wife of three weeks, entertaining your mistress in the very same house!"

"Get your fan out of my face," he told her, his blue eyes darkening to the color of a storm.

She realized she'd been somewhat demonstrative with the implement, but she wasn't ready to back down. "Or what?"

"Or you'll need to buy a new fan."

"I'll put it on your account." She poked the end of the folded fan into his chest once more for good measure.

With a sudden move, Cameron smacked the fan out of her hand, and it flew in an arc directly into the fireplace.

"I warned you," Cameron said.

"That fan was my sister's!" she whispered in anguish. Gen's sister Grace had died two months before Gen married Cameron.

"God *damn* it." He dove for the fan.

Gen screamed when she saw his hands in the flames. She lunged toward him, the force of her attack pushing him to the side of the fireplace. He stumbled and fell, bringing Gen down with him.

"What the hell did you think you were doing?" she said furiously, completely oblivious to the fact that she was sprawled on top of him. "Fire burns, you dolt!"

"Yes, so I've heard," he said. "Besides, what do you care if I catch fire?"

"I don't care!" she huffed. "You can burn. I just don't want a pyre in my study. The smoke will stain the wallpaper."

He caught her by the waist, his hands heating her skin through the thin fabric of her dress. "Did you intend to sit there all night?"

Gen said, her cheeks now burning as hot as the fire itself, "No! Get off me!"

"Technically," he pointed out with a quirk to his lips, "you're the one on me, so you have to get off."

She gave a little strangled scream as she pushed herself up and away from him.

"Did you want this?" He offered her the fan.

"Oh, mercy." Gen gasped in surprise. "You saved it."

"Well, it was your sister's."

Gen snatched the offered fan, gripping it tightly to her heart for a moment before she examined it closely for damage.

"What's the condition?" he asked, standing up and straightening his jacket, looking every inch a lord.

"Scorched," she replied. The silk would need replacing, but the ivory ribbing appeared to be undamaged. "But salvageable."

"I seem to be in the same condition," he said, looking over his attire. "You're welcome, by the way."

She glared at him. "You were the one who threw it into the fire in the first place. Don't expect an ovation."

"You certain you didn't ask me here just because you needed a more lively interaction than your dinner guests can provide? If I'd known you planned to jump on me, I would have arrived earlier."

Good Lord, was he *teasing* her? Gen bit her lip, trying to decide whether to be annoyed or...extremely annoyed. "Cameron. This is not a time for jokes. I require cash on hand to continue a very important project that will benefit a great number of children. The other members of the Society have donated as well—quite generously—but we need more. And I will not do this by half measures. If I am to go forward, I must know that we have the capacity to see it through to the end."

"We?"

"The Society. Lady Stanfield and the rest of the board, and those who offer their aid. There are too many children in this city who have been neglected and ignored by those who should care for them. Their parents are dead or imprisoned or ill. The church offers platitudes and scraps of bread. The government does nothing, except to hire men to run them off the streets where the sight of them offends their betters. As if it's better to ignore a child than help her! If I can't…"

Cameron caught her wrists gently in his hands, stopping her homily. "I see your point, Genevieve. Money for children."

"In a nutshell. Yes." She took a long breath. Speaking out on her chosen cause—whether to one person or a crowd—always made her emotional. Fortunately, she had plenty of practice, since she'd taken elocution lessons and had been encouraged by her parents to become quite a natural public speaker. It was part of their plans for her to make a good match.

"You truly have thrown yourself into charity," he said quietly.

"What should I have done?" she asked. "Sat at our palatial country seat, receiving the vicar and the local hunt club? Or perhaps raising the children I don't have? You left me with nothing. So I made my own way."

Cameron's eyes widened slightly during this statement. He let go of her wrists, saying, "I have an offer."

"Is it an offer to jump into the Thames and drown while I look on and laugh? Because I'm unlikely to be interested otherwise."

"An exchange. I can give you something you want."

"You have nothing I desire."

"That's not true. Will you listen?"

Genevieve looked at him uneasily. "Go on."

He pointed to the desk. "I will sign that paper on the day you confirm your pregnancy."

Gen opened her mouth to retort, then registered what he'd said. "What?"

"You said you wanted children. And as both our families and all of London knows, I need an heir. We're already married, and it's not as if you found the process so terrible."

She blushed, remembering the *process* he alluded to. "That was before. I hate you now."

"Affection has nothing to do with it." He leaned even closer. "Even if you hate me, you won't hate our child."

"I would love our baby," she whispered. How cruel was this, for Cameron to dangle the one thing she truly wanted in order for her to get what she needed? And now, after all these years?

"It's the one thing I can give you," he went on. "I'll leave afterward, if that's what you want. You don't have to endure my presence day to day. But you do need me if you want a child."

"I can't believe we're discussing this as if it's a transaction."

"What else can I do? We're long past affection, as you said. But we're bound to each other, so why not make the best of it now? And in a matter of weeks, I'll be able to tell the world an heir is on the way, and you'll have your capital to pursue whatever charity project you wish. Do we have a deal?"

"A child for a signature," she said, her voice stunned and distant even to herself. "All right."

"Let's be clear on the details," he said. "I come to you every night till you conceive."

Her heart dropped into her stomach. "Every night?"

"Every night. Will that inconvenience you?" His eyes narrowed. "Do you have another nightly visitor I should know about?"

He caught her arm before she could slap him.

"How dare you," she raged, struggling to reclaim her wrist.

"So that moral indignation is real? You took no lovers since I left?"

The way he was looking at her nearly made her catch fire. He was asking if *she* had a lover. The audacity! "Of course I haven't!"

Cameron's expression relaxed. "Then I see no reason why I shouldn't come to your room every night. If you want to get me out of your life, this is the price. The more often we…"

"Oh, don't *say* it!" she gasped.

"…the sooner you'll be with child," he finished with a slightly vicious smile. "Deal?"

Genevieve was all too aware that Cameron was the son of Lord Lionel, a consummate politician and legendary negotiator. He'd learned plenty of tricks by watching his father. "Are there other aspects to this deal I should know about?"

"Yes. You must be civil to me while we live together. You don't have to pretend to love me, or even like me. But I will not tolerate rudeness, histrionics, or this ice princess act. Is that clear?"

Her heart was pattering wildly, like a rabbit's in a trap, but she nodded curtly. "I expect the same from you, then. Don't belittle me, and don't act like you own me…or you'll regret it."

"I already regret it," he said. "If I could turn back time, I would have never married you."

She inhaled sharply, and felt as if he'd hit her.

"For your sake," he amended quickly.

"This is going to go badly," Gen muttered.

"We'll find out tonight, won't we?"

"*Tonight?* Absolutely not! I have guests awaiting my return."

"They're leaving after dinner, yes? Tonight."

She gritted her teeth. "You've waited one thousand nights already. One more will make no difference. You may resume residency tomorrow. And come to my room tomorrow night."

"Very well."

His acquiescence surprised her, but then, this whole evening surprised her. An hour ago, she knew what the shape of the world was. Now, she was wandering in a fog, and the only certain thing was that her lying, cheating husband was once again a part of her life.

Cameron picked up the Greyslake contract and tucked it into a jacket pocket. "I'll just keep this until it's needed." He winked at her, as if he hadn't completely upended her entire existence.

"Don't lose it," she said, numb from the events that had just unfolded.

"You may rely on me, sweet Gen," he said, using the endearment from their courtship. "Do tell the staff that I'll be moving back in. Ainsworth doesn't care for surprises, if I remember correctly."

"He's not alone in that," she returned, thinking of how the butler might very well suffer heart failure at the news his lordship would be moving back in.

"Then I'll see you tomorrow. I trust you'll dream of me until then."

He left before Gen could explain that she would not dream of him, because she didn't think she'd sleep at all.

♊

AFTER CAMERON LEFT THE HOUSE, Gen had to return to the dining room and pretend all was well. She was just able to exchange a meaningful glance with her friend Sabine, Lady Stanfield, who was seated on the other side, resplendent in an amber-hued gown. Sabine was also a member of the Society, and in fact was the person who first showed Gen that charity work—one of the very few outlets for wealthy women to express their own interests—was an effective remedy for loneliness.

Gen presided over the meal as best she could, even announcing that she expected a speedy resolution to the matter of raising the needed capital for the next project. She didn't say how of course, because she'd die of embarrassment first.

Finally, when all the guests had left except for Sabine, the two ladies all but dashed into Gen's study.

"Was that him?" Sabine asked, her eyes bright.

"It was him."

Sabine was thrice married, thrice widowed, and therefore a woman of considerable experience. Genevieve had met her shortly after her own marriage deteriorated and rather naively asked the silver-haired lady for guidance. Instead of an airy comment, Sabine instead offered a shoulder to cry on, and then shepherded Gen through the thorny realm of being a society wife brushed with scandal—a topic Sabine was intimately familiar with.

"What a turn of events," Sabine declared. "Tell me everything. No, wait, pour us some sherry first. Then tell me everything."

Over the drinks, Genevieve told the facts of the matter, which did not take long.

"So the Viscount Deverall is back in residence," Sabine said at the end.

"He will be by tomorrow night."

"Have you two made up, then?"

"No. But he needs an heir." Gen did not reveal the other part of the deal, feeling ashamed about it. She would be using her body for money. Yes, he was her husband, and yes, the money was in some sense already her own. But it felt wrong.

However, Sabine only knew the part about the heir, and she nodded at hearing it. "I must say it's very sound-minded of you both to acknowledge the reality of the situation."

"But after so long, and after what he did to me…I don't know what to do."

"Well, the simplest thing is just to lie there and let him finish."

"Oh, mercy." Gen covered her face with her hands even as she laughed. "That is *not* the advice I need, Sabine."

Her friend smiled. "Nor is it the advice I'll give, but I wanted to be sure you still had your sense of humor about you."

Genevieve tried again. "I mean, how should I go about my life when he's here, without even an apology or a nod to what happened? And what if he chooses to make things difficult?" Cameron in the same house could make any number of things difficult, from awkwardness at the dinner table to possibly another mistress strolling through the garden.

Sabine frowned as she sipped her sherry. "Do you fear he'll use the nights as punishment for your recalcitrance? After all, no matter what he did to deserve your wrath, Deverall has endured a certain amount of…censure from the *ton* and his circle for how both of you have lived apart. A man is not well respected when he can't control his own wife."

"He never tried! He walked out of the house and I barely saw him since then."

"True. But still, there is talk."

"I don't think Cameron is planning any sort of retaliation against me. He was clear enough that all he wants is an heir."

"And you said he was very considerate of you before. In bed, that is."

Gen nodded. It was true, and it was one of the most vexing parts of her relationship with Cameron, because as awful as he'd been to her, he'd also frequently been *not* awful—wonderful, really—and trying to reconcile the two aspects of the man drove her to madness sometimes.

She'd been a virgin on her wedding night. Her mother explained her marital duties in an embarrassed sort of way, so Gen understood the basics of the act. But that was very different from actually going to bed with a man for the first time, and she'd been so nervous she almost lost her dinner while she was waiting for Cameron to knock on her door.

However, he'd been incredibly kind to her, not rushing her into bed but rather taking a long time to calm her. She remembered a lot of gentle kisses and him repeatedly asking her if she would permit him to go on. She said yes every time, partly because she didn't know what else she could say—he was her husband and she wanted so badly to please him—but also because those kisses did hold some power to set her at ease and make her want to know what the next step was, right up through the act itself.

It had been painful, though not as painful as she feared after her mother's warnings. And Cameron had apologized profusely, even though she knew the pain was inherent in a woman's losing her virginity and he could only do so much to relieve it. And afterward he'd stayed with her for a while, which was something her mother suggested would *not* happen. But they'd talked, and she'd confided her hopes for a child not just for duty but because she truly loved children. Few things gave her more joy than spending time with young people. She liked their way of looking at the world.

Cam had promised to give her as many sons and daughters as she wanted, saying that he knew she'd make a perfect viscountess, and some day, a perfect marchioness. And Gen thought herself very much in love with him.

For a week, he came to her every night, and she slowly grew more comfortable, though she never could abandon the sense that she shouldn't actually enjoy the act—ladies weren't supposed to be wanton, even in a marriage bed. She got the sense that Cameron was perhaps slightly bored with her. And perhaps he was too big for her, because she never quite got over how…full she always felt when he was inside her, how she felt as if she might lose all sense of herself if the act went on too long. She most assuredly didn't want to lose herself at such a time.

Then her monthly courses arrived, which meant she wasn't with child. She'd been unaccountably upset, though her mother assured her that it was just timing, and Cameron said—with an odd smile—that he never quite trusted any bride who announced a pregnancy within a week of the wedding.

He stayed away from her bed while she was indisposed, and then he was called away on some family business that he didn't share with her. Not unusual—men didn't speak of those sorts of matters to their wives. He returned several days later, telling her how happy he was to be back home. She was excited to host their first party, a gathering of some thirty people, all of whom were members of the *ton*.

And then, during the party they were hosting, she'd walked into a room only to find Cameron alone with a woman who'd been standing by his desk with her rumpled skirts hitched up to her hips, or so it appeared to Gen.

And Cam was giving her *money*.

Gen remembered that moment with as much clarity as her wedding night, and the emotions were just as vivid. Shock. Alarm. Shame. And over it all, the deep sense of betrayal.

"I can't forgive him for what he did in the end," she said, more to herself than to Sabine.

"Many men have mistresses," her friend pointed out, quite correctly.

"In our *home*." There were unspoken rules of society, and one of them was that while men could have both a wife and a mistress, they never allowed the two to meet.

"Yes, that was terribly indiscreet," Sabine conceded. "I suppose every man turns into a fool when it comes to dipping his wick."

"But now he expects me to act as though he's done nothing wrong. Just husband and wife…all's well! I wonder if he'd go with me to church if I asked."

Sabine laughed at the image of Lord Deverall at Sunday services. "If you get him to agree, let me know so I can attend myself. The church walls themselves might get scorched from the hellfire he'll bring."

"Sabine, I don't know what to do."

"My dear, you must not give him more power than he's already got. He's in the house again, yes, but that's just for convenience. As you say, once you're with child, he'll leave again and you may resume your life."

Gen nodded, though part of her quailed at the thought of Cameron leaving her *again*. The first time had been humiliating enough. Could she endure a second time, while pregnant? Even if it was at her own request?

"Unless you fear he'll change his mind and want to stay?" Sabine asked, her sharp gaze on Gen. "Men are so changeable. They want one thing today, another tomorrow, and of course they go up in smoke if you point out their inconsistency."

"His moral direction would not be welcome when it comes to rearing a child," Gen said. "Though he had the gall to criticize my gown. He said it was scandalous. It's not, is it?"

Sabine rolled her eyes. "Your outfit is beautiful and perfectly appropriate, my dear. I suspect he'd not have said that if the gown was worn by any other woman."

"The next few months promise to be very difficult," Gen said.

"Just remember that he needs you, whether he likes it or not. You're the key to the Deverall family line now, and that gives you considerable leverage should you want something else. Such as help with our cause in Parliament. Remember what we discussed at the last meeting? Clean water for all of London would be a marked step forward for our children."

Gen took a deep breath and nodded. Then she said, "Enough of this subject. I need distraction. Tell me something. Anything, as long as it has nothing to do with Lord Devil-Take-It-All."

"Hmmm, it's getting difficult to come by good gossip now that half the *ton* is already gone from the city for the summer. Let's see. The son of Lord Brookmire has decided, most abruptly, to head to America." Sabine lowered her voice, despite them being alone. "He was caught cheating at the gaming tables."

Gen's eyes widened. Of the many transgressions a man might commit, few were unforgivable. But cheating at cards was one of them. "He was actually caught?"

"Red handed. Called out for a duel that moment, and he accepted, but then fled. Society will never let him back in, not after that."

"His family must be mortified."

"I wonder that his mother didn't faint with horror. And her with three daughters to marry off! They'll have a hard time of it now, poor girls."

Yes, such a stain carried over to the whole family. Gen winced, thinking of the innocent sisters who would suffer for the brother's act, being ostracized by association. "Please tell me something else."

"Well, the Bailey family home was broken into a few nights ago, and a maid reported that the Black Mask is the responsible party. Apparently quite a number of jewels were taken, including the family sapphires."

"Indeed?" Gen asked, her interest piqued. For years, there were recurring rumors of a criminal known as the Black Mask.

"The maid said he kissed her hand like a true gentleman. I hope he tries to rob my home," Sabine mused, her hand fluttering at her neck. "I'd demand more than just a kiss."

"Sabine!"

"Why not? If I find a dashing man in my room one evening, I should have *some* say in what he's doing there."

"You are a wicked widow," Gen scolded. "You'd probably scare the man with your appetites."

"Ah, for the chance to find out…" Sabine smiled a very wicked smile indeed, then sipped the last of her sherry.

"You really ought to go," Gen said, thinking of the late hour, "lest I be corrupted by your worldly influence."

"One thing to keep in mind, dear…" Sabine said, her smile softening as she stood up. "If he does wish to make amends, you should listen. My first marriage would have been much more harmonious if either Bertie or I could have backed down once in a while and simply listened. But it was not in our natures. You, however, have a chance to start…well, not anew, but again. And that is not something every woman gets."

Genevieve stood up as well. "I suppose I ought to inform Ainsworth and the household of the change, and make sure everything is in order when he arrives."

"Good luck, my dear. Keep me informed. Do you expect that you'll still be able to join us on Tuesday?" Tuesday was one of the days the members of the Society gathered to serve meals to the children who came to their building, knowing that food and shelter was available.

Gen nodded. "Nothing will keep me from my work, not even my lord and husband."

"That's the spirit!"

♊

CAMERON RETURNED TO GEN'S HOME—no, *their* home—
shortly after eleven the next day. He was accompanied by
his man, Quinn, who held the title of valet, but was much
more than that. Quinn always seemed to know what
Cameron needed before he could think to ask. He knew
Cameron's schedule by heart, and he performed every
task with competence. The only flaw in Quinn's personality was a distressing tendency toward honesty. Most servants would be sacked for telling their masters the absolute, unvarnished truth. Cameron, however, kept Quinn
around.

Cameron looked around the front hall, the first time
he'd seen it in daylight for over three years. The whole
house was sparkling, and he suspected the staff had barely
slept in anticipation of the master's arrival.

Genevieve herself was at work in her study, and only
came into the front hall when the fuss of his trunks and
cases and whatnot got too loud to ignore.

He saw her framed in the doorway. She was just as
lovely from the neck up, though her outfit was worlds
away from the fashionable confection of the previous
night. Now she wore a plain, even dowdy, day dress of
brown linen. He wondered if she was making a statement
with her gown, because she certainly wasn't making a

statement with her words. Instead, she just stared at him, her gaze cool.

"Give me a smile, Genevieve. I thought you were looking forward to seeing me again."

She offered a too-sweet smile as she said, "Of course I was looking forward to seeing you again. I'd hoped it would be right before they started nailing down the lid on your coffin." And then she turned about, her skirts rustling, and retired back into her study. The conversation was over.

"A kinder welcome than I had anticipated," Quinn murmured from behind him.

Cameron took the stairs to the upper floor, where his long-abandoned master's suite awaited him at the back of the house. When he got inside, Cam immediately shrugged out of his jacket, which had grown warm the second he'd seen Gen.

"I'd forgotten what a wit she is," he remarked out loud. "Is it illegal for a man to cut his wife's tongue out?"

"It's frowned upon in these modern times, sir." Quinn was his usual unflappable self. As the footmen arrived with the trunks and cases, he directed the items to the correct spots, then gave the whole suite a thorough going over. "The maids have been vigilant. No hint of dust or mildew. I expect they aired everything out regularly, despite your continued absence. Lucky."

Lucky? Cam's first reaction was offense at the idea that any household staff would be unprepared for the master to return at any moment. But he then had to admit that the state of the suite was rather better than he would have guessed. Gen could have locked the room and ordered the maids to ignore it completely. Instead, it did look as if it had been well cared for, even though he might never have come back after that one fateful night.

It had started out as an excellent evening…Cam and Gen's first party, in fact. He was proud of Gen for arranging everything so well, though of course it was the sort of event she'd been trained to organize with grace and style. That was what a political wife did, and eventually that's what Genevieve would be. In any case, even three weeks in, he thought she was embodying the image of a viscountess perfectly.

Then he got the most bizarre note, stuffed into his hand by a footman. He slipped away from the party, certain that whatever strange thing was occurring, it would interrupt him for a moment and then be over.

He was a fool.

Cameron never should have let the woman in at all. Strange women pounding on the glass of one's study were in general not good omens. But Genevieve was quite absorbed in acting as hostess a few rooms away, and Cameron had thought a quick intervention would be better than ignoring the woman. Then he could send her on her way.

So he let her in. His first mistake.

Then he listened to her story. Second mistake.

The third mistake was not locking the door to the room, because it was at the worst possible moment of that encounter when Gen walked into the study and saw them together.

Cameron couldn't tell her the truth at that moment, so he let her believe what seemed to be right in front of her eyes, even though it twisted him in knots to keep from defending himself…and the woman who was trapped in the middle.

Cameron had got the woman out of the house, and faced Gen's judgment on his own. And what a judgment it was—Gen had been mortified and hurt and deeply, deeply angry. She'd never been good at hiding her emotions, and Cam could read every single thought inside her as she railed at him.

Then, of course, others at the party heard what was going on, and sidled closer, and absorbed the unfolding scandal with equal parts delight and horror. Cameron let Gen unleash her rage, hoping that she'd tire soon enough and let him defend himself…or, if not defend himself, at least try to make some attempt to patch things up until he could think up a better lie, or do something that would get him back into Gen's good graces.

Cam had been far too optimistic. He underestimated both the scale of her feelings and the viciousness with which the *ton* reacted to all the rumors.

But now he was home again. At last.

"Where do you want this?" Quinn asked, holding up a wooden box. "Somewhere out of sight, I'd imagine."

He took the box from Quinn and set it on the bed. A key from his pocket unlocked the box, and he lifted the lid to reveal a space three-quarters full with folded letters, every one of them from the same sender. Cam withdrew another letter from an inside pocket of his jacket, and added it to the contents.

"It'll be awkward getting those here at the house, sir," Quinn noted in a quiet, deliberately disinterested tone.

"I'm the only one who opens my letters," Cam replied. After locking it again, he handed the box to Quinn. "Put this in some dark corner of the clothespress, would you?"

Approaching footsteps made them both look to the door. It was Ainsworth, the butler, who entered.

"Good day, my lord," the man said, standing much as a soldier on a parade ground would. "I trust everything is to your satisfaction?"

"You exceed expectations, Ainsworth, just as I'd expect," Cameron replied, enjoying the slight confusion that flit across the butler's face. Then, so as not to assault the man's dignity any further, he added, "The rooms are all up to snuff, but my stomach is not."

"Nuncheon has just been prepared for you, sir."

Of course it had. Ainsworth would never let the lord of the house go hungry for a moment.

"Excellent. Is my wife waiting to sit down?"

"No, sir. She's gone out."

Cameron frowned. So Gen fled not a half hour after he arrived.

"Her ladyship," the butler added helpfully, "is usually out from eleven to four, whether for social calls or her charity work. Today, she remained long enough to ensure you'd arrived."

"Oh," Cameron said. "Well, then I shall enjoy the kitchen's efforts on my own. It's been far too long since I've had Mrs Baxter's cooking."

An expression of satisfaction lightened Ainsworth's features. "You will not be disappointed, my lord."

Cameron was not disappointed, for Mrs Baxter had prepared some of his favorite dishes, evidently well remembered. He ate heartily, sent sincere compliments to Mrs Baxter, and wondered where the hell his wife was.

Irked by the idea of staying home while Gen was out, Cameron also left that afternoon, but the whole time, he wanted to get back home, back to Genevieve, back to this life he'd made a bargain to restore.

When he returned to the house after visiting his club, he was informed by a maid that the lady had just gone up to bed.

Well. Time to make good on his side of the bargain. He went to his own rooms to cast off his jacket, but before he could change out of the rest of his clothes and into a dressing robe, which would have made sense, he found himself moving to the connecting door between their rooms.

Cameron knocked before opening the door, feeling uncharacteristically nervous.

"Come in." The invitation was issued in the least enthusiastic tone imaginable, but then, this wasn't about pleasure. It was about duty.

Gen sat on the edge of her bed, clad in a simple shift. It reminded him of the very first time he'd entered this room, on their wedding night, and then he realized that she was wearing the exact same shift, now rather worse for wear. The once crisp white had yellowed, and the lace looked ragged.

So Gen's feelings about this arrangement were clear.

Cam bit back a comment. He didn't want to fight with her every moment. Especially not this moment.

"How was your day?" he asked, striving for a neutral question.

"Rather disrupted," she replied, her expression cool.

"You'll get used to it."

"Or perhaps we'll be lucky and neither of us will have time to get used to it," she countered. "Let's…" She waved a hand, indicating he should take the lead in what she'd already dismissed as a distasteful task to be completed as soon as possible.

Cameron removed his own clothing, noticing how she resolutely avoided looking at him, except for a few glances beneath her eyelashes. He wondered if she was looking at the scar on his forearm, and if it bothered her. He often forgot he had it, since it was the result of a childhood accident that he'd long ago put out of his memory. But the scar itself was raised and about six inches long, whiter than the surrounding skin, and certainly not an enhancement to his appearance.

Then he caught the direction of her gaze. No, it was not his *arm* she was peeking at. He almost laughed. She was acting a skittish as a virgin—and Cameron knew she wasn't, because he'd taken care of that years ago.

He pulled back the covers for her and Gen wordlessly climbed in, her shift still on.

"No," he said flatly, getting a fistful of the fabric before she could hide under the sheet. "This thing comes off."

"Very well." But she made no move to do so.

He removed the shift, balled it up, and flung it somewhere far into the shadows of the room. Gen watched, but said not a single word about the careless treatment. Perhaps she knew the article of clothing wasn't worth more consideration.

Then she sighed and lay down.

Cameron noticed the rapid rise and fall of her chest—she was nervous. He wanted to be more playful, remind her that she'd once enjoyed being with him, but he also knew that if he did so right now, he'd likely get reprimanded for it, or just receive a scandalized, wounded look for daring to bring pleasure into this very serious business of making a child.

"Is there a problem?" Gen asked. "You look like you're taking an inventory and you've been shorted."

"I assure you, I don't see a single defect." Except for the lack of interest. "May I go on?"

"That was the intention of joining me in bed, yes?" She looked off to the side, as if hoping for something more diverting to occur over there.

So much for a heartfelt reunion.

Despite her scorn, he still reacted to her physically.

He'd always thought she was beautiful, and despite the rumors of him as a devil-may-care lord, Cam hadn't actually taken a woman to bed since Gen kicked him out. He had far too much to think about to add an affair to his schedule. Yes, he'd flirted outrageously, and when necessary he did a bit more than flirt—a kiss or ten could do wonders to gain an ally, if done right. But never more than that. And now, with Gen naked in bed beneath him, all his other thoughts flew away, replaced by sudden and now undeniable need.

Cam forced himself to slow down—Gen was far from feeling the same need. Nor did she show any interest in prologue. The moment he brushed his hand between her legs to judge her readiness, she tensed.

"Is that necessary?" she asked, her voice husky in a way she probably didn't intend.

"Yes," he said. "I don't want to hurt you."

"Oh." Gen blinked several times, as if clearing her head of the idea that he *would* hurt her. Cameron felt immensely offended, and then shoved the offense back in his mind—he'd deal with it later.

He touched her as gently as he could, though his state of arousal was making it very difficult to think of anything but being inside Gen *right now*. And she did react to his touch, though he could tell she hated letting even the smallest gasp of pleasure out, which she did when his strokes drew out the moisture inside.

"If you want to wait for a few nights," he said without realizing what he was saying. "Until you're more comfortable…"

Please don't tell me to wait.

She shook her head. "This first night was always bound to be awkward. It will be less so next time. Do you think?" The question, spoken in a rush, revealed a vulnerability in her eyes.

"It will be better," he promised. "We just need to get used to each other again."

"You seem…used to me again," she whispered.

If by that she meant that his cock was painfully hard against her thigh, and that his balls ached, she was absolutely correct.

He took her faster than he wanted, unable to hold back after so long.

Cameron swore under his breath. Gen was *so* tight, and he was so overdue. He lasted an embarrassingly short time, but Gen didn't complain when he finished mere moments after entering her, though she tensed again when Cam kissed her soft shoulder just before he withdrew.

His body now infinitely more relaxed, he rolled to the side of the bed, knowing she'd reject any further attempt to make this encounter congenial.

"Was that more or less awkward than you feared?" he asked, suddenly very curious for the answer.

"The anticipation was worse than the act," she responded evenly, not looking at him. "Is our business concluded for the evening? I'd like to get to sleep."

Business. "You and I are done, yes." Shaking his head, Cameron got up, and gathered up his clothing before he walked to the connecting door. "Good night."

Gen didn't answer at all.

♊

GEN WAITED UNTIL CAMERON HAD closed the door after him to grab her pillow and plow her face into it. She wanted to cry and she wanted to scream, but she didn't dare do either while he was only a room away. She thought she'd be able to handle his presence in the house, and in her bed. She told herself that she'd be cool and collected, and that whatever happened was simply in the course of duty. They both knew that.

But her poor body didn't know that. She'd been racked by all the emotions she'd ever felt about Cameron, from the beginning of their courtship, to their infinitesimally short honeymoon of a marriage, and all the rage that came afterward.

Feeling him inside her threatened to break the last bit of composure she had left, and thank goodness he didn't prolong the act. Instead, he finished with such speed that she knew he could hardly stand to be in the same bed with her anymore. And just when she was reminded of how exciting it was to be close to him.

So she huddled into the large down pillow and clung to it, hiding her gulping breaths from the rest of the world. Lord, what had she agreed to? Was a child worth this humiliation of being in bed with a man so indifferent to her?

Eventually, she calmed down a little. She heard

movement in Cameron's room, and then the sounds of conversation between Cameron and his valet, Quinn. A door slammed. She got up and dashed to her own door that opened to the hallway. She eased it open an inch, just in time to see Cam, now dressed to go out, walking toward the stairs.

Quinn hurried after him. "You're certain?" he was asking.

"Why not?" Cameron said over his shoulder. "The night is young, and besides, I don't like to think I'm missing something."

"I'll secure a hack," Quinn said in resignation, just as the two men disappeared down the stairs.

Gen shut the door again, as if she'd been caught eavesdropping. It was nearly midnight. Granted, gentlemen such as him held to a different sort of schedule, but this seemed absurd. What might he be missing at this hour?

A flash of heat shot through her body as she thought again of how she'd been imitating a statue in bed. He was missing what he didn't receive from her, and now he was off to find it.

"This will never work," she said out loud. No agreement between them would ever last long enough to produce a child, and certainly not when he was dashing out to amuse himself moments after leaving her bedroom. It was infuriating. It was mortifying. And, worst of all, it was understandable.

What wife could compete with the sort of women who made pleasure their profession? Genevieve hadn't the slightest idea what Cameron wanted, and even if she did, to behave in such a way went completely against her whole upbringing as a lady. She'd been instructed to endure sexual congress, and never to enjoy it—though she could tell that it would be very, very enjoyable if she dared to let herself go, to let Cameron know what she was really feeling.

But could she ever trust him with her heart like that? If only she actually *knew* something about her own husband. Then she had a thought. She could easily slip into his room and perhaps learn a little about him from what he'd brought home.

She retrieved her discarded nightshift and pulled it on, further destroying an already loose bit of lace from one sleeve. Over that, she pulled on her summer robe, once a pale and pretty blue, but now stained with watermarks and more than a few wax splotches from unwisely held candlesticks.

Cameron's rooms were dead quiet, and very tidy, with the exception of the outfit he'd peeled off before bedding Gen. It now lay in a crumpled heap on the floor. No doubt Quinn would attend to it later.

Two gigantic clothespresses stood on either side of the window looking over the back garden. But there was nothing in them but clothes, and she already knew that side of him. Cameron had an impressive collection of clothing—he seemed to sport the latest looks almost the same moment the looks emerged. Brummell would be proud.

But wait…it was not just clothing. She found a long wooden box with the coat of arms of his family, containing a pair of gorgeously made shooting pistols. Cameron wasn't much of a hunter as far as she knew, but perhaps he shot at targets with his compatriots. Gen put the gun case back.

She looked around the room, wondering what of Cameron was truly in it. Perhaps Cameron was as shallow as the gossip suggested, gossip she should have listened to years ago, instead of falling for those eyes that seemed to be so deep.

The table by the bed had a few books stacked on top. Ah, promising. One was a new translation of Boccaccio. Not surprising, as he was one of Cam's favorites. His mother was an aficionado of the great classics, and Cameron had very nearly been named Decameron in honor of the writer's best-known work. The marquess, however, thought that a bridge too far, thus they settled on the compromise name of Cameron. He'd told that story early in their courtship, laughing the whole time.

Under that, there was a volume of poetry by Rochester —and not from his penitent Christian period either. And under that, a novel titled *Cynthia, or An Education of a Young Lady Abroad, Told with Unvarnished Honesty*. The slim volume was bound in dark red leather, and the few pages Gen scanned made her blush. Someone *wrote* this? And *published* it? And people *purchased* it? Not just other people, but her very own husband? Shocking. She put the book back quickly—well, after reading a few more pages, just to assure herself she was correct to be scandalized. She hoped she stacked the books back in the proper order.

The bedside table was actually a cabinet, a single compartment with a single door. But when Gen tried to pull it open, she found it locked.

But Gen was the lady of the house, and now a very curious lady, so she fetched her great ring of keys and sorted through them until she located the small brass key that matched this lock.

It turned easily, and revealed a compartment with two more novels of similarly salacious content, as well as a black leather case somewhat smaller than a doctor's bag. It felt quite heavy.

She opened it. Why did he unpack everything but the

contents of this small case?

Inside, she found a strange collection of objects. A coil of thin, braided rope. A flask of what smelled like the strongest alcohol ever distilled. A rolled piece of dark silk. And an even smaller leather case that turned out to hold a set of what seemed to be small, very sharp knives.

What could Cameron possibly want with this strange assortment, and why here, next to his bed?

As she replaced the leather case of little knives, the edge of a broken nail caught in the roll of silk.

"Oh, blast," Gen whispered. She snatched her hand away, but succeeded only in partially unraveling the silk. She took a breath and carefully extracted her nail to avoid a run in the fabric. She held up the unfurled silk. It wasn't a cravat, as she first thought. It was a...

"...blindfold?" Gen asked herself. The strip of silk was far too long for any proper necktie, but it could certainly be used to tie around someone's head.

The black silk blindfold, paired with the rope, made her flush. She'd heard hints of some of the less conventional ways people enjoyed themselves in the bedroom— Sabine loved to gather and share some of the more saucy gossip that circulated in London, and Gen listened, half-rapt, and half-horrified. Was Cameron one of those people? No wonder she'd bored him to death in bed.

Either that, or he planned to take up piracy if his family disowned him.

She stifled a nervous laugh, then rolled the silk up as it was and put it back. She shut the lid of the case and shoved it into the cabinet where she'd found it.

This was what came of prying into people's secrets, she told herself. Invariably, the truth was uncomfortable. If it wasn't, they wouldn't keep it a secret.

Gen locked the cabinet again, swearing to herself that

she'd not try to discover more about her husband. The lesson of Bluebeard came to mind, and another nervous laugh burst from her, loud in the otherwise silent room.

Nonsense. She was in no danger from Cameron. He was the most harmless man in London. A debonair, lazy charmer who could do no worse than disappoint his wife and family.

Wasn't he?

♊

WHILE HIS WIFE, UNBEKNOWNST TO him, spied on his private things, Cameron sat in a rattling hired coach and wondered what the hell he was doing with his life, and why he'd agreed to become a spy for the Zodiac in the first place.

"She took it rather well, if I may say," Quinn noted from his seat on the opposite side. "Your presence in the house, that is. In fact, the whole household seemed…well, *happy* isn't the word. *Relieved*."

"People like it when the world is predictable," Cam said, staring moodily out at the darkened streets, only occasionally punctuated by a lantern or candlelight from a window. "I shouldn't have stayed away so long." He knew things wouldn't be easy, but he was set back on his heels by the sheer distaste Gen held for him, in bed and out of it.

Well, he'd worked hard to build his persona. He shouldn't be surprised when people believed it.

"It all worked out, sir. Let you act even more like the man you aren't." Quinn knew quite a lot about acting like who he wasn't, and Cameron took the comment as it was meant—a vote of confidence.

Cameron thought about all the things he'd done over the past years to create the impression of Lord Deverall as a useless, harmless man who no one feared.

"Think it will be Gemini or Black Mask the Zodiac needs this week?" Quinn asked then.

"That's what this meeting should reveal." It was always Gemini or Black Mask who took action. Not Cameron. That was the core of the deception. No one would ever suspect that a foppish, lazy lord would also be a black-clad criminal who scaled walls like they were garden walks. Cameron spent a lot of time maintaining his body so he could do all the things the Black Mask needed to do—climb a rope a few stories up, run from any people or dogs pursuing him, even to lift something heavy that might be in his way. And he had to do all that training in secret, because Lord Deverall never lifted a finger as far as anyone knew.

It was a good deception, and it let Cameron get information no one could get in any other way, because he had the knowledge and background of an aristocrat, able to see the subtle hints of something wrong in a letter concealed in someone's house. Yes, he sometimes took items, but more often he just took his memory of them back to the Zodiac, where his information was added to an evergrowing mass of files, to be assessed and added to what the Zodiac already knew from other sources.

He was proud of the work he was doing, though he could tell no one about it. Society looked down on spying. It was seen as ungentlemanly, even vulgar. Spying wasn't honorable, according to the notions of honor that preferred men to march boldly onto battlefields and shoot each other dead according to long-held rules and rituals. Cameron was willing to give up some personal honor if it meant fewer battles and fewer people dying. Fewer widows and orphans. Fewer wars.

But no matter how much he kept telling himself that it

didn't matter what people thought of him, it did matter. He'd grown to hate his persona as a lazy lord, not so much among the general public, but among his family and friends. And Genevieve.

Quinn had ordered the coach to drop Cameron off at Powell and Gate Streets. He'd then told the driver to continue to a location not far ahead, where a certain tavern operated outside the bounds of the city's licensing laws. "Meet me there, sir."

Cameron waited until the coach rolled off and then made his way across the street to a large building that looked as if it functioned primarily as offices for various businesses, which it did. However, that was not all the building contained.

Inside, the building's many hallways and stairs contrived to form a sort of maze, the result of frequent hasty, unplanned renovations. Cameron made his way to an office on the fifth floor. He knocked smartly, and the door opened a moment later.

"Come in." The invitation was issued by a woman. Her ash-blonde hair was pulled back into a bun, from which a significant portion of the hair already escaped. Rather than a gown, she wore two separate items: a rather masculine cotton shirt tucked into a long grey woolen skirt. Over the shirt, she wore a cropped jacket in a plaid tartan with red and black as the principal shades. The effect suggested a woman who cared nothing for others' opinions, and that effect reflected the truth.

"Evening, Miss Chattan," Cameron said politely. "Got your note. Anything urgent?"

"Not exactly," she said, a smile passing across her features like a brief glimpse of sunlight through clouds. "Thank you for coming so quickly though. You must be in the midst of reestablishing yourself at home."

The last line was delivered without inflection, but Cameron shot her a look. "Honestly, must you rub in your knowledge of everything?"

"When one's business is keeping secrets, it's quite therapeutic to reveal one now and again. I get so little opportunity."

"That's true, so don't begrudge Miss Chattan her fun," said a new voice. "Good to see you, Gemini."

"Good evening, Aries." Cameron looked to the doorway of the inner office, where Julian Neville stood. Julian was six inches shorter than Cameron, with sandy-colored hair and a pleasant face that looked like it belonged to anyone but a spy—which made Julian an exceptional spy, and indeed the day-to-day leader of the Zodiac, or in the parlance of the group, the First Sign.

"Let's sit and talk," Julian said, gesturing to his office. "Chattan, can you bring that file in?"

Cameron often wondered why Julian only addressed the woman by her last name. It was an odd practice...but then, the Zodiac was an odd institution. He'd never heard her first name, not once in years of working as a Sign. He concluded that Julian hid the information to protect her identity, though he couldn't see why she needed protecting. Miss Chattan seemed extremely capable of protecting herself.

Chattan returned with the file. Julian took it with a nod and a murmured thanks.

The two men had worked together for years, and Julian was actually the one responsible for the creation of his thief persona. Cameron wasn't the first Gemini to work for the Zodiac, but he was the first Gemini to have an additional identity—the Black Mask.

Most of the Signs traveled overseas frequently, and were heavily involved in spying on specific countries. But traitors were closer to home as well, especially since the exodus of the French aristocracy following the Revolution, and the advent of Napoleon's various wars. Julian needed a Sign dedicated to hunting down dangers in England itself. A man with the proper social standing to get in the highest places, the money to be listened to, the wiles to get into the lowest places, and the intelligence to get out alive.

It meant structuring a persona that looked utterly nonthreatening. And Cameron was very, very good at it. People liked him. They thought he was amusing and a little scandalous, but not anyone they'd have to watch their words around. Meanwhile, he collected and remembered every little scrap of information, passing it on to the Zodiac. That was his work as the Sign of Gemini.

Cameron learned a lot by listening, but sometimes he had to get information that no one was talking about. So he'd become the Black Mask whenever it was necessary to procure a letter or a document that was hidden away in a locked drawer or a safe or a hidden room.

"So. What happened?" Julian asked then, looking up and catching Cameron with his direct gaze.

"Ah, isn't that usually my question for you?" Cameron replied.

"I meant, what happened to cause you to move back to your house? Will it influence your ability to work for the Zodiac?"

"Not in the least," Cameron answered, a little stiffly. "The summary is that my wife and I agreed that we have some mutual goals, and thus living together is necessary."

"Ah." Julian undoubtably caught the true meaning of that, but it wasn't something Cameron wanted to discuss. "As you say. Well, I do have another assignment, one uniquely suited to the Black Mask side of your persona."

"Tell me." Pleased to learn that he'd be working as the thief, Cameron eased back in his chair.

"There's a Frenchwoman who goes by the name Mireille Lambert. She's a trusted agent of Napoleon."

Cameron nodded. He didn't even think to question how the Zodiac got that knowledge—he'd long ago learned that the organization had resources far greater than one would expect, considering there were never more than twelve active agents at any given moment.

"Mireille is in London now, and your job is to find out exactly what her plans are, so we can prevent her from carrying out any work detrimental to England or our progress in the wars."

"That's not a lot to go on."

"Alas, the French spies do not announce their intentions when they arrive here. Quite rude of them, but then, they're French." Julian slid the slim file across the desk. "Her current whereabouts, known contacts, and a physical description."

Cameron nodded again. He didn't possess an eidetic memory, but he practiced tricks to help him memorize most things that came his way.

"I may need a little help," he said, thinking of the difficulties in tracking a well-trained agent in a city the size of London.

"We've already put a few Disreputables to work. Someone is watching her rented home around the clock, and they'll stay in contact with you through Quinn."

Cameron nodded again. Of course the Disreputables would be involved. The cadre of former criminals—now nearly all household servants in respectable homes—had become invaluable aides to the Zodiac. It was how Cameron met Quinn in the first place.

"All right." Cameron stood up, leaving the file on the

desk. He'd memorized it all. "With luck, I'll have something for you in a few days."

"Be careful," Julian told him. "If she's on British soil, she has a definite objective. Don't underestimate Mireille. Our sources say she's remarkably intelligent, in addition to being the usual sort of seductress."

Cameron left the Zodiac office in search of Quinn. The entrance to the tavern was difficult to find, being down a narrow alley, with a door that looked as if it hadn't been opened in a century. Cameron knocked and offered a very particularly coded greeting to a massive doorman, who opened the door just wide enough to let him through.

Inside, Cameron was given a thorough look by several of the tavern's patrons, all men of various ages. Their looks were interested but covert—Cameron wasn't a regular here.

Quinn was a regular, it being one of the few places where he could act a bit more like himself.

He found Quinn at a corner table. "You like to make me meet you here because you find it amusing."

"I like it because it's discreet, and your work is a discreet sort of work. And it's funny to watch you fail to fit in."

Most of the Disreputables fell afoul of the law because they'd grown up as pickpockets, smugglers, jewel thieves, or some other type of criminal. They were grifters and con artists.

Quinn was none of those things, and never had been. Yet he'd seen the inside of a gaol several times, and was nearly executed alongside violent criminals.

His crime was being interested in men rather than women. From the age of twelve, he had to learn about certain parts of London's underworld very quickly in order to survive. He knew who he could bribe if he got caught, and which judges were sympathetic (or not) to a well-told tale about how he was an innocent victim. And as he got older, he learned more about a particular *demi-monde*, a network of men and women who hid their interests from an unforgiving world, choosing to live and play in selected houses and taverns and other such places where they could be relatively free.

But it was hard to remain free, and Quinn was often caught in raids or simply hounded by a Charley with an agenda. And that was how he met the Disreputables.

Once Quinn became a Disreputable, he used his knowledge of the city to help Cameron on various assignments. And in exchange, Cameron helped others like Quinn when he could. It was not uncommon for a man hiding one sort of secret to fall prey to hiding another. Such a man was easy to blackmail, and more than one of Cameron's missions had resulted in evidence that would expose someone's "unnatural" impulses. And while the Black Mask didn't usually steal the physical documents he found, Cameron always took those…and destroyed them.

"I've received my assignment," Cameron said quietly, "and I'm afraid it means very little rest for either of us for the near future."

"Back to work, then," Quinn said, drinking the last of his ale. "For King and country."

♊

GEN SLEPT BADLY THAT WHOLE first night, thinking of all the ways that Cameron's return could ruin her peace of mind, and possibly her life. She rose early and dressed in a silk morning gown, which at one time was green but now had faded to a sort of apologetic khaki. She disdained a cap.

Her lady's maid, Kincaid, always brought her breakfast in bed, since it was silly to lay out all the dishes and set the table for one in the dining room. However, when Kincaid appeared in the bedroom that morning, she bore no tray and instead asked if Gen would like to go downstairs to dine with the master.

"Oh, mercy." The very first event of the day showed Cameron's propensity for disruption. But if the food was already out, there was no sense in wasting the effort.

Gen didn't truly believe Cameron was at home, let alone awake, until she clapped eyes on him. But not only was he there, he was alert, perfectly dressed, and digging into a plate of food far more extravagant than Gen ever allowed herself. Bread and jam, but also hot ham, sausages, sweet buns, and a full pot of coffee.

"Morning," he said with far too much cheer and warmth for a man who'd practically run from his wife's bed the previous night. "Sleep well?"

"Does it matter?" she asked, surveying the embarrassment of dishes on the sideboard. "What is all this?"

"Breakfast. You should try it."

Gen stiffened up. So she was too skinny for his liking, was that it? She regarded the ham with malevolence, and assembled her usual selection of toast and honey. She never had much appetite in the morning, and Cameron's presence cut her hunger entirely.

Nor did he let the subject lie, as a sensible man ought to.

He eyed her plate. "That's not enough to go on."

"I'll have coffee as well," she said defensively.

He took that as an order, and before she could say a word, he poured some coffee into a cup, and splashed in warm milk from a nearby pitcher.

Gen stared at the drink, dumbfounded that he'd remembered she preferred *cafe au lait* to plain coffee.

"That's right, isn't it?" he asked, the cheerfulness now sounding a bit forced. "Or have your tastes changed?"

Why did she read multiple meanings into that question? "No, I'm just as I was. Except thinner, apparently."

"Not much thinner," he said quickly. "But I hope you're not approaching every meal with such apathy."

"Why should you care?"

"You want to feed yourself well. And feed any baby you might find yourself with."

True. Gen could be with child any day now. Yet she resisted his paternalism…on every level. "I will eat as I see fit."

Cameron waited a beat, then said, "What are your plans for the day?"

"I have several calls to make," Gen said. "Some members of the Society, to discuss the children's home we're building, and a few friends…no one you'd care to see, I'm sure."

"I've got to do the rounds as well. I assume you're changing into something else before you leave the house."

Gen put her cup down carefully, lest she hurl it at him. "Yes, my lord. I am capable of attiring myself in accordance with the whims of polite society. Indeed, I've done many things all on my own for the past three years. Independently, as it were."

Cameron's jaw set, and though Gen had almost never seen him act in anger—the incident of knocking the fan into a fire had been totally unexpected—the Bluebeard fairy tale echoed in her mind once more, and the image of ropes and knives and blindfolds all carefully packed in a case flashed before her eyes.

But then the shadow was gone. He got up from the table, having polished off the last of his meal. "Well, I'll leave you to it. See you tonight."

The implication lingered in Gen's mind, but the man himself was gone before she could reply.

Gen spent the day making a series of social calls. Then there were calls on acquaintances from whom Gen hoped to raise some funds for the construction of the new children's home and hospital. Usually she could wrangle a small pledge from people after she told them of the terrible poverty that children faced. The members of the *ton* typically did not have much sympathy for the rabble of London, viewing them as lazy or shiftless. But when Gen argued on the children's behalf, she could make some headway. It was hard to blame an innocent child for their predicament, and harder still to say they should starve simply because they were unlucky.

Some people did argue just that, of course. They appealed to fate or simply quoted Scripture to the effect that "the poor are always with us," as if it was an admission of defeat rather than a call to arms. The fact that Genevieve avoided working with religious institutions also made some people suspicious. But Gen didn't want some distant bishop deciding what the children of the slums needed. She thought the people living there knew best how to improve their own lot.

She'd gathered pledges from a few ladies that day, and feeling flush with victory, she arrived at the home of her mother-in-law, Edith, the Marchioness of Bainbridge. She'd got to know Cameron's parents during her engagement, and even after Cameron's awful behavior, she remained close to them. Indeed, his mother stood staunchly on the side of Genevieve in the wake of the scandal. Edith never hid her disappointment in her son, and Cameron never once showed a hint that he cared.

Genevieve entered the foyer with a smile, which dissipated the moment she saw who was standing in front of her. "Cameron. What are you doing here?"

"It *is* my parents' home," he said dryly. "What are you doing here?"

"Though they are my parents by our marriage only," she retorted, "I make it a practice to visit regularly, as family should."

His eyes narrowed, the blue darkening as her barb hit home. Cameron had behaved awfully these past years, and he knew it.

A maid had gone in to announce the unusual combination of callers.

"What?" A feminine cry rose from the next room a moment later. "Both of them, together?"

Cameron glanced at Gen. "Prepare for an onslaught of motherly emotion. Someone should have warned her."

"How? Neither of us knew we'd be here at the same time. Besides, your mother is far stronger than she pretends."

The maid appeared at the door and frantically waved her hands to beckon them in.

Lady Edith stood by the window, her face lit by the summer light, softened through the veil of the sheer silk drapes. Her blue afternoon dress was a marvel of tucks and folds along the high bodice, with even more embellishments at the hem, the fabric folded and worked into elaborate rosettes. Genevieve tried not to calculate the number of meals the price of such a gown would buy for the children in the slums. Instead, she greeted her mother-in-law with a cheerful face.

"Have we surprised you?" Gen asked as she reached the older woman.

"Indeed. Here you are, together." Edith shot a look at her son. "This better not be a prelude to asking for something."

"Speaking of asking for something," Cameron said, his voice as sharp as his mother's gaze, "is the pater around?"

"He's hard at work, as you should know."

"But Parliament isn't in session now."

"There's still work to be done before we leave town for the summer," Edith returned. "Your father is very dedicated." She did not have to add that Cameron could learn something from his father. Her tone did it for her.

"I'm not here to ask for anything," Cameron said, in a slightly more conciliatory way. "Genevieve wanted to see you."

"Always so thoughtful." Lady Edith's porcelain perfection eased into a smile. "And it is good to see you both together."

"Marriage is marriage," Cameron responded, helping his mother to the long divan liberally scattered with cushions. "We both know what we're responsible for."

The line was vague enough that Lady Edith could read into it what she liked, and sharp enough to remind Gen that Cameron didn't really want to be in the same house with her.

Remember that you need his approval to sell the estate. Yes, Gen had to keep her larger goal in mind. She could help hundreds of souls simply by enduring this sham of a marriage for a little while, and surely that was worth it.

Cameron was about to sit in a chair by his mother when she snapped open a fan and ordered him to sit by Genevieve instead. "You two have so much lost time to make up for!" she cooed. "And of course I must hear how you made amends."

Gen went cold—they had no story to tell that would be appropriate for his mother to hear. She glanced at Cameron, who put his hand over hers very briefly and squeezed.

"Leave it to me," he murmured.

Oddly, Gen felt a surge of relief at his words, and a warmth in her chest from his touch.

But in fact, Cameron wasn't able to tell much of any story, whether true or false, because they were not left alone to discuss it. A parade of Lady Edith's friends and acquaintances stopped by to call, and all were greeted by the image of Viscount Deverall sitting next to his very own wife as if all was well between them. The chatter remained light, though Gen grew hot under the many knowing, smug glances sent her way.

Rumors would fly around London and beyond. After today, people would be gossiping about how Lady Cameron finally took her husband back, even after he embarrassed her so thoroughly.

People were tactful enough not to raise the subject

directly in front of them. Topics ranged from whose daughter had the best Season, to the discussions likely to be taken up in Parliament next session, to that oldest of chestnuts, the weather.

A short while later, Cameron rose from the couch, bringing Gen up as well. He bowed over his mother's hand and promised to visit again soon.

"You both must come to dinner before we leave town," Edith replied. "It's been far too long since we've had everyone under one roof."

"We'd be delighted," Genevieve said. She doubted Cameron would be delighted, but if they were going through this sham, why not play it to the hilt?

In the carriage, Cameron sat across from her, his expression thoughtful. "Practically the whole *ton* will flee the city for summer," he said.

Gen said, "Perhaps, but I've not left the city in summer for the past few years."

He shook his head. "Why did you not go to Greyslake? You said it was your favorite place when you were a child. Boating on the lake, and hiking to the top of your very own mountain among the pines."

She'd told him about her childhood during their courtship, but she was surprised he remembered all those little stories. However, seeing Greyslake again just before she sold it would break her heart. "I have to remain here," she said. "My charity work does not stop just because the seasons change."

"What tasks are so essential that you can't direct them via letter?"

In truth…very few. Genevieve just felt so useless in the country, or anywhere that she couldn't focus on her chosen efforts. She never liked the endless rounds of visiting, or the slow, often stifling pace of country life. "I just prefer to be available, if needed. If you want to leave town, you're welcome to."

"Leave?" His eyebrow rose. "With our contract not fulfilled? Surely I can prove my dedication to something in my life, and this way I can do it lying down."

She bit her lip and stared down at her lap. Why did she still get flustered when Cameron teased her? He *was* her husband, so she ought not feel ashamed. Yet, the reminder that Cameron intended to join her in bed for the foreseeable future still made her nervous and flushed. The image of him unclothed came into her head. He *was* extremely nice to look at. And she'd get to look at him every evening, like clockwork. Until…

"If I find I'm with child soon and you want to get away…out of the city," she said, "you'll sign the Greyslake papers before you leave?"

Cameron watched her for a moment, his expression almost blank…but not quite. Then he leaned back against the seat and yawned. "Of course. A deal is a deal."

She wasn't sure she'd read his face correctly. It was dim in the carriage, and Cameron had never been the sort of man to show strong emotions. Nothing seemed to affect him very much. His quickness to laugh and his ability to set people at ease was one of the things that had first caught her attention when they'd met years ago. He seemed so approachable, in spite of his family name and his wealth.

"When might you know?" Cameron asked then. "Just for curiosity's sake."

Gen blinked. "That's a rather intimate question."

"It's an intimate matter that concerns both of us."

"Two or three weeks, at the earliest," she murmured, embarrassed of the need to discuss this with him. "My cycle has never been very consistent." It was a source of annoyance to her, since she never knew when to expect her courses. The first few days were often marked by pain and cramps and a sour mood that turned her into the most unpleasant person imaginable. Her maid had a special tea blend reserved for just those days—the secret ingredient was a liberal splash of brandy.

"Well, you'll announce it the moment you know, I'm sure. Probably along with a second copy of your Greyslake papers, an inkwell, and new pen."

"And you can call for a carriage the moment you're done signing," she added, thinking of how fast he'd want to be gone.

"You won't give me time to have my things packed?"

"I assumed you'd just direct your man, Quinn, to have them packed and follow after. You must miss the particular comforts of your own home."

He was about to reply to that when the carriage stopped. He looked out the window. "Ah, speaking of home. We've arrived."

♊

THEY ATE AT HOME THAT evening. Just the two of them, dressed for dinner and with very little to say. Genevieve looked beautiful as always, but fidgeted with her salad fork, then her dinner fork, and finally her dessert fork.

Unsurprisingly, her nervousness didn't dissipate in the bedroom later. Cameron tried to soothe her, he really did. But Gen didn't seem to want to be soothed. And Cameron didn't want anything other than to explore every inch of her, a desire that made his brain once again lose the battle against his cock. He lasted longer than the previous night, but not much longer. And he knew Gen didn't enjoy the encounter nearly as much as he did.

After he withdrew, his body satisfied and his mind anything but, he lay next to Gen, thinking he'd have better luck pleasuring her now that the obligatory part of the evening was over.

She didn't object when he put his hand gently on her belly, nor when he ran it up between her breasts. But the moment he shifted, sliding his palm across one of her perfect, luscious breasts, she wiggled a few inches away from him.

"I thought we were done," she said.

"We don't have to be."

"But we *are* done." Gen blinked rapidly, looking a little confused. "You seem quite…finished."

It was almost funny, the way she looked at everything except him. Yes, he had a hell of a finish, and he was no longer painfully aroused. But that could change quickly if she let him stay in the bed with her.

Cameron reached for her—she hadn't wiggled *that* far away. Cupping one breast, he murmured, "Why not start again?"

"You mean…with all the…touching?"

"Yes, with all the touching, though I didn't touch you nearly enough. Let me do that now."

"It's not necessary," Gen said quickly. "I'm quite content to not do all that again."

Despite her words, he saw veiled interest in her eyes, and when he pulled his hand away from her just a fraction, she leaned forward enough to make contact again.

So he was fairly confident as he said, "What if we do all that again tonight, and it results in you conceiving?"

"Oh." Gen's breath rushed out, tickling his chest as the air hit him. "Well, that would be…good. I mean…but we wouldn't know."

"No, we wouldn't know for certain. But isn't it worth a try?" He was up for it. Or he would be soon.

Gen lay very still beneath him for a long moment, clearly agonizing over the decision. He let her agonize while he teased her breast and thought about the odds of her allowing him to use his tongue to get her ready. He'd never done that yet, but God he wanted to.

"I think I might be too sore," she whispered at last.

Cameron winced. He must have been rougher than he thought. "Did I hurt you?"

"No! It's just a bit…uncomfortable as yet. I'm sorry."

"Don't be sorry." Neglecting her for three years was definitely something he should apologize for, not her.

"In fact, you should leave," she said abruptly. "I need

to sleep. I don't keep your sort of hours." She slipped out from under his hand, and wound the sheet around her like a protective shroud. Only then did she look back over her shoulder. "Do you have any idea how odd it is to have you in the house at all? I barely was used to it at first, and then you left for so long... You can't just pick up as if nothing changed."

"Is that what you think I'm doing?"

"I think it's what you hoped for," she returned, with far too much acumen. "But it's not as simple as that."

No, it wasn't simple at all. He'd been too optimistic, thinking that once he moved back in, Gen would want to return to their old life as much as he did.

But, as she hinted, they never *had* an old life. Just a courtship and a few weeks of marriage. There'd been no time to settle into a routine.

"Gen," he said, unsure what point he wanted to make, just that it was important he didn't leave without making some point. "I am trying."

"I know you are," she said after a moment. "And we are agreed that a child is necessary, for both of us. But don't pretend we're like other couples, Cameron. We're not, and we never will be."

Cam left Genevieve and went to his own room. Gen's comment was more cutting than she probably intended. They weren't like other couples, and it was entirely due to Cameron's secrets. He'd been selfish to marry anyone while his life was not entirely his own.

But he craved the normalcy that marriage was supposed to offer. Taking a wife was meant to have made his life simpler—no more difficulties at balls and social events with mamas foisting their daughters on him. No more questions about the fate of the Deverall line. An easy, uncomplicated arrangement. That's what was supposed to have happened.

And now things were more complicated than ever and Genevieve was stuck in the middle of a web that she couldn't even see.

Cameron hadn't set out to make a love match. Genevieve came from a very suitable family line, and was herself quite acceptable—more than acceptable. She was well-educated and quite willing to apply her mind to any problem she found interesting. That was the thing that attracted him most. Not just her looks, though he approved of those, especially her sweet smile and the way the left side of her mouth twisted when she was trying not to laugh. He liked the way she stood up for what she cared about, and advocated as fiercely as any MP. She'd entered into a political discussion with his father during a dinner one evening—Gen never raised her voice, but over the course of ten minutes, she told the marquess that his position on a matter in the House of Lords was flat-out wrong, and proceeded to counter each of his defenses with well-reasoned arguments.

If Cameron hadn't noticed her before, he certainly would have then. Gen's cheeks grew pink as she argued her case. Her hands were animated, outlining her vision in the most compelling way. And her eyes glowed with the sort of passion that any man would want to see directed at him—not some obscure motion in Parliament.

He'd made a point to call on her the next day. And the next. And the next.

Everything he learned over the course of those carefully chaperoned, very proper meetings convinced him that Genevieve was well-prepared to be the wife of a politician, because she was gracious and clever and had no hint of scandal about her. She'd make a perfect wife for him.

However, Cameron hadn't yet realized that he wasn't the perfect husband for her. Not even close.

He couldn't match the openness Gen brought in their marriage. He had only layers of secrets and lies. And all too soon, one of those secrets trapped him in a spiral of deceit that hurt Gen as well, forcing him to stay away from her for years.

Why should this time be different?

Because I'll make it different.

Superficially, Cameron settled into his new life. He spent his mornings training. Then he returned home to carry out the often inane and superficial tasks of a member of the *ton*. He made social calls, responded to invitations and letters and such, and took care of whatever social obligations his rank demanded. Then an evening out. Then home again to bed Genevieve. Then out again to do whatever he had to do as Gemini.

Sometimes that meant attending a party as Deverall and listening far more carefully to the words dropped by certain people concerning this new French spy in town— she seemed to lead a very quiet life, however. The Disreputables said she went shopping and wrote a lot of letters, but nothing to signal why she was in England.

Sometimes it meant wearing all black and shimmying through a window as the Black Mask. And then he dragged himself back home to sleep a precious few hours until it all began again.

It wasn't much different from his old life of the last few years, with the exception of needing to fool Genevieve and the household into thinking that his absences weren't interesting or nefarious. The household, from Ainsworth down to the lowest scullery maid, knew better than to question the master. And Genevieve didn't seem to care one way or the other what he did—after the first few days, she rarely asked where he went, and only occasionally did he catch her looking at him with a hint of skepticism.

But she said nothing, nor did she thaw much in the bedroom. He didn't want to rush her, so he didn't suggest anything beyond what they'd done together before. But it made him antsy, to have such a gorgeous woman in his arms and yet no hint of pleasure or interest from her. Perhaps she'd secretly found her pleasure elsewhere?

"You're certain you haven't had a single lover over the past three years?" he asked one time after she'd risen from the bed and pulled on her shift.

Gen arched an elegant brow. "Are you asking me that because you think I might have forgotten such an event? As if I'd ever find myself in bed with a man who isn't my husband but then be too flighty and—*poof!*—misplace the memory of the encounter. And in any case, why would I want to engage in such an act for no purpose but diversion? It's a preposterous idea." She huffed and resumed her previous activity, which was covering up all her lovely flesh under the dull and tattered dressing gown.

Cameron avoided mentioning that several parts of the city were devoted to establishments catering to that particular diversion, not to mention most of the scandals among the *ton* also centered on who was enjoying such diversions with whom. Did Gen dislike it? She didn't seem to mind, but she also seemed, well, relieved to have it be over. And she certainly hadn't achieved any release, or she was *very* quiet about it.

Then it occurred to him that because Genevieve was such a proper lady, it was possible she didn't even know the extent of the pleasure she could be feeling. The first part of their marriage, he'd been too preoccupied with getting her comfortable with him that he frankly hadn't got to the more pleasurable aspects of sex. He'd assumed they'd have plenty of time for that.

And then the incident during the party had ruined everything.

Cameron watched his wife dress, and he realized just how little he knew her. That was not an ideal situation. He resolved to alter the terms of his contract with Gen. Cameron would not just give her a child, he'd make her love the whole process of creating a child, and he'd make her understand exactly what she'd been depriving herself of all these years.

Cam thought that Genevieve was slowly growing used to having him in the house. Over the next several days, she stopped jumping in surprise when he greeted her at breakfast, emerged around a corner, or passed her by in the hallway. However, he was not used to her mode of dress, so he took some steps to improve it.

When a large number of pasteboard boxes arrived at the house one morning, he made a special effort to accompany them to their recipient. Kincaid preceded the train of footmen, and then Cameron, into Gen's bedroom. "These just arrived for you, my lady!"

"A mistake. I didn't order anything," Gen said. She was still in bed, though obviously awake, for she held a newspaper in her lap.

"I did," Cameron announced.

"What are they all?"

"One way to find out," he countered, as the footmen deposited the boxes and left.

The packages turned out to contain several morning gowns, and two chemises he intended to be seen nowhere but in a bedroom, by him. Everything was well-made, from the fabric to the intricate stitching to the lace embellishments. The maid ran the back of her hand over the blue silk of the first morning gown, humming in approval.

"Very fine, ma'am. And new," she added pointedly.

"Put them away," Gen said, her forehead pinched with disapproval. "I'll continue to wear my own things."

"These *are* your own things, ma'am." The maid looked to Cameron for support.

"Kincaid, why don't you go downstairs. I want to speak to my wife alone."

The servant made herself scarce, and it was just Cameron and Genevieve, staring at each other.

He'd better head off any arguments she would make. "You needed new things," he said.

"I certainly do not. What I have is perfectly adequate."

Cameron gestured to the ratty morning robe she had on. "Don't be obstinate, Gen. That gown is an abomination."

"It's comfortable."

"The new ones will be comfortable as well," he said. "More comfortable. They damn well better be anyway, considering the cost."

"The cost is what concerns me."

Enlightenment nudged him. "You funneled all your pin money into your charity work. You don't spend anything on yourself."

"I buy things," she protested. "Gowns for parties and events and such."

"Because you are representing your Society there," he guessed. "But at home, you wear rags."

"It's my choice. Anyway, you are entirely too presumptuous in thinking you could pick out my clothing for me."

Seeing that Gen was spoiling for a fight, he changed his tactics. "Perhaps. Would you just try one?"

She pursed her lips but said, "Very well. Put it on me." She slid out of the bed and stood imperiously, daring him to refuse, or to complain that he wasn't her maid.

He picked up the blue silk one, divested Gen of the original robe—resolving to burn it later—and slid the new morning robe over her arms and reached around to tie the ribbon that held the front closed, fastening it under her chest. He ran his hands over the shoulders of the gown, feeling the buttery silk. "Tell me that's not better than the old one."

Gen sighed, and he instinctively worked his thumbs into her muscles, drawing a longer, softer sigh from her.

"It's better," she said, sounding far more relaxed. Lord, if a simple massage could improve her mood, he'd have done it far earlier.

You should have been around far earlier, an inner voice taunted him.

Well, he was here now. He bent his head, murmuring close to Gen's ear, "I thought this color would look perfect on you."

He continued to rub her shoulders, enjoying how she seemed to melt against him as he worked. The silk aided his efforts, the fabric warming as it glided next to Gen's skin. He kissed her neck because he could, and her reaction was enough to make him want to remove the gown again immediately.

Gen gave a tiny moan and laid her head back against his shoulder, leaving more of her neck exposed. Cameron's blood surged at the move, the first real indication of Gen wanting something from him just for pleasure. He kissed her neck again, very gently.

"More?" he asked.

"Hmmm, yes."

He obliged, laying a trail of open-mouthed kisses from the base of her neck up to her hairline. He brushed his lips against her ear, saying, "Did you know how soft your skin is, sweet Gen? I could kiss you all day."

She just gave another little moan. He could take her to bed this moment, show her that there was no reason to confine their encounters to late nights.

He kept kissing her neck, and reached to untie the ribbon again. "Seems a shame to both be here in this room, with this bed, and not make use of it."

"I haven't eaten breakfast yet!" she objected.

"I'll help you build up an appetite." He plucked the morning robe off, revealing the old shift underneath. "This thing," he said with distaste. "I'm going to rip it off for the last time."

"You're more interested in changing my wardrobe than bedding me."

"I'm equally interested in both," he said.

She shook her head. "Let me go."

"Not till you say you want me to come to your room tonight."

"We already agreed that you're going to be here every night," she said, not looking at him.

He touched her cheek. Her eyes widened as he leaned in to kiss her. Gen resisted for a moment, but he felt the moment when her irritation turned to acceptance, her lips softening under his. And then the acceptance turned into something better—interest. Hesitant, shy interest. But when he slowly pulled back, she leaned forward, fully engaged in the kiss.

Until she broke it off with a ragged little inhale, a necessary breath for a woman unused to the rhythm of something as simple as kissing.

"Forget the agreement, sweet Gen," he said, keeping his voice low and steady—unlike his heartbeat, which was already anticipating a move to the bed. "I want to hear you say you *want* me to be here."

He saw her pulse thrum against the delicate skin of her throat, and he knew his heart wasn't the only one affected by the kiss. "Cam…" she started.

"You don't have to do anything more than say it, Gen. Then you have the whole day to yourself." *And you better think of me the whole time.*

"I want you to come to my room tonight," she whispered, each word dropping from her mouth unwillingly, precious stones she would have preferred to hoard.

"Why do you want me here?" he asked, drawing her out.

"You know why," Gen murmured, her cheeks going delightfully pink again.

He slipped his fingers into her hair, still unbound in this morning hour. "I want you to tell me."

"Because…" She trailed off.

"Because you do want me in your bed?"

"Yes."

She spoke so softly he could barely hear the word, but once he did, he immediately pressed, "Because you want me to kiss you, perhaps on the neck as I just did?"

"Yes." Again, her answer was hardly more than breath.

"Because you want to feel my hands on you?"

Her face was flaming now, the color high in her cheeks. She mouthed the *yes* but no sound came out.

"Hmm. Well, then I'll be here," he said, just as if he'd agreed to a second cup of coffee. "Does midnight suit you?"

"Y-yes."

"Excellent." He pushed her away, mostly because if he kept hold of her, there was no way he'd wait till midnight to bed her.

"Cameron?" she asked.

"Yes?" *Beg me to take you right now.*

"Thank you for the new gowns. It was very thought-ful." She reached out as if she wanted to touch him. But then she blinked, like a woman waking from sleep. She shook her head once, a much more Gen-ish expression covering her face. The competent lady who didn't let herself be diverted.

She stepped away, and said, "You ought to leave. I need to get ready for the day. I've got to go to Bond Street, and then to a meeting of our board, and then some errands…" She rattled off a list of tasks in a nervous, flustered way. "You're occupied as well, I'm sure. No time to waste…"

Her gaze slid to the bedclothes, as if he might toss her on top of them after all. Which he wanted to, very much. But he actually did have things to do, things that no one would expect Lord Deverall to be remotely involved in.

"You're right," he said. "But tonight, Gen. I'll be back here."

"Midnight," she said softly.

"Not a minute later. Wear the new pink chemise."

A very shy smiled graced her mouth. "If you like."

"I do like. See you tonight, Gen."

* * * *

After Cameron left her room, Gen was in a complete haze. She spent far too long admiring the new gowns, for his choices mirrored her own tastes surprisingly well. Or perhaps not so surprisingly. Kincaid bundled the old things up and took them away, leaving Genevieve dressed in a new, lovely gown suitable for her later errands.

She tried to work. Every time she picked up a book or a paper or a letter, the words blurred in front of her eyes and all she could picture was Cameron. The way he'd held her that morning, the way he'd touched her just enough to make her so distracted and dizzy and dreamy…

Perhaps he was a little interested in her after all.

Gen pulled herself together in time to go downstairs to meet a carriage. She dropped a few letters to be posted onto the tray in the hall. There was another there, the street direction written in Cameron's bold hand. It was addressed to M. Metcalfe, Summermaid, Trace Street, London.

The letter was sealed of course, though not with the seal of Cameron's family crest that he used for his correspondence. A sudden suspicion blossomed in her mind. Why not use the seal? Was he trying to be discreet?

A little late for that, she thought. Trace Street. Gen didn't know the street, but that meant little, with the way London was growing so quickly year by year. That street might be in any neighborhood—she'd have to ask to find out just where the place was.

Just then, Cameron entered the foyer. And he was holding the small leather case she'd seen in his bedside cabinet that first day he returned home.

The case with the thin rope, and the strange little knives, and the blindfold.

Genevieve caught her breath. "Are you sure that you'll be back tonight?"

"Certainly," he said easily. "If you'll be here."

"I'm home every night," she said, her gaze locked on the suspicious leather case. "Where are you going? What hostess is demanding you at this hour?"

He shifted the bag to the other side of his body, looking at last a little discomfited. "No one you'd care to know, Gen."

Irked by the evasive answer, she swept past him, seeing the footman open the door to reveal a carriage at the end of the walk.

"Have a *lovely* time," she muttered as she crossed the threshold.

Gen stewed in the carriage, her thoughts locked on that leather case and its contents. If it was full of items intended to be used in a bedroom, then why was Cameron carrying it out of their house? Where was he going to spend his day? Presumably with someone less staid than her.

She was so foolish to have thought he'd changed. She denied him this morning, so he was off to see his mistress, just like the rogue he was.

"I'm being unfair," she said, the words unheard over the clatter of the carriage wheels. "I'm being unfair." Truth be told, Gen couldn't be sure what Cameron needed that case for, just as she had no proof the letter in the hall was anything other than innocent.

She laughed out loud. When had Cameron ever been innocent? All the stories about him suggested at least a little rakishness, a little edge, a little more excitement than most of the gentlemen of the *ton* had. And wasn't that part of what attracted Gen when she first met him? Cameron, Lord Deverall, the handsome, charming, intriguing gentleman. The man who looked at Gen with a twinkle in his eyes when he told her he loved watching his father the marquess lose an argument to a lady. The man who asked her to dance one night, and then easily persuaded her to stroll through the gardens without a chaperone—just for a few minutes, just long enough to make her feel deliciously daring, just short enough to get her back to her mother without any raised eyebrows. The man who always seemed just out of reach for Genevieve.

She'd been astonished when he continued to call on

her, continued to court her. And when he told her that he wanted her and no other woman for his wife, Gen felt as if she'd fallen into a dream.

But that dream was long ago, and Gen had to live in the world she made. She paid a few crucial social calls, and then went to the building where the Society for the Improvement of Friendless Children served food to those who came in the doors. Despite the name, the Society refrained from specifying an exact age that made a person a child or adult, and in fact many orphans of London weren't sure how old they were. Gen remembered many times a young woman of fifteen or sixteen years would linger by the doors, fearful of being turned away. She especially liked to invite those girls in, watching their expressions turn from wariness to hope.

On this particular day, Genevieve and Sabine stood side by side at a large table. Sabine wielded a large knife in one hand, and was efficiently sawing large loaves of crusty bread into manageable hunks for each child. Gen dipped a ladle into an iron pot and one by one filled dented metal cups with a vegetable soup.

A pair of children approached the table, a young girl of about seven, and an older boy of perhaps twelve, his arm protectively around her thin shoulders.

"Good day," Gen said. "Bread and soup for you, miss." A daughter of very proper parents, Genevieve thought that etiquette was a useful thing for all children to see. She handed the food to the girl, who looked almost ecstatic to receive it.

"And for you," she said to the boy.

"We don't have money for one meal," he said. "Sure not two."

"No one pays to eat here," said Sabine.

The boy, older and wiser than his sister, narrowed his

eyes. "Why?" the boy asked bluntly. "Why just give out bread?"

"Because we have bread, and you need bread," Gen replied just as bluntly.

The boy considered her words carefully, then nodded and took the food. He nudged his sister to walk to an empty bench where they could eat.

"Do you feel there are more children each month?" Sabine asked in a quiet voice, sawing away at a fresh loaf.

"I know there are. Laurel sits at the door every day, and she doesn't miss her numbers." One of their children had taken on the role of counter, mentally recording how many children entered and ate. She reported her tally with confidence, and Gen saw no reason to doubt her.

"The sooner we can break ground on the new building, the better. I would dearly love a bakery on site." Sabine smiled at a dark-haired child who came up to her. "More bread, dear? Certainly."

During a lull, Gen asked Sabine, "Do you know anyone named Metcalfe?"

"Why?" Sabine asked, her eyes narrowing.

"Oh, just something an acquaintance mentioned at tea the other day. I thought it might be someone we could discuss the children's home with…but I can't remember any name but Metcalfe."

"Hmmm. Well, there must be dozens of families by that name in London. There are the Essex Metcalfes, but I think they are hardly in society. Wouldn't go there for assistance. What about the Somerset Metcalfes? Mr Michael Metcalfe?"

"It does sound familiar. Large family?" Gen probed.

"The usual. More daughters than is advisable for financial solvency, but there is a boy as well. Also a Michael, if I recall."

"And the daughters?"

"There is a Rose and a Margaret. There was the eldest daughter, Amelia, but she passed away."

"Did she? When?"

"My word, years ago." Sabine's voice sharpened as she began to recall the long-dormant gossip. "Shame—she was a diamond of the first water. The parents hung their hopes on her face bringing the whole family up to higher levels, and then she took sick and died within weeks. The other daughters are plain as old bread, poor things. No hope for an advantageous marriage there."

"Sabine!" Gen chided.

"What? I'm just reporting the facts. If Amelia had lived, she'd have been on the arm of an earl at the very least. And instead, her mother buried her and tried to marry off the younger misses, who don't have a tenth of the late Amelia's grace. They probably married some old country gentleman in need of a second or third wife. *C'est la vie*," she finished.

Well. That line of enquiry resulted in a dead end. Gen must look elsewhere for a likely Metcalfe. Perhaps it wasn't even a woman Cameron was corresponding with. It could be a matter of business. Some solicitor or other. Completely innocent. So what if Cameron was writing letters to one of them?

After serving what food they had, Genevieve went home, and was not surprised to find Cameron still out. She ate dinner alone, and then read a gothic story in one of her favorite monthly journals. This one was by Gratia Fitzwilliam, a writer new to Genevieve but who was fast becoming a reliable favorite.

But the whole time she read, a thought lurked in the back of her mind—where was Cameron, and who was he with? Mr Metcalfe? Miss Metcalfe? Or was it Mrs Metcalfe? And if it was, did the contents of the leather case have anything to do with the meeting?

She put the magazine down on her knee. She sighed, annoyed with herself that the issue mattered so much to her. Genevieve was not in love with Cameron. She had no desire to be the sole fixation of his lust. Indeed, she'd agreed to their contract only because she did want to be a mother, and Cameron needed an heir.

The arrangement was simple, and what he did on his own time was his own affair.

She winced thinking of the word *affair*.

Thank goodness she wasn't in love with him. That would be a tragedy.

When midnight chimed, Gen was waiting in her bedroom, a single candle burning on the nightstand. She wore the new pink shift. The silk rippled across her skin, a pale pink that didn't seem too revealing, until she put it on and realized how easily one could see the flesh under the fabric when the light struck it just so.

She wondered what Cameron would think when he saw her in it.

By quarter after twelve, she wondered what was delaying him.

By half past, she wondered if he'd forgotten where he lived.

By one in the morning, she took off the new shift, pulled her old one back on as a matter of principle, and curled up under the covers, trying not to cry.

She wasn't sure if she was angrier at him or herself. He'd promised to come to her room at midnight. He'd wrangled the request out of her in the most embarrassing way. Gen should have known better than to believe his promise, and she certainly should have known better than to hope anything would be different this time.

Gen wasn't going to fall into that trap again.

Even buried under blankets and a down pillow, she heard every little creak of the house, every footstep from the servants downstairs. She'd hear if Cameron walked up the stairs and opened his door. Or hers.

But there was nothing.

Eventually she fell asleep, her restless slumber broken by strange sounds and dreams of dark hallways, and once, of Cameron's voice, promising more promises he'd never keep.

♊

AS IT HAPPENED, CAMERON *WAS* going to another woman's house later that day, and the contents of the leather case were extremely important to the escapade. Genevieve likely would not have been comforted that the woman in question was not named Metcalfe, but was rather a ravishing French agent.

Evening came. Cameron, blissfully unaware of the specifics of his wife's concerns, whistled a tune as the closed coach he and Quinn were riding in passed by Hyde Park and proceeded toward a fashionable square of the city.

"You're in a good mood," Quinn said. "Eager to catch a spy?"

Cameron, now dressed all in black with his mask in his hand, just grinned back. He was in an astoundingly good mood, but it had nothing to do with the robbery he was about to commit. It was because the moment it was over, he was going back home to Genevieve, who'd finally admitted that she did want him in her bed.

The sun had set a half an hour ago, and the bells of a nearby church tolled nine o'clock. Three hours, he thought. More than enough time.

Shortly after, the coach rolled to a halt near an alley. The smell of horses and manure hinted at the nearby mews which would serve the residents of these few streets and the houses of the square the French agent was inhabiting.

Cameron nodded to Quinn. "I'm off."

"Stay out of trouble."

"I won't run into trouble," Cameron said. "No matter how wily this Mademoiselle Mireille is, she can't catch smoke." And when he was the Black Mask, Cameron might as well be made of smoke. He opened the coach door, slid out, and proceeded down the dark, cluttered alley as if it were a promenade.

He reached the house he wanted and settled down in the appointed spot to wait. Her rented house had been under surveillance for days now, so the Zodiac could learn her patterns and decide when it was best to attempt to enter. A boy sidled up to Cameron while he was concealed in the bushes outside.

The boy took in Cameron's mask with appraising eyes. "You ready for the task?" the boy asked.

Cameron merely patted the leather case at his side. "All the tools I need."

"Right, then. The lady of the house went out an hour ago. The best room to enter is on the righthand side of the house, looking from the front. Middle story, second window in. Be careful."

"Many thanks," Cameron murmured.

"Don't mention it," the boy said, sounding much more mature than he was, for he looked no older than twelve. Cameron knew the Disreputables selected for talent, but this boy seemed very young indeed. Perhaps if Genevieve ever got her children's home built, boys like him would be off the streets and never fall into crime in the first place.

He climbed the outside wall of the house easily,

thanks to a sturdy ivy vine. The window slid open after only a bit of struggle, and then he was in. After peeking in a few rooms, he saw the one most likely to contain the agent's correspondence. Nothing on top of the desk was likely to be helpful, but Cam sorted through it anyway.

He needed to find out Mireille's reason for being in England, and he had to do it without alerting her that she was under surveillance. Hence the extremely cautious approach—watching the house, noting patterns, using multiple Disreputables to follow her around the city. Ordinary people might assume that the goal was to catch a spy as quickly as possible. That was not the case. It was often far more enlightening to let them operate, thus learning far more about their missions, contacts, and objectives than one would ever learn through interrogation.

But sometimes, an agent had to hurry things along, so Cam was willing to take the risk of searching Mireille's flat.

He turned his attention to the locked drawers of the desk. Cameron went to work on the lock using his set of picks, and a short while later he had a whole cache of papers in his hands. He used the moonlight to read though letter after letter, stowing away the interesting phrases in his mind.

And there it was. A very interesting phrase. And a shockingly interesting name. He held up the letter, squinting since the moon had gone behind a cloud. He read it again. Yes. This was his clue.

Mireille Lambert was going to Worcestershire. Which meant Cameron would be too.

He replaced everything just as he found it, then slipped out the window. He pulled it shut, so the agent would never know someone had been inside. He emerged from the lot into the mews, feeling rather pleased with himself.

Then he heard the barking.

A skinny young man ran toward him, hauling a bulky sack over one shoulder. The dog was barking desperately, its chain preventing it from giving chase.

The man hurtled directly toward Cam, who avoided getting knocked over only due to his quick reflexes. He stepped to the side and grabbed the young man, who looked deeply annoyed.

"Who stands in a dark ally in all black at night?" he growled. Then taking in Cam's appearance more carefully, his eyes widened. "Hey, you're—"

"The Black Mask!" a new voice called from down the alley. Both of them turned to see a man standing there, gripping the leash on a different dog, a mastiff.

What were the odds? The one night Cam robbed the French agent's home, a commonplace thief was robbing another house on the same street. And his clumsiness would expose them both.

"Charleys," the young man muttered. "Bad luck."

Bad planning, Cam thought, who always made sure the houses he robbed didn't have dogs, or had dogs that could be hushed in one way or another.

"We need to get out of here," he said. They began to run, in the opposite direction of the advancing lawman.

"Oy, you!" the Charley howled from down the long alleyway behind the houses. "Both of you! Stop there!"

Cameron did not stop. He ran faster.

The Charley loosed his mastiff, and the dog began to give chase.

"Split up!" he ordered the young thief, pointing him to a gap between two stables. The man dashed down it.

But the dog continued to follow Cameron. The mews opened to a narrow side street and he turned down it.

Then a whistle up ahead, as another Charley ran toward him. They were out in force tonight.

He swerved down another alley, and slowed as a figure stepped out of the shadows.

Quinn.

"What did you do?" the valet snapped out, running alongside.

"It wasn't me!" Cam kept up the pace, creating a bending, twisting path through the neighborhood. He was making for the river, knowing that the posh houses would soon give way to less congenial surroundings, where they had a better chance against pursuit.

The whistles faded, but the baying continued, the dogs on their scent. One got close enough to nip at the back of the black shirt Cam wore. He surged ahead, eager to avoid being devoured.

Cam crossed a street and paused, Quinn lurching up beside him. "Those dogs aren't going to give up."

"There's a place we can go," Quinn got out between heaving breaths. "Follow me."

They took off again, Quinn leading this time.

Cam was in good condition, but he thought his legs were about to give out when Quinn suddenly turned down an alley so narrow two people couldn't walk side by side.

He looked around in confusion. The dead-end alley was dank, and all the residents appeared to be rats.

Quinn walked further down, urging Cam to keep close. "This is a safe place, but we still have to be circumspect. You'll have to take your mask off. And your shirt."

"What?"

"Sir, you currently look exactly like the Black Mask. Head to toe black, with Charleys on your heels. We can hide in here, but they can't know what you are."

"So I'll be more discreet half-dressed?"

"Yes," Quinn said. "And anyway, in here, half-dressed is not odd at all."

He ripped off the mask, and then the shirt. Quinn grabbed them both and bundled them into a tight ball. "Let me do all the talking."

They proceeded to a narrow door nearly obscured in the darkness. Quinn knocked on the door in a rapid, syncopated pattern that Cam couldn't catch and wouldn't be able to duplicate.

The door popped open, and an arm reached out of the darkness, grabbing Quinn, who in turn grabbed Cameron.

They were yanked into the building, the door slamming shut behind them, followed by the sound of several bolts sliding home.

"Thanks," Quinn said to their nameless, faceless host. "There are Charleys outside."

"Aye, we could hear the baying of the dogs. The Charleys in this neighborhood love to run with mastiffs. They after you?"

Quinn shrugged. "A misunderstanding."

"Isn't that always the way?" Their host gave a laugh with little humor in it.

A candle was lit and Cameron saw that their host was a small man, five feet tall at the most. He had thin, silvery hair in an old-fashioned queue. "Haven't seen you in a while, Mr Quinn."

"I've been otherwise occupied."

"And your friend?"

"This is Mr, er, Black."

The man surveyed Cam—right down to his bare torso and the distinct scar on his arm—with an expression of resigned amusement. "I'm Rawlins. Proprietor of this fine establishment. Welcome."

"We just need to catch our breath and wait out the

Charleys," Cam said, even though Quinn warned him against talking.

"Fear not, you'll be able to do both of those things here. We've got lookouts on the street, and they'll tell us when it's all clear."

Rawlins led them into the main part of the house, which was far more comfortable than the alley entrance would suggest. It was well lit, and well furnished, with many small rooms that seemed to serve as private parlors. Some were occupied. The guests were all men, in twos and threes. Some were drinking, some were flirting, and a few were doing more than flirting.

Their host yanked the door shut on one such couple. "A little decorum, please!" he yelled through the door, in a tone that suggested he'd yelled the same instruction many times before and had no expectation that his words would be heeded.

Finally, Rawlins entered a larger room, and Cam saw that not all the inhabitants were male. A young woman in men's clothing lounged on one of the couches in a corner. Her red hair was tied back in much the same manner as Rawlins's.

"How's the street?" Rawlins asked her.

"Busy," she replied, making a face. "A whole pack of animals sniffing their way past every door. Oh, and their dogs are with them."

Rawlins chuckled. "Keep a keen eye out, my little mouseling."

"Always do." She nodded to Quinn and the shirtless Cam, and then turned around, rising up on her knees to face the curtain-covered wall. But then she twitched a curtain aside, and revealed a strange apparatus, like a periscope. She peered through it, with the patience of someone who'd be staring for hours.

"Drink?" Rawlins asked. "You might be here awhile."

"We don't have a while," Cam said.

Rawlins reached for a bottle and two glasses anyway. "You have until those Charleys give up, which might be longer than you think. They know there's a house of ill repute around here, but they never quite figured where we are or how to get in. They and their damn dogs will scour the streets and wake up the neighbors until they think they've turned every stone."

"Hours?" Quinn asked.

"Possibly. Relax and have a drink. Rawlins's is a place where men leave their worries at the door." The host smiled. "Excuse me. Must check on a few other patrons."

He left, and only the woman he'd called a mouseling remained in the room, intent on her surveillance of the street.

Cam explained what had happened in the alley. He finished with, "The worst thing is that the Charleys will assume he was with me. The Black Mask does not work with amateurs."

"Aren't you snobbish for a criminal," Quinn noted.

Oil lamps burned, providing a warm glow to the room. And the brandy was first-rate. Cam wished he could enjoy it. He closed his eyes and thought back to the document he'd seen in Mireille's house. It was still surprising, but perhaps it shouldn't be. After all, if the woman was a French spy, wasn't it logical that she'd been trying to contact one of the most important Frenchmen on English soil?

"You look perturbed," Quinn noted in a low voice. "But not because you nearly got your leg wiped off by a mastiff."

"No. I saw some information that means a completely new direction. Worcestershire."

"Never been," Quinn said with the superior indifference of a born Londoner.

"I have. You're not missing much. But I'll need to alert"—Cam left the Zodiac's name unspoken—"to let them know as soon as possible. And I'm expected home."

Quinn raised an eyebrow. "That's your priority?"

"My priority is the assignment," Cam said stiffly. But he'd promised Gen he'd be home. And the clock hand was moving with distressing swiftness toward ten.

Then to eleven.

And then past eleven. The law was using the excuse of chasing a criminal to knock on doors and barge into houses. The calls of residents grew from a low grumble to a louder altercation, and through it all, the barking of dogs continued.

The Charleys were thorough, according to the mouseling who was watching. Cam guessed her to be about sixteen, and suspiciously well-spoken for a girl in this neighborhood. From her commentary, he gathered that Rawlins hired not just her but also a few other women to keep watch at various spots in the house, and also to assist with serving patrons food or drink as needed.

As for her unusual mode of dressing, she said bluntly, "Why shouldn't I? Men get to wear comfortable clothing. And here at least, we can drop the nonsense we've got to pretend outside."

"I can see why you like it here," Cam muttered to Quinn.

"It's quite relaxing," he said. "So long as we don't get arrested coming or going."

The young woman nodded at that. "Speaking of, what do you need to get you on your way, Mr. Black? Your lack of shirt suggests either a disregard for convention…or a dearth of funds."

"A sartorial mishap from earlier in the evening," Cam replied. "Could you get me a replacement? Something plain, but not laborer's wear. Like a clerk or a man of business."

"Our neighbor does laundry," she said. "I think there will be something in your size. Give me a few moments, sir."

She left.

Just then, Rawlins declared to the house's patrons that the search had finally been abandoned. "You can head out if you like, one at a time, please." He continued to mutter out loud about Charleys who thought they could go anywhere they liked.

"They think the law protects them from breaking the law themselves," he said, not for the first time. "Think they can knock on doors in Seven Dials as if they were collecting for charity. At night. Five quid says not all of them return to their employer to report."

"Wouldn't that be a shame," someone else muttered from somewhere in the dim room as patrons who'd been kept there prepared to leave.

The young woman came back with some folded clothing in her arms. "Miss Bella had what we needed in the laundry. Dry and pressed." She handed them to Cameron, and pointed to an unoccupied room where he could change. He did so, finding himself now looking like an ordinary clerk, in dark trousers and a coat, with a crisp white shirt, and no hint of decoration that Viscount Deverall would sport.

He stepped out again.

The woman swept him with a critical eye. "Fits well enough to get you home, sir. Miss Bella will need those back, lest she lose a good customer."

Cameron nodded. A laundress couldn't afford to have

clothes go missing in her care. "I can see that Quinn gets the clothing back tonight."

"That will do. Quinn, you be careful." She gave the valet a kiss on the cheek, then opened the back door and looked out. "Clear. You both be off."

Despite the hour, Cam insisted on going to the Zodiac offices. And Miss Chattan was still there. She listened to Cam's report, gravely issued an order on Aries's behalf, and told Cam to go home.

Even at that hour, the city wasn't completely asleep. Night workers trod the streets, and on a few corners, prostitutes waited for late customers. A few coaches clattered along, the sounds of the horses' hooves more sharp and lonely sounding than in the middle of the day when they all blended into the general din.

At his house, Cameron chose to enter his room through the window, not sure if a servant would be up very late or very early. Quinn waited below while Cameron changed out of the borrowed clothing and dropped it in a bundle out the window. Then the valet disappeared into the gloom.

The clock on the mantel told Cam it was now three in the morning. He'd missed his assignation with Genevieve, with no good excuse for why. His hand fell onto the latch of the connecting door before he fully realized he'd walked over there. The impulse to see Gen was strong, and even though he knew it was foolish, he eased the door open and stepped in.

She was asleep, her body drawn up into a little knot, her arms wrapped around one of the down pillows. *It should be me she's clinging to*, Cameron thought, seeing how tightly she gripped the pillow.

He didn't sit on the bed, fearful he'd wake her. But he said in a tone just above a whisper, "I'm sorry, Gen. I didn't mean to stay away so long. I promise I'll make it up to you." He wasn't sure how, since his work in the Zodiac was demanding and the timing out of his control. But he wanted to promise anyway. He wanted Gen to be able to rely on him. "I swear I'll find a way through this, no matter where it leads."

He left before she woke up. Cameron retreated to his rooms to think. He needed a damn good story by morning. Unfortunately, he sat on the bed to do his thinking, and he fell asleep a moment later, without having thought of a single worthy excuse to tell his wife.

♊

THE NEXT MORNING, GEN ORDERED Kincaid to bring breakfast to her. She couldn't bear the idea of seeing Cameron across the table, knowing he'd chosen some livelier diversion than her the night before. She never should have let him back into the house.

"And he's broken our stupid contract," she muttered out loud, inadvertently spilling toast crumbs onto the bed. She ought to bring that up the next time she saw him, and demand he sign the Greyslake papers immediately. That's what a solicitor would advise.

She ought to wake him up by slapping the Greyslake papers in his face. Was he even home? Or was he sleeping off his excesses in some other woman's arms?

Vengefully wearing her old brown linen gown—though she thought longingly of the buttery soft silk she'd worn yesterday—Gen yanked open the connecting door.

Cameron was sprawled out on the top of his bed. He hadn't even pulled the covers back. He wore only a dressing robe, the deep red paisley one that had hung unused for three years.

She could tell that Cam was cold. The fire hadn't been lit last night, so the room was chilly. And why was a window open? Gen pulled the window shut and latched it, then walked back to the bed and grabbed the blanket that hung over the footboard. She shook it out and laid it over Cameron.

He made a sound in his sleep, a little hum as the woven blanket covered him. Gen bit her lip. He didn't deserve to be babied like this. And yet, she was his wife. There was a contract there too, a far more sacred one than the Greyslake-for-child abomination, and she would not be the one to break it.

As she walked away, her foot nudged something on the floor. She bent to pick up a letter that had fallen, and even as she moved to place it on the table nearby, she glanced at the script on the front of the pale blue paper. It was addressed to Lord Deverall—no surprise there. But the hand was flowing and feminine, and not one she recognized. She knew the handwriting of Cameron's mother. Who was this who was writing to him? The plain seal on the letter was intact, and Gen was sorely tempted to break it and learn who'd signed it.

But no. She wasn't going to stoop to that level. It was one thing to peek at what books he had at his bedside table, and quite another to break the seal on a letter not addressed to her. Gen let the still-folded letter slide to the floor again.

She went down to her study and spent the next hours intent upon several letters to potential supporters of her project, and then—more fretfully—examining the ledger which detailed all the expenses of the Society for the Improvement of Friendless Children. The final figures were worryingly low. She might have to raise a loan to keep the project going, even if she soon got the deed to Greyslake clear.

There was a quiet knock on the door, just at the time the post usually arrived. A footman walked in with several letters on a tray.

"One from Italy," the footman announced with a trace of a smile, for he knew just how much Gen liked to hear from her brother.

Gen put aside her ledger. She read Roger's words eagerly, thinking of the places he saw, and the people he met. He finished with,

...I saw a painting in Florence today, of two little girls in white dresses. It reminded me so much of you and Grace. Next time you visit her grave, buy some flowers and tell her they're from me. I miss all my sweet sisters.

With great affection,

Roger

Gen smiled as she laid the paper down on the table. Her brother was such a darling.

There was another knock at the door. Surely not another letter so soon. Was it a social call?

"Who is it?" Gen called. "Tell them I am not at home." She wasn't attired properly to receive callers.

The door opened, and Cameron walked in, now awake and alert and dressed as perfectly as always. "You're at home to me," he said flatly.

Gen looked up, willing her gaze to be as frosty as she could manage. "It doesn't seem to matter whether I'm at home or not, my lord. Last night, did I miss something in our agreement? Some subclause that permits you to ignore the single edict you insisted on? Do you want an heir or not?"

"Who's writing you?" he asked, ignoring the jibe and pointing to the letter instead.

"Roger. He's in Florence, or was at the time he wrote."

Cameron's lip curled slightly, and Gen frowned. To her knowledge, Cameron had met Roger only three times. Once at a party in town, once at a dinner at her family home shortly after their engagement was announced, and finally on the day of their wedding. The men had been perfectly polite to each other, and Gen couldn't imagine why Cameron now revealed distaste for her brother.

"Quite the extended trip," he commented.

"There's no crime in a Grand Tour, or in appreciating art."

"Yes, I'm sure he's appreciating all Italy has to offer." Without even glancing at the letter Cameron said, "He wants money from you?"

"How did you know that?"

"So he did ask for money?" Cam pressed.

"He requested a small sum to tide him over while he sorts out some difficulty with a bank."

"And what of all the friendless children on the streets of London? Tell Roger your money is already spent."

"It's just a little! And anyway, if you signed the papers for Greyslake, I could sell it and there wouldn't be an issue of money. Which reminds me! You violated our agreement last night, and that means you are in breach of contract. You can sign the Greyslake papers right now." She reached for the copy she had in her drawer.

"Hold on a moment. It wasn't my fault. I was delayed due to circumstances beyond my control." He sounded genuinely upset about it, though he didn't offer any details.

Gen bit her lip, but then said, "Regardless, a breach is a breach. It doesn't matter why you didn't come, just that it happened."

"No mercy from the justice?" he asked, stepping around the desk to meet her.

"We both agreed on the terms," she said, inhaling the scent of his skin and suddenly wishing she could sit down.

Cameron reached out to put a hand on the small of her back, drawing her a little closer. "I'm a few hours late, but we can fulfill the terms of the contract right here if you like. It looks like a very sturdy desk."

"Cameron!" Did he really mean he'd take her on the desk itself?

"Is that a yes?"

"No!"

Rather surprisingly, his eyes were sparkling. "Who's breaking the agreement now?"

Lord, he was *enjoying* teasing her.

"Cameron, I'd have to be mad to agree to that."

He leaned a little closer, his lips brushing hers. "A little madness can be very liberating."

Gen parted her lips to object, but he took it for an invitation to deepen the kiss. And Gen found herself rather immersed in the sudden sensations he was stirring up. His mouth caught hers, his tongue teasing her lower lip in a way that made her whole body delightfully shivery.

Then both his hands were in her hair, making a wreck of the simple twist, releasing curls with no regard for her decorum. The long pin holding the twist in place clattered to the surface of the desk.

Cameron didn't seem to notice, because he was too intent on kissing her over and over, not just her mouth now, but her cheeks and her neck, tipping her head up so he could reach every bit of exposed skin.

Gen sighed as his lips moved over her. His hands slid down her back, to her bottom, and with a quick move, he lifted her up and set her on the edge of the desk.

"Cameron!"

He murmured an apology if he set her down too hard, and then his hands were on her knees, parting them so he could step closer. His mouth returned to hers, his tongue doing things that felt far too pleasurable for the surroundings.

And yet Gen kissed him back, encouraged by the sound of his voice, the satisfied moans that escaped him every time she leaned forward.

His hands moved gently over her body, a touch here, a squeeze there. A stroke along her leg and then a quick rush of cool air as he pushed the fabric of her skirts away from her lap.

He pressed against her newly exposed thighs, and she could feel just how aroused he was, with a very noticeable bulge straining against the falls of his breeches. *He would really do this*, she thought. *Here in the study. With the door unlocked. In the middle of the day.*

Suddenly, she remembered walking into his study that fateful night. He'd been at his desk then too, with a woman close at hand. Her desire shifted into anger, the heat of one emotion easily flowing into the other.

"Stop this at once!" she said. Did he think Gen was just like that other woman? "This behavior is wrong."

"What's wrong about it, sweet Gen?" he murmured, unaware of her change in mood. "Everything about this feels right to me."

It did feel right. Too right.

"Well, it's not right, and I won't indulge your...absurd predilections for sex on furniture."

He raised an eyebrow. "If the study isn't to your liking, I'll take you upstairs." He grazed his fingertips along the neckline of her gown, making Gen nearly faint with the frisson of pleasure his touch created. "Please."

"No. It's midmorning."

"Yes. I'll be able to see you in the light."

"Cameron!"

"And you can see me—you pretend not to look, darling, but I catch you at it, you know."

"I don't!" Oh, Lord, she did. But only because Cameron was so damnably attractive. Not because she liked him.

His voice became low, beseeching, flatteringly intense. "Genevieve, come upstairs with me. Then we can have some real privacy. Believe me, it won't be the same in Worcestershire."

She blinked, confused. "Worcestershire?"

He went still for a second, then sighed as his lust evaporated. "That's what I meant to tell you when I came in. I just found out. We're going to a house party."

"Ugh!" The exclamation burst out of her the second she heard the word *party*.

"What's the matter?"

"I just don't like house parties," she said, flustered for a whole new reason. "They're an exercise in tedium."

He laughed, surprising her. "God, yes. Half the time I want to run to the stables, saddle the fastest horse, and ride out."

"Then why go at all?"

Cameron's smile vanished. "Because I have to."

Gen was puzzled. As the only son of a marquess, Cameron most certainly chose how to spend his time. Perhaps he meant a more intangible obligation—it was possible his father asked him to go, and he had to do his filial duty.

Then he said, "You could look on it as an opportunity to ask for more support for your cause from the others who are wasting time there. No reason you can't get something out of the visit."

"Other than a child?" she retorted, before she thought better of it.

Cameron's smile returned. "Who knows? Perhaps all that fresh country air will be vitalizing. You can leave the windows open when you prepare for bed."

"You're incorrigible."

"That's what people say." He touched her neck with a fingertip, his expression longing. Then he shrugged one shoulder and stepped away.

"In any case," he said. "We're going to Worcestershire in three days. You should direct Kincaid to begin packing everything you'll need for a month in the country."

Gen frowned at the short deadline. "Three days is not much notice. I can join you later."

"No." He regarded her carefully, his hands going to her shoulders, kneading the tension spots that had already formed at the very idea of spending a month in the country. "We have an agreement, don't we?"

"Yes, but…"

"No objections. The sooner we arrive, the sooner we'll be able to leave. Or so I hope."

"You didn't say why you have to go. Where is it precisely? Who's hosting it?" She already felt the tingling in her chest and stomach that she got when confronting anyone of the *ton* she didn't know well. So many of them thought Genevieve's work was silly, or worse. "I won't fit in at all."

His eyes narrowed. "You're the Viscountess Deverall, Gen. You'll fit in. I'll see to that." He sounded very different from the lazy, careless lord she usually saw. She wondered if this Cameron—the one who seemed eager to defend her—was a sort of show. He might want to get the business of an heir settled so much that he'd pretend to be the sort of man she wanted.

And she was beginning to realize that she did want him, very much.

"The house?" she prompted.

"The house is called Thorngrove. Apparently quite a place."

"And the hostess of the party?"

"Alexandrine Bonaparte. Her husband is Lucien Bonaparte."

Gen felt lightheaded. Surely she'd misheard… "Did you say *Bonaparte*?"

"Yes. Brother to the other one." Cameron smiled thinly. "Surprise."

♊

GENEVIEVE HAD NO IDEA HOW Kincaid managed it, but within three days, all her trunks were packed and ready for a trip to Thorngrove. Cameron had as many trunks as she did, so it was decided they'd take the best carriage with the most important items, and Quinn and Kincaid would follow in a second carriage with the remainder of the luggage. Cameron declared that he didn't trust their possessions to a third party, and considering the stories Gen had heard about unscrupulous couriers, slow coaches, and highwaymen, she agreed.

The journey was barely tolerable, the roads pitted and rough. The first night at an inn, Gen was so tired and sore from travel she went up to the room and collapsed onto the bed. The next few days were no better in terms of comfort—coach travel was an ordeal even for the richest on earth. She and Cameron sometimes talked, usually of inconsequential matters, as they seemed to be the matters Cameron was most comfortable with. He did, however, ask Gen about her proposed project to build a secure and healthy home for as many orphans as she could manage to house.

Since Cameron made the critical error of asking about it when he could not escape the carriage, he learned far more than he probably wanted to. She enthusiastically outlined the details. Separate buildings for girls and boys. A hospital wing to treat the children who fell ill from the many diseases and injuries that afflicted the London poor.

A garden and a yard for animals like goats and chickens and geese, to help the home provide its own food for the kitchen. Schoolrooms and places for children to practice common trades before seeking apprenticeships when they were ready.

"We'll hire people to speak to seamstresses and milliners and shoemakers so that we can place older children in apprenticeships to help them become self-supporting by the time they're grown."

"What of the ones who don't care for a trade? Will you tell the boys they can join the navy? Enlist in the army?"

"I suppose we ought to have a list of recruiting officers," Gen mused. "Do you know who I could speak to about that?" She realized even as she said it that Cameron was the unlikeliest person in England to know a military contact.

Indeed, he had a completely careless air as he said, "Not my thing, Gen. Not my thing."

No, it wouldn't be. And yet…was there something just a little theatrical about his response? She didn't know how to press him on it, and then the moment was over.

When they weren't talking, one or both of them dozed. Gen tried to read a book until the bouncing rattled her eyes so much she couldn't focus on the words. Cameron tried to read something as well—not one of the erotic novels she'd happened upon, Gen noted.

Finally, they passed through the village of Grimley, which meant they were near their destination.

Not long after, the carriage turned down a driveway flanked with tall stone posts and iron fencing that disappeared into the trees. They proceeded through a little greenwood filled with mature beech trees. Sunlight filtered through the high canopy, casting everything in a soft greenish light.

Cameron rolled up his sleeve and put one hand out of the open window, letting the light and shadow play over his skin. Gen watched, mesmerized by the sight of him. It was his scarred arm, and she was a bit surprised he revealed it, since he usually took pains to hide it from... well, everybody.

He noticed her gaze, and gestured to the window. "You do it."

Gen would have to remove her gloves, and that would not be proper. "I can't. And you should button your sleeve again and get your jacket on. We're almost there, aren't we?"

He sighed, not doing as she asked. "It's a month in the country, Gen. You can let go of some of the rules we're forced to follow in London."

"As if you ever follow any rules," she retorted. She shouldn't start a fight, not now, not so close to their destination, but she couldn't help herself. She was sitting primly on one seat, while Cameron sat sprawled out opposite her, looking like he hadn't a care in the world. Without his jacket on, no less.

She picked up the jacket lying on the seat beside him. "Cameron. You're the Viscount Deverall. Please act like it."

"I most assuredly will act like it," he muttered, though more to himself than her. Then he leaned forward to take the jacket. His hand covered hers when she offered it. "Gen, I know we haven't spent much time together... around people. But if you follow my lead, you'll be fine."

"You speak as if I'm in the middle of my first Season," she said. "I assure you, Cameron, I don't need your oversight to conduct myself properly as a guest."

His hand tightened. "Of course you don't. You're a

perfect lady, Gen. You always have been. I just meant…I want to make things easier for you."

"Then put on your jacket and try to look presentable. Please."

In the space of three minutes, he managed to restore his appearance to that of a proper lord. He tugged on his cuffs and asked, "Well? How do I look?"

Stunning. Gen could never deny how handsome he always looked. His well-shaped mouth. His cheekbones. And his eyes. Always those wonderful blue eyes, the ones that could still make her heart race if she didn't warn herself about the man behind them.

"Quite appropriate," she said out loud. "And just in time."

They arrived at the main house. Cameron stepped out of the coach first, and then helped Gen out. He slipped one hand around the small of her back, whispering, "It won't be so bad, sweet Gen. A few weeks, a month at most."

She nodded, but then made the mistake of looking up at the house itself. It was magnificent. The stone facade seemed to take up half her vision, and well-manicured gardens and grounds filled up the rest. It was hard to describe what made this house different, because Gen had been to many country estates. Her own family possessed more than one.

But Thorngrove had a certain majesty about it, a hint that somehow more interesting things were going on inside the walls. Perhaps it was simply the fact that the exiled Bonapartes were the owners.

And then, a middle-aged lady dressed in the height of Continental fashion swept out of the main doors and stopped at the top of the steps.

"Lord Deverall," their hostess proclaimed. "We've

been expecting you. And your wife," she said to Genevieve.

Cameron bowed politely, and then spun an entertaining, much exaggerated story of the tiresome journey from London, and mentioned how Genevieve needed to recoup before supper.

They were shown to the upper floor, where two connecting bedchambers awaited. Both were large, well-appointed rooms that faced the pond on the western side of the great house. Gen looked at the elaborate wallpaper, the new silk draperies, and the heavy furnishings of her own room, and asked, "Why are we here? Is there some family connection?"

"No," Cameron replied as he surveyed the view outside the window. He'd looked his own room over, but stayed with Gen for the moment, a fact she appreciated more than she'd admit out loud. "Come here."

Gen joined him at the window. He pointed to a couple walking by the edge of the water. Even from that distance, Gen spied the bright red nose and the rounded belly that marked a man fond of his drink. The woman was perhaps one third his mass. "That's Lord Newsham and his wife. He's in close with the prime minster. Absolute bore. She's pleasant enough. I don't know how she stands him."

"You know everyone here?"

"Oh, no. Hardly anyone, at least at the moment. But we'll get to know all of them, whether we want to or not. And our host."

"Lucien Bonaparte." Gen still wasn't over the shock. "Why is he here again? Not Thorngrove in particular, but in England?"

Cameron said, "He's not welcome in France any longer, so he fled to Italy for a while. Then he attempted to sail to America—Lucien is a true revolutionary after all. But his ship was intercepted by our navy, and now he's here."

"I wonder why the government permits him to stay."

"The government is insisting that he stay. The official word is that he's a private citizen, and one who apparently has many friends in this country. He's never declared war against the English, and it seems that he's on the outs with his more belligerent brother. But the reality is that he's forced to stay here on the estate, with occasional trips to the village. This house is a very fancy prison."

"Why do you know so much about Lucien Bonaparte's situation? And why do you want to meet him?"

"I just want to see what he's wearing." He'd never sounded so sarcastic before. Cameron continued to stare out the window, his grim attitude utterly unlike his usual charm.

"Are you angry?" she ventured. Cam must have some hidden opinions. After all, he was going to be a marquess and enter the House of Lords eventually. Perhaps he thought more about the wars than he seemed to. "Angry that a Jacobin like him is here? Are you worried he'll stir up dissent?"

Cameron turned to her, surprise on his face. "Why, no. What he does is nothing to me."

Oh, it's something to you. "Nothing at all?"

"Let the man do what he likes. After all, I do what I like."

"But you must…"

Cameron's eyes were locked on her, and she suddenly forgot what she meant to ask. Then his hands slid around her waist in a way that turned all her good intentions to jelly.

"Gen," he whispered. "Let's try out this bed."

"We're expected to join the others before dinner!" she

objected, though it was difficult to argue with intent when he was kissing her neck the way he was right now.

"Plenty of time," he said. "Besides, we'll need to change for dinner anyway. Why not take off every stitch now and save time later?"

She sighed, but refused to succumb to his seduction. "No. We must behave properly, or what will people think?"

"Who cares what they think?"

"I care." It was difficult enough being here in the first place. She couldn't stand to think other ladies were snickering behind their fans at the insinuation that the first thing Lord Deverall did on arrival was to disrobe.

"Why? You're better than all of them. They should crave your approval."

"That's not how it works."

"That's exactly how it works."

"Cameron, if you want the other women here to accept me, then they need to see me. Dressed appropriately. And not…just…tumbled." She stepped away.

He laughed. "Are you a milkmaid? When have I ever *tumbled* you?"

"You know what I mean."

"But do you? I could tumble you, just in the interests of education—"

"That's enough! We both need to dress for dinner, and you need to stop talking."

"All right, but then what should I do with my mouth?"

"Cameron!" She was aware that she sounded like a scandalized matron. "Go to your room!"

"As you wish. But I'll be back later."

"*Cam.*"

"To take you down to dinner," he added innocently, with no innocence in his eyes.

♊

FOR THE FIRST DINNER AT Thorngrove, Genevieve needed to look like a proper viscountess, so she wore one of her new gowns. The outfit had a long train-dress of soft white satin, elegantly worked and embroidered in a border of blue and gold. The short sleeves were made entirely of white lace. Since it was evening, she wore a headdress—a very modest tiara of gold set with blue stones, which held back her mass of curls. She had white kid shoes and gloves to complete the outfit, and in the end was feeling quite satisfied in her fashionable appearance. It *was* fun to dress up, and she didn't always have to deny herself, did she?

While Kincaid worked, Gen asked her, "How was traveling with Quinn? Any issues?" She was wary of any man who had access to a woman in such a private setting as a closed coach.

But Kincaid smiled. "No, ma'am. He's a gentleman, I must say. Very proper and polite, and so many stories of London! I quite enjoy his company."

Gen breathed a sigh of relief. Quinn had been Cameron's valet since…always. She'd hate to have to fight about his servant's misbehavior as well as his own.

Cameron knocked on the adjoining door before entering her room. Kincaid curtsied and hurried out of the room. She'd spend her evening among the many servants below stairs.

He surveyed Gen's outfit with obvious approval, which was unsurprising, considering he'd arranged for the new wardrobe to be made.

"Like the dress?" he asked.

"It's lovely."

"I agree." Cameron had been hiding one hand behind his back, and now he pulled it out and placed a small box in her hands.

"What's this?" Gen asked.

"A sort of apology for dragging you here."

She opened the hinged lid. Against white satin, a single sapphire glowed. It hung from a thin gold chain, which looked almost too delicate to support the weight of the stone.

He reached for the necklace, obviously intending to put it on her.

Gen let him. He stood behind her and fastened the chain around her neck, then pivoted her around to face him. He smiled. "I thought the blue would look well with the dress, and it does."

"You can't solve all your problems with a pretty gift."

"I know, but I am about three years behind when it comes to getting you pretty gifts, so you can expect a few more." He ran his hand down the side of her sleeve and then her bare arm. Cameron leaned forward. "Kiss me?"

Gen tipped her head up slightly, intending to kiss him on the cheek. But she found his mouth instead. The touch of his lips instantly summoned a warmth in her lower belly, a little coil of need that only more of his attention would satisfy.

His hands on her shoulders, running down her arms, settling on her waist, drawing her closer...

No. She broke off the kiss.

"Cameron, we ought to go down to dinner." The excuse sounded weak in her own ears—she wanted to be convinced to stay, to have the dress rumpled and torn under his hands, to forget the obligations of dinner entirely and just stay in this room all evening long.

This is what lust feels like. Genevieve flushed as she realized just what was happening to her, and felt annoyed that a mere kiss could lead her to such places.

"Let's skip dinner," Cameron murmured. "We can escape out the window, climb down the wall, and steal two horses from the stable. We can go anywhere. Anywhere but here."

Gen giggled at the idea of Lord Deverall shimmying down a brick wall like some sort of thief. "Don't be absurd."

He sighed. "I suppose stealing horses is illegal."

Now she laughed outright. "Not to mention we're expected downstairs. You're the one who insisted on attending this house party."

"So I did. Shall we go down into the lion's den?"

Thorngrove was designed for parties. The rooms glittered with candlelight, reflecting on mirrors and refracting through crystal everywhere Gen looked. They stood in one of the anterooms, sipping drinks from etched wineglasses while meeting what seemed like an army of houseguests.

Their hostess, Alexandrine Bonaparte, did the honors for the first few minutes. The lady was disarmingly open, insisting that her guests were quite free to use her Christian name, as her family name was not dear to English speakers at the moment.

They met Lord and Lady Newsham. Then Mr and Mrs Calverley. Then someone else. And someone else. Gen already wanted to sit down.

She was looking for an unoccupied chair when she heard Cameron say in a low voice, "There she is."

At the end of the room, Gen caught sight of another woman, and immediately felt the pain of the wallflower when in the presence of a hothouse bloom. This woman was brilliantly blonde, with fair skin and wide-set china-blue eyes. Something about her was at once innocent and knowing, and all the men present seemed to react to her almost without volition.

Gen could feel the shift in Cameron's attention and wanted to melt into the shadows of the room, unable and unwilling to compete with this beauty, who was now walking toward them with an airy grace that Gen could never achieve. Her richly dyed, deep green silk gown was almost an afterthought, a final flourish to her appearance that already rendered men speechless. She wore emeralds around her neck.

Alexandrine indicated the newcomer. "Ah. Mademoiselle Mireille Lambert. I shall ask her if she wishes for you to be introduced to her."

Gen's throat tightened. From the way the blonde woman's eyes raked over Cameron, there was little doubt she would very much like to have him introduced to her.

"Lord Deverall, may I introduce you to Mireille Lambert. My dear Mireille, the Viscount and Viscountess Deverall."

"How do you do," Cameron said. The words were proper, but the interested tone set Gen's teeth on edge.

"*Enchante*," Mireille murmured, her gaze locked on Cameron.

Gen said nothing, certain that any words would fall on deaf ears.

But then Mireille greeted her with a sunny smile. "My

lady, I do hope we shall be friends while we're here. It is so restorative to be in the country, is it not? And the countryside is beautiful here. At times, breathtaking." She looked at Cameron as she spoke.

"Ah, there are the Woxleys," Alexandrine said. "My lord, I do wish you to meet them."

"I'm just going to sit down a moment," Gen said quietly. "Please go on."

Cameron cast her a look of concern, but Mireille hooked her arm in his and drew him toward the oh-so-important guest and he was gone.

Genevieve sank onto a nearby chair and opened her fan. She wasn't overheated and she wasn't fatigued. But her chest was constricting and she felt an overwhelming sense of loneliness creep over her.

She scanned the room, watching the dozen or so guests who were assembled. Then she noticed a man watching her. He was wearing a dark coat over a white shirt, well-tailored but not embellished at all. Nor did the clothing conceal his thin, lanky frame and essential clumsiness. He walked like a man who'd never quite mastered all his limbs.

He noticed her appraisal and came over. "My lady. We've not yet been introduced, but if you'll forgive the impudence, I'll introduce myself. Mr Valentin Brodeur."

"How do you do." From her seated position, Gen extended her hand.

The Frenchman bowed politely.

"Are you a friend of the family?" she asked.

"I am merely secretary to Monsieur Lucien," he explained diffidently. "I'm only present at this dinner to avoid having thirteen at the table. Madame Alexandrine is a bit superstitious. I do not have the lineage of the other guests."

"Well, I am honored to make your acquaintance, Mr Brodeur."

A smile broke over his face—a wide, crooked grin that lacked any sophistication and was all the more sweet for it. "I am grateful. This is a unique situation."

Genevieve found herself smiling back. "But unique situations are more interesting than the usual ones, and give us all a chance to experience something we'd otherwise miss."

Valentin beamed at her. "Indeed, my lady! I am lucky to be here."

"You've been part of our host's retinue for some time?"

"Oh, yes. Since we all left France for Italy," Valentin said. "It is my duty to facilitate all kinds of business matters, large or small, that Lucien requires."

"That sounds rather daunting, especially being confined here."

"I'm the only resident of Thorngrove who has permission to leave the area of parole," he said. "I'm often called upon to travel to meet with various officials regarding the matter of our, er, length of stay in this country."

"So you are granted more freedom than your master."

"My freedom is purely for the convenience of the British government," Valentin said with a wry smile. "They'd rather I sit in a coach on the road to London, not the other way round."

Gen grimaced, for the pain of travel was all too fresh, and she was sure she had bruises on her bottom to prove it. "A true show of loyalty," she murmured, earning a laugh from Valentin.

After a few more minutes of small talk, a servant rang the bell for dinner. Genevieve looked around, wondering if she'd missed something. "How can we go into dinner when our host is not here?"

"Oh, Monsieur Lucien is often too engrossed in his own pursuits to remember to come to dinner. Madame Alexandrine is quite used to being a sole hostess." Valentin offered his arm, a little shyly. "May I escort you into the dining room, my lady?"

Gen glanced toward Cameron and saw, with an unpleasant jolt, that he'd already offered his arm to Mireille.

"Thank you," she told Valentin. "I should be very grateful." More grateful than the skinny man could know.

Fourteen people sat at dinner that evening. Genevieve resolved to say as little as possible and simply get through the ordeal. Through the first three courses, her plan worked. Conversations bubbled around her. She smiled and added only the briefest agreements to appear polite. She tried not to notice how much Mireille sought out Cameron's opinion on even the most trivial topics, and how he responded to her every. Single. Time.

Gen stabbed her lamb a little too viciously after hearing Cameron share some joke with Mireille in a low voice. The clink drew a few eyes, but she merely bit her tongue. But then, during the pause before the fourth course was served, someone asked how Lady Deverall spent her time in London.

Genevieve looked up, startled. Lady Newsham across the table was the one who asked.

"I—" *I spend it in the slums, and am too tired to dance later*. Hardly a politic response.

"My wife," Cameron said suddenly, "doesn't have much time for parties, since she dedicates so much of her life to charitable causes."

"Oh?" Alexandrine said, looking interested in Gen for the first time.

"Yes," Cameron continued. "She's much too modest

to boast about it, but she's been a force for improving the lives of hundreds of children in London, and she has even grander plans to provide food and education for the poor." Cameron smiled at Gen, and her stomach flipped over.

"Surely raising funds does not take so much time?" Lady Newsham asked, sounding truly puzzled.

"It takes more time than you might think," Gen answered at last, "but my husband was referring to the time I spend with the children."

"You go into those dreadful streets *yourself*?" the other lady asked in horror.

"On Tuesdays and Thursdays," Gen replied. "How can I ask for money if I don't see how it's spent? Besides, it's very fulfilling to hand a hungry child a piece of bread and see them devour it before your eyes."

Alexandrine nodded approvingly. "You have a mother's instinct, Lady Genevieve. You must have children of your own."

"No," Gen said, the brief moment of peace over.

"Not *yet*," Cameron corrected.

"When you do," Lord Newsham pronounced, his bulbous nose seeming to grow redder with every sip of wine he took, "you will doubtless devote yourself to your own family. Not at all proper for a lady to mix with the lower classes."

"I'd be terrified," Lady Newsham confessed. "Those streets are swarming with pickpockets and murderers. They'd pull a woman out of her carriage and steal every last ring and then shoot her dead in the street."

Gen repressed a sigh. "I've not yet had that experience, my lady. Perhaps not all the residents have been told how they are expected to behave."

Mr Calverley looked thoroughly uncomfortable at the turn in the conversation. "Shot dead in the street! We can't have that sort of talk at the dinner table. What excursion shall we plan for tomorrow if the weather holds?"

"Perhaps a bit of shooting?" Cameron suggested, his expression perfectly bland.

"Capital!" Mr Calverley agreed. "I think it is just the right time of year to get some grouse, and this is prime territory!"

"Oh, I love a good hunt," Mireille chimed in.

Gen was quite certain she did. And from the way Cameron had already wandered blithely into her snares, she'd have her trophy soon enough.

♊

DINNER SEEMED TO LAST AN eternity. Cameron thought he'd slice his own ears off before the evening ended. He was used to making small talk, and he was used to joking and laughing and wasting time, because that's what Lord Deverall did. But it felt different with Genevieve at the table.

He never should have brought her here.

But he also never should have made that bargain to get back into her life.

He had a hunch that the presence of Mireille was going to make things very awkward. The French spy obviously used seduction as her primary weapon, and she appeared to practice it on any man in her sights. Cameron hadn't missed her appraisal earlier. Neither had Gen, and he hoped that she wasn't completely enraged.

Mireille didn't have much reason to try to seduce Cameron, since as far as she knew he had nothing to do with whatever assignment she was here for. And what *was* she doing here? Cameron still had no idea. Of course, it was only the first day. He'd scout around the house, see who she spoke to and how she spent her time.

After dinner, he stayed with the men for the usual round of brandy and smoking—he didn't smoke himself, but it was the time that he often got the most useful information out of people.

Then they rejoined the ladies in the parlor, and he slowly made his way over to Genevieve, who stood near the garden doors with a glass of sherry in her hand.

"Did you enjoy dinner?"

She shrugged, not looking at him. Yes, she was irritated.

"Who was that who escorted you in?" Cameron asked. "I didn't catch his name."

"Mr Brodeur was kind enough to offer to escort me in, which was fortunate as you were…occupied."

"I should thank him for stepping in when I was too far away to be any use. Though I'm not sure if he was a living man or a scarecrow."

"I liked him," she said staunchly. "Even if he looks odd. This whole"—she waved her hand to encompass Thorngrove and its collection of guests—"is odd. Imagine saying a year ago that the brother of the dictator of France would be living on a country estate in England, his wife hosting a house party indistinguishable from any other."

"Well, there are some differences. The family can't travel further than the village of Grimley, or the army will come after them."

"They seem quite content here."

"For now." Cameron looked around at the gracious surroundings. "Even a gilded cage is still a cage."

That finally made her look at him, a speculative expression on her face, perhaps because as Deverall, he wasn't known for making insightful comments.

Genevieve excused herself shortly afterward, saying she was fatigued from travel. He caught her uncertain glance as she left, asking him with her eyes if he still intended to come to her room. He raised his chin a fraction, then mouthed *midnight*.

He wanted to go to Gen's room immediately, but duty was going to delay him. He needed to get to know the house so he could move around it without getting lost. He offered his good nights to the other guests a while later. He didn't go directly upstairs, but rather wandered the rooms of the ground floor. He affected a slightly dizzy manner—like a man who'd had one drink too many—but inwardly he was recording the location of every room and door and window with precision.

He'd practiced memory tricks for years, essentially turning the task into a game for himself, coming up with little hints to help him picture places later. So the *b*illiard room had *b*lue carpet and two *b*old doors on the south and north walls. He named the portrait hanging in there *Boring Baron Bill* (in reality Lord William, the fourth of his line and perhaps a lively wit in his day). The tricks helped him remember how to move through the house later.

About fifteen minutes into his wandering, he paused, recognizing the deep green skirt of the dress that Mireille wore at dinner. Where was she going?

Cam gave her a few minutes, then followed and rounded a corner to see her in a small sitting room, standing with her back to the door. The other occupant was none other than Lucien's secretary, who'd escorted Gen into dinner. Mireille had all but pinned him against the wall, not allowing him to escape. He looked alarmed at having the woman's barely covered chest thrust up so close to him.

Evidently, Mireille hadn't wasted time, for they were already well into a discussion.

"I'll stay in England as long as he needs me to!" Valentin was saying in French, his tone low but vehement. "Who are you to question my loyalty?"

Mireille's response was inaudible, since she was facing away from Cameron and spoke more quietly. But whatever it was, it was intended to soothe the man's temper.

Valentin's next words were calmer, but no more encouraging. "I can't do what you ask, even if I wanted to. And in any case, it's all petty nonsense, worth no one's time."

Mireille's tone dropped to a whisper.

Valentin listened, swallowing nervously, but at last he nodded, very reluctantly. "I'll consider it. But my duties to Lucien are paramount and I won't be distracted from them!"

"Just try," Mireille said, now in a conversational tone. "As a favor to a friend."

"We're not friends."

She just chuckled, warm and knowing. "There are many kinds of friendship."

"Then let us be distant friends who never write each other as often as we promise." Valentin finally managed to shift sideways and get free of Mireille's reach. He bowed stiffly and made his way out of a discreetly placed wood-paneled door on the opposite side of the room.

Mireille didn't follow him. She just stood there, looking thoughtfully at the many bookcases.

She might remain in the room, but Cameron had seen enough for one night. He moved silently back down the hall until he reached a door. He opened it into another room, this one facing the gardens. He darted in and closed the door, not wanting to alert Mireille that she'd been overheard.

Why speak to Lucien's secretary? Did she think she could get to Lucien more easily that way? She must be trying to get something from Lucien Bonaparte, something that she couldn't just sneak in and grab on her own, or charm out of the man. She needed a little bit of help.

Fortunately, Valentin hadn't sounded inclined to help her. Though he may not have realized exactly what she wanted, just that Mireille wanted something to take back to France. Luckily, he seemed fiercely loyal to Lucien.

Cam got back to his own room unnoticed, and changed from his evening clothes to the dressing robe laid out by Quinn earlier. Then he knocked on the connecting door to his wife's room, hearing her tell him to come in.

The moment he saw Genevieve sitting in the chair, wearing nothing but the pink chemise and the thin silk dressing robe over it, he shoved all thoughts of espionage aside.

She glanced at the clock. "Five minutes until midnight, my lord. You're early."

"You're ravishing." He walked over to her, appreciating the view. Her body was a continual source of delight to him. It seemed impossible that any woman so interesting as Gen should also be a pleasure to look at—all too many ladies who were gifted with physical beauty were steered away from any attempt to improve their minds. Intelligence was considered a detriment on the marriage mart.

Cameron reached her and sank to his knees, thinking that Gen hadn't been properly worshipped lately. But the moment he knelt at her feet, she stiffened up, anticipating something out of her realm of comfort…which, to be fair, was a very small realm.

"If you intend to"—she froze before simply saying the words, her breeding not permitting her to discuss, well, breeding—"we should move to the bed, shouldn't we?"

"In a moment." *God damn, Gen. Let me make you happy.* He didn't say the words out loud. Maybe he should have. Instead he took one bare foot in his hands, rubbing it slowly. "You said you were tired from travel."

She sighed, relaxing a little as he massaged her foot—a sensual but not overtly sexual touch. Nothing to startle her or disturb her deeply ingrained notions of what she was allowed to enjoy. He'd have to remember that. With Gen, he always had to go slowly.

"I am quite tired. But we have a deal."

He kept his attention on her feet. "You stood up for yourself tonight," he said. "Newsham is more of a boor than I've been led to believe."

"I'm afraid I was rather rude to him," she said.

"No, he was rude. You were perfect."

"If you'd not been there to speak for me at first it would have ended quite differently."

"Then I'm glad I was there." He bent down and kissed the top of her foot, finding the skin gloriously soft and delicate there.

"Cameron," Gen breathed. "I don't think you're supposed to kiss my *feet*."

"Because you're not a monarch?" he teased.

"Because...I don't know."

He recognized that she was dangerously close to sending him away, using the excuse of being too tired. He stood up, taking her by the hand to help her up as well. "You suggested moving to the bed."

He was guiding them back into familiar territory. She let him lead her to the bed and remove her clothing.

The kisses went well, Gen leaning into him and responding to his touch. When he urged her to open her mouth, she even slid her tongue against his, a simple gesture that was nevertheless devastatingly effective. He could feel his legs and groin tighten in reaction.

She let out a gasp, almost a whimper, when he eased his hand between her legs.

"It's fine to like it, Gen," he told her.

"I do," she said quickly. "I just need to…acclimate. In bed, I mean."

Cameron bit his lip. He wanted to hear her tell him what she needed in bed, but the words he had in mind did not include *acclimate*.

"I had a dream last night," Gen whispered then. "That I was riding with my daughter. She had eyes like yours."

Cameron paused, the image of Gen as a glorious, happy mother bright in his mind. "That's a good dream."

"You'd prefer a boy, I know. You need an heir."

"One step at a time, sweet Gen."

He continued, one step at a time, until the inevitable conclusion that left him drained and satisfied, and left Gen gasping, closed-eyed beneath him, clearly torn between maintaining her poise and allowing herself to enjoy the moment. Poise always seemed to win. God, he wanted to hear her cry out with need. One night, she would do that, just for him. He had to believe it.

* * * *

The next morning, Cameron woke in his own bed—Gen having sent him off after their "business" was concluded for the night. He'd been dreaming of what might have happened if she'd not sent him away, and the state of his body revealed just how powerful those dreams were.

To distract himself from more salacious daydreams, and because he had other business at Thorngrove, he spent much of the morning riding around the estate, learning the layout of the main house and the grounds. The stableboy saddled an exceptional stallion, night-black, with powerful muscles rippling under the glossy coat.

"This is Alexander the Great," the boy announced, as

proudly as if he'd raised the horse himself. "Master Lucien purchased him special. He's the fastest thing I've ever seen."

Indeed, Cameron could hardly wait to let the creature run flat out when he reached an open meadow. It would be the closest thing to flying a human could experience.

But first, the work. He saw the so-called Observatory, where Lucien apparently spent a large amount of time. He even noticed when the gangly secretary hurried in and out of the Observatory, a leather case under his arm and a purposeful expression on his narrow face. Had he warned Lucien about Mireille? Did Lucien know what Mireille was after? Did he have latches and locks to keep the Observatory secure?

He'd have to wait until Lucien left the place in order to examine its security.

Continuing his ride, Cameron went farther out, almost to the edge of the property, when he noticed a pair of British troops riding along the narrow road on the other side of the meadow. It was the road that marked the boundary of Thorngrove, and the soldiers' eyes were fixed on the estate.

He watched the soldiers pass by, returning the polite wave one offered, since they were much too far to actually speak. As they proceeded up the road, Cameron considered his options. The Zodiac wanted him to gather information, but Chattan had been clear that he was free to choose how best to do that. *We trust you*, she'd said. He could work as Gemini, using his charm to learn what others were hiding. But if Mireille wanted to take a physical object from Thorngrove, the Black Mask was a better choice. It would be a race to reach the prize, and the Black Mask would have better luck than Gemini if it came to stealing something.

The military guard around the estate wouldn't pose a practical problem for him because he wouldn't actually be running away in the middle of the night. But people would expect the Black Mask to run—and he definitely didn't want anyone to think the Black Mask might be someone staying at Thorngrove. He needed some form of misdirection to complete the illusion of a thief on the run…and who successfully evaded any pursuit.

Poor Quinn, Cameron thought with a smile. He was going to be involved if the Black Mask was needed. The Black Mask was known to have committed some virtually impossible robberies—and he'd only been able to do it because they were actually committed by more than one person.

Once Cameron felt confident he knew the surroundings, he took Alexander the Great to a wide-open field and gave him the freedom to gallop at top speed. The world blurred as they shot over the ground. Cameron reveled in the purity of the horse's stride, his complete focus on speed. There was no hiding, no calculation, just movement and balance. The horse was doing exactly what he was designed to do.

At the end of the meadow, Cameron reined the horse in, patting his neck affectionately. "Excellent, my boy. You needed that, didn't you."

The horse nickered, shaking his neck to toss his mane to the other side. Cameron would swear the horse nodded.

He rode back at a leisurely pace, feeling better about the whole assignment.

At the stables, a different person took the reins after Cam dismounted. Unlike the young lad from before, this was a full-grown man, somewhere around twenty-five years of age, and he moved confidently, like a king of a very small realm. Cam guessed he was in charge of the stables, trusted with the care of all the horses, no small responsibility when the horses included stock such as Alexander the Great.

"Enjoy your ride, my lord?" the hostler asked politely. His accent marked him as a native of the shire.

"With a mount like this one, how could I not? Lucien has a good eye for horseflesh."

"Alexander is remarkable," the hostler agreed. "He knows he's the finest creature on this estate, and he could put on airs, but he doesn't." He patted the horse's neck fondly. "You just want to be free to run, don't you, my boy?"

The horse nickered in response, turning his head and nosing toward the hosteler's vest pocket.

"You beggar!" The hosteler laughed, and pulled out a piece of apple, which Alexander the Great received with joy.

Cam was about to issue the request he usually gave to stablehands—namely, to be certain to rub the horse down and not neglect a good watering. But he saw the genuine affection the man had for the animals in his care, and knew the warning was not just unnecessary but would be actually insulting. Instead, he pulled out a small coin and handed it to the hostler. "To keep Alexander in apples."

The man took the coin with friendly acknowledgment. "I'll see that he gets his treats, my lord. And should you wish to ride him again, tell any of the boys that Mallory said you've permission."

"You're Mr Mallory, I presume? Master of horses?"

"And master of nothing else." Despite the words, the hostler sounded content with his life.

"Does Lucien ride much?"

"Not as much as *I* would, if I had Alexander the Great to call my own. He's up half the night in his Observatory, scribbling away at whatever he's about. The horses are sadly ignored."

"Well, I'll certainly be back to take advantage of the opportunity," Cam said. "In fact—"

"Ah, I thought I heard your voice, my lord!" Mirielle stood at the entrance to the stables. "I was just passing."

Cam bowed politely. "Mademoiselle Lambert."

Mallory disregarded the woman entirely, totally absorbed in caring for the horse. Cam took that as his cue to move off. He joined Mireille at the door and offered his arm, because he couldn't do less without appearing churlish.

"I was heading back to the house," he said. "If I may escort you a little way?"

"How very kind," she purred.

Cameron walked with her and chatted, as he was expected to, but he extracted himself as soon as he could. On the way to his bedroom, he sent word for Quinn to meet him there.

"Here." He tossed the second set of black clothing toward his valet when he appeared.

"I trust you want me to press these," Quinn said, looking askance at the items.

"I want you to have them ready to wear. Over the next few nights, I'll be exploring the house, and if by chance I'm spotted, you'll need to give the impression that the Black Mask has somehow escaped the house. And you'll need to do it in a way that you can be almost caught leaving the property, but still vanish into the darkness."

Quinn picked up the clothing. "Live to serve, my lord. You're certain you're not just doing this to keep me out of trouble?"

Cameron raised an eyebrow. "We've been here for less than a day. How could you have met someone you'd want to get in trouble with?"

"Oh, I saw him immediately," the valet noted smugly. "One of the hostlers. He's hard to miss."

"Name of Mallory, by chance?"

A flush colored Quinn's cheeks for half a moment. "You met him?"

"After my morning ride. For what it's worth, I like him."

"So do I," Quinn said with more of his usual wryness.

"And...he'd be interested in getting into trouble with you?" Cameron asked.

"Guaranteed. I know what to look for."

"Please be careful. Remember that we're here for a reason, and that reason is not romance. I need you to be available, in one piece, not distracted, and not in gaol."

"I know."

Cameron knew he knew. It was one of the reasons he always trusted Quinn, who'd developed a finely honed danger sense over the years.

Quinn sighed, refolding the dark clothing almost without thought. "Very well, my lord. I shall be prepared to assist in your clandestine and illegal activities, rather than indulging in my own. Do you require anything further?"

♊

GEN SPENT HER DAY CLOSE to the house, not wishing to venture farther out until she felt much more confident about her surroundings…which would take only a century or so. Cameron's valet had informed her that the lord was out riding, and Gen felt a little drop in her stomach at the realization that he'd not even attempted to invite her to join him. She then berated herself. Their arrangement covered only a few very specific activities late at night. Cameron wasn't expected to ask her to tag along all the time.

She was left to her own company, unless she wanted to join the other guests lounging around the various rooms and gardens, enjoying the lazy, daylight hours. Everyone greeted her, with no trace that they were thinking of the scandal that chased her as Cameron's long-separated wife. Or of her odd choice to visit slums on a regular basis.

She spread her hands down the front of her dress, smoothing away imaginary wrinkles. This dress was another new one, made of fine thin kerseymere perfect for the hot daytime. The sleeves and front were French cambric, trimmed with crepe of the same color—a soft sky blue that made her eyes and dark hair especially prominent. She wondered if that had been any consideration in Cameron's head when he ordered the gown. But probably he'd just specified a certain number of day dresses, a few evening gowns, a few chemises to suit. All the details of color and embellishment must have been left to the seamstress. Why would he concern himself?

Then Gen remembered when he put that first morning gown on her, telling her how he'd thought the color would suit her. So he did plan it.

Or it was an easy, pretty lie made up on the spot. Gen couldn't forget that he was fundamentally a liar. No matter how many times he complimented her, or kissed her feet, or made her whole core nearly melt with anticipation when he stretched over her in the bed...

Stop it. She ought not be thinking such prurient things in the middle of the day. Such thoughts brought a rash of heat across her chest and an uncomfortable—but interesting—ache in her belly.

She was looking toward the stables as she was considering this, and just then, Cameron rode up on a magnificent black horse. It was lathered in sweat, but not tired, just strong and satisfied after its exertion.

Not unlike Cameron last night.

Will you stop it! Gen chided her baser thoughts. How was she supposed to act normally when her mind kept leaping to such places?

She watched as Cameron dismounted, and stroked the horse's neck with obvious pleasure. He spoke a few words to the stablehand who'd come up to take the rein.

Then Cameron turned to face the house, and Gen had to catch her breath. His hair was damp after the morning ride, and he pushed it back from his face in a careless manner. The gesture lifted his jacket enough to show one side of his torso, the shirt clinging to his body, exposing the excellent condition he kept himself in. Strong shoulders and stomach, narrowing to his hips, obvious under the tight riding gear. In short, a perfect specimen of a man.

And he was hers. Gen started to smile, only to feel her satisfaction evaporate as she saw Mireille Lambert stroll over to him from wherever she'd been lurking.

Gen couldn't hear the words exchanged, but the flirtatious tone was unmistakable. Mireille must have considerable practice, Gen thought sourly. But worse was Cameron's response, the way he smiled back at her.

What did the woman say to evoke such interest? Gen suspected, but also knew that the answer wouldn't help her. She'd never learned how to flirt, and hadn't spent enough time as an eligible miss to observe more than the tamest, safest interactions between men and women.

"Lady Deverall!"

She heard Alexandrine call, and pasted a neutral expression on her face.

Her hostess extended a personal invitation for Genevieve to join her and her daughters for a light luncheon in the gardens, and Gen couldn't refuse.

The two daughters, Charlotte and Letizia, were dressed in crisp white muslin dresses, with their hair curled in long corkscrews. They exuded childish confidence. Charlotte, the elder daughter, asked several questions about Genevieve's work with London's street children.

"They have *nowhere* to sleep?" Charlotte asked, her eyes wide with horror.

"Many do not, and those who have a roof may not have a bed," Genevieve explained. "That's why I am planning a big new building to provide a safe place for them to sleep and eat and go to school."

"An exemplary endeavor," Alexandrine said.

It soon became clear why Alexandrine was so approving of Gen's work with homeless children. She herself considered the role of mother to be paramount. She focused on the care and training of her own brood to the exclusion of almost all other concerns. They spoke English better than their parents. And her children were always perfectly attired and gloriously polite.

Still, a knot remained in Gen's stomach all through the meal. She was waiting for the veneer of politeness to drop, and for the others at the house to say what they really thought of Gen's interests and personality. That she'd been selfish, shirking her duty as a wife to dabble in hopeless causes.

Then again, Alexandrine had a few dreams of her own. While Lucien worked on his epic poem about Charlemagne in the so-called Observatory (for he looked to his pen and paper far more often than he looked through the telescope), Alexandrine worked on her own literary endeavor, a poem about a medieval lady named Bathilde, who Alexandrine regarded as a sort of saint for French Republicanism. Apart from her children, the only thing Alexandrine exhibited passion about was the book she was writing. Alexandrine spoke of it to anyone who asked, and the need to tell the story clearly burned in her heart.

Her impromptu lecture was cut off only when two gentlemen strolled up together—none other than their respective husbands.

"Ah!" Alexandrine said to Lucien. "You emerge from your glorious isolation. Have you met Lady Cameron yet? Obviously, you have been speaking with her husband."

"Greetings, my lady." Lucien bowed over Gen's hand. "Welcome to Thorngrove. We have only been in this house a short while, so I hope you have found everything you may need as a guest."

Gen knew the line to be a gracious lie—the family would never have invited guests unless they were certain the house would be ready to receive them. She smiled. "Everything is beyond expectation. Such a lovely house, and the grounds are just as magnificent. I see you are planning even more gardens. Am I right that you intend that spot east of the house to be a parterre?"

"Indeed. I have read about many innovations and wish to try them all here. Eventually, they may serve as a model for others who are committed to modernizing ancient agriculture."

"So you intend to stay in England," Cameron said.

Lucien gave a laugh that was half snort. "I have given up predicting the future, my lord. My family and I are here now, so we shall make the best we can of the small world we have been given."

"That is all any of us can do," Gen noted, trying to smooth over the awkward silence.

Cameron squeezed her hand. "Wise words." Then he leaned over and brushed a kiss against her temple.

Gen went still, not prepared for either the compliment or the touch. To her surprise, no one else seemed find the affection he displayed as inappropriate. The French really did see things differently.

Lucien considered what she said. "Spoken like a woman with a firm mind, my lady. I think you shall enjoy the company at Thorngrove. I look forward to speaking with you again."

Then he left, saying some important work could no longer be put off. Cameron bowed to the others and requested permission to steal Genevieve and escort her through the gardens.

She rose, surprised by the attentiveness he was showing. He was acting like a devoted husband. If only she hadn't seen him flirting with another lady not an hour ago.

"So that's Lucien Bonaparte," Gen said when they were alone. "He's not what I thought he'd be." Then again, what did one expect the brother of a tyrant to act like?

"He seemed taken with you," Cameron said.

"I'm surprised he showed up at all. Apparently, he spends all his waking hours in that summer house. He calls it the Observatory, since he keeps his telescopes there."

"But stargazing can't occupy his daytime hours," Cameron said.

"Oh no. During the day, he writes," Gen said. "His wife told me that his current project is a poem about Charlemagne."

"It will probably be an epic once Lucien is done with it," Cameron said. "But he's indefatigable. One of those men who can pursue a dozen passions at once and never tire."

He's not the only man here who fits that description, Gen thought. How many passions did Cameron have? And how foolish was Gen for hoping that he'd be different than he used to be?

They continued walking through a well-kept herb garden, the scent of lavender enshrouding the path in a heady, summery haze. Gen inhaled. "So wonderful, the smell of lavender."

"Reminds me of Bainbridge House," he said, referring to the vast estate where he grew up. "We used to run though the rows of it when we were young."

She looked at him curiously, trying to picture the worldly Cameron as an innocent young child. "Did you?"

"Oh yes. Usually well behind all the other children. I was the youngest of the local lot."

"I always had my sisters and Roger," she said. "I don't know what I should have done without them. And now Grace is gone. And Roger so far away."

Cameron said nothing to that, but a moment later he asked, "Were you able to repair that fan? The one I threw in the fire?"

Gen was touched that he remembered. "I sent it to have the silk replaced. I'll pick it up when I return to London. Whenever that may be."

At the far end of the cultivated herb garden was a hedge maze, and Cameron walked directly to the entrance.

"Oh, we shouldn't," Gen protested.

"Why not? What's the point of growing a whole maze if no one ventures in?"

"But we might get lost."

He smiled. "I doubt it. Come on."

They went down one tall green corridor and then another. Gen tried to remember the turns and the number of openings in the maze that they skipped, but was it two left turns and then a right and another left, or…two lefts?

"We're lost."

Cameron seized her shoulders and spun her around. "Does that help?"

"No!" She put her foot down to stop the spin. "Cam, not everything is a game."

"A maze is. It's a puzzle expressly made to provide amusement. That's what a game is."

"Until you're lost and hungry," she objected.

"You just ate lunch, and you're not lost. Thorngrove is on the other side of the hedge."

"Says you."

"Says me. I will get you out of here, Gen. And we won't be here for hours. Unless you want to be." He leaned over and laid his mouth on hers.

Gen drew her head back. "Cameron! It's one in the afternoon!"

"I can tell time," he murmured. "One kiss, sweet Gen."

"This is not what we agreed to. Why are you acting so…husbandly?"

He straightened up, surveying her closely. "I hate to break harsh news to you, Gen, but I am your husband. I thought you'd want me to act like it while we're here."

"Oh? Is that why I see you flirting with Mademoiselle Lambert every time I turn around?"

"It's harmless banter," he said instantly. All the warmth in his expression vanished, and he looked like a different man. Edgy, wary.

"It's not banter. And it's not harmless. Not to me."

"You're exaggerating what's going on. I've talked to other guests here and you haven't noticed anything wrong with that. Mademoiselle Lambert is just a little more… outgoing."

"You'd better not be going out anywhere with her."

"Jealous?" he asked, raising an eyebrow.

"I'm not jealous. All I ask is not to be made a fool of mere weeks after we've supposedly reconciled. Or is that the absolute total length of time you can bear to be associated with me?"

"Don't go on about this topic," he warned. She could feel Cameron's mood grow cold, and she shivered as if a cloud had blocked the warmth of the sun. "I'm doing exactly what you asked me to do. Every night."

She turned to leave, then realized that she didn't know which way to go.

"That way," Cameron said, pointing to an opening in the hedge. "Then a left at the statue of Venus, fifty more paces, right at Neptune, and…do you want me to take you?"

Gen bit her lip, hating to need him. "Yes, please."

After Cameron led her out of the maze garden, Gen excused herself and made her way back toward the house. Cameron didn't attempt to join her.

When Genevieve returned to the gardens closest to the main house, she heard the unmistakable sound of Mireille, and almost spun on her heel to retreat. But she'd been spotted by the other ladies, so she had to advance, willing herself to look braver than she felt.

Alexandrine was speaking of her writing to Mireille, and had evidently been doing so for some time. Gen expected the blonde woman to be condescending, but she seemed genuinely interested in the topic. After a few moments, Gen realized that Mireille was not only being polite, she was asking sharp, attentive questions about Alexandrine's work.

"What actions of Bathilde are most reflective of what we would now call an ideal Frenchwoman?" Mireille leaned forward, clearly hanging on Alexandrine's answer.

"She defended her people against the oppression of a foreign power, yet still submitted to her husband and to God. This is the balance and the test of the modern woman as well—how do we hold true to our beliefs when it is so easy to succumb to the tides of power? Bathilde did so and her example is just as instructive for the Frenchwoman living today as it was for a noblewoman or peasant living through that evil, dangerous age. I strive to convey not just the excitement of Bathilde's life, but her powerful will. That is why I wish to write the story as a poem, not as a novel or historical essay."

Mireille put her hand to her breast. "I never would have thought of that, yet you are correct. Verse lends a dignity that no prose can match."

"Exactly." Alexandrine gazed warmly at Mireille, with the pleasure a teacher feels in gaining a bright pupil.

"And here is Lady Deverall," Mireille said. "Another devotee of poetry, I hope?"

"I have not the training to appreciate much beyond a simple sonnet," Gen demurred. "I would not dream of attempting a work on the scale you are, madame," she added, looking at Alexandrine. "But I wish you the best in your endeavor. Please excuse me."

Gen went up to her room but didn't sleep a wink. She stretched out on the bed and wondered how terribly awkward it would be to return to London on her own. Just leave Cameron behind, say she'd heard of some emergency…no, she couldn't do that. It would be cowardly and it would hand Cameron the excuse he needed to never agree to anything again.

Lord, what a stupid bargain. She never should have sent that note to Cameron in the first place. What had it got her? Not the money she so desperately needed. It got her nothing but distress, mortification, and some of the most soul-rending nights of her life.

The things he made her feel. The way he could run one finger along her skin and make her want to give him anything, *any*thing to keep the delicious wonder surging through her body. Thank goodness she hadn't given in to those feelings, the unfamiliar, terrifying seduction that she knew would result in her losing the last dregs of sanity she had left. Surely no one wanted to feel that way.

But didn't he feel exactly that way? Gen was fascinated by the expressions that passed over Cameron's face when he joined her in bed. He seemed to want the chaos, to look forward to losing his control.

That's what she needed him to do, if she wanted a

child.

She just didn't want to fall into the same chaos. It was too horrifying to contemplate.

If only the first part didn't feel so good.

Memories rushed up at her, inescapable. Nor did she try hard to escape, instead reexperiencing all the times he'd come to her, growing heated and impatient for the night.

But first she had to make it through evening. Gen rose from the bed, irritable and bothered on too many levels to assess. She rang for her maid and considered which gown to wear. She chose an evening gown in dark blue silk, with a minimum of embellishments. She selected a white silk shawl and wrapped it about her shoulders.

Downstairs, she entered the main room only to stop short when she saw Cameron, who was dressed in a dark blue coat and tight buff-colored breeches that accentuated all his many attributes.

He was surveying Gen from where he stood near the fireplace. Putting his aperitif aside, Cameron made his way over to her.

"That's not one I ordered for you," he said when he reached her. He ran the back of his fingers down the dress, along her side. It was an innocent enough touch, but it sparked more of the uncomfortable warmth in her body.

"I didn't hurl out my old wardrobe the moment you returned, you know," Gen said, rather more tartly than she'd intended.

"You look lovely. That's what I meant to say," Cameron said, holding his arm out for her. "Truce?"

Gen slipped her hands around his forearm, wishing she didn't enjoy the feeling of being so close to him. "Truce. I should not have said what I said in the garden."

He shook his head. "An entirely reasonable concern, Gen. I apologize for being thoughtless."

Polite, distant. Gen knew that their truce was just a truce.

And then she felt his attention shift away from her.

Mireille.

Standing in the doorway, Mireille commanded attention. She wore a gown that was decidedly French. Over the past few years, French and British design had diverged in women's clothing. The war did not encourage exchanges among the fashionable classes, and the embargo of French ports and Napoleon's Continental system, adopted in retaliation, all but guaranteed that ladies wore different fabrics and accessories, depending on their source.

The French look was more daring, with more exposed skin and skimpier layers. British gowns had been similar at the turn of the century—there was a madness for classical naturalism. But the past few seasons pulled back on such daring looks, and English ladies now wore slightly more modest gowns for the most part.

Mireille embraced French fashion, of course, and she wore it well...which was to say that she looked as if she scarcely wore it at all. Her evening gown was spring green silk, so filmy that her underthings could be glimpsed if one really tried to look (a challenge most of the men seemed up for). The neckline was so low that a cough might completely destroy the pretense of covering her breasts, and the tiny cap sleeves seemed to be all that held the bodice up. Her long gloves did cover most of her arms, but Gen suspected that every man was preoccupied with wondering just how he might peel them off.

The only items competing with her natural beauty were the magnificent necklace and matching bracelet she'd worn before. The necklace hung in four golden strands, the longest strand supporting a large, vibrantly green emerald that nestled in the valley between her breasts. The bracelet was also gold, with a number of smaller emeralds in the same shade of green set into it at intervals. She wore her blonde hair up, held by a gold-shot ribbon that allowed several long curls to escape.

She looked stunning, the picture of carefree, seductive beauty. And Gen wanted to hide behind one of the brocade curtains.

Cameron noticed Mireille—who couldn't?—and Gen's shoulders slumped.

Dinner passed without incident. Mr Calverley spoke of the hunting and riding to be enjoyed at Thorngrove, and Cameron agreed. Mireille wished for continued good weather so all the house guests might take part next time.

"It is no good to ride out if the sky is at all threatening," Alexandrine said. "We have seen fearsome storms while living here, and I am told that this has been a mild year."

Then Alexandrine announced that since the weather was perfect that evening, a special treat was planned. Dessert and drinks would be served outside on the gravel veranda, with a display of lanterns and candles in the gardens beyond.

The guests filtered outside, where the nearby gardens had been transformed into a fairyland, dotted with candlelight on the paths and colored paper lanterns hanging from the branches above.

Everyone oohed and ahhed over the display, with the last lingering glow in the west to accent the glimmer of the hundreds of individual flames. Gen walked to the balustrade and just looked over the sea of lights in wonder. It was magnificent, though part of her remembered the children back in London, who so often spent the nights in darkness.

Mrs Calverley walked up to her, delight on her face. "Isn't it a vision, my lady?"

"Beautiful," Gen said.

"Life here is just a dream," the other lady went on. "So peaceful. I love house parties. One can simply enjoy oneself without the demands of daily life."

Gen nodded but said nothing.

"You must be enjoying your time here as well. Lord Deverall is a very handsome gentleman."

"That is true," Gen said. Really, her life would be easier if Cameron were not so devilishly attractive.

"And you get along so well. Just look at your outfits this evening! The dark blue of your gown complements his jacket just so, as if you might pose for a portrait."

"A coincidence."

"Nonsense. It means you think alike, and that is very important in a marriage."

The serving of dessert interrupted their talk. Dessert— a luscious spiced mousse—was served in little cups so no one had to sit. And therefore, the end of the meal flowed into the evening without the usual break of the ladies leaving the dining room for the men to indulge in a smoke. Now guests simply broke into small groups, chatting idly. Gen chose to remain by the balustrade, looking out over the garden rather than engaging in any chitchat.

She did drift toward Cameron, who was speaking to a clutch of other men at one end of the veranda, where the smoke from their cigars and pipes would not trouble the ladies.

She caught the last part of the men's conversation, which seemed to be about the war generally, and in particular how the Emperor Napoleon planned to expand his territories over the next year.

"He'll be lucky not to lose what he's got," one guest said. "Half the French ships are at the bottom of the sea, and he can't march his men across the Continent on empty stomachs. Trust me, there's a change brewing in his fortunes."

There were both grunts of agreement and sounds of argument. Cameron looked noncommittal. He looked up and saw Gen standing there, and his expression transformed into one of relief. He stood up and excused himself, walking briskly to Gen.

"Get me out of here," he breathed out as he gave her a quick kiss. He offered her his arm and started walking toward an empty spot at the balustrade, overlooking the vast sunken garden that dominated the landscape near the house.

"Did you need rescuing?" she asked once they were well out of earshot.

"That conversion was getting deadly tedious."

"What's all the talk about ships?"

Cameron sighed. "The same old news. The French navy has been severely depleted...not that it was ever a match for ours. But evidently the emperor is getting rather desperate for ships. He's begging neutral countries to sell ships or supplies to build them."

"Begging?"

"Not personally. He sends envoys. Not that they'll have much luck. There are very few truly disinterested countries in Europe now. Even those without official alliances rely on trade with Britain for their goods. They won't risk economic ruin just to sell some lumber or supplies to France."

"You sound very certain."

"This has happened before," said Cameron. "The

perennial problem of going to war against an island nation…we're rather difficult to invade. And we've built up a very impressive navy over the years."

"What about America? They're friendly with France."

Cameron shook his head. "They've no navy to speak of. Any ships or supplies they have would be used for their own efforts. And remember, America's alliance was with the old French regime. I don't think they care much for emperors over there."

"Oh." That seemed logical. A nation of rebels probably didn't want to prop up a man claiming to have power over half of Europe.

"Never mind about the ships," Cameron said then. "Mrs Calverley was talking about the riding around here. Let's go enquire about that. Thought it would be a better diversion for us than endless games of whist."

"Do you know about Bathilde?" Gen asked on the way.

Cameron blinked. "Is that a new guest?"

After Gen recovered from her fit of mirth, she said, "No, Bathilde is the subject of Alexandrine's poetic work. Some medieval queen. I wonder where I might learn about her…Bathilde, that is. It's clearly something that Alexandrine is very passionate about."

"They have an expansive collection of books. No doubt there is something in the library."

"Of course you're right. I'll look tomorrow."

And at the end of the evening, he took her up to bed, and fulfilled their contract…and then excused himself. Gen's heart twisted. She almost asked him to stay, wishing their relationship were real. But by then he was gone to his own room, away from her.

Would she never learn how to live with him?

♊

GENEVIEVE FOUND THE MAIN LIBRARY early the next day —there was more than one, as the family was committed to education. She looked for books on Bathilde, and quickly became overwhelmed by the sheer quantity of words in the room. Many in French, English, German, and Latin. A few in Greek. One in what she guessed was Chinese.

It was all too much, especially when her head was swirling with emotion. She'd woken from a nightmare in which Cameron promenaded through Rotten Row with Mireille at his side and the unknown woman from three years ago on the other, shamelessly flaunting his infidelity.

Though it was only a bad dream, Gen couldn't shake the embarrassment she felt at the coming shame. For surely it was coming. Cameron was an incorrigible man, and she would never change him.

She paged through a volume of French poetry, and sighed as the ink wiggled across the page, thwarting her attempt to read it.

"I hope I am not interrupting, my lady?"

Gen looked up to see Valentin standing there. "Not at all. I was just reading," she said, putting the one down, "or trying to. My French is less than perfect."

"I should be happy to help translate."

"That is kind of you, but surely not why you came in here today."

"No. I hoped to speak with you. I wished to say…" he began, sounding a little unconfident in either his English or the subject he was about to broach. "That is…your words at dinner the first evening. About the poor. I was very moved."

"Oh!" She hadn't expected that to be the subject.

"You see, I know firsthand how it is to be hungry. I wasn't born to a wealthy family. And life after the Revolution was hard for many. My mother worked herself to the bone to provide for me and my siblings. She paid for my school—I don't know how she managed. There were many nights of no food, but at least we always had a place to sleep. And it drove me to better myself. To learn to read and write and speak the languages I needed to advance. Fortune was kind to me, but there are thousands and thousands of children who were not so lucky. In Paris, in London, in every city."

Gen blinked back tears, thinking of how small her efforts seemed in the face of what he described. "I only wish I could do more."

"Does your childhood hold the reason for your compassion, my lady?"

Valentin's simple question evoked a deep memory. One time, when she and her siblings were all young children, their Aunt Eliza took them to London. It was an exciting trip, full of new sights and sounds and wonderful, sparkling experiences for the children. Gen thought London was a fairy-tale city. Everywhere they went, buildings were large and gracious. They were served the tiniest meals. And each day, they received new and delightful things—lacy frocks for the girls, toys, a porcelain doll, delicious little sweets.

And then Aunt Eliza's carriage drove through a different set of streets. Young Genevieve had looked out the window and saw girls just like her, except they were dressed in rags, had no dolls, and looked starved and angry in the muddy streets.

She told her aunt to stop the carriage, that there were little girls like her out there who needed help.

Eliza had sniffed. "Nonsense. Those people are beyond aid. They're barely civilized and they would hurt you if you dared approach them. Close that window shade, Genevieve. We ought not give them any hints about who we are."

"Why not?" Grace had asked.

"Because they live in one world and we live in another. That is simply the way it is, and there will never be any changing it. The poor are always with us."

Gen dutifully pulled the shade down, but she peeked around the edge once her aunt was distracted. She didn't understand Aunt Eliza's words. Clearly, they were all in the same world. And if Gen had extra food, and the little girl on the street had none, wouldn't the right thing to do be to share it?

The images she saw that day stayed with her, appearing nightly in dreams for several weeks, and then receding to a deeper level of her mind, not as sharp, but still potent. And when Gen grew older, she started to assert her own views, despite the discomfort of her family and friends.

"My lady?" Valentin prompted, as she'd been lost in the memory.

"Not directly," she said at last. "I lived a very comfortable life, especially at Greyslake with my brother and my sisters."

"I know so little of England. Where is that?"

"North of here," Gen said. "It was where my family

spent summers when I was younger. Many people who can afford to leave London do so in the warmer months."

"And it is a lake?"

"Well, no. There *is* a lake, and the estate takes its name from it. But it is a whole estate, with farm-fields and forest—mostly forest. A perfect setting for children who wish to be adventurers!"

He smiled. "So you were an adventurer, my lady?"

"I liked to dream about it. We sailed our tiny boat on the lake. We fished. We sought butterflies and beetles for our collections. We marched through the woods on journeys that seemed very daunting for ten-year-olds."

"It sounds wonderful." Valentin's eyes lit up. "The woods, tell me more of that."

"Oh, they were my favorite to play in. There is a part of the forest that's all pines, ancient trees that were never once cleared to make way for farmland. The tall ones, you know, old and towering. Just the sort of trees that go up and up and up."

"Like ships' masts."

"Exactly like that! I think in earlier days, they even cut some and sold them for the purpose. But not while my grandmother or mother lived there. They'd never stand for it." Gen felt a twinge of guilt. Her mother no longer had any say in what happened to Greyslake, not since Gen's marriage to Cameron.

And Gen loved it too. But it was selfish to keep such an estate for her private enjoyment when she could use the profits from a sale to finance the desperately needed hospital and home for the children.

"I am afraid, actually, that Greyslake will not be mine much longer." And then, without realizing she was going to do it, she shared the plan to sell Greyslake for her cause. All she held back was the specifics of her deal with

Cameron, saying only that she required his permission to sell and he was reluctant to grant it.

Valentin sympathized with the conundrum, telling her that the goal was noble and she was quite courageous in pursuing it, rather than sitting idly by.

Sitting idly by.

"Mr Brodeur…I wonder if I may ask for some advice on another matter."

"Of course, my lady."

"It will sound quite forward, but I've no one else to ask. You're a man. If you…if a woman wanted to get a man's attention, what would be the best way of going about it?"

He smiled. "Here is the difference between the English and the French. English women are so meek and shy and agreeable that a man hardly knows what they prefer. When a Frenchwoman wants something, she lets the whole world know."

"Yes, that is evident," Gen replied, thinking of Mireille's outlandish, devastatingly effective flirting. "But I am English, and can't change that." She realized that she'd revealed that her question was not hypothetical at all, but the clever secretary probably knew that from the outset.

"Men are not complicated," Valentin said, choosing his words carefully. "If you wish to get a man's attention, all you need to do is…well, forgive any impertinence, but you are an extremely striking woman, Lady Deverall. In the right gown, you'd be the center of attention without saying a word. All you'd need to do is smile at your target, and Cupid's arrow would do the rest."

"I wish I had your optimism. Oh, this is foolish of me. I should just return to London."

"No, no, no, my lady. Try it and see. Tonight at dinner.

The worst that can happen is you'll be admired by everyone present."

Genevieve had many gowns to choose from, but that night, with Valentin's advice in mind, she knew there was only one choice to make.

"You're certain, madam?" Kincaid asked when Gen stated her choice.

Gen nodded as the maid pulled out the gown in question. It would get Cameron's attention, and his attention was what she desired.

So Gen descended the stairs in the flowing pink gown that Cam had reacted to so strongly the night he came to the house. She was terribly aware of the low cut, the light layers, but she kept her head up high.

And everyone did seem to notice.

Mrs Calverley told her that the color was very becoming. Charlotte, being permitted to join the adults for dinner this night, said she wished for a gown just like that, and Alexandrine replied that Charlotte was years away from carrying off such a look.

When Valentin saw her, he gave her a nod and said, in a low voice, "Ah, madame. You are a vision. Well done. Anything you ask would be granted."

Anything? *Maybe I could try to bring Cam around to my cause*, Gen thought. Then she shook her head. She couldn't even get Cameron to sign a form for a property sale without getting snared in a life-changing bargain. How could she convince him to advocate for her cause in Parliament? She wasn't skilled at the sort of persuasion *he'd* respond to.

Her cheeks grew hotter when she remembered finding that woman in the room with him during that party so long ago. She'd pushed it out of her mind during the last few weeks, striving to focus on the present, but in truth, the thought was never far below the surface. Cameron had kept a mistress he valued far over his new wife, and there was nothing Gen could do that would change that fact. And he'd *still* never apologized for it.

Not in words, she countered to herself. But wasn't this month a step forward? He was acting differently. He was acting like a husband, and a very attentive one at that.

But was it just acting? How would Cameron react once Gen was with child? He'd likely revert to his old ways, ignoring her completely because he'd already got what he needed from her.

Isn't that exactly what you asked for? She'd made her bargain with Cameron. She knew what she was getting into, and she had to see it through to the end.

And then Cameron entered the room. He saw her, went still for a moment, and then advanced upon her in a direct line. His eyes were storm-cloud dark when he reached her.

"I told Kincaid to burn that gown" was his only comment.

"Perhaps you did, but Kincaid works for me. And she knows the value of well-made clothing. Besides, everyone else approves." She smiled triumphantly.

"We'll talk about this later," he warned.

"Oh, I very much look forward to that," Gen replied, not bothering to hide her sarcasm.

"So do I." He didn't sound angry then, and Gen felt a spark in her belly. She'd certainly succeeded in making him notice her.

Dinner was a pleasant affair, if slightly nerve-racking. Every time she looked over at Cameron, he was looking back at her, often with a tiny smile at the corner of his mouth. And sometimes with a look in his eyes that sent a jolt of heat down to her toes. What was he doing, flirting with her? Right there across a dinner table?

She found it more and more difficult to focus on simple conversations, and when it came time for the ladies to move to the drawing room, she couldn't help but glance back at Cameron, who was regarding her with an expression that seemed to say *don't go too far*.

In the drawing room after dinner, Alexandrine also noted the effect of the gown. "Lady Genevieve, you turned every head tonight."

"Especially Deverall's," Mireille added, sounding girlishly excited rather than jealous. "He is well and truly conquered."

If only that were true, Gen thought with a little twinge of despair. She might have caught his eye tonight, but only because Cameron liked pretty things. He probably looked at Mireille just as much, and naturally Mireille was too intelligent to mention it!

The men customarily shared a drink and smoked for a brief time before rejoining the ladies. Gen guessed she had perhaps ten minutes before the drawing room would be invaded again, and this part of the evening would be torture, since it relied so heavily on entertaining others through displays of womanly talents like pianoforte or singing, neither of which Gen did well. If only discussion of food distribution or water sanitation was considered an art!

"The heat is getting to me," Gen said quietly, hoping that only Alexandrine would hear. "I think I shall retire. Please give my apologies to the others. Good night."

Gen retreated upstairs. At her bedroom door, she paused, surprised to see candlelight from the gap below, lighting up the wooden floorboards to a warm golden glow.

Hesitantly, she opened the door.

♊

SHE FIRST THOUGHT THAT KINCAID must be a mind reader, to know that Gen needed assistance long before the other guests were done with their evening. But when she opened the door, it wasn't the maid she saw, but Cameron, standing there still in his evening wear, looking expectantly at her.

"You…you aren't in the dining room," she said, feeling idiotic, because of course he wasn't.

"The conversation was not compelling enough to stay," he said, his gaze raking over Gen and her gown, looking just as flirtatious as during dinner. Cameron walked to where she stood like a stunned creature, with her hand still on the handle. He gently lifted her hand and pushed the door closed, his intention very clear.

"I…need my maid.…for gown." She plucked at the fabric of her skirts, somehow not able to frame a basic sentence.

He backed her against the door, his body preventing her from moving. "Forget the maid. I'll help you disrobe."

That woke up her muddled brain. "Oh, no! You'll make a mess of it." He'd send every button flying and rip the silk to shreds. Which sounded…a little exciting.

But he shook his head. "I will not. I know how to undress a woman. Don't glare, sweet Gen. I didn't mean it like that."

"Is there another meaning that could possibly make sense?"

He paused, thinking, then said, "No. But please indulge me. I'll treat every garment like gold. I promise."

"You said you wanted it burned."

"A mistake. I've decided I quite like it."

She rolled her eyes at his changeability, but then gasped, because he sank to his knees in front of her, lifting the hem of her skirt, and suddenly she was having difficulty breathing.

"What are you doing?" she gasped.

"Shoes off first, yes?" He gave her a too innocent smile, and lifted her hem an inch higher. "Give me your left foot."

She lifted one foot, and he slid off her shoe. Then the other. And then he slid his hands right up her leg above her knee and expertly untied the ribbons that held her stockings up.

"Cameron!"

"What, did I tickle? Does your maid ever tickle you?" he added curiously.

"No! And good Lord, give me some warning when you do something like that!"

"Fair warning: I'm going to roll down your right stocking." And he did so, his fingers grazing her bare skin as he removed the thin silk. Gen felt the rush of heat between her legs, which only doubled when he removed the other stocking, and then ran both hands up her legs again, sliding up to her thighs. Gen tried to flatten her skirts down with her palms, but he just slipped one hand around to her backside and delivered a light spank. "I said to leave everything to me."

She pressed herself against the door so he couldn't

spank her again—not that it hurt in the slightest. "Cameron, what exactly are you doing?"

"You want more warnings?"

"Yes!"

"Very well. I'm going to kiss and lick—"

"Don't say another word!" she ordered, her mind reeling from the possibilities of what he might utter next.

To his credit, he didn't say another word…but he did duck his head right under her hem and proceeded to kiss her feet, then her legs, all the way up to her inner thighs, where the kisses turned into little bites that made her knees buckle. His hands, now at her hips, braced her against the door, even as his mouth inched closer to the apex of her thighs, his tongue marking a trail of heat along the way.

Gen's breath went shallow when he encouraged her to spread her feet just a little wider. He teased her, his tongue flicking at her skin until…yes, he did it, licking her just where the most intense heat was building.

She stopped breathing for a moment, because she was too distracted by just how very good it felt to have his tongue touch her there. Soft but wicked. Gentle but nerve-racking.

He pinned her there, pleasuring her in this completely new way, until Gen felt her whole belly winding up into a coil of tension, and her legs were going weak.

She felt as though she was about to fly apart somehow, and it scared her. "Cameron," she managed. "I'm…I need to lie down…please…"

He stopped his assault and stood up again, releasing her from his grip for the barest second before he stood up again. He drew her a few steps into the room, then moved behind her to help her out of the dress. He didn't say a word, but she heard his breath over one shoulder, the quick inhalations of a man who was very intent on his mission.

Gen slid out of her gown. The stays fell away next, and then the thin chemise. Cameron put everything over a padded chair nearby.

"Get in bed," he ordered hoarsely.

She slipped under the covers and watched as he discarded his own clothing with none of the care he'd shown to her own.

He put his hand to the covers, and she said, "Cameron, you have to blow out the candle. Please."

There was brief moment of blackness as Gen's eyes adjusted to the lack of light. In that moment, Cameron slid into the bed, moving over her in place of the covers he'd pulled aside.

But he didn't stay there. Instead, he moved down so he was kneeling between her legs, and Gen felt the first twinges of panic when she realized exactly what he meant to do, *again*, and how much part of her wanted him to do it.

"Cameron, this can't be proper."

"Define *proper*."

Define? That would require her mind to operate correctly. "I can't."

"Then don't worry about it, Gen. Just let me do this."

He bent down, his head dipping between her thighs. "Wider, sweet Gen," he whispered, his breath hot on her skin.

After a moment, she spread her legs out farther, finally accepting that she did want what he was offering. She wanted to know what would happen if she didn't shy away, didn't turn him away.

And what happened was…nothing. Gen squirmed in anticipation, wondering why he was waiting. "Cameron."

"Yes, love."

"What are you doing?"

"Honestly? Exulting."

"Oh, please." She huffed out an exasperated breath, ready to call an end to this nonsense.

And then his tongue rolled against her skin, and Gen whimpered as pleasure radiated through her. "Oh, please," she gasped with an entirely different meaning.

He laughed, which she felt as vibrations through her core, lovely ripples to match the lovely strokes of his tongue against the hard bud at her center. Quick little strokes, over and over, until Gen's hips were lifting up in a natural response to his attentions.

She ran her hands down her stomach and then reached for his shoulders, gripping them tightly as a means to hold on to something while her own body was shivering into chaos.

Gen probably said his name a dozen times, but he didn't stop licking her. Slow, then fast, then slow again, always making her moan a little louder as the waves of pleasure increased.

"Cameron." She didn't even know what to ask for, and didn't realize how hard her fingers dug into the bunched muscles of his shoulders, rhythmically echoing the thrusting of her hips. "Don't stop. Whatever you're doing, don't stop."

He sped up, flicking the tip of his tongue at her center until she dug her nails into his back and gave into a final stroke that undid her.

A slow wave of pure ease rolled over her body, and Gen for once didn't fight back against the *petit mort*. She let the warmth and the joy spread through her, every limb relaxing after a long moment of blissful nothingness.

Cameron moved, shaking off her now-lax hands, and

sitting up so he could survey her in the dimness. She gazed back though lowered lids, partly because she was too dazed to open her eyes the whole way, and partly to avoid the look of smugness he'd surely be wearing.

But no, there was no smugness, no pride. Just raw need as he looked her over, and then let his hands do what his eyes were doing, covering every inch of her.

"Gen," he said, his voice rough. "Tell me you're ready for more."

His cock was rigid, big, throbbing. Whatever he'd done to her, it aroused him as well.

Without thinking, she reached for him. His whole upper body convulsed when she wrapped her hand around him. Cameron growled once as she eased the tip into the folds of her sex, shockingly wet after he'd given her his tongue.

Still kneeling, he slid his hands around to her waist and then to her back, lifting her off the bed, pulling her to him.

"Like this," he instructed.

She sheathed herself over him while he wrapped his arms tightly around her waist. The sensation was enough to make her moan. He was so hard, and she could feel every inch.

He moved then, thrusting up, his body slick with perspiration. "Gen, you feel so good. You are so perfect. You're still so tight, even as wet as you are. God, one night soon I'm going to look up at you while we're together. Your hair…" He lifted one hand to sweep her hair over her shoulder, his eyes following the movement.

"Cameron," she whispered, mesmerized by his fascination.

He kept thrusting, his pace quickening. He sought out her breasts, and licked one nipple frantically.

She shifted, giving him the other breast, then threw her head back as he moved his hand to grip her hips, driving her body onto his in a pattern that brought jolts of pleasure to her every other beat.

The same chaos was rising inside her again, the same wave threatening to break over her once more. She didn't ignore it this time. She tried to find it, located the spot within her body where the feeling was strongest when Cameron pushed into her and then, yes...

Gen cried out as the ecstasy broke over her again.

Cameron held her against him for an endless moment, then thrust in a furious burst, a dozen rapid movements. Then he went completely still, his muscles rippling, his breath caught.

A moment later, they'd fallen back together onto the bed, legs and arms tangled up, their skin slick with sweat. Gen's thoughts floated through her mind, unconnected and unconcerned with the real world.

Cameron's lips grazed her skin as he settled himself beside her in the bed. "Gen," he murmured. "Say something."

"What am I supposed to say?"

"You could start by telling me you enjoyed it...which I think you finally did."

Enjoyed it? It had shattered her. Everything Cameron had done to her reduced her to a puddle of need. She tried to think of what she should say. "Enjoyment isn't the purpose."

"Then think of it as an unintended consequence."

"I think you were quite intentional in making me feel that way."

"Guilty." He kissed her again, his tongue teasing her ear. "Will you let me do it again next time?"

"Is it necessary?"

"Why are you so concerned about feeling pleasure, Gen? We're married. What we're doing isn't a sin."

"No, but doesn't emphasizing the pleasurable part of it indicate a sort of moral…laxness?"

He gave her a knowing smile. "I only noticed a certain physical laxness when you finished. And I happen to like it when you're so soft and sweet after coming undone, so I'm not at all concerned. In fact, I'm adding a new subsection to our contract."

"That's not how contracts work."

"You're not a solicitor, Gen. Want to hear the subsection?"

Gen wanted to point out that Cameron didn't have one more day's worth of legal education than she did, but she was also curious. "Tell me."

"I'll continue to come to your room every night, but I refuse to engage in any intercourse until you come undone first."

"Cameron! That's not fair!"

"Why not?"

"Because, what if I can't *do* that again?"

"I'll dedicate myself to ensuring that you will."

"Is this some form of humiliation?"

He blinked in confusion. "What?"

"That you should force me to be so naked in front of you."

"You were naked before, sweetheart."

"I meant naked in the sense of…" She trailed off.

His eyes narrowed. "You mean because when you came undone, I could see something you'd rather hide from me? That I'd see the tall and regal Genevieve feels desire after all? That she has emotions and loses control of herself? Or that just perhaps, she needs me a little bit, not just to get a child, but to give her something no one else can?"

Heat rolled through her, the unpleasant burn of embarrassment. Or shame. "Stop it."

"I won't," he said. "I've waited long enough to come back to our bed, Gen. Don't be surprised when I want to enjoy it fully."

"You say it as though it was my fault!"

"I say it because *you* kept me away. Remember, Gen. I came to you the moment I received your letter. I'd been waiting for *you*."

Gen went still, so surprised she couldn't move for a moment. She hadn't known that. How could she? "It was your house. I was your wife."

"So what? I was supposed to storm back and haul you up to bed and fuck you because I own you? Did you really think I would do anything against your will, whether it was living in the same house or fucking in the same bed?"

"Stop talking like that."

"Don't object to the language to avoid the argument. My point stands."

"I didn't know what to think," she said. "I didn't know you."

"You still don't." He hurled the words back at her so fast she flinched.

"What?"

Cameron leaned down, his expression contrite. "Gen. I'm sorry."

She evaded what was meant to be a kiss. "What did you mean by that? I still don't know you?"

He froze for a moment, then shook his head. "Just that…we don't know each other very well, do we? Superficially, yes. But I don't know what you were thinking those three years, and you obviously didn't know what I was thinking."

"True." She sighed. "I can't argue any more tonight. I'm exhausted."

"You're banishing me to my room, I take it?" Cameron was already shifting to sit up, clearly intending to leave.

"Why would you want to stay?" Gen asked.

He looked back over his perfectly formed, muscular shoulder. "We used to sleep in the same bed."

"That was before."

"I thought we'd agreed to try to behave like a married couple."

"Yes, but we never said anything about sleeping…I mean, actually sleeping…I don't know, Cameron. You have a way of getting more than you bargained for."

He raised an eyebrow. "But not tonight."

"Don't force me into agreeing."

Cameron stood up, his body outlined against the pale light coming through the window. "Gen, I would never, never force you into anything. You know that, at least?"

She bit her lip, trying to recall a single instance where he'd directly violated her wishes, and couldn't. They'd argued, he'd ignored her, he'd left her, but he'd never pushed her into acquiescence, or threatened her. And honestly, was asking to sleep in the same bed such an outsized demand?

"I just need more time," she whispered.

"You can have time," he assured her, gathering up his discarded clothing. "You can have until tomorrow night, when I come back to your room. Remember we have an agreement."

Gen closed her eyes, wondering if she would ever have a child, and if it would be worth it. "Yes, Cameron. I remember."

"Good night, sweet Gen." He walked to the connecting door and opened it. A distorted rectangle of gold light was cast onto the floor—his room was still illuminated by candles lit by some servant.

Gen blinked, dazzled by the sight of him, utterly nude and not in the slightest bit modest. "Good night," she mumbled.

"Oh, and Gen?"

"Yes?"

"I'm going to fall asleep dreaming of what we'll do tomorrow night."

She couldn't see his face, but she could hear the smile in his voice, the promise in his words. How could he keep flirting with her, even after all they'd said and done? "Good *night*, Cameron."

"Sweet dreams, sweet Gen."

♊

THE NEXT FEW DAYS PASSED uneventfully, in terms of espionage. Cameron continued to sneak around the house in the wee hours, hoping to find some trace of Mireille's efforts. It was murder to have to think and operate rationally after leaving Gen's bed, but it was his duty.

As the Black Mask, he searched the Observatory once, finding many items of academic interest, but none to suggest that Lucien was working with his brother or had any real knowledge the emperor would want.

During the days, he used his skills as Gemini to wheedle more clues and information out of anyone who seemed remotely connected to government or the war. Nothing.

Frustration began to eat at him. He needed results soon.

Worse, he was distracted the whole time.

After the night he'd finally coaxed Gen into relaxing enough with him to allow herself to climax, he'd assumed—foolishly—that things would be easier from then on. That it meant she'd finally accepted him in her life and in her bed.

Well, she did accept him in her bed. The following night, she'd been waiting for his knock, dressed in that sheer pink shift that hid exactly nothing. A good sign.

And she'd melted in his arms, her body soft and so

incredibly smooth under his touch, and so wet between her legs when he eased one finger into her. Also a good sign.

And she'd come undone again. Cameron loved listening to her moan and plead for more, begging him to show her how to achieve the lovely feeling again. A very good sign.

And she'd nearly clawed his back raw while taking him in, which he was fine with.

But afterward, she'd told him it would be better if he let her sleep alone.

He felt like he'd been dropped off the side of a mountain, forced to climb up again.

Three more days and nights like that, ecstatic highs and miserable defeats. Gen refusing to desire anything more than what their stupid contract covered.

Cameron had a problem. Every time he looked at Gen, Cameron practically forgot what he was supposed to be doing. All he could think was, *My God, that's my wife.* She'd been his wife for years, and one would think he'd have got used to it by now. But that long separation must have been like a stupor, because he felt like he was still waking up, astonished by the reality of her.

She was so comfortable with the children in the house, natural and composed as if she'd known them for years rather than a few days. The older girl, Charlotte, seemed especially enamored of Gen. Cameron heard the girl—a child of Lucien's previous marriage—suffered from some sort of deformity, though she looked perfectly normal to him. Apparently, she was required to recline in some special apparatus that was meant to mold her spine into a better position, and while she was in it, she could do almost nothing. Therefore, Charlotte desired someone to read to her during that time, and Gen had graciously done so in the mornings.

Cameron loved that Gen volunteered, though considering her interest in young people it wasn't surprising that she'd jump at the chance to help a girl in need.

It was Gen's sweet nature that was really undoing him. Yes, he wanted her in bed every chance he got. Making Genevieve happy was his primary drive during the hours of darkness, and he rejoiced in the fact that he was succeeding at last, that she was responding to him and letting him give her all the pleasure she'd been denied for the years they'd lived apart.

But as satisfying as the nights were, it was all these daylight moments when he caught sight of her and remembered *My God, that's my wife* that were destroying his concentration. He was supposed to be studying Mireille, learning what her purpose was here at Thorngrove, and how to stop her. But his eyes kept turning to Genevieve.

Cam's problem was simple. He was wildly in love with his own wife. And she was not in love with him, and likely never would be. Because she saw exactly what she was supposed to see, and he could never reveal his true self completely.

It was increasingly difficult to maintain his persona of the carefree, self-indulgent Lord Deverall. He was doing everything he was supposed to be doing—flirting with all the ladies, playing cards with the men late into the nights, subtly watching Mireille. But it was straining his reserves like no other assignment before. And it was because of Gen's presence, and the way it was tearing him up to be Cameron for her, and Gemini for everyone else.

In fact, it was time for the Black Mask to take over. An exploration of the spy's private bedchamber was long overdue.

He spoke with Quinn, who listened carefully to servants' gossip. One day, the valet discovered that Mireille intended to visit a neighboring estate for a ride and then stay for supper.

"She should be gone until very late. Possibly she'll not return until tomorrow."

"Perfect. Then the Black Mask will visit her room via the window. You'll keep watch as usual." Not that anyone had sighted him yet in the previous nights he'd stalked the house as the Black Mask. He was always careful.

That night, he left Genevieve in her bed, asleep and alluring. Cameron dressed in his working clothes, then slipped outside the house. He tied the mask on while standing under the window he intended to climb into.

This window did not feature a convenient trellis or nearby chimney, but the Black Mask always had a plan. Cam uncoiled a rope with a hook at the end. He knew that Quinn was hiding a short distance away, keeping watch in case a light went on in her room or the adjacent rooms. They had a series of signals arranged.

Cam swung the rope, and a short while later he entered the upper floor window, feeling that he was right where he was supposed to be.

That, of course, was when a light flared.

Cameron found himself looking into the wide-set blue eyes of Mireille Lambert. She must have just entered. She held a candlestick in one hand, which started to tremble.

He reached out and steadied her hand, not wanting to start a fire in the room.

"Did I startle you?" he asked. "I do apologize."

"Thief!" she said, though with no trace of fear in her voice. "Are you here to rob me?"

He had to think quickly. "Only if you're Madame Alexandrine. I've heard quite a lot about the jewels of the

Bonaparte family, you see."

"Alas, I'm only Mademoiselle Mireille. You seem to have infiltrated the wrong room."

"These country houses…I never get confused in London."

"I've heard about you," she said. The breathiness in her voice seemed to settle around him like fine mesh—weightless but hard to escape. "You're the Black Mask."

He bowed. "Guilty as charged. Not that I intend to ever stand trial. Now if you'll excuse me, I've got to make my escape, and then find the right window."

"Oh, not so fast, stranger. I've heard that you're quite…appreciative of the ladies you meet in the course of your work."

The Black Mask was known for chivalry, and there was no way he could leave without playing his part fully. He reached to take Mireille's free hand and bowed, kissing her hand. "I try, mademoiselle."

"Then you'll obey a lady's request. I'll let you go only after a kiss."

"I don't wish to take advantage of a mistaken window."

"But I do. And if you don't kiss me, I shall scream. Unless you'd rather make me moan." Her eyes were locked on him, and her moistened lips parted, taking his answer for granted.

He could hardly refuse. It would be out of character for the Black Mask.

He kissed her, tasting anise on her breath as she sighed and leaned into him. Kissing a beautiful woman wasn't exactly an ordeal, and Mireille was definitely a beauty, though she'd be more beautiful if she wasn't working for the enemy.

Mireille wound her arms around his shoulders, keeping him close as she deepened the kiss. She was an expert, her lips warm and very inviting, her open mouth all but begging for more. Her tongue flicked against his lower lip, a deeply sensual move designed to make him want her tongue everywhere. And it did evoke a physical response in his groin, a desire to feel more of that dark, base pleasure he felt now.

Mireille's hands found his, and then she ran her fingers up his arms under the loose sleeves. "So strong," she murmured. "I'd like to see what I can already feel."

But all he could think of was how to get the hell out of this room, away from this woman who would undoubtedly kill him in his sleep if she knew what he really was. That thought kept his mind cold even when his body was being assailed by Mireille's unabashed sensuality.

If Gen found a masked man standing in her room, she'd have slapped him…or possibly just swung a candlestick at his head. The image made him smile.

Mireille thought the smile was for her. "Shall we move to the bed?"

He extracted himself from her arms, taking a long breath. "Tempting. But if we continue much longer, I won't want to leave," he said. The words came out mechanically, the sort of platitudes that sounded pretty and meant nothing.

Her white teeth flashed like a cat's fangs in the moonlight. She reached for his shirt, tugging the fabric to encourage him to take it off. "Must you go? After all, the night is young."

"And I must make my living, which means I've got plenty of work before dawn, and as desirable as you are, mademoiselle, I can't sell *you* to a fence—I've got some morals." He stepped back.

Her lip quirked. "A gentleman thief, indeed. Do you

want me to remain silent about your midnight visit?"

"I'd never ask a lady to keep a secret she didn't feel she ought to. Tell the world if you like—no one will ever catch me." He moved to the window.

"Do be careful on the way down, *mon ami*," Mireille warned, just as if she were advising him to take a heavier coat on a cold day.

He *was* careful on the way down, and smiled when the rope fell into a coil beside him. Mireille had unmoored the grappling hook, removing the only physical evidence of his having been there. He gathered up the rope and hook and melted into the shadows.

Then Cameron quickly headed back to where Quinn was waiting.

"The light came on too late to warn you. What happened?" Quinn asked, his voice tense with agitation.

"Mademoiselle Mireille was there."

"Bloody hell. I'm sorry. The maid was adamant that Mireille would be gone until late."

"Never mind. We'll try again."

"But what if the lady raises the alarm? There's no telling if she might get spooked…"

"The lady won't say anything until tomorrow, and we'll manage any outcry in the usual way."

"What did you do?" Quinn demanded, eyes narrow. "If you threatened her…"

"Nothing of the kind. I just gave her a little good-night kiss."

"Oh, my God," he groaned. "Do you never stop…"

"I have a reputation to maintain. Don't worry, Quinn. There's something in that house that I want, and the Black Mask has never not gotten what he came for."

He inhaled, realizing that his breath now smelled of anise. He decided he didn't particularly care for anise.

♊

THE NEXT MORNING, THE HOUSE was abuzz. Gen walked into the breakfast room and confronted what seemed to be every guest in the place awake and chattering.

"What happened?" she asked the nearest guest, who had most of a croissant in their mouth.

"The house was robbed last night!" the slightly muffled reply came. "By none other than the Black Mask!"

Gen thought it highly unlikely such a clever thief would try to rob a house so heavily guarded by British soldiers. "How can one be sure it wasn't just some other man wearing a mask?"

"Hear her tell it." The guest returned to his croissant.

None other than Mireille Lambert was holding court in the center of the room. She breathlessly retold her account whenever a new person asked, and it sounded like a nearly ecstatic experience.

"Such a bold, relentless gentleman," Mireille was saying at one point. "He quite stole my heart."

"But not your jewelry?" Gen asked, puzzled. Mireille had those fabulous emeralds after all.

"Oh if he'd tried anything I didn't like, I would have given the alarm, and he knew it. No, he left out the window, bearing nothing more than he came with other than my sincere admiration for his…talents." She smiled slyly, putting a soft hand on her chest, drawing attention to the low cut neckline. She left the extent of her meeting with the Black Mask to the imagination, but didn't shy away from hinting that it had been more extensive than a mere kiss on the hand.

"Well," said Lord Newsham. "I shall speak to our hostess and demand more protection. What is the point of having soldiers patrolling the estate if a thief can simply waltz up to the house itself?"

"The Black Mask is said to be far more wily than an ordinary thief," another guest said. "Perhaps the challenge of breaking into Thorngrove appealed to him."

"Perhaps we should all stand watch tonight," Cameron, who'd been standing by the window, suggested. "A night watch, with drinks to help pass the time!"

His proposal was met with enthusiasm by several male guests.

The chatter continued, but Gen lost interest in the specifics. Evidently, it was only attempted robbery, so no harm was done. Still, how strange for the Black Mask to appear here in the country! Did even criminals leave the city during the hot summer months?

As she took a plate and began to scan the sideboard for breakfast items, Valentin Brodeur approached her. In a quiet voice, he said, "My lady, do you have a moment?"

"Certainly," she said, laying the empty plate aside.

"A walk through the gardens, perhaps?" Valentin asked, offering his arm.

Outside, Valentin said, "I have been thinking of your conundrum…the matter of Greyslake. I looked at it as a puzzle. How can you keep your beloved home and still have the funds for your important work?"

"I don't suppose you've found a way?"

"Well, I may have. The crux of the matter is that your

husband is not in agreement with you, and he controls the sale of the land."

"Yes," Gen said sourly.

"So don't try to convince him at all. Instead, you can make a different arrangement. Sell some crops off the land. You can make a tidy sum—not as much as selling a whole estate, but that is better than nothing."

"But Greyslake has no crops to sell."

"It has pine trees, you said. You could arrange to have them cut and sold. Your husband need not even know, and in any case new trees can be planted."

"Sell the forest?" she asked. The idea of denuding Greyslake of its beautiful forest made her sick at heart. But she had to do *some*thing, and who knew if Cameron would ever sign the papers to sell the estate itself?

Valentin looked at her earnestly. "I hope you will forgive me, my lady. I took the liberty of broaching the matter with a Scottish merchant I happen to know. Not the details, of course. Just that if it were possible to purchase a stand of pines for commercial use, would he consider it? And he would. If it is your wish, Lady Genevieve, I could arrange the sale and everyone will overlook any slight irregularities in the signatures."

"Is that possible?"

"Why not? It is backward that a married woman can't be her own agent in such matters. The Revolution brought some dark times in France, but it also brought many things to light, including the unfairness of relations between the sexes. Shouldn't a woman have as much right to control her property and her destiny as any man?"

"You *are* a revolutionary, aren't you?"

Valentin straightened his thin frame. "I envision a better world, my lady. And I am not the only one."

Bolder words than that were probably not wise to

speak out loud, considering that the gardens they were now strolling through were actually part of a revolutionary's elegant English prison. Gen didn't press the matter.

"I'll have to think about it. I don't suppose you have a…a figure in mind?"

"I would need details of the number and condition of the trees. For example, for every ten hectacres of quality pine, my employer might go as high as a few thousand pounds."

Gen's eyes widened. "For trees?"

"For a particular kind of tree, yes. Would you like me to pursue this on your behalf? It's a simple matter of sending an agent to assess the property. You need not make any commitment at this time."

"Oh. I…yes. Yes, that sounds very…correct."

Valentin's crooked smile reappeared. "My lady, you should not feel as if you need to know every step. Let me help you. Out of respect for your work. Indeed, it would be an honor to do so."

Gen walked back to the house, but her interest in eating vanished, replaced by excitement at thinking she might have an answer to her problem, an answer that would not involve her not-quite-trustworthy husband.

The day passed as so many others did at a country house. There was a morning ride. There was luncheon. There was whist. There was a stroll through the gardens. There was an hour to read, hoping that no one would pop in and ask her to join a game of croquet to ensure the proper number of players.

There was, finally, dinner. Gen dressed for it with little enthusiasm. This evening featured the same guests as usual, except for the addition of the local vicar, Mr Martin, and his wife. When someone mentioned that the Viscountess Deverall was interested in the plight of children, the vicar's wife leaned forward and said, "An interest of mine as well. Perhaps you would come to tea one day soon, my lady. It is always a pleasure to discuss matters of such import with those who understand."

"I look forward to it," Genevieve said. Perhaps she could learn something new.

After the meal the ladies went through to the parlor. Little cups of a light punch were served while the ladies waited for the gentlemen to rejoin them.

Mireille was still talking about her encounter of the previous evening, and her account—while not altered— seemed to be a bit more vivid with every retelling.

Gen sipped her punch as she stood nearby and listened. She wondered what she'd do if put in the same situation. A masked man, alone in her room?

She'd scream and run out the door, certainly.

But what if he was as charming as the Black Mask was said to be? Would she also succumb to a kiss, or more? What would Cameron say if the Black Mask visited her in the night?

A giggle escaped her, and she quickly drained her punch to distract herself.

That was when Cameron and the other men came in.

Mireille offered a flirtatious greeting to all the men, though her gaze was locked on Cameron.

He returned her greeting in his typical fashion—which was just as flirtatious. But then he turned to Gen. "Holding up, darling? Do you need anything? That cup looks distressingly empty."

"A little more punch would be appreciated," she said.

Cameron took the cup from her. "Then I shall return forthwith." He headed for the punch bowl.

"Such an attentive gentleman," Mireille noted with a little wicked smile. "He dotes on you. He must come to your room every night."

Gen blushed, mortified that Mireille was discussing the subject so openly, and equally mortified that the woman was so observant.

"Come, *cherie*, you need not pretend. I am not like these English matrons. There's no shame in admitting such things occur. Especially since he's your husband and you don't need to sneak around!"

"We very much want a child."

Mireille blinked, not expecting this response. But then she sighed and guessed, "So he does come to your room every night, but he is gone within a quarter hour, his duty done."

Gen bristled, compelled to defend Cameron's behavior. "It's nothing like that."

"He stays all night?"

"Yes," Gen snapped, her anger pushing her to assert more than was strictly true. "Not that it's any of your business!"

Mireille actually took a tiny step back. "I meant no offense, madame. I merely worried for the other ladies in the house. After my ordeal, I thought of how vulnerable a woman might be. All alone in her room…asleep…defenseless…"

Why was she making it sound like a seduction? Genevieve said, "After the Black Mask's visit, I'm sure Alexandrine will take steps to increase the security of the house. Perhaps she can arrange to lend you one of the hunting dogs to sleep at the door."

Just then, Cameron returned, offering Genevieve a fresh cup of punch.

Mireille shot Gen a mischievous look. "How lucky you're here, my lord. We were just discussing a very interesting subject."

Gen almost choked on her punch. Surely Mireille would not be *that* bold.

"The Black Mask," Mireille went on, and Gen could breathe once more.

Cameron waved his hand as if to brush the whole matter away. "A common criminal with a somewhat uncommon style. The ladies of the house have nothing to worry about. Lucien contacted the local magistrate as well as the troops who are in charge of watching Thorngrove. Gave them something of an earful, though it was mostly in French—thank goodness, most of the soldiers probably didn't understand a word. But the thief will surely not come back."

"But he could," Mireille said, sounding more inviting than frightened. "After all, he didn't get any jewels. And this is such a prize…Thorngrove and all the guests have such pretty baubles lying about!"

Cameron shrugged. "You'd have to ask him."

"Yes, I would," she agreed. "To be honest, I rather hope he comes back so I can interrogate him…in my own way."

Gen frowned at the Frenchwoman over her cup of punch. "That seems very foolish. He might have been charming to you in the moment, but he's obviously a dangerous man."

"That is a wise observation." Cameron spoke easily, but then he looked at her with a little concern. "Are you feeling entirely well, darling? You look somewhat flushed."

If she was, it was undoubtably due to Mireille's incessant flirting and her bizarre conversational jabs.

Cameron took her by the elbow and pointed her to the open French doors. "Let's step outside onto the veranda so you can cool down. Excuse us," he said politely to

Mireille, who nodded back graciously, though with a little spark in her eyes.

"Do watch out for danger, my lord. Who knows what you may find in the dark."

* * * *

Cameron couldn't wait to get Gen away from Mireille, who obviously suspected that the Black Mask's visit to her room last night was not a coincidence. She must have been trying to wheedle some information out of Gen, who of course didn't know a thing. He took a long, quiet breath. As much as he wished he could share everything with Gen, it was safer for everyone when Cameron kept his secret work separate from his daily life. No matter how difficult things got with Gen, at least she was safe. That was all that mattered.

She stood looking out at the manicured landscape, not saying anything. The nearest gardens were once again illuminated with lanterns on hooks as well as rows of candles marking the main paths. A few couples were walking along them, the ladies' dresses terrifyingly close to the flames at times.

Gen said, "It's so serene looking, isn't it? If only everything was as peaceful as this garden looks right now."

"Let's walk," he suggested, wanting to get her farther from the din—and the listening ears—of the ballroom guests. They started down one of the candlelit paths.

"You looked upset when you were speaking with Mademoiselle Lambert. What were you discussing?" Cam didn't like using the tactics of a spy with his wife, and prying out information under the guise of seeming concerned certainly counted as a tactic. But then again, she was his wife, and he *was* concerned.

"The Black Mask," she said. "You were there for the end of it."

"But why should that upset you? Was that all you talked about?"

"Not all," Gen said unwillingly. "She was also inquiring in my personal life. She's very nosy!"

A few more questions pried it out of her, and Cameron had to be impressed by how Mireille went about trying to ascertain his whereabouts the previous evening. Luckily, Genevieve's adorable sense of propriety drove her to defend him even when he didn't deserve it.

They'd reached a secluded corner of the garden, one missed by both the hanging lanterns and the candles along the ground. He put his hand on the small of her back and drew her closer, facing him.

Gen's expression was startled. "What are you doing?"

"Admiring the beauty of my wife. That's allowed, isn't it?"

She narrowed her eyes, trying to see if he was mocking her. "Is that what you're doing? Then why must you do it in virtual darkness?"

He smiled, because she made an excellent point. But he was not interested in a debate at the moment. "Gen, you're very clever, you know that?"

He kissed her before she could respond.

She made the tiniest gasp of protest before her hands slid up his chest to curl around his shoulders. Her lips were incredibly, perfectly soft under his, and he loved the way she raised herself on the balls of her feet when he drew her more tightly to him.

Cameron wasn't going to do anything more than a kiss —not here anyway—but his body didn't know that, and reacted strongly to having Gen so close. So strongly that he mentally calculated just how far the maze garden was and how fast he could get there with Gen in his arms.

She broke off the kiss that moment. "You can't do this, Cameron. People will see!"

"Let them. Not only are we married, we're actually married to each other. We're providing an example for today's dissolute youth. Society should thank us."

Unexpectedly, she laughed, probably drawing more attention to where they stood than the silent kiss had.

Still, he smiled to hear it. "I love it when you laugh, Gen."

"When do I laugh around you?"

"Not as much as I'd like," he admitted. "But that's my fault. I know we haven't had much to laugh about in the time we've actually had together."

She nodded, her face growing serious again. Always so serious. Or upset. Usually at something he did.

Then, astonishingly, she said, "Walk me to the maze garden."

Not questioning his luck, Cameron did. Gen barely spoke while they made their way through the paths to the entrance, but talk couldn't improve the summer night. He watched her face as she took in the candlelit scene in the gardens, and the brightly lit house behind them.

The maze was darker, and thus more delightful to walk through, especially since Gen clung close to him as they went. He thought about the possibility of seducing her in some secluded cul-de-sac.

"Cam," she said then, her hand in his. "You do know where you're going, don't you?"

He looked back. "Don't you trust me?"

She shook her head, smiling. "Not in the least."

"That is a most unwif—"

At the sound of other voices in the maze beyond,

Cameron broke off and pulled her aside. He whispered playfully, "We don't want to be caught where people will see."

Gen made a face, but remained quiet, evidently content to be toe-to-toe with him, his arms around her waist.

Then he heard the conservation.

The first man said, "It is a sensible bargain, sir, and you know it. Where else would you take such a product and expect such a return? No one would offer more than a quarter of the price."

"The price is not the issue," someone he recognized as Lord Newsham said. "I must think it over, you know. My reputation, my place in society… It's all very delicate!"

"It is a business decision, nothing more." The words of the other speaker were polite, but tone sharp. What voice was that? It was familiar, but Cam couldn't place it. The voice went on, "You must make it on that basis. I will not trouble you further tonight, sir, but you must decide soon."

The voices moved away. Gen's forehead was wrinkled in thought.

"That was Lord Newsham," Cam said. "Do you know the other voice?"

She shook her head very slowly. "I'm not sure I could say."

"Well, no matter." But it was an odd conversation. Though it didn't seem to have anything to do with Mireille, it sparked his interest. He'd expand his searching to cover

Newsham—if he was involved in anything nefarious, Cam wanted to know. And he also had a good idea of how to make Newsham sweat a bit, if he was concerned about money.

Gen said softly, "I think I should like to go up to bed

now. Perhaps you could take me there?"

Oh, yes he could. Putting aside the matter of voices in the garden, he took Gen back to the house. He thoroughly enjoyed the game of Make Gen Lose Her Composure, and even more thoroughly enjoyed the sound of her gasping his name over and over as she came undone. She looked glorious when she was finished, and it nearly killed him to leave her there, lying among tangled bedsheets with her dark hair streaming over the pillow, her bare skin glistening with sweat.

But he had a job to do.

He had to steal some jewelry, and he had to be seen doing it. It had to be very clear to the inhabitants of Thorngrove that the Black Mask was interested in money, not secrets.

Quinn was ready to help in case things went badly like they did the previous night. There were more guards, but Cameron knew exactly where they'd be.

Therefore, stealing Lady Newsham's jewelry was ridiculously easy. A child could have done it. Indeed, Cameron knew at least four children among the Disreputables who probably could have done it faster than he could.

At three in the morning, Cameron snuck into Lady Newsham's room while she was snoring, broke open her large jewelry case, and absconded with a large collection of shiny baubles.

He made very sure to be seen as he dashed out of the French doors into the gardens. Quinn aided by shouting unhelpful directions to the guards who gave chase. Cameron even thoughtfully dropped a few pieces so everyone would know what the Black Mask came for.

He snuck into the maze garden, hid the bag of stolen jewelry for Quinn to retrieve later, changed out of his black clothing, and waited to skulk back into the house via a door he'd left unlocked earlier.

Five minutes later, one of the house's guards encountered a perfectly dressed Lord Deverall, who staggered a bit and had the smell of brandy on his breath. Cameron played the fool when the guard asked if he'd seen anything, and the guard bought the act completely.

His alibi was set. But he was exhausted when he finally got to sleep, and he knew he couldn't take many more of these late nights.

When Lady Newsham was awoken by the guards and discovered the extent of the theft, she screamed to bring the house down. Cameron slept through it, and thus missed the chatter about how the Black Mask was *non pareil* as a thief to be able to sneak into a sleeping woman's room.

"He'll never return here, not after that. He must have gotten away with a thousand pounds worth of jewels!" one guest proclaimed.

If Cameron had been awake to hear that, he would have been pleased.

Genevieve, who did hear it, was relieved.

Mireille gave a little sigh, possibly of regret.

Cameron awoke in full daylight, much refreshed, happy that he'd have at least a day and a night free of worry before he resumed his work.

He was completely and utterly wrong.

♊

LATER THAT MORNING, GENEVIEVE WAS sent an invitation from the vicar's wife for tea that afternoon. It was written with sunny confidence that Gen would have nothing better to do…and as it happened, Gen didn't have anything better to do. But still, it was a bit presumptuous.

Ignoring a twinge of misgiving in her gut, she wrote a brief reply to the effect that she would attend, and then had Kincaid help dress her in a sweet blue gown with lace at the sleeves. She put on the necklace Cameron gave her a few days ago, hoping he'd notice she'd done so.

But Cameron didn't notice a thing, because he evidently slept all morning long, and thus missed the hubbub about the Black Mask's return. Lady Newsham was inconsolable about the loss of her jewelry, citing the merits of each piece as though it were a beloved child. The ruby brooch. The strand of Indian pearls. The onyx cameo, Lord, the onyx cameo! Irreplaceable! And the diamonds! So many diamonds.

"The Black Mask is a monster," Lord Newsham declared, his face redder than ever. "How am to replace such heirlooms?"

"I am so sorry to hear of your loss," Mireille told him, looking quite smug—she'd not lost any jewelry after all. She smiled at Genevieve as she spoke, and then asked, "What are your plans for the day, my lady? A ride with your darling husband?"

"I am going to Grimley to have tea at the vicarage," Gen replied politely.

Mireille looked as if Gen offered up a plate of potted eels gone off. "Oh, how…bucolic. We shall miss you here, of course."

Gen doubted it.

In the midafternoon, she rode to the village of Grimley in a carriage driven by one of Thorngrove's footmen. He stopped in front of the vicarage and jumped down to help her out.

"I'll be here when the clock strikes five, my lady," he said with a bow.

Genevieve advanced up the white gravel path, through a beautiful cottage garden full of summer flowers. Bucolic, Mireille had said. Well, it was.

Mrs Martin greeted her with enthusiasm, and introduced the other guest, Mrs Woolman, to her. "We handle much of the charity work here in Grimley," Mrs Martin said.

Over tea and cakes, the talk was pleasant enough at first, though Genevieve quickly surmised that Mrs Martin was looking for a new patron to finance her work, rather than discuss the new directions that people like themselves might take.

Mrs Woolman said little, and was perhaps embarrassed that the vicar's wife was angling so hard for contributions.

"You don't work with the church at all, my lady?" Mrs Martin said at one point. "But surely that is the best avenue."

"The church often ignores the plight of the city's poor," Gen explained. "Not to mention that many of the children are wary of such institutions."

"Children, you call them. Surely some of them are not so innocent. I've heard stories of ten-year-olds acting like hardened criminals thrice their age."

"All the more reason to offer hope."

Things went worse from there, with Mrs Martin acting sugary on the surface, but revealing a vinegar soul. Gen resolved to merely get through the meal and leave. Politeness costs nothing and reveals everything about a lady, her mother used to say.

Well, let this afternoon reveal my patience, Gen thought.

Then the vicar himself entered the room. "Good afternoon! I trust you ladies are having a lovely time."

"Of course," his wife said stiffly. "You remember the Viscountess Deverall."

Mr Martin nodded knowingly. "Of course, we've heard about your husband *Lord* Deverall."

"Yes, I've just the one," she said, irritated that the vicar stressed Cameron's title with such disdain. Was there really a question as to who her husband was?

"An honor to see you again, my lady. Your reputation does *not* precede you."

Genevieve felt her social footing start to slip. No one at Thorngrove acted half as catty as these people. Why invite her to tea if they hated her so?

Mrs Woolman said in a rush, "We were speaking of Lady Deverall's charity work. Most interesting."

Gen nodded. "I was just about to say that I've wanted to build my new project because it will house both boys and girls. Girls are often neglected. Charity pupils are often limited to boys."

"Young girls only?" the vicar asked.

"All the girls we may help." Gen was puzzled. Did the Martins not think that older girls needed food and shelter? If anything, they faced more difficulty.

Mrs Martin frowned. "You can't be serious, Lady Deverall. Throwing good money after bad girls? What a waste. Everyone knows that once a young woman has given away her virtue, she can never recover it. She may eventually be taught to behave modestly, but a fallen woman's soul is likely to be as sooty as a devil's face."

Genevieve struggled to breathe. The sheer cruelty of the statement took her breath away.

She stood up. "It is rude to insult me or my husband, as you have done. But it is beyond the pale to impugn the character of young girls you have never met, and who, though they have been born poor and unlucky and have every reason to curse Providence, have shown more Christian charity in their daily hardscrabble lives than you have shown here today surrounded by comforts they could only dream of. I am appalled for the people who attend your church, and I pray they will soon get a shepherd worthy of the name. Goodbye."

The vicar's wife stood as well, though she made no sound and her cheeks were stained with bright red circles.

Mrs Woolman said hesitantly, "My lady, you cannot leave. Your carriage, your driver…"

Gen narrowed her eyes, realizing that her driver was likely at some public house in the village, whiling away time before the expected end of tea. "Mrs Martin will send word to wherever he may be, and he can drive the carriage along the road to Thorngrove. I shall be walking it."

"But the sky has darkened so! It will surely rain…"

"I would prefer a deluge to this company," Gen said. "I am going."

She did just that, carried out of the vicarage on a wave of righteous anger on behalf of the children who'd just been slandered by these smug, parochial, self-satisfied folk. She turned sharply to the left began to walk the way the carriage had brought her. The distance to Thorngrove couldn't be all that far, and anyway her driver would be along in a few minutes.

What was important now was to get out of this hideous village before anyone else might try to speak to her or hail her or say a word, because Gen knew that the next person foolish enough to open their mouth would bear the brunt of her fury.

How dare they. A vicar, of all people, and his lace-and-ribbon wife. Such arrogance to think they knew the mind of the Lord enough to condemn thousands of souls they'd never even clapped eyes on.

She glanced back at the western sky, which had darkened considerably in just the short time since she'd left the vicarage. The storm front had seemed much farther away before. A rushing wind tore her hat from her head. Gen turned to chase it, but it was a lost cause, the straw object now sailing into the tops of the trees.

She ought to find somewhere to get out of the wind immediately. Problem was, the wind made walking west toward the village nearly impossible, and there was nothing to the east but the road entering the woods. Dubiously, Gen hurried toward the shelter of the trees. Where was that carriage? Surely the driver could see the sky and know to hurry?

Then the rain started, fat drops hitting the dirt road. One, two. Four. A dozen, spattering dust up at her skirts. Gen left dignity behind and ran for the nearest tree.

Alas, the nearest tree was poor shelter, since the strong wind was blowing the rain drops nearly sideways. Gen sighted a larger tree a bit farther on and made for it. She'd wait for the carriage there.

The carriage did not come, but sheets of rain did. And then the lightning began to flash. The branches above soon turned from protecting her to drenching her. Once again, she ran ahead, crossing a little ditch to get to a spreading oak.

Her relief was short lived. More lightning sizzled and thunder cracked soon after, and the dry ditch she'd just crossed began to fill as the rain began to seek the low ground.

Gen watched in dismay as the ditch grew into a long puddle, and then a stream, and then a small river. She couldn't cross back to the village now, not by this path.

She cut into the forest, moving toward where she knew the road to Thorngrove to be. But she had to navigate tangled thickets and sudden rivulets, and within a few moments, she was not entirely sure where she was, or whether she could find her way back to the road.

Lightning struck somewhere and dazzled her eyes. Under a large oak, she looked around, but couldn't see a hint of anything but more trees, already obscured by wind and rain.

The next lightning strike was so close Gen could feel the air change, and there was only an instant's delay before a crash of thunder boomed through the woods. She clapped her hands over her ears, already smarting from the sound.

"Oh, Lord, please preserve me!" Gen huddled against the massive trunk, hoping that the ancient oak would keep the worst of the torrential rain away. But the wind picked up, growing into a powerful gale that chilled her to the bone, despite the air itself not being that cold. Gen wrung her hair out and wound her mostly sodden wrap about her head in an attempt to keep herself warm. It was likely futile, but what else could she do?

She remained next to the trunk, her body succumbing to a bout of shivering that chattered her teeth. She ducked her head and tried to make herself as small as possible, like an urchin in a hedgerow.

Gen had no idea how long she remained there. Hours? She must have been dazed for a bit, unable to stay alert. But after a while, she became aware that the wind had died down, and the rain was slowing to a few random drips.

She stood up, her very bones aching, but knowing that she had to get out of these woods, which were now dark. But she was a stranger here, and her wild run into the deeper woods meant that she was now completely turned around. Lost. The cloudy night sky offered no hint as to which way was east.

She began to walk, then hesitated. What if she chose wrong and wandered farther from help?

She leaned against a tree, trying not to cry and lose her courage entirely.

"I will walk," she said out loud. "If only to keep warm."

So she walked. Slowly, haltingly, but in as straight a line as she could manage.

She walked for what seemed like a long time. And then she saw it. A light bobbed in the distance, a fairy gleam behind trees.

"Here!" Gen screamed. "I'm here!"

The light vanished, and despair gripped her. Was she hallucinating? Dreaming of a rescue that would never come?

But no, the light flickered into being again.

"Here! Over here!" She kept shouting as loud as she was able, but her voice was growing hoarse. She stumbled in the direction of the light.

The light loomed closer and at last Gen saw who was holding it. Her knees buckled. "Cameron."

♊

HE HAD HER IN HIS arms before she could fall, holding her close. "Gen, it's all right. You're found."

"It was my fault," she babbled. "The vicar's wife made me so angry, I just couldn't stay, and then I didn't know where the carriage had gone, and I thought it wouldn't be too terribly far, but I misjudged the distance in the country because it's rather different when one is riding, and then the storm—"

"Darling. Don't worry about any of it," he said, pushing her hair back from her face. "It was just bad luck."

"The stream was impassable," she went on, "so I had to try to find another route, and it got dark…"

"Gen, don't worry about it," Cameron repeated gently. "Let's get you back to the house."

Then he simply picked her up in both arms and started walking. Gen wrapped her hands around his shoulders to keep herself balanced. She objected, rather weakly, that he could not possibly carry her all the way to the road. He countered that he damn well could, and Gen's sole duty was to stay warm and not fuss.

So Gen let her body nestle into his, amazed at how steady his pace was, even with the sodden, slippery path and the extra weight of her in his arms.

"I can walk on my own," she said at one point, fearing

she was far too much of a burden.

"No need, we're almost there."

Their vehicle of salvation was a cart normally used by the gardeners. A footman sat on the front bench, holding the reins. A huge draft horse waited, its coat steaming in the cool air. Without any fanfare, Cameron lifted Gen into the back of the cart and jumped up beside her.

"Back to the house, quickly," he said. He shrugged out of his coat and draped it over Gen.

The footman encouraged the horse to trot, as eager as everyone else to get back to shelter.

Gen sagged against Cameron, who wrapped one arm around her and held her close to his body, and with his free hand rubbed some of the warmth back into her icy fingers.

He didn't say anything at first, and Gen thought he was angry. Then he kissed her forehead over and over, murmuring, "I don't like losing you, Gen."

"I'm sorry."

"It wasn't your fault, sweetheart." He kissed her again, and Gen burrowed closer, craving the warmth radiating from him. "But all the same, I don't intend to lose you again."

Before she could think of a suitable response, Cameron nudged her and told her to wake up. How had she managed to fall asleep in the rattling back of a cart? Her eyes snapped open at the sight of the great house all lit up from within.

Servants helped them down, and a maid brushed the errant straw off the jacket Gen still wore before Cameron reclaimed her, putting one arm around her shoulder once more. He looked disheveled and dashing in his shirt, the sleeves rolled up to his elbow, revealing the scar on his forearm that he normally was quite circumspect about, more to preserve others' feelings than out of his own discomfort. Gen almost offered to return his jacket—a gentleman should never appear in company without it—when she recalled the sheer oddness of the situation. No one would be thinking of Cameron's outfit just now.

Indeed, Genevieve was the absolute center of attention when they crossed the threshold into the blazingly bright foyer. Normally silent and well-bred servants couldn't stop looking at her, and several actually offered her a smile, and in one case a maid gave thanks to God for Gen's safe return.

Cameron led her to the east parlor, where a fire was burning in the fireplace, and several ladies stood waiting anxiously.

At the sight of them in the doorway, Mireille gave a little cry. "Here by the fire, my lord! Bring her right here."

Cameron steered her there. Mireille rushed forward, taking her own wrap from her shoulders. "Everyone from Thorngrove and the village has been out looking for you! You poor thing, you've been half drowned." She removed the already damp jacket, and draped the fine woolen fabric around Gen. Cameron released her from his grip, and the French lady helped her to sit down on a padded silk bench that would surely be stained forever. Gen's legs were shaky, and she couldn't stop shivering. The fire was glorious, the dry heat causing her clothing to start steaming.

"Tea!" Mireille ordered a maid standing by, who immediately left to retrieve some.

Alexandrine appeared a moment later, with profuse sympathies for Genevieve's ordeal. She and Mireille chattered to each other, largely in French, and Gen understood only that she must look very bad indeed, that a bath was already being drawn for her in her room, and that it was only divine Providence that spared her during the storm.

Mireille put a cup of hot tea into Gen's hand, cautioning her to hold it steady. Gen sipped the tea, feeling the warmth seep into her body, radiating out from her throat and then her stomach. Her muscles slowly unclenched. "Thank you," she murmured.

"Are you strong enough to walk upstairs?" Mireille asked.

"I can carry her," Cameron said, and Gen's heart flipped over at the words. He was once again wearing his slightly damp jacket, his appearance restored to normal— or as normal as possible under the circumstances.

Mireille shook her head. "You've done quite enough, my lord. You're as soaked as your wife, and you too must change unless you wish to catch cold. Now go! We women will take good care of her."

And so they did. Genevieve was pampered and babied. A doctor from the village of Grimley came to the house, gave her a very brief examination and pronounced that all she needed was rest.

He left, and Mireille returned.

"A little broth before you sleep," Mireille announced as a maid set the tray down. "You must have heat to counter the cold you suffered. The more you get, the faster you will recover."

"You sound very sure of your methods."

"It is common sense! Those pompous doctors will go on, but in the end it is simple medicine of good food and long sleep and plenty of warmth which will heal most people. And if those do not work…well, better then to call for a priest than a doctor."

Gen laughed weakly. "I hope it shall not come to that."

"You'll be yourself again tomorrow," Mireille assured

her with a kind smile.

Kincaid entered the room. "The doctor says her lady-ship must sleep as soon as possible."

Mireille excused herself, but the moment she left, the door opened once more, and Cameron stepped in. He'd bathed and changed, and looked ready to walk into Al-mack's.

Gen's stomach dropped. He was here for the bargain. After all she'd been through, he was going to act like nothing had happened.

♊

THE SIGHT OF GEN NESTLED safely in her bed let Cameron take his first free breath in hours.

Kincaid was moving toward the door even before her mistress dismissed her. The moment she left, Genevieve looked over to Cameron and shook her head. "I can't tonight. Not after all that. This day…"

"God, Gen. I'm not here for that. I'm just putting you to bed. Making sure you have what you need to get a good night's rest."

She gestured to the array of bottles and the tea things and the broth on its warming stand on the nearby table. "I've got all I could need and more."

He refused to be put off by her attitude. Tonics were one thing, but she also needed him, whether she would admit it or not. He sat on the edge of her bed, carefully avoiding any hint of amorousness. "I'll go in a moment, as soon as you're lying down properly and not trying to keep your eyes open."

"And then you'll tuck me in?" she asked with a tired laugh.

"I'll even give you a bedtime story," he teased back, responding to her tone. If she wanted to joke, he'd joke. Anything to keep her talking to him.

"I don't think I'll stay awake long enough for a whole

story."

"It's a very short story." He gestured for her to slide down from her sitting position, and took away the largest pillow so she could settle comfortably. He drew up the blanket to her chin, and said, "Once there was a beautiful princess named Genevieve."

Gen gave a skeptical, unladylike snort.

"Hush," Cameron reprimanded. "One day the princess was walking through the forest, and got caught in a rainstorm."

"Is this a bedtime story or a newspaper report?"

"I said hush. Every time you interrupt I'll kiss you." He enjoyed the way her eyes widened. "Now, Princess Genevieve was caught in the storm, and had to hide under a large tree until the rain and wind stopped. And by then it was dark. So dark she couldn't see any path, or any moon or stars."

"She couldn't stay out all night," Gen said.

Cameron leaned down and kissed her lightly on the cheek. "That's for interrupting. The princess started to walk because she knew she couldn't dare remain where she was. And she wasn't the helpless type. As she walked, she sometimes heard a twig snap on one side, or a growl from the other side. She wasn't helpless, but she also wasn't stupid. So when she heard those things, she'd veer in another direction, just to be safe. And then the sounds would stop for a little while. And when she heard them again, she just turned in a different direction, zigzagging her way through the woods.

"Eventually, she saw the edge of the forest and the lights of her castle beyond, and she knew she'd get home safely. The moment she reached the meadows, she moved faster and left the forest behind."

"This is not much of a story," Gen said, though she

was smiling softly.

He kissed her again, on the other cheek. "I'm not done. After she left the trees, she didn't notice a masked man emerge from the shadows and watch her until she reached the castle gates."

Gen shivered, but didn't say anything.

"He waited until he knew she was safe from all harm," Cameron explained. "He was the one who made the snapping sound of the twigs whenever she veered off the right track, and whenever some animal or criminal with cruel intentions approached her, he'd make the growling sound to scare them away."

"Why didn't he just announce himself and lead her home?"

Cameron kissed her forehead. "You're a terrible story listener, darling. He didn't introduce himself because he didn't want to frighten her, or make her think he was an enemy trying to hurt her. He was content to help her without being seen. And then, once she was safe, he went back into the forest and went to his hideout and went to sleep. The end."

Genevieve looked thoughtful, then said, "It's interesting, but it needs work, especially at the end. There's no happily ever after."

"I'll revise it," he promised. "Good night, sweet Gen."

He fought the urge to kiss her again, and got up, walking to the connecting door.

"Cameron?"

"Yes?"

She swallowed nervously. "Nothing."

"Gen, what?" What was the matter?

"Would you...would you...stay with me?"

He immediately retraced his steps and then pulled the chair to the bedside. "Of course I can stay till you're asleep." She must be afraid of nightmares, unsurprisingly after the storm she endured.

But she shook her head, reaching out one hand. "I meant…in bed. Sleep by me. If you don't mind."

Mind? "I'll be back in a few moments."

In his room, he rang the bell, then stripped off his clothes and yanked on the robe. Quinn appeared just as Cameron was splashing water on his face.

"Sir?"

"Don't wake me till I ring. And inform Kincaid she has the same orders. No interruptions. Gen's exhausted and needs rest."

"Yes, sir." Quinn stooped to gather Cameron's discarded outfit. "Nothing more till tomorrow morning, then?"

"No. You should feel free to take the night off, Quinn."

The valet's eyebrow rose. "Oh?"

"Yes. Provided you promise to be *careful*."

"I'm very careful. Enjoy your evening, sir." With a slight smile on his face, Quinn left.

Cameron returned to Gen's room and pulled the covers aside. He slipped in next to his wife, who reached for him and twined her body around his.

"I'm so selfish," she whispered. "I kept you away, but the moment I don't want to sleep alone, I make you stay with me."

He reached up to stroke her hair. "I'm delighted to stay with you, whatever the reason. Do you want me to keep the candle burning?"

"No, you ought to blow it out. No sense surviving a storm only to die in a fire."

He shifted to do so, but instantly returned to the position where he could hold her close to him. In the soft silence of the bedroom, Gen's breathing sounded quick.

"That storm was extraordinary," he said, not sure how to make her feel better. "I've never seen lightning strike so close before. You had to be terrified."

"I knew you'd find me."

He paused, not expecting that. "You did?"

"Yes. I don't know how, but for some reason, I knew the first person I'd see come through the storm would be you, Cam."

She tucked her head under his chin and nestled into his side. The gesture made his heart skip, and he didn't intend to move an inch all night if it would mean disturbing Gen's rest.

It would be ironic if this was the night she was meant to conceive, and it was also the one night they didn't make love. *Well, no matter*, Cameron thought. If it took another month, or two, or eight, until she was pregnant… he'd just suffer through every glorious night.

How many more nights will you have to sneak away on assignments for the Zodiac? He pushed the unwelcome thought away. Keeping his true secret from Gen was damned inconvenient, but he'd manage something. Honestly, he should be trying to spy again tonight, waiting until Mireille either left her room or fell asleep so he could discover exactly what she was doing here.

But that would require leaving Genevieve, and he would rather die than leave her tonight.

II

FOR THE NEXT FEW DAYS, everyone treated Gen as if she were a fine glass figure instead of a living person. The doctor from the village visited daily, but did little more than tell her to rest and eat good hot broth as much as she was able.

She was not able to eat much more than that, because the chill of being out all night in the rain had given her a terrible cold. For three days, she sneezed constantly, her throat itched, and she felt horribly sick to her stomach.

Kincaid was kept busy washing handkerchiefs until, at last, Gen didn't feel that her nose was about to fall off her face. But though her head cleared, her gut did not, and the mere mention of food was sufficient to send her to the chamber pot to retch.

Meanwhile, Cameron spent those few days discerning exactly what went awry so badly that Genevieve ended up alone in the woods during the worst summer storm in years. And from what Gen could glean from Kincaid's reporting, this wasn't the charming, carefree Lord Devil-Take-It-All asking. No, this was an incensed future marquess who conducted the inquiry, and everyone who encountered him was chastened by the experience.

Evidently, the driver had never been alerted that her ladyship needed him to pick her up on the road back to

Thorngrove nearly an hour earlier than he'd been expected at the vicar's. He quite logically assumed that the rain would keep her at the vicarage longer, and so he was slow in leaving the pub where he was cooling his heels.

Mrs Martin was the primary culprit, for she failed to do her duty as a hostess and send word to Gen's driver, or offer another option when the weather looked so threatening. She instead fumed that her guest disagreed with her, until the thunderstorm was upon them.

The vicar tried to smooth things over. He expressed regret for Gen's soaking, and begged Cameron for indulgence over the little minds of squabbling women. That had been the wrong choice of argument, and the vicar was now living in fear of his own patron revoking his position…for as it turned out, Cameron's father the Marquess of Bainbridge knew the earl quite well.

More than sufficient response, Gen thought. She didn't crave revenge, but she also didn't think that man and his wife had any business caring for the souls of others.

Sympathy and kind messages were sent by the earl and several others in the area once they heard of the event, which was already being romanticized, the terror stripped from the long cold night now that the lady was safe—if sniffly—at home.

Only when her nausea outlasted her sniffly nose by three days did Gen think to count when her courses should begin. Her body was never reliable, but even if she went by the longest time between courses she'd experienced, she was overdue. That, plus the nausea, plus the way she wasn't losing any weight despite her lighter appetite, made the conclusion fairly obvious.

She was pregnant.

And that meant her agreement with Cameron was concluded. He'd sign the Greyslake papers, and she'd never have to see him in her bedroom again.

But now that she had what she asked for, she wasn't at all sure that's what she wanted.

"I have to wait a little while," she told herself. "I have to be sure."

Gen *was* sure, in her own mind, but putting off the announcement calmed her nerves.

She waited one day, two days, three.

In the aftermath of her ordeal, Cameron was incredibly attentive—except when he wasn't. He saw her every morning and asked her how she felt. He made her sit outside in the shade to recover in more interesting surroundings than her own room. He escorted her to dinner and back to her room…and didn't once try to make love to her.

Saying that she needed rest, he simply slid into bed with her and held her, which was dizzying in its own way. Despite the lingering sniffles, and the growing unease surrounding her condition, she'd never slept so well. A few times, she'd half awaken in the middle of the night to think that Cameron was gone, but then she'd close her eyes and it would be morning. Cameron was there in bed with her. He'd kiss her awake, and only leave when the dawn brightened through the windows. He preferred to wash his face and get shaved and get dressed in his own room.

The only times that he got distracted were when Mireille passed by his sight, or her laugh was echoing somewhere through the house. Then he'd look up, stiffen for a moment, and be as distant from Gen as the moon.

And then he'd shake it off, and smile at her, and pretend that nothing was wrong.

It hurt, every time, and it was worse because Gen had no proof that he'd done anything untoward with the woman. He was merely enchanted by her—and was that a crime? No. It wasn't Mireille's fault that she was beautiful and vivacious and caught men's eyes. It wasn't Cameron's fault that he was drawn to beauty. If there was fault, it was with Gen, who expected too much.

Ever since the storm, since he'd held her the whole night as if there was nothing he'd rather do, Gen knew she needed Cameron far more than she'd been pretending she did. Having him near was maddening and unpredictable... and she couldn't imagine returning to her old life.

Of course, she wouldn't be returning to her old life anyway, since she'd soon be a mother. And Cameron would drift away again, his duty done. Why would he stay?

She didn't say any of these things out loud, naturally. It was too mortifying to admit.

One afternoon at Thorngrove, Genevieve sat outside with Cameron. The air was sultry and still, and only the shade from the house made their spot bearable. Gen fanned herself slowly, a book of poems unopened on her lap. Cameron was reading some hefty tome, looking fully absorbed. He was a well-educated man, and a great reader all his life. For someone known to be so social and indeed shallow, he was also able to sink into a book and read for hours, not needing or wanting the company of others. It was another of his quirks, and one of the reasons Gen doubted her assessments of him. Every time she thought she understood her husband, he surprised her.

She didn't want to disrupt his reading, so she kept quiet and surveyed the grounds.

Lord Newsham strolled by with his distinctly unbe-jeweled wife. Both called out a greeting.

Cameron looked up, returned the greeting in a dis-tracted way, and sighed. He closed the book, obviously torn from the world he'd been in.

"That man was probably an interfering plague from birth," Cam muttered, still smiling.

"I suppose I should know this by now, but is Lord Newsham an important man?" Gen asked softly, waving to Lady Newsham.

"Depends on what you mean by important," Cameron replied. "He comes from an excellent family, very influential. His financial outlook is a little bleak, I've heard, but one can wield a lot of power with just a name. That's what he does. Always makes a point of telling people he's got connections in the House of Lords and the Home Office…friends in high places. Why?"

"No reason. Just when we overheard him speaking in the garden, it sounded like they were speaking of trade. That confused me, because he's a lord."

Cameron chuckled. "I wouldn't be surprised that he's dabbling in trade to get out of debt. I am surprised he'd talk to anyone about it. Most of the *ton* would rather die than discuss trade."

However, Lord Newsham *had* discussed trade the night in the garden when she and Cameron overheard him talking. And Gen knew who the other speaker had been.

"That night," she said suddenly, "it was Lucien's secretary he was speaking with. I wasn't quite sure then, but I am now." She felt a wave of relief at telling Cam the truth, despite the white lie of not being sure initially.

"Lucien's secretary? That's odd. For a few reasons."

"Everything about this place is odd." She closed her eyes, feeling the warmth of the humid air against her forehead.

"You look a little peaked," Cameron said. "What if you went upstairs and slept for a while before dinner? This heat isn't going to abate before sundown." He shifted, about to stand up. "I'll take you."

"No, no," she said. "I'm capable of finding my own way. You enjoy your book."

Gen made her way upstairs, feeling the heat more every moment. Another wave of nausea sent her to the bed, where she lay quietly, praying it would pass before she lost the meager lunch she'd forced down earlier.

"Oh, Lord, tell me this isn't punishment for wanting a child too much." Gen sighed. No, she was being silly. She was meant to have a child. And what was more appropriate for her to want? Every marriage she knew of occurred to keep family lines growing, the brides and grooms carefully selected by families and society to ensure that everything would go on as it always had before, world without end.

So it doesn't matter if he loves you or not.

But it did matter. Gen wanted a child. But she also wanted a family. A family of her own, built on shared love. Perhaps that was where she was being selfish—desiring to not just fulfill her duty as a wife but to also enjoy her marriage.

The nausea faded, and Gen lay back on the bed and curled up to nap.

She slept through the worst of the heat, and made it through dinner and the rest of the evening with no mishaps or embarrassing urges to vomit.

She had to tell Cameron about the pregnancy. She was going to go mad if she was the only one who knew.

Assuming, of course, that she was correct. But all the same, it was time.

After Kincaid helped her change from her formal gown into her night things and left for the night, Gen knocked on the connecting door, hoping to hear Cameron tell her to come in. She heard nothing, and in her impatience, she twisted the knob and stepped in.

The room was empty.

His outfit from dinner lay carelessly across the bed. Clearly Quinn hadn't yet been in the room to tidy up. But the dressing robe he always wore to bed was there as well. If Cameron changed out of his evening wear but not into his night clothes, where *was* he?

Then she noticed a paper on the floor where it had fallen. It was folded into a sort of pocket, as it were meant to hold something small.

The note was written in pencil, and the handwriting suggested an educated person who was nevertheless in a great hurry. It said: *M's key. Room available until midnight.*

There was no key in sight, and the clock ticked a quarter to midnight.

Available? Gen's hands trembled in rage, the paper rustling. Was that what Cameron was up to, why he was so distracted earlier this evening? He was just waiting for an assignation with his new French mistress, and Gen was supposed to wait in patient ignorance in her own room, the good little wife. The one who was dutifully carrying his heir while he dallied with another.

Well, she wasn't going to wait around a moment longer.

Gen left his room through the main door and marched down the hall to Mireille's room. The door was shut and she heard only the faintest sound on the other side. She took a deep breath, terrified of what she would see— Cameron and Mireille in some passionate tangle that would cause Gen's heart to break finally and completely. But wasn't it better to know the truth than to wander about in this fog of uncertainty?

She eased the door open. If she was going to catch

Cameron cheating, she'd do it without warning. Then he couldn't pretend any longer.

The room was lit only by a few candles.

In the far corner, near a large bureau, she saw Cameron from the back, inexplicably wearing a very dark shirt and no jacket at all. She knew it was him though. She recognized the shape of his back and the slope of his shoulders. There was something on his head, Gen noted in confusion.

He was opening drawers one by one, then closing them silently. He was acting like a...thief.

"Cameron, what in God's name are you doing?"

He spun around, his eyes going wide behind the mask he wore. The *mask*.

The mask? Gen stared at him, completely dumbfounded. "Cameron?" It was unmistakably him, yet not.

He looked furious. "Christ. Why in hell are *you* here?"

That snapped her out of her daze.

"What am *I* doing here? What are you doing here, in another woman's private bedchamber? And why are you doing it in the middle of the night, skulking around, dressed up as if you're the Black Ma—oh."

Her knees suddenly felt shaky.

He rushed toward her, taking her by the shoulders, though more to keep her in one place than to keep her upright.

Cameron's voice was iron. "Genevieve. I need you to not speak for five minutes. Later, you can speak. You can yell. Whatever you need to do. But now, just stand there and behave yourself."

Then he turned and marched back to the drawers he'd been rifling through. He muttered, "I need to find some evidence of what she's here for. She knows someone's looking for it—she keeps moving things around, making it impossible to search properly...."

"You're looking for jewelry?" The Black Mask had stolen Lady Newsham's jewels before. But Cameron was well off...he was Lord Deverall. She struggled to understand what was happening.

"Jewels?" he echoed. "No, that's misdirection. Mireille has papers. I've seen her tucking them into her reticule at odd moments. She's taking something from this house..."

"Check inside the books," Gen advised. "I've kept papers folded into my bookshelves at home."

Wordlessly, he turned to the bookcase. He started running his hands along the tops of the books. He pulled one off the shelf, letting it fall open. He found a folded paper, made a grunt of satisfaction and then continued on. He found more and more, one or two sheets at a time.

After a few moments, Gen saw that the papers in his grip were threatening to escape. She moved to the bed, yanked one of the pillowcases off a fluffy feather pillow, and held the case open in her hands.

"In here," she directed. "Just dump them in, we'll sort them later."

He paused for a bare second, watching her. He was probably astonished that she was not in hysterics, not to mention actively helping him. She was equally astonished by the fact. Then he continued on with his search, moving efficiently and relentlessly through the books. Gen held the pillowcase, opening it whenever a new paper appeared.

What am I doing? she wondered. I'm helping him steal things from another woman.

Then the clock chimed midnight.

"Christ," Cameron muttered. "She could come back any minute. These papers will have to do." He took Gen by the elbow and steered her to the door. "Peek out and check for anyone, please."

She did, and saw no one. Cameron pushed her out, then shut and locked the door, and propelled her to his own room without another word.

Once the door was shut, Gen flung the pillowcase onto a chair by the clothespress.

She spun toward Cameron, the black-clad, masked Cameron. "Tell me exactly what is going on."

♊

GENEVIEVE WAS DONE WITH BEING left in the dark. She demanded, "What were you doing?"

After a second's hesitation, the masked man in front of her replied, "I was stealing papers from Mireille Lambert."

"I could see that. Why?"

"I can't tell you."

Gen flung herself at him, her hands balling into fists as she struck his chest. "I'm your *wife*. You aren't supposed to have secrets from me! Especially not...whatever this one is!"

Cameron caught her wrists in his hands before she could do any damage. Not that Gen could do much against him, as sleekly muscled and well-built as he was. *Far too fit for a lazy lord*, she finally admitted to herself.

He said, slowly and deliberately, "It's better if you don't know."

"I'll decide what's better for me! Don't stand there in a mask and tell me that you're the moral authority on secrets!"

"Not moral. Just practical. If I've got secrets, it's to protect you, sweet Gen."

That endearment, at a time like this. She looked up, and was caught by his blue eyes, the only part of his face not hidden by the mask. Well, that and his mouth. His mouth that kissed her so well.

"You need to take this outfit off," she said. "What if someone else saw you? You look…"

"I look what?"

Gen quested for the word she wanted. She wanted to say *ridiculous*, but in fact he didn't look ridiculous. He looked…appropriate. Dashing. Daring. Rather piratical. Definitely intriguing.

"Just take it off." She reached for the shirt, bunching the fabric in her fists. Suddenly, it was not at all about preserving his identity. It was simply about getting his clothing off, as quickly as possible.

She peeled off his shirt, running her hands over the body that belonged to a thief and not a lord. No more hiding his reasons for looking the way he did. No more hiding her desire to reach out and touch him.

The muscles under her fingers contracted in response.

"Gen," he breathed. He reached up and pulled the mask off, the black fabric falling to the floor.

She saw his face fully before she knew what she intended to do, she pressed herself to him, kissing him with a desperation she'd never felt before.

He responded instantly, his hands on her shoulders, pushing the open robe off and onto the rug. Then he slid his hands down her back over the silk of the chemise, keeping her as close to him as their remaining clothing allowed.

Gen opened her mouth, newly excited by the touch of his tongue on hers. It was difficult to catch her breath all of a sudden, and sweat beaded on her skin.

"Take me to your bed," she whispered in between kisses.

He said nothing, but picked her up and walked the ten

feet to the tall four-poster bed where he laid her down.

He started to reach for the thin straps of her chemise, but she put her hand on his chest to stop him. "No. You first."

Cameron went still. She stared at him, at his fierce expression, wondering what would happen.

Then he straightened up. "You want to see me."

Yes. She wanted to see all of him, to try to understand this man she'd assumed she knew. This man she'd been wrong about.

Cameron practically kicked off the few items of clothing he was still wearing, and then stood in front of her, not trying to hide anything. Not his pride, or the scar on his arm, or the fact that he was hard with arousal.

The candles in the room were still burning, and in the glow, he possessed the body of a Greek god, slim and sleekly muscled. With a boldness she always tried to tamp down before, she now let her eyes drink him in.

"You still want to do this?" he asked.

She nodded slowly. She shouldn't. It was madness, getting herself in deeper with a man she'd just discovered had sides she never dreamed of. But yes, she wanted this. She wanted him.

"Come take this off," she invited, plucking at the strap of her chemise.

She saw the ripple of the muscles in his throat as he swallowed. Then he stepped to the edge of the bed.

Instead of reaching for the straps again, he put his hands on her legs and began to slide the fabric up, up, up. Exposing her skin, but never taking his eyes off hers.

Her thighs, then her hips, then her stomach. Cameron knelt between her legs as he pushed the chemise over her breasts, deliberately rubbing the silk across her nipples.

Gen gasped, and he smiled at last.

"Arms above your head, gorgeous."

The simple compliment tripled her heartbeat, and she raised her arms up.

He lifted her an inch off the bed to remove the chemise, so easily. The silk whispered past her face, over her arms, and then she was wearing nothing. She'd been naked with him before, many times. But this felt entirely new.

He bent down to kiss her. A wash of heat flowed over her, and she kissed him back eagerly, her body triumphing over her mind. She reached out to touch him, her hands roaming over his chest and arms, feeling the athletic muscles contract as she did so.

Cameron used all his knowledge gained from their previous nights to pleasure Genevieve into insensibility. He eased his finger between her thighs and Genevieve let her head roll back when he touched her, a moan escaping from her throat. Slowly drawing his finger out, he drew the slick wetness of her body along.

She shook as he caressed her, feeling him fill her. Then he laid his thumb on the sensitive bud just outside her entrance, and she thought she'd die. No wonder they called it the *petit mort*.

"Cameron," she hissed, instinct making her thrust her hips toward him. The tightening of her body was growing unbearable. She wanted release. She pushed her body closer to him, her skin growing glossy with moisture. "Please, Cam."

She was more than ready. She was aching for him. Why was he not already inside her?

Without saying a word, he rolled so that he was on his back and she was straddling him. Gen stared at him in surprise. Her unbound hair spilled down around them both. He parted the smooth waves to cup her breasts, then traveled down to take a firm hold of her hips, raising her up on her knees.

He nudged her center, the tip of him wet with his seed. Genevieve pushed against him, desperate. He groaned as her body began to take him in. Genevieve felt the thickness of him plunge into her, and she wondered how her body could always open so much for him. Gen sucked in a huge breath at the sensation. The feeling was almost too intense, and she struggled to keep her thoughts in line.

"How is this?" he asked.

"Good," she managed.

"Make it better." He took her right hand and guided it to where their bodies met. She circled two fingers around the base of his cock.

He pulled her hand away. "Not me. Touch yourself. You know what your body needs."

Shyness besieged her. "I can't."

"You can. Close your eyes." He entwined his fingers in hers.

She closed her eyes, and whimpered when she felt his fingers, still laced with hers, cover her most sensitive place. He pressed her own fingers to her skin, in a little circling motion. Lord, was she really that hot? That wet?

She kept touching her body, finding the right rhythm to make those waves of pleasure repeat over and over, feeling the hard length of Cameron inside her, and realizing from the way his breathing matched hers that he could feel the same sensations.

Cameron held still, his hands gripping her hips.

Only once did he speak, his voice rough. "Gen, you're perfect. Just watching you would finish me off."

Something about his confession made her moan. She surrendered herself to the act, her breathing becoming ragged and fast. He pushed deeper within her, until Gen let out a shaky little whimper, and felt the ripples of her undoing run down her body. He held still for a moment, letting Genevieve recollect herself.

Still deep within her body, he began to thrust strongly. Gen murmured incoherently, and sighed his name when he came within her.

He drew her down to him, kissing her roughly.

"You are mine, Gen. You're mine," he said in a growl. "You're mine."

She opened her eyes at last. "Yes. But who *are* you?"

Cameron reached up to cup her cheek. "I'm the same man you've always known, Gen."

She shook her head. "Which man? The noble or the thief? My God, Cam, I don't understand. You're a viscount. You don't have to steal."

He lifted her off of him, laid her on her side, and turned to her.

"Perhaps the Black Mask isn't after what you think he is after."

"What does that mean?" Genevieve bit her lip, frowning.

"Don't bite your lip. Let me do that."

He distracted her for a delicious moment that brought her to gasping, but she soon recovered herself. "Don't try to put me off, Cameron. You owe me the truth."

He paused for a very long time, physically close but clearly miles away in his mind. Just as Gen was about to give up, he said, "All right, Gen. I'll tell you on one condition. You can never speak a word of it to anyone. Not your family. Not your friends. Not anyone in authority, no matter how important or how urgent it seems."

"Who would ask me?"

"Please promise, Gen. It'll make sense after you hear."

"Very well. I promise to stay quiet."

He nodded, but didn't speak again for a long moment. Gen waited in increasing distress, anticipating ever-worse revelations.

"Let me tell you a story," he said finally.

"Your last bedtime story wasn't a masterpiece."

He smiled, which eased Gen's soul. "This one is more intriguing. So. Once upon a time, a very important person on this island decided that there were too many secrets in the world. Secrets dangerous to the British crown and the whole country. Secrets that might lead to losing a war, for example. So this person wanted to devise a way to learn those secrets. Let's call this person the Astronomer, looking through a telescope at little specks far away. But instead of stars, this person gazes at secrets.

"And this Astronomer needs help, people to go where he can't, see things no one else can see. A group is formed, a small group of trusted people. Thoroughly vetted. Reliable. Trustworthy. Loyal. People who look for secrets and bring those secrets back to the Astronomer, who puts all the information together."

"So you're a spy?" she said, trying to make sense of everything.

"In a word."

"But you work *in* England?"

"Not everyone on this little island is a perfect citizen, Genevieve. And the war on the Continent has made some people rather conflicted about their loyalties."

"Traitors, you mean," she said flatly.

"Again, in a word. And one of the ways to get those unreliable people to give up their secrets is to be a useless lord who doesn't seem to care about anything. From the moment I accepted my role in this group, I worked hard to appear to be what the group needed me to be. I know what people think of Lord Deverall. Well-read, but only to make better jokes. A good dancer, handy when invitations are issued. And absolutely indifferent to politics and the world beyond my clothespress."

"Lord Devil-Take-It-All," she noted, remembering how Cameron's personality had seemed to alter from a sensitive soul into the foppish libertine depending on the audience.

"I hated it, if you want to know the truth. I still hate it. But by pretending to be something I was not, I was able to learn all sorts of things. People let their guard down around me. I learn a lot of things that way, more than you'd expect."

Gen digested that information for a few moments. Then her eyes fell to the discarded silk he used as a mask. She pointed to it. "All plausible, but charming your targets at parties doesn't explain the Black Mask. He's a thief. *You're* a thief."

"I am, when I have to be. That's my other role as spy. Traitors always have proof of their treachery if one knows where to look, and they often have information from the enemy that could help us."

"So you're not after jewels?"

He laughed softly. "What would I need jewels for?"

"What about Lady Newsham? You did take her jewelry."

"If there are jewels missing, people assume that's all I came for."

"But Mireille will certainly notice her notes missing."

He sighed. "Yes. It's unavoidable in this case. Normally, I prefer to simply find the information and memorize the contents."

"You always seem to remember everything," she agreed.

"I work at it. So I only take the actual articles when

it's necessary. Only when it is so damning I couldn't leave it behind, or when it's essential to prove something later."

She frowned, thinking it over. "Wait. How can you be both the Black Mask and...you? These past several nights, you slept here with me."

"Well, Gen, the thing is...you're a very sound sleeper." He smiled apologetically.

"You snuck out of our bed to commit robbery, and then snuck back in? You used me for your alibi?"

"That wasn't my intention." He paused. "Though it helped."

She gaped at him, then said, "I should slap you."

"Please don't. I much prefer it when we get along." He reached for her, and against her better judgment, Gen let him draw her into an embrace. "Believe me, it was not easy leaving you in the middle of the night. You're so soft."

He nuzzled into her hair, then swept it away from her neck to lay a kiss on her skin. "And warm. And you smell..." He inhaled. "I don't even know what you smell like. Something wonderful. I sleep so much better with you, sweetheart."

"Cameron, don't do this."

"Do what?"

"Talk sweetly like this. You used me, and no amount of kissing is going to make me forget it."

He narrowed his eyes. "No amount?"

"I said stop it!" Mercy, she shouldn't be giggling. And yet.

Cameron seized on her lapse and kissed her on the mouth, silencing the giggle. Then he said, his lips over hers, "I'm sorry I couldn't tell you, Gen. I was trying to keep you out of it. For your sake."

She sighed, wanting to believe him.

He must have sensed her wavering, for he went on, "No more secrets, Gen. I promise."

"No more secrets," she said. She'd promise the same, but she had no secrets. Well, she had one. "Cameron, about earlier, when I followed you."

A trace of frustration showed on his features. "Yes, why were you following me? Why tonight of all nights?"

"Because I had to tell you something and I thought we could speak alone and—"

"It couldn't have waited for later?"

"I'm pregnant," she said. Then all in a rush, she added, "Please don't leave me."

♊

HE HAD HER IN HIS arms before he fully registered what she'd told him. "I'm here, Gen. As long as you need me to be."

Her answering sigh was one of relief, and she let him hold her for several moments. He lay back against the pillows, his mind still trying very hard to catch up. His body was no help at all, exhausted and satiated.

This is what I wanted to hear, he thought to himself.

If Gen knew she was already pregnant, then it meant the encounter tonight had nothing to do with the contract. She just wanted him.

Finally.

Or perhaps she was just hedging her bets.

"You're certain?" he asked at last.

"Yes! My courses didn't come once since we…well. And I haven't been able to keep my breakfast down for the last week, which I've heard is an excellent sign."

"Good," he said. "At least if I die in the line of duty, someone will carry on the family line. If it's a boy, that is."

"Cameron! I don't need that sort of reminder now."

"What do you need now?"

"I don't know. I didn't expect that the first person I told would be London's most notorious thief!" She frowned. "Your work for this agency seems extremely dangerous."

"The danger is no greater than on a battlefield." He smiled. "Does that mean you worry for me after all?"

"Cam, I don't know what I would do if you were hurt, or…"

He held her tightly, bending to kiss her. "Let's never find out, then."

"You're entirely too confident."

She rolled onto her side, her hip rising in a way that nearly made him push her right back onto the bed. But she clearly had more serious things on her mind.

"Speaking of your thieving, how did you get the key to Mireille's room?"

Cameron took a long breath. He said, "It was stolen, of course." He didn't mention it was stolen by Quinn.

"She didn't give one to you? I thought you were…and Mireille…" She trailed off.

"Gen, did you seriously think that after we finished every night, I simply got up and sought out *another* woman's bed? Aside from the fact that you're the woman who I want to be with, what makes you think I could even physically manage it?"

Her cheeks went pink. "Well, you always seem so ready every time we're together, I just thought you were…"

Cameron bit his lip to stop a smile. "I'm flattered by your assumptions about my stamina. But believe me, everything I have, I'm giving to you, and it's probably only the three years of withholding that's letting me be as vigorous as I am."

"Three years?" Her eyes were wide with shock. "You never…"

"Not with any other person, sweet Gen. Any release I

got was courtesy of my own hand and my own imagination."

"Oh." Gen looked away, then back at him, her gaze sharp. "*Never*?"

"Never."

"Why not?"

He paused. Was this a trick question? "Because you never asked me back?"

"I meant why not with another woman? You had to have considered it." This was the new Genevieve who was asking, the woman who understood far more of life than what ladies of the *ton* were thought to know. The Genevieve who fed children who grew up on the streets and saw sides of life other ladies did not.

"I considered it." After all, he had a pulse. And a cock. And three years was a long time to have both of those things and not do anything about it. "But my life isn't quite as dissolute as I've been pretending it is. So the opportunities were not quite as frequent as you'd think. And even when I had an opportunity...I guess I just didn't want it enough. Affairs take a toll, Gen. Even casual encounters do. I'm speaking from prior experience here, darling. Before we got married."

"I'm aware that you had experience prior to our marriage," she noted, her gaze becoming just a little sly. Definitely the more knowledgeable Gen speaking.

Cameron found he liked it, and his body reacted predictably. "I want to add a new subclause to the contract."

"The contract is over. You got what you wanted."

"No. I mean yes, but I want more. Let me continue to come to your room. Even though you don't need me for a child."

"Is that wise?"

"Well, toward the end, we might have to restrain ourselves. But until then, let me be with you."

"Every night?"

"Not just nights."

Her eyebrows rose. "Days?"

"I mean…living as a proper couple. I want to be a proper husband to you. Give me a chance."

"Have you got the time?" she asked skeptically. "You have your spying and your thieving…" She looked over at the pillowcase half stuffed with papers. "What did you take from her?"

"That's a good question. I'm not sure yet. All I know for certain is that she's a French spy. My task was to follow her and find out what she wants from this house."

Gen blinked, as if just now putting all the pieces together. "So all of this—the party, the flirting, the nonsense—was all so you could get here and discover what she's up to?"

"Indeed. If it were up to me, I'd never have come. I really do hate house parties."

"You hide it well."

"I hide a lot of things well," he said with a trace of boasting. He remembered something Miss Chattan had said, something about the pleasure in revealing a secret when one's job was to keep them.

"How can you just let them sit there?" she asked. "You must be dying to know what's in them."

He should be. And yet, with Gen in his arms, nothing else seemed to matter that much.

But he had to look at them sooner or later.

With regret, he released Gen and then slid out of the bed, grabbing Gen's clothing from the floor and offering it to her.

She climbed out of the bed, watching him with alert, curious eyes as she dressed.

Cameron then asked Gen to light a few more candles while he hurriedly put on some nonblack clothing. Moments later, he was seated on the floor of the bedroom, papers splayed around him. He picked one up, then another, turning some so they were the right way up. The first step was to get them in proper order.

While he was frowning at the separate pages in his hands, Gen sank to the floor as well.

"How can I help?" she asked simply.

"The papers need to be laid out, all right-side up, on the floor. In a grid. Then we'll move them about as needed."

"Like a jigsaw puzzle."

"Precisely." He was too excited by the potential of what he had to consider the wisdom of letting Gen even see the papers, let alone help sort them.

They arranged the papers into a rough grid.

"This page is dated in the corner," Gen said, pointing to one. "Last Monday. That was just a few days after we arrived."

Cameron nodded. "Good. Let's put it up on the top row."

He returned to the paper he was holding. He read out loud, translating from the French as he spoke, "'A woman can affect the governing of kings from the kitchen.'"

Genevieve tipped her head. "I hope she's not advocating poison."

"Who knows?" It was a strange phrase to be sure. "This cache must not be everything she had. I did get interrupted," he reminded her.

"Will you go back to her room?" Gen asked. "Do you need to get more pages?" She held up the long rectangle of black silk that he folded up and tied into his mask. Leaning over the papers, she offered it to him.

Cameron took it, but shook his head. "Too dangerous. I didn't like to take these, but I wasn't having any luck otherwise." He rolled the silk up. Ready to stow the mask, he pulled out the little leather case from under the bed.

"Oh!" Gen said, sounding surprised…and surprisingly relieved. "So that's your case of thieving tools?"

"What else? Hold a moment. You've seen this case before?"

Her cheeks were on fire. "Yes."

He raised one eyebrow. Why was she so embarrassed over a seemingly random collection of silk scarves, rope, and…wait. "You thought I used these items in the bedroom?"

Gen struggled to respond, looking more mortified by the second. "The possibility occurred to me."

"How do you even *know* about that sort of thing?"

"I, um, once heard someone talking."

"Who, pray tell?" Cameron asked.

"My friend Lady Stanfield is rather knowledgeable, and once she explained the, um, theory to me when something similar came up in conversation. That is, a rumor of a couple who'd been found in a most comprising position, where masks and rope and knives were, um, involved."

"Hmmm." Knowledgeable Gen was fascinating. "I'll admit that a blindfold or a silk binding can add interest to an evening, but I've never personally understood the appeal of pain."

"It was the knives that I found frightening in the story that was going around," she confessed. "Apparently, it was…requested?"

He nodded. "Some people get more excited the rougher the play is, and that's between them and whoever they choose to spend their private time with. But as I said, I don't want to add pain to the experience, for me or anyone else. These tools are picks," he added, holding up a jagged, sharp-ended one. "They break locks, not skin. Does that set you at ease?"

Gen exhaled. "Yes."

Cameron put the tool down, and raised one hand to cup her cheek, his thumb caressing her face. "When did you first see these things?"

"The day you moved back into the house."

"And you worried about it ever since then."

She nodded.

"Gen, if you'd just asked…"

"How does one ask about something like *that*?"

"Out loud, to begin. The words don't have to be perfect, Gen. You just have to make the attempt. If you'd asked—"

"You'd have lied to me. If I hadn't walked in on you literally in the act of stealing, you'd never have told me what you're really up to. Admit it."

Cameron felt a stab of remorse, because she was absolutely right. "Yes. I probably would have lied. Telling you anything at all is a violation, in fact. One I hope I won't regret."

"Are you implying that I can't keep my mouth shut?"

"I'm just saying that secrets are best kept by telling the fewest number of people possible. I never intended to let you know about this side of my life, because I don't want you to have to worry about me."

"Well, I will," she declared, her hand drifting to her belly.

Cameron felt like a heel, again. Of course she would worry about whether the father of her child was going to end up dead or missing, the victim of a secret war. He'd taken steps to ensure that Gen would always be taken care of if he died—it would be irresponsible for him to marry without doing that—but he hadn't considered the emotional toll it would take. In all honesty, he sort of thought that she'd be glad. Three years of silence had that effect.

Unwilling to pursue the tangle of his relationship with Gen, he tried to focus on the pages in front of him. However, nothing seemed to indicate what Mireille was after. "Bathilde." He frowned at the page. "I've heard that name before."

"I told you about her," Gen said. "She's the subject of Alexandrine's book."

Cam shook his head. "That makes no sense."

"All the same, that's who she is."

He closed his eyes, thinking hard. "It must be a code. She heard the name and used it as a placeholder for whatever she's really working on."

"She gathered information and recorded it this way?"

"Yes. There must be some message hidden in here. A few words that don't fit, that will tell us what Mireille and the Bonapartes are up to."

"I don't understand," Gen said. "Is Mireille working with Lucien Bonaparte or against him? And what does Alexandrine have to do with anything?"

"I don't know. It's what I've been spending my nights trying to discover. Initially, I thought Mireille was here at Lucien Bonaparte's request. That she's a courier between the brothers. But Lucien barely spoke to her—in fact, I think he avoids her. Certainly, he's not given her anything, and he hasn't told her anything. If it were a matter of a simple exchange, Mireille wouldn't linger here. But she is still here, still writing all her odd notes and then concealing them in books."

Gen frowned. "So her target is not Lucien."

"She's only been conversing with Alexandrine." He gathered the rest of his black clothing and balled it up, thrusting it into the clothespress. He shouldn't advertise his other identity.

"And only about Alexandrine's novel," Gen added. "At least, that's the only thing Alexandrine speaks of when she's not discussing her children. I guess that's what gave Mireille the idea."

"Maybe." What did Alexandrine know? She didn't seem like the sort of woman who'd be passing on messages to Napoleon. The self-styled emperor tried to get Lucien to divorce her after all. So why would she help one of Napoleon's agents? Or perhaps she wasn't. Cam was still missing an essential key, the one element that would link all this information together.

"Cameron?" Gen asked hesitantly. "Are you going to put these back?"

It would be the safest course, assuming Mireille hadn't come home and already discovered them missing. But Cam felt in his gut that he had to keep them. "No," he said decisively. "I need to study them. But I do need to put them in a safe place."

"My room," Gen offered. "She wouldn't suspect me of taking them."

"It's too dangerous."

"No more dangerous than her finding them in your room, proving that you're not who you say you are, *my lord*."

Knowledgeable Gen might be a lot of trouble.

"Please leave the espionage to me," he said. "I've got my own ways of hiding things. Your sole duty is not to think about it."

"You can't be serious."

"I am, Gen. Forget what I told you. Keep on thinking of me as your vexing but admittedly charming husband."

She shook her head and smiled. "That is a true description."

He leaned over to kiss her. "Think about our child. Not me."

"I do think about you," she responded with a heat to her voice that he'd rarely heard before, and wanted to hear over and over again.

It was hours before dawn. He pulled Gen closer, murmuring, "Stay with me tonight?"

She put her hands on his shoulders, then leaned in to kiss him, hard.

He took that as a *yes*.

♊

CAMERON SLEPT VERY WELL, BUT he awoke abruptly when he felt Genevieve shift and then scramble off of the bed. She hurried to a chamber pot in the corner. On her knees, she hunched over, obviously in distress.

He sat up and reached for his robe. By the time he crossed the room to Gen, she was already sitting back up, wiping her mouth and looking rather miserable.

"Are you well?"

"I'm pregnant," she responded with a little shrug. "This phase will pass eventually. I hope. My sister Gloria dealt with it for eight weeks unbroken."

"Can I get you anything?"

"Water."

Cameron hurried to the water pitcher. He was annoyed at himself for not knowing that Gen was suffering through this, even though she'd avoided telling him. That was what came of his sneaking off in the night and slipping away too early in the morning. He wanted not to bother her, but the result was that he missed the opportunity to help her.

When he returned with a glass of water, he first helped Gen stand up, her legs visibly shaky.

She drank the water, then sighed. "That's better."

"Can you eat?"

Gen winced. "Don't talk about food just yet."

He let Gen return to her own room before summoning Quinn to help him shave, dress, and get ready for the day. He took the quarter hour of privacy to hide the papers in a place he'd preselected for such events.

Quinn arrived looking slightly more cheerful than usual. "Morning, sir. Lovely day today."

"What's got into you?"

The valet smiled. "Nothing I can say in mixed company, sir." He tapped the chair where Cameron sat to be shaven. "Let's begin, shall we?"

"Who's the maid assigned to help Mireille?" Cameron asked a little while later, running a hand over his newly smooth face.

"That'd be Nadette."

"If you have the chance, ask her if Mireille seemed out of sorts either later last night or this morning."

Quinn nodded, used to such random requests.

Cameron knocked on Gen's door before going down to breakfast. She opened it and stepped out, wearing the light blue morning gown he'd bought her, along with the sapphire necklace. There was no outward hint of her condition now, but he thought she was growing more beautiful. Though he was hardly an objective judge.

"Come down to breakfast with me?"

"Yes, but I'll just have tea," she said.

"And toast."

"Don't bully me."

"No one has ever bullied another with toast," he argued.

"I will *try* to eat some toast, if you promise to stop hovering."

"No hovering," he promised. That would be a promise he was sure to break. Gen was going to be a mother. The thought still made him a little giddy. "When will the baby come?"

"I don't know," she said with a shy smile. "I'll need to confer with a doctor. Early next year, but I'm not sure what month."

"How do you feel?"

"Apart from the nausea, very happy."

"Really?"

"Yes. This is what I hoped for. A child."

Not a family. Cameron smiled, even though he knew he was reading too much into her response. "You'll be a splendid mother."

"Thank you."

He wasn't sure he'd be a splendid father, but he'd try. He had to speak to his own father as soon as he could.

The room where breakfast was laid on the sideboard was sunny and bright. Several other guests were already there, eating or reading the newspapers sent from town.

Cameron looked around, but didn't see Mireille at all. Perhaps she was sleeping in, or taking breakfast upstairs. If she'd discovered the papers missing, she might well be scouring the books, or just fuming and plotting her next move.

Gen sat at the long table, and Mrs Calverley was already offering her tea. Cameron took two slices of toast from the warming basket on the sideboard, buttered them, and placed the plate in front of Gen, who rolled her eyes slightly before she thanked him.

Just as a demonstration, Cameron then loaded his own plate with as much food as could fit. He glanced at Gen, who took a tiny nibble of her toast in retaliation. He almost laughed out loud. Gen was fun.

He'd barely finished eating when one of the footmen came up and murmured that Quinn needed to speak to him.

Cameron got up, catching Gen's concerned look. He smiled before he left.

In the hallway just outside the kitchens, he saw Quinn waiting anxiously.

"What's happened?"

"Mireille is gone, my lord. Apparently, she left before dawn, taking everything she had with her."

Cameron wasn't sure what he expected, but it wasn't that outcome. Why would she disappear immediately? Did she think that the loss of the papers would mean she'd be accused and arrested as a spy? An agent as experienced as Mireille obviously was tended to be confident in their ability to bull through a lot of obstacles. Then again, experienced agents also knew when to retreat.

"What do you want to do?" Quinn asked.

"Start packing my things and tell Kincaid to pack Gen's things. We'll leave tomorrow."

"Yes, sir." Before Quinn spoke, there was the slightest hesitation, and something flickered in the valet's eyes.

"Something wrong?" Cam asked.

"No sir. Just…tomorrow?"

"Tomorrow. Will this inconvenience you?"

Again, that flash in the eyes. But Quinn said, in a stiffly formal tone, "Of course not, sir."

"But you have a thought about it?"

"Just…that's not much time to…"

"To what?" Cam pressed, irritated by Quinn's uncharacteristic mood.

"Say goodbye," Quinn said, so quietly that the words were nearly lost in the air.

Cam's annoyance evaporated when he finally realized the distress the other man was in. In all their years together—years of unequal footing, yes, but also friendship—

Quinn had rarely even mentioned a specific person he was interested in, let alone worried about saying goodbye. Whatever had happened with the hostler Mallory, it was enough to shift Quinn out of his usual habits.

But Quinn only showed the briefest glimpse of his emotions, and then the veneer of the perfect servant slid over him again. "No matter, sir. I'll have everything ready by tomorrow morning."

"Wait. I have a better idea," Cam said. And he shared his new notion with Quinn, who accepted that it was indeed a better plan.

Afterward, Cameron returned to the breakfast room, strolling over to Gen as if he had no cares in the world. "How about a turn around the garden, my lady?" he asked.

Gen's eyes flickered with concern, but she smiled and let him help her up.

In the middle of the lavender beds, he told her the news.

"She just up and left?" Gen asked, incredulous. "What must Alexandrine think?"

"You should ask her," Cameron suggested. "Though I'm sure the answer will be a story about a sick relative or something similarly vague."

"Then what? Do you know what's going on?"

"I wish," Cameron muttered. "But we're not going to learn what it is here at Thorngrove. Darling, I'm going to be a complete coward and use you as an excuse to get out of here. I need to get back to London to follow this clue. And you're not staying behind."

"Thank goodness," she breathed.

"I don't want to arouse any more suspicions, so I'll confide to our hostess that you need to return to London to see the family physician to confirm your happy state.

That gossip will provide more than enough justification for our leaving early."

"But if you return to London and the Black Mask starts robbing likely houses there again too, won't someone start thinking about your similar travel plans?"

"No, because Quinn is remaining in the village for a few days—just long enough to commit one robbery at a nearby estate that I can't possibly be connected to."

"Ohhhh." Gen blinked. "Quinn knows?"

"He does. I couldn't creep around robbing places without my valet knowing. How would I explain all those ripped and torn black outfits? And I'm certainly not doing my own laundry."

"But to ask him to…"

"He's a very unusual valet," Cameron assured her. "And he's got all the skills necessary to act as the Black Mask for a night."

"Cameron, someday you'll have to explain how you got into all this."

"Someday, love. But for now, enjoy your last day in the country. We leave for London tomorrow."

"I'll be glad to get back."

"The first task for you is to see your doctor. Then we'll talk about Greyslake."

She shot him a dark look. "You said you'd sign the papers!"

"I did," he admitted. "But Gen, you adore Greyslake, and I don't want you to sell it. I'll instruct my solicitors to look into other options to raise the money you need. Land is too valuable to give up, especially when it's not just land, but a place you love."

"Do you mean it? You'll help raise the funds?"

"Of course. We'll find a way, one that doesn't involve you losing your childhood home."

"Oh." Her eyes filled with tears.

"Easy now, darling. Your delicate state is affecting your moods. Don't cry."

"I'm not sad," she said, wiping tears from her eyes. "I just…oh, I don't know."

"Gen," he said, pulling her into his arms. "Is it so surprising that I'm on your side?"

"A little," she murmured, laying her forehead against his chest. "Sometimes I feel like I don't know you at all."

"You know me better than anyone else does, sweet Gen. And you can believe me when I say I'll help you."

"It may cost more than you're willing to pay."

"We'll discuss the cost later."

Gen straightened up and stepped back, her face now lit with a smile. "When we made our agreement, I never imagined we'd be in a place like this, talking about anything we've discussed in the last twelve hours."

She walked a little ways down the path, stooping to pick some lavender sprigs. He remained where he was, struck by how different she was today from the woman who'd made the bargain with him. She looked radiant in the mellow sunrays of the late morning. He wished he could tell her more, tell her everything. Gen knowing about him being the Black Mask, and his work with the Zodiac, lifted some of the weight of his soul, but not all of it. There was still the secret of Amelia, the woman who'd been with him in his study at exactly the wrong moment.

It sat between them, an invisible but ugly thing that neither of them could discuss or ignore.

He could make something up, something about how Amelia had been supplying information and he was just paying for her expenses. Cam knew how to spin a story, and there was no audience more receptive than someone who wanted to believe.

But that would mean lying to Gen, again. And Cameron refused to do that. After three years of stony silence, she had allowed him back into their home, and her bed, and most importantly her life. And now she was carrying their first child. Cameron couldn't sully all that careful rebuilding with a lie.

A lie would be so much easier than the truth. It would hurt her less than the truth.

Cameron shook his head, trying to ignore the cold, practical voice. He'd maintain the old lie—the one she already believed about Amelia—because the damage was done. But he wouldn't tell any new lies, or spin new stories to trick Gen into a temporary state of peace.

Because lies weren't safe places to live. No one knew that better than Cameron.

♊

THEY RETURNED TO LONDON. THE city was hot and rife with the stench of the river and the garbage and the vermin that made London London. Genevieve didn't care. She was in a daze of contentment. She understood her place with Cameron now, and she was going to have a child, and what else mattered?

For his part, Cameron doted on her whenever he could. And when he had to leave at strange hours, sometimes carrying the small leather case, she knew why he behaved so oddly. Most of all, she knew he'd be back.

She decided that the sound she liked most was when the door was opened and Cameron's distinct footsteps echoed in the foyer. It calmed her when she was in her study or lying down in her bedroom, a faint but certain promise that she'd see him moments later.

The first day after they'd returned, Genevieve sent word to Dr Follett, her family physician, to come see her. He confirmed her condition, congratulated her warmly, and predicted a date of mid-March for the baby's arrival. He also suggested that she leave the city again as soon as possible.

"Go to one of your family's country homes, my lady. The fresh air and good food will do you and the child wonders. The miasma of the city is not at all healthy. I wonder that you came back at all."

"Who should I trust but you?" Gen asked, to his obvious pride. "And we are only here for a short while. My husband has obligations here which cannot be put aside."

The doctor hefted his medical bag as he prepared to leave. "Pleased to hear that his lordship is recognizing his duties. If you have any questions at all, my lady, you know where to find me. Good day."

After he left, Gen set about writing a slew of letters. One to her sister Gloria. One to her mother, and Cam's mother. One to Sabine. One to Roger. She probably should wait, but her excitement didn't let her. She wanted to reassure her parents that everything was going as it should, at last. And to tell Sabine the best possible outcome happened. And to hopefully convince Roger to finally come home after so long away.

Sabine was the first person to call on her, sweeping into the house dressed in a confection of white cotton and brilliant yellow trim. Her hat, covered in gold mesh ribbon, was a sight.

"My dear," she said, swooping down to kiss Gen's cheek. "Congratulations. You have done brilliantly. You've brought your wandering husband to heel, and you will be the savior of the family line, and you look gorgeous as ever. How can you live with yourself?"

"Well, I don't live with myself any longer. Cameron is going to remain a resident of our house."

"How delightfully domestic! His moniker will have to be changed."

Yes, Lord Devil-Take-It-All wasn't appropriate any longer, Gen thought smugly. It never was appropriate, really. Now that she knew of Cameron's secret life and how hard he'd worked to appear as if he never worked at all, she was much more forgiving of his behavior.

"You look immensely satisfied," Sabine noted. "I do

hope your reconciliation was…thrilling."

"I have no complaints," Gen said, hiding her smile.

"Ah. You say only a tenth of what you feel, my darling friend. So I know that you must be delighted with your lover."

"My husband!"

"The two are not always separate," Sabine said dryly. "Only in most cases."

"Sabine," she chided.

"I only speak the truth. However, in all seriousness, I'm happy for you, my dear. You deserve to have some peace at home after what you've been through. I should warn you though, that such about-faces are not always lasting. He might be the adoring husband now, but…"

"We've talked," Gen said quickly. "I think much of our difficulty was simply because Cameron and I hadn't fully understood each other. And now we do."

"Did he apologize, then? For that business with the mistress in the house?"

Genevieve took an unsteady breath. No, he hadn't. Neither of them had brought it up. But she couldn't bear to go through it all again. So she said, "It was an indiscretion. It won't be repeated."

"You forgave him." Sabine regarded her as if she were a mythical creature. "I could not have forgiven any of my husbands had they transgressed in such a way. You are a marvel, Genevieve."

After Sabine left, her mother stopped by.

"Genevieve," Lady Jane said breathlessly. "We received your letter, and your father and I are so happy for you. At last, after we'd all lost hope for your marriage. But you endured, and now you are to be a mother. How wonderful."

"Thank you, Mama," Gen replied, already feeling the

role of daughter steal over her, like a cloak she'd forgotten the weight of. "I couldn't wait to tell you, though we will not announce the news publicly for some months yet."

"Oh, indeed. There is so much to be done. You'll have to make plans for your confinement. No lady can be wandering about the city in such a condition. Will you go to Greyslake?"

"We have not discussed it yet, Mama! I am months away from that."

"Oh, but it would be ideal. You were born there, your sisters and brother were born there. And it's so peaceful. The forest, the lake, the hills. It soothes the soul. Just what an expectant mother needs."

"I will bring the matter up with my husband."

"You are on speaking terms, then."

"Yes, Mama. All is as it should be." Gen refrained from saying more. She'd never had a terribly close relationship with her mother. She loved her, but she didn't confide in her. There was too much pressure to be good and say the right thing to please. Lady Jane was, it must be said, a rather reserved individual. She had been shocked and horrified by Cameron's action three years ago, but it was the silent, pinched-nose horror that didn't allow for discussion. Her father was even more distant—a benevolent but unapproachable man. Roger had just left England. Gloria was younger than her. And Grace had passed away.

Genevieve had been on her own.

Now her mother chatted with her about inconsequential, innocent things. Gloria's latest gowns. Roger's amusing letters. His promises, ever delayed, to come back home.

She stood up at last, saying she had other calls to

make. But she smiled at Gen and said she intended to be back frequently. "Extend my congratulations to Lord Deverall," she added, ever proper. "And discuss going to Greyslake. Don't let him drag you to his family's estate. No matter how magnificent Bainbridge House may be, it's not home."

"Yes, Mama."

In fact, there was a lot concerning Greyslake that she needed to talk to Cameron about.

Earlier, on the same day of her mother's visit, she had received another letter. This one was from Valentin Brodeur, and it was written in much the same tone as he spoke—hesitant and kindhearted.

My lady,

I do hope you will excuse my continued presumption in writing to you, but you left Thorngrove before I could relate my latest news on the topic. I have consulted with my contact in Scotland regarding the matter of the pines...

Gen continued to read, astonished by the final sum Valentin said that his buyer would offer. He concluded with his assessment that the price was a good one, but that it was naturally Genevieve's decision.

He concluded,

I know you will act in the interests of the children you aid. If I can be of further assistance, you may write to me either at Thorngrove or the location I stay at while in London.

He offered a street address that Gen recognized as being very close to the buildings of Parliament. That must be where the secretary had to go to deal with the various complexities of Lucien's incarceration in England.

Gen put the letter away hastily, still feeling guilty for considering cutting down the beloved woods at Greyslake. Of course, she'd begun this endeavor with Valentin before she knew she was pregnant, and before Cameron told her that he'd help her raise funds without selling any land.

Perhaps she should write to Valentin and simply explain that his kind intercession was no longer needed.

But something stopped her.

Because a little voice in her head told her that Cameron, wonderful Cameron, had made promises before, and then broken them, along with her heart.

She'd turn down Valentin's offer when she had the funds in hand. Until then, the letter stayed in her desk drawer, a bulwark against betrayal.

And next to Valentin's letter, she saw the scrap of paper on which she'd written the street direction for the letter Cameron had sent to the mysterious Metcalfe. Cameron had rushed her out of London, and so Gen had not got the chance to find out where the person lived. And in truth, she'd forgotten about it.

But she was back in London now.

A quarter hour later, Gen was being driven through the city toward a less fashionable quarter, where Metcalfe's letters were all sent. After winding through streets that were less and less attractive, the carriage rolled to halt.

"Here we are!" the coachman yelled.

"Excuse me?" Gen called back.

He leaned down to open the door, not leaving his high perch.

"Summermaid Public House, ma'am. That's the address you asked for."

She looked to where he pointed, toward a tall building with a hanging sign of a buxom, laughing woman holding a bunch of grapes in either hand, and the name "Summermaid" underneath.

"Mercy," Gen murmured, stepping out. She paid the man the cost of the ride, and turned to the pub.

Swallowing nervously, she walked inside, feeling quite out of place. She wore an understated white muslin gown and a short cotton cape in green linen, one that was intended to keep dirt and wetness off, not to keep her warm. Still, her outfit was much finer than that of the tavern's other clients, who ranged from solid working classes to rather shabby.

"Can I help you, ma'am?" a barmaid asked while Gen stood in the foyer, peeking into the area where several men drank.

"Where might I find the manager of this establishment?" Gen asked.

"Mr Johnson? I'll fetch him."

Moments later, a round-faced man in an apron stood before her. Gen put in her request.

"Metcalfe? No, ma'am. No one lives here by that name."

"But there are letters that come to this location, quite regularly."

"Oh, letters! You see, ma'am, I do accept and hold letters for a number of folks who might find it convenient. Cost of one shilling per quarter, in exchange for me keeping such parcels safe. If this Metcalfe is one of them, they could live anywhere."

"Can you tell me if it was a man who picked the letters up, or who paid for the service?"

The proprietor made a noncommittal sound, and a single glance at Gen's reticule.

"Oh, mercy," she muttered. Digging out a coin, she pressed it into his palm.

"I remember now, ma'am. It was a woman who paid and picked up the letters. Quite a handsome one too. But quiet. Never said much other than good day. And no, I don't know where she lives. Another coin won't help with that. I just don't know."

"I see. Thank you for your assistance." Gen turned to leave.

He called after her, "She talked like you, ma'am, when she talked at all."

Outside, Gen managed to flag down a passing cab.

She gave the driver the direction to her home, and got in, slumping against the back cushion of the bench. Another attempt to learn about her husband ended with defeat. Metcalfe remained a mystery.

Perhaps Metcalfe was a contact. A supplier of information. Perhaps Cameron wrote to her to ask for help in his spying. And paid her for the answers.

Would that explain why an unknown, unrespectable woman might have come to him late one night, on a night that he was otherwise occupied at a party? Perhaps she had information that couldn't wait. And he paid her.

And when Gen over saw it happening, he couldn't explain why without exposing his life as a spy and compromising the woman as well.

Gen's heart beat faster. It could explain the situation. Barely. But it could work.

♊

CAMERON'S RETURN TO LONDON WAS also marked by meetings. In the discreet and rather shabby office from which the Zodiac was run, he related all he'd learned, which seemed pitifully small. But both Julian and Chattan were pleased with the results so far, especially the stolen papers.

Julian was only worried about one thing. "The newspapers are full of speculation about the Black Mask and where he might strike next. Lady Newsham claims over a thousand pounds worth of jewelry was stolen."

"I stole her jewelry as a distraction, and it worked," Cam said. "The papers can talk about jewelry and silver and the Black Mask and whatever else they choose. But no one is talking about the notes I got, or the fact that Mireille Lambert more or less disappeared immediately after. I did exactly what you needed me to do."

"I didn't need you to take a thousand pounds worth of jewelry."

"Trust me, the total value is closer to fifty pounds. Nearly all of her collection was fake."

"You're saying Lady Newsham exaggerates her worth?"

From the outer office, Chattan gave a cough that just might have been a poorly concealed laugh.

"All I know is that she won't have to pay that much to replace what was lost. Or rather, Lord Newsham won't. It may be worth looking into his finances, by the way. I suspect that he actually sold the real versions of her jewels to get funds he needed. I overheard a conversation where he was discussing going into trade in some way, so he must be desperate."

"Noted." Julian turned to the stack of stolen notes. "These papers you took from the agent's room. You think they're in code?"

"They must be." Cam explained how they appeared to be innocuous notes for Alexandrine's planned book—hardly on the level of a state secret, since she spoke to literally everyone she met about it.

Julian gave the notes a thorough look, then called Chattan into the office. She took one glance and said, "If it's a code, Pandora will know." She shuffled the pages together into a tidy pile. "I'll contact her, and she'll report back when she's broken it."

"How long will that take?" Cameron asked. He didn't like the idea of sitting idle.

Chattan cocked an eyebrow. "Only the codebreaker will know that, Gemini. Leave the notes here. You'll be contacted with the results."

"Yes, ma'am."

Julian said, "We kept a watch on the agent's London flat while she was gone, just in case. No one's reported anyone coming back other than the building's housekeeper and maid. Since the lady hasn't returned, it would be a prime opportunity for the Black Mask to get a better look at what's inside. Good hunting, my friend."

Cameron knew he was dismissed and left the office. His next meeting was going to be more uncomfortable.

He had to speak to his father.

His family's townhouse was quiet, as his mother was out of town, thank goodness. She always looked upset when Cameron came around, mostly because she too believed that Cameron was exactly what he appeared to be. It was nearly as painful to him as Genevieve's earlier disdain. The time when he appeared with Genevieve was a rare exception.

So Cameron avoided the house for the most part. The maid who opened the door looked surprised to see him, but said she'd see if his father was at home. Yes, Cameron had succeeded so well at creating the image of Devil-Take-It-All that even his own father would have to consider whether he'd be at home to his son.

Then Lionel, Marquess of Bainbridge, appeared at the end of the hallway. "Cameron. In here."

He obeyed, walking into Lionel's personal study, a new room built at the back of the house, which shared only one wall with the original structure. The other walls featured a surprising number of windows, and looked out onto the back garden. It looked lovely, but more importantly, it was extremely difficult for anyone to eavesdrop without being seen. The marquess liked his privacy.

Lionel closed the door after Cameron, and then turned to regard him.

The marquess was an imposing man, broad shouldered and still in good condition, despite an inordinate love of sponge cake. His once dark hair was now salted with silver, and Cameron realized with a jolt that his father was… older. That he was not unchangeable, immortal, the way Cameron had subconsciously assumed. Though he knew it was foolish, he'd always trusted that his father would be there. And that was plainly not going to be true forever.

"Looks like you've got something on your mind," Lionel said. "Sit. Drink?"

"No," Cameron said, sitting on a wide chair that faced the gardens. "I...well...a lot has happened recently."

"I've heard some of the news." Lionel poured himself a glass of brandy, and the scent wafted toward Cameron, an aroma he'd associated with his father for years. "You've reconciled with your wife."

"Yes," Cameron said, sounding more uncertain than he meant to. "We had a discussion several weeks ago, and agreed that we needed to try again."

"Was it Genevieve who asked, or you?"

"She asked me there on a matter of business. I proposed the plan for living together again."

"You must have been very persuasive. The poor girl seemed unable to forgive what happened. The separation drove your mother to tears some nights."

"I'm sorry."

"You made a decision," Lionel replied calmly. "Naturally, there were repercussions. Sure you don't want a drink?"

"Quite. I need to have my head clear."

"Tell me."

Where to start? The good news? "First, Gen is expecting."

Lionel paused halfway through taking another sip of brandy. A smile suffused his face, showing new wrinkles in his skin. "Indeed?"

"Yes." Cameron couldn't stop an answering smile, one of pure pride. "We think the baby will be born in March of next year. She's very happy. So am I, naturally. But Gen's happy." That was what mattered.

"Congratulations." Lionel took the sip at last. Even though he tried to hide it, Cameron could see tension leave his body. He'd worried about the family line, and now he had one less worry. "Have you told your mother?"

"Gen sent a letter."

"That's truly marvelous news. I'm grateful you came in person to tell me."

"So am I. But that's not all."

"No?"

"I have another problem."

"Well, out with it. If you can't tell your old father, who can you tell?"

Indeed. "Genevieve knows I'm a spy."

Ⅱ

CAMERON FELT ANOTHER WEIGHT LIFT off his shoulders as soon as he spoke the words. Aside from Gen, the only other person in his family who knew about his being part of the Zodiac was his father, because his father had once been Gemini too.

Cameron was fifteen when he learned the truth about his father. The man was not just an aristocrat. He was an agent of the crown, and his frequent absences were usually due to the secret work he did in the shadows, not the social rounds of titled gentlemen.

Lionel, who'd recently become marquess following the death of his own father, made a point of taking Cameron out for a long ride the day of his fifteenth birthday. Cam had been excited—as a child, he rarely got his father's undivided attention. But on that day, he got it, along with the truth of Lionel's commitment to the crown, and an invitation to do the same.

And Cameron, overwhelmed, had agreed to everything. Every rule, every restriction, every order.

The understanding was simple: Cameron would work as a member of the Zodiac until he became marquess himself. Then he'd leave the organization, just as Lionel did before, just as (Cameron was astonished to learn) his grandfather had done before that. The burden of marquess would be too difficult to manage along with work as a spy.

One of the most important restrictions had been that he couldn't tell anyone outside the organization the truth. It was too dangerous. Everyone—Julian, Chattan, Lionel—had been clear on that.

His father had said once, "Speak to me, should you need to vent any frustrations—I can sympathize, believe me. But when you marry, as you will, your wife can't know. I never told your mother and I never shall."

"Did you not trust Mother?" Cameron had asked.

"It's not a matter of trust! It's a matter of care. I wouldn't dream of placing that burden on her. Knowing that I was involved in such activities, worrying when I was gone a day too long, or acting a bit out of character. It's not at all fair to involve an innocent woman in the affairs of the Zodiac. Better to keep her ignorant, for everyone's sake."

Cameron had nodded, though he also suspected his father had been a *little* concerned that his mother might accidentally reveal the truth to the wrong person. In any case, the fewer people who knew, the better.

Now, Cameron's father looked at him with an alarmed expression. "You told her?"

"Only because she'd walked in on me working. It's very difficult to explain away the Black Mask."

"That damned thief! I knew it was a mistake to ask you to play so many roles. Gemini is enough, and the Zodiac should have known that. I never gallivanted about the roofs of the city dressed in black."

"I made a decision," Cameron said. "There were bound to be repercussions."

"Don't be smart with me, boy." But Lionel smiled to hear his words turned back on him. Then he sobered. "All right, the details. How much does she know?"

So Cameron gave his father the whole account—what he'd told Gen and what still remained secret. At the end, Lionel sighed. "A sticky situation."

"I trust Genevieve not to say anything. But now I'm more worried about her getting into trouble simply by association."

Lionel shook his head. "As long as she keeps quiet about it, she'll be as safe as she was before. The risk lies in her saying something to the wrong person, not out of spite, but concern."

"I know. But what's to be done other than reminding her constantly not to do that? Gen is not going to appreciate those reminders." She'd regard it as condescending.

"Are you thinking of leaving the Zodiac?"

"What? No." But he had. More than once since telling Gen the truth. And since she'd told him about the baby. "I'm committed to staying in just as long as you did. It's our tradition."

"Tradition is important. So is staying alive. Don't let any Aries or Astronomer—current or future—tell you otherwise."

"Aries has said nothing. Though he doesn't know about Gen."

"Don't tell him, is my advice. I never worked with this incarnation of Aries, but Julian strikes me as a man who's very mild on the outside, and deadly when he chooses to be. You don't want anyone thinking your lovely wife is a liability."

That thought made Cameron want a drink. He instead flexed his fingers open and closed, trying not to form fists. "How did our family get involved in this?" he asked without expecting a reply.

Lionel just chuckled. "Gives us some experience of the world before we enter politics. Can't tell you how useful my time as a Sign was in shaping my perspective. I understand politics, and politicians, far better than I would have otherwise."

"Using secrets to your advantage?" Cameron teased.

His father straightened up, looking comically prudish for a moment, though a twitch of his lips gave him away. "The idea offends me to the core. It would be highly un-ethical to use any knowledge I gained while in the Zodiac in my political life."

"So you don't have some secret information that Lord Kirkhall is a traitor and that's why you vote down any-thing he suggests?" The rivalry between the men was well known.

"Of course not," Lionel said in his usual tone. "I op-pose Kirkhall's motions because the man is an ass. Also, he once treated your mother quite rudely at a party. And he never apologized."

"You didn't call him out?" Cameron asked, only half joking. His father was an excellent fencer, as well as an extremely good shot. Cameron just assumed, probably with a son's naive faith, that his father could win any con-test.

His father chuckled. "Oh, the thought was tempting, believe me. Could have got away with it too, back in those days before all this nonsense sentiment against duel-ing. But I had my own reasons for keeping the matter quiet. And in any case, this is a better form of revenge. Call a man out and you only get one chance to shame him. Whereas I've killed over a dozen proposals he's championed, and isolated him from his peers." His father grinned, revealing the ruthless, competitive streak that had served him so well as a spy.

"Well, I don't know how I'll do in politics, consider-ing the sort of man people think I am." Cameron couldn't quite hide the bitterness.

His father's grin widened. "My boy, you're preparing a political trick of a magnitude undreamed of, and you're not even appreciating the impact you can have. You'll have to plan the revelation for something big—something where a single vote will be pivotal, something where you can speak up for a cause that matters. When you become marquess and reveal your true self after years of pretending, you'll stop everyone in their tracks. I only wish I could be there to see it!"

Because when Cameron became marquess, it would be because his father had died.

♊

GENEVIEVE SPENT THE DAY IMMERSED in work. First, she met with a few other members of the Society, discussing the latest plans for the new building. Then, she went to the large space the Society rented as a place to feed the children who came to the door. The old warehouse was cavernous and drafty in cool weather, and still smelled faintly of malt in the warmer months.

She and the others ladled out soup from large pots, served seemingly endless quantities of bread, and poured cup after cup of clean water for the children to drink. Many children had no cup of their own, and thus shared with friends—or strangers. Gen never thought the practice entirely sanitary, though she couldn't say why. She just noticed that when a child who was coughing or sneezing violently shared a cup with a healthy child, the healthy child very often took sick soon after.

It was a long, dreary day, with clouds sweeping in and rain falling. She came back home just after dark, grateful for the luxuries she had. Dry clothing, warm slippers, a delicious supper with hot tea afterward.

In her study, she read an article about a new project in the city of Philadelphia, the Fairmount Water Works. The city was attempting to correct the mistakes of the past with a new, modern, entirely innovative system with a pumping station and a reservoir, and plans for a dam across the nearby river. She would write to the architect and discover if any of his ideas could be used for her own project, which needed quite extensive plumbing and wells.

Cameron had not come home, and she assumed he was up to no good, a phrase that she privately used because it felt familiar to think about Cameron being up to no good, and because she became rather distraught if she thought too long about the danger of *espionage* or *thieving*.

Shortly after midnight, she went up to bed.

As Genevieve stepped into the bedroom, a gust of air blew her candle out. "Blast," she muttered, glad no one was there to hear her unladylike curse. With her luck, she'd trip over something as she made her way to the bedside table. And which foolish chambermaid had left the window open on a rainy night like this? She picked her way forward carefully, hands out in front of her. Suddenly, she froze. She heard a footstep.

"Hello?" she said uncertainly. "Is someone there?"

A rustling sound right in front of her caused her to jump and drop the candlestick. But rather than a crash, she heard only a slight grunt and the dull flash of the metal base. Someone, quick as a cat, had caught the candlestick.

Terrified, Genevieve began to scream, but a hand covered her mouth, choking her off.

"Calm down, sweet Gen," Cameron murmured close to her ear. "You're in good hands."

Genevieve closed her eyes when she felt him brush her cheek with his lips. He trailed a series of light kisses across her face until he found her mouth in the darkness. Her lips tingled at his touch. He deepened the kiss, delving tentatively with his tongue, parting her lips and darting inside. Gen gave a little moan of pleasure, setting a humming vibration through their kiss.

Lost in the swirling pleasure of the kiss, Genevieve instinctively raised her hands, and felt the fabric of the silk mask beneath her fingertips.

"Cameron! You weren't crawling about London as the Black Mask in the rain tonight, were you?" Then she remembered the draft. "Did you come in the *window*?"

She closed the window in question, then relit the candle. In the gold light, she was immediately drawn to the man standing before her.

"I did. In fact, I was just looking for the right woman to steal," Cameron replied in a low voice. "You'll do nicely."

"Impudent thief, I'm promised to another," Gen said primly, then giggled.

Cameron's eyes lit up at her impromptu roleplay though. "If you've got someone, then why isn't he here?"

"Real gentlemen don't lie in wait in dark rooms. Only rogues do."

He kissed her, then asked, "Do you want a rogue in your bed right now?"

"How do you know I haven't always got a rogue in my bed?"

"Because you just told me you were promised to a real gentleman. So he can't be a rogue as well."

"In truth," Gen said, "he may be both a gentleman and a rogue."

"Sounds intriguing," Cameron murmured, his tongue tracing unknown patterns on her neck.

"He's very intriguing. I'm not sure I understand him at all. I may have…misjudged him earlier."

Cameron went still. "Tell me more."

Gen chose her words carefully, or as carefully as she could in the arms of a dizzying, seductive man. "There was a time, years ago, when I thought he was a rogue, and worse. I drove him away and swore he'd never get near me again."

"But now?" Cameron's breath was shallow.

"Now I wonder if his behavior only appeared roguish. And that he might have had a reason to hide the truth from me. Such as a secret side of him that he never revealed to me. Perhaps the scene I saw him in—with another woman—was not what it appeared."

Cam stared at her from under the black silk mask, then reached out to stroke her cheek with the tips of his fingers. "No man in his right mind would want to hurt you, sweet Gen. And if you'd be truly willing to give him a second chance, he'd be grateful."

Gen sighed. "I'm just scared to trust him again, after what happened. Oh, I'm confused."

"Never be scared, sweet Gen," he murmured, brushing his lips against hers. "It's all right to be confused. Lord knows I am—I've got more identities than I know what to do with. But we're here, together."

He took off the mask, which unfurled into the long rectangle of black silk that she'd first found in the case. She'd missed the eye holes in her brief examination of it.

"I thought this was a blindfold the first time I saw it," she said.

"It can be," he replied with a lazy smile. He twisted the silk and a second later, it was a long, thin strip. "Curious?"

She inhaled.

"Oh. You've been *thinking* about it. Don't deny it."

She looked at the silk. She *had* been thinking about it, more than any lady ought to. But she shook her head.

"Just the blindfold," he said softly. "And if you decide you don't like it, I'll take it off that instant. Admit it. You're a little curious."

Her chest constricted as she felt a heat all the way through her torso and down into her legs. "A little."

"Then it will be a little experiment. Turn around, love." He tied the silk around her head. "Too tight?" he asked, his breath teasing her ear.

"No, it's fine. I'm fine."

"Tell me if that changes, Gen."

He proceeded to undress her, and though he'd undressed her before, it hadn't felt as sensual as what he was doing now. He undid the buttons at the back of her gown one by one, and Gen felt the cool air caress her skin as he exposed it. She felt like she'd faint when his hands ran along the lower part of the stays under her breasts.

When he untied the stays, she was left wearing only the thin silk chemise.

Gen then felt the heat of his mouth on her breast, kissing her through the fabric. Gen whimpered at the sensation of the suddenly wet silk across her nipples. "Cam," she gasped.

His arms circled her waist, and held her to him as he continued to lavish attention on her very sensitive breasts. He licked and sucked until she was moaning, bending her body to match his. "Cameron, that feels so good," she gasped. "Why does it feel so good?"

"You know why, Gen," he responded, cupping her breasts in his hands while she writhed against him. "Take away sight, and all the other senses compensate. Your hearing means more, your senses of smell and taste, and best of all, your sense of touch and feeling. You don't know where I'll touch you next, so every time is a surprise."

She felt his thumbs graze her hardened nipples and she gasped.

She thought she could almost come undone purely

from the way he was fondling her. Before she could stop herself, she whispered the guess out loud, and heard Cam's ragged breath in response.

"Let's find out," he said in a low growl.

He peeled the silk down from her shoulders to her waist, and then laid her on the bed, moving carefully so the blindfolded Gen didn't so much as get a bump from a misplaced step. Then he straddled her and proceeded to drive her completely mad with his lips and tongue and hands. Gen couldn't see a thing, and didn't need to because she felt each move like a bolt of lightning through her body, making her muscles tighter and tighter until she was begging him to bring her to a release.

His breath was hot against her breast when he hissed, "Feel this."

Something pinched her nipple and Gen lost her breath when she realized he was raking his teeth across her skin, and she loved it. She loved it so much that she arched her back to push herself toward him, only to buckle when her body began to shake with the unstoppable peak he'd brought her to.

She said his name over and over while the feeling shot through her, and moaned in agony when he suddenly pulled away.

"No, don't leave me," she said, reaching for him, not knowing where he'd gone, only that he was away from her.

"One moment, Gen," he said, his voice tight. He sounded close by, but not close enough. The sounds of piece after piece of his clothing hitting the floor filtered through to her ears. Then his hand roughly pulled her shift off from where he'd left it at her waist.

A naked, fire-hot Cameron covered her body again, and Gen wrapped her arms around him. "Why do you like to do this to me? The blindfold?"

His fingers ran over her face. "It heightens everything. Anticipation. Enjoyment. Everything." He slid his hands under her, drawing her to him.

His mouth covered hers, and she melted as he captured her in a long, slow kiss. His tongue traced her lips and then teased the inside of her mouth. She moaned, giving herself up to it.

Cameron sucked her lower lip and then said in low voice, right by her ear, "You know what's best about this, Gen? The fact that you let me do this at all. The fact that you trust me enough to let me enjoy you this way."

She stilled, realizing that she did trust him. And it was more than trust. She loved him.

"I want to do something I haven't done yet," she said.

"Besides wearing a blindfold?" he asked, a low laughing voice in her ear.

"Yes, besides that."

"What, sweet Gen? I'm at your service. Tell me what you want."

"I want to know what my mouth can do to you."

He exhaled heavily. "So do I."

Gen ran her hands along his body, finding that a lack of sight was joined by a lack of inhibition. She touched him with a boldness she never had before, her fingers finding new ways to learn about his shape and his sensitivities.

She moved lower, running one hand along the hard length of his erection, listening to how he breathed in faster when she squeezed a little harder and how he exhaled in time to her strokes.

Then she opened her mouth and gave an experimental lick across the tip.

Cameron moaned, and she couldn't stop a smile. She

licked again, and then slid her lips over the tip. He held very still for a moment, and then put a hand gently on her head. "Keep going, love. Take all of me in."

Encouraged, she opened her mouth. She sucked gently, and was rewarded with an inhale from above. "Oh, Gen. Yes. Taste me. However you want to. Suck me, lick me, bite me—not *too* hard, love. Oh, God."

She experimented with all those choices, finding that Cameron seemed to love every one. He kept a hand on her hair, guiding her movements without pushing her too roughly. Mostly, he just seemed to want to ensure she'd not stop, based on his repeated pleas of *don't stop*.

She paused when she felt him pull her hair gently, halting her attentions.

"Get up on your feet, gorgeous. And then turn around. Trust me. That's right."

He leaned over her, his hands tight on her hips. "Another time I'll let you finish me with your mouth, sweet Gen. But I need to be inside you right now."

She needed it too, needed to feel him spend himself in her body, not to give her a child—they'd taken care of that—but just to feel him need her that much.

She did as he asked. Gen spread her legs and moaned when she felt him enter her from behind, his thighs against the backs of her legs as he slid farther into her body, sheathing himself in her.

They were both so close that the end was inevitable. She came undone just as he did, and an easy warmth seeped into her bones. It was odd to think that she'd once been afraid of feeling so good.

Cameron withdrew a moment later, and fell beside her on the bed, breathing heavily. He drew her down next to him, her back to his chest.

"You've still got the blindfold on, Gen." His fingers

fumbled at the knot, failed, and then he just slid the whole thing off. "Christ, you surprised me."

"You thought I'd never keep it on?" She kept her eyes closed as he swept her hair back.

"Gen? How are you?"

"Lovely. Would you hold me?" she asked.

"God, yes." He drew her back against him, and wrapped her in his arms. Gen sighed, happy with the heat seeping into her body from his. She felt his hand drift downward to her belly, his fingers splayed wide across it. "I'll hold you both."

A frisson of joy arced down Gen's spine.

Cam went on, "We'll have to think of a name. Two names. A boy's name and a girl's name, just in case."

Gen nestled closer into him. "We have months to decide," she said sleepily.

His arms tightened around her shoulders, cradling her close to his chest. "I love holding you, Gen."

"Holding," she repeated wryly, thinking he'd done a lot more than hold her.

"Yes, holding. Whether it's after sex, or just because you want to be held. Nothing makes me happier than seeing you in my arms, Gen. Knowing you want to be in my arms after all. Those years without you were torture, Gen. Loving you but not being able to show it at all."

"Loving me?"

"God yes. I love you, Gen. I pursued you because you were the woman I wanted in my life. I already loved you when I asked you to marry me. I wasn't going to let you get away."

Cameron loved her? A glow suffused her whole body, even more glorious than the *petit mort* she was now very familiar with. How perfect, to be loved by someone she loved too.

♊

GEN SLEPT THE NIGHT IN Cameron's arms, and woke up feeling as if the world was brand new. She looked over at her still sleeping husband. He was everything she hoped for—she just couldn't see it under the public face he'd worn to protect himself. She was grateful he'd finally told her the truth, even though part of her wished he'd done it deliberately, and not just because she'd caught him. Did he not trust her with the knowledge? She would never speak of it. She'd never hurt him. She loved him too much.

Then she realized that she'd never told Cameron that. Oh, she'd told him how happy she was when they were engaged, and probably some twaddle about the high regard she had for him. All measured, ladylike words and nothing as true as a profession of love. And of course, during the three years of separation, she'd thought she'd hated him.

But now, she could admit that it was indeed love. Not just because he was her husband and the father of their child, but because he was smart and kind and funny, and deeper than anyone knew. And so attentive and caring when they were alone together.

The time for her confession had come at last. She laid a hand on his shoulder. "Cameron, wake up. I have something important to tell you."

His eyes flicked open, alert and alarmed. "Gen? What's wrong?"

"I love you."

Cameron went still for a moment. Then his lips curved into a slow smile. "You do?"

"Yes. I should have said it before."

"I'm happy to hear it anytime." He pulled her into an embrace, dropping kisses along her neck, burying his face in her hair. "Oh, Gen. Isn't this better than being apart?"

Yes, yes it was. She didn't want to be parted. Ever.

His kisses grew more sensual, as he whispered suggestions for how to start their day.

A knock at the door interrupted them. Gen pushed Cameron away, giggling even as she ordered him to look respectable. He made a face as he pulled the sheets and blanket up over his gloriously naked body.

"Come in," Gen called.

Kincaid entered, looked startled on seeing two in the bed, and immediately dropped her gaze to the carpet. "It's ten, my lady. Shall I get your morning dress so you can come down to breakfast?"

"Tell Mrs Baxter we'll have breakfast brought up this morning," Gen told Kincaid. She was in no mood to leave the comfort of the bed, not today, not when she was so content.

"Yes, ma'am."

"I'll have toast and jam. And tea." Her nausea was faint today, but she didn't want to take chances.

"Mrs Baxter knows what I like," Cameron said, obviously not thinking of food at all.

"Yes, my lord." Kincaid kept her eyes on the floor, but Gen detected a smile—rather embarrassed, but happy—on her maid's face.

He added, "Oh, and Kincaid, if there was anything in the post, tell them to bring it up as well. And the newspaper."

Kincaid nodded and left.

Gen giggled again. "She was not expecting you to be in the bed, my lord."

"She should. It's technically mine, along with the rest of the house."

"And me?"

"And you, my fair wife." He pulled the sheet down, exposing her upper body. "Speaking of breakfast…"

"What are you intending?"

"Just need to get something in my mouth. I'm starving. Not for food. For you."

He proceeded to use the short while they had alone to tease and pleasure Gen to the point of distraction, going no further than her breasts. He didn't have to go further, not when his attentions had her whimpering beneath him, arching her back, and then going pliant in his arms.

Another knock on the door made him growl with frustration. "Later," he promised, before sitting back in a semi-respectable position.

Kincaid and another maid entered at Gen's invitation, bearing breakfast trays and a small platter with the newspaper and a few letters. They put the trays down and excused themselves, no doubt full of gossip to report below stairs.

Gen poured herself some tea, then looked to the stack of letters Cameron was sorting through. "What do you have there?"

"Just few letters for me. Oh, and you have one from your vagabond brother."

"Roger wrote? Let me have it."

Cameron started to hand her the sealed letter, but retracted it at the last moment. "If he asks for money again, you're to say no."

"Cam. We've been over this."

"Yes, but you didn't heed me the first time. He's taking advantage of your good nature."

"You don't know him."

Cameron expression grew dark. "I know his type."

"Oh please. Give me my letter!"

"Very well, but I require a tax first." He leaned over and kissed her deeply. Gen melted into him, reveling in the touch of his mouth on her, and all the little shivers it sent through her body.

Cameron ended the kiss, only to place another on her nose. "Tax paid." He pressed Roger's letter into her palm. "Here you go."

Gen shook her head, laughing at Cameron while she broke the seal and unfolded the letter. She didn't even look at it yet, too consumed by Cameron's blue eyes.

"One more kiss," she insisted.

He obliged, and Gen glowed with happiness.

Then she looked down at the letter in her hands. She started reading, frowning, more and more confused by what Roger was saying, until in a flash, she realized Cameron had handed her the wrong letter. This note was meant for his eyes, not hers.

By the last paragraph, hints of the truth seeped into her brain.

Though I wish to avoid it, I must ask for money once more. Peter is no better, and I have run out of other options, save that which your support has so far permitted me to avoid. You know how much to send, and where to send it. In the absence of his father, these coins are all Peter has to aid him. I urge you not to delay. Peter relies upon you, though he does not know it. And I of course will never tell him the ugly reality.

Amelia

"Who is Peter?"

Cameron had been scanning the newspaper, went still. "What?"

"Who is Peter? Who is *Amelia*?"

He snatched the letter from her, stared at it, then looked at the others letters still on the tray. The one from Italy, from Roger, lay on the top.

Realizing his mistake, Cameron closed his eyes, but said nothing.

"Well?" Gen asked. Happiness drained away, replaced by a wave of cold, a sudden certainty that everything she'd thought she had was vanishing into a fog. "This is what those letters are all about."

"What?"

"I saw those letters—some of them, or the outsides of them anyway. Some person who wrote to you practically every week. Letters you always tucked away as soon as you got them, not like all the other letters you received. I told myself those letters were part of your work. A contact. And when I told you that, you let me believe it."

"Gen."

She shoved her breakfast away, the tray and dishes falling to the floor with a clatter and a crash as the porcelain pot cracked open. She scrambled off the bed before he could stop her.

"Tell me who she is," Gen insisted from where she stood. Naked, vulnerable, but with anger now propelling her. Had she just told him she loved him? How he must have laughed inside.

"She's not a contact," he said quietly.

"Obviously. Because contacts don't ask for money for sick boys. Her child?"

"Yes."

"Your child?"

"No!" At that, he leapt out of bed too. Another breakfast set was lost, turning into a pile of shards and spilled coffee and cooling food.

"You expect me to believe you?" Gen found her robe and wrapped herself in it. The nausea which had thus far been faint now surged up, the worst it had ever been.

Cameron grabbed his own robe, and advanced around the large bed. "Gen, I can explain."

Before she could yell at him to stay away, the urge to vomit overwhelmed her. She barely made it to the pot kept for the purpose. On her knees, she lost what little she had in her stomach, and then suffered through dry heaves as her body tried desperately to purge whatever it could. *Get this love out of me*, she thought. *Get this stupid fool love out*.

Cameron's gentle hands were on her shoulders as he knelt beside her. "Gen, are you all right?"

"Get away from me." She tried to jerk out of his grasp, but she couldn't. Instead, he pulled her up to her feet, keeping strong hands on her, cradling her to his chest.

Gen pushed away, or tried to. The last thing she wanted from him was coddling, as if she were incapable of caring for herself. She didn't want anything from him.

Finally, she pushed hard enough that he let her go. She stumbled over to the bell pull and yanked down hard, too hard. "You lied to me."

"That's the last thing I wanted to do."

"She was a mistress back then, and you kept her this

whole time. And there's a child. God, I'm such an idiot."

"You're not. Gen, she's not…"

"Shut up. I am through with all your damned lies. You must think I'm so…*gullible*." And she had been, desperate to believe the lovely things he told her, desperate to mistake passion for love.

Cameron looked stricken, but also…fierce. The hints of darkness she'd seen before were back. "You don't understand, Gen."

"No, I don't and I don't want to. I will never believe you again. You'll not see *my* child a moment longer than decency demands. You will never bed me again. You will never sleep under the same roof as I do, ever again."

"Gen…"

"Do you hear me? Get out. Get *out!*"

Kincaid opened the door, having been summoned by the bell. She stared at the broken dishes, the couple that had been so happy in bed before now up and furious.

"My…lady?" Kincaid asked hesitantly.

"Kincaid, my morning dress. Now."

"You're in no state to be dressed. You need to wash…"

"I said get it now." Whatever slender thread of control she had over herself was about to snap in two.

Cameron walked to the door, telling Kincaid, "Take care of her. I need to speak to Quinn."

The moment he left, Gen sagged onto the edge of the bed.

Kincaid rushed to her. "My lady, what can I do? Should I send for the doctor? Lady Stanfield?"

"My mother. I want my mother," Gen gasped out, not even aware of her words. "Mama," she whispered, her world crumbling around her.

♊

GENEVIEVE WAS LOST IN A daze, and only dimly knew that people were talking to her: Kincaid, then Dr Follett, then her mother. Not Cameron.

Someone offered her a sickly sweet drink. She put her hands over her face and hid from the world, curling up into the softness of whatever surrounded her. And she drifted.

Memories collided with strange fancies, as Gen walked down paths she didn't recognize, looking for people she'd never met. Rain began to fall, and she was back in the woods where the thunderstorm had struck. But this time, Cameron wouldn't find her and bring her home.

Lightning flashed, a creak of thunder followed, and Gen woke up.

"Oh, my dear!" Her mother stood at the bedroom door, a bright lamp in her hand. "I thought you'd still be sleeping. Kincaid sent word that you'd taken ill."

"Not ill," Gen said, but her mother was already hurrying toward the bed, putting the too-bright lamp on the table.

"Hush, darling. Don't trouble yourself. He's gone. He left the house."

"Cameron?"

"Yes," her mother said reassuringly. "He's gone."

Paradoxically, the news made Gen want to curl back

up into the blankets. Why should she want him near after learning what she'd learned? But she did want him, desperately.

"Did he say anything?" Gen asked, her voice rough and dull. How long had she been asleep? She glanced at the windows, and saw that the curtains were all drawn.

"He was just leaving when I arrived earlier. He told me that he was leaving the house to give you peace and quiet, and he could be reached at his former rooms—he still rents them, I suppose."

"He has a mistress," Gen blurted out.

Her mother took her hand, not saying anything, but with her eyes full of compassion.

"The same one as before," she went on. "This whole time he let me think he was starting over, that he cared about a family and…me. And then I saw the letter."

Again, her mother squeezed her hand. "You must try to stay calm, dear."

Gen nodded. She could be miserable, but she still had a responsibility to her child. "I don't know what I'm going to do."

"You lived on your own before, darling. You are much stronger than anyone thought. And of course you'll have our support for the baby."

Yes, she'd lived on her own for three years. But that was before she'd completely lost her heart. Could she keep up appearances with this ache in her chest?

"The doctor gave you something to help you sleep earlier. Would you like more?"

Gen remembered the sticky sweetness in her mouth. "No. I won't have another fit. I promise." What a spectacle she must have made of herself.

"You were distraught, darling. I quite understand."

"How could you?"

Her mama's smile was sad. "Your own father was not always faithful to his vows."

"What?" Gen gaped, not just at the revelation but also the fact that her proper mama was actually discussing such a distasteful matter.

"It was years ago, when you all were little children. I daresay he was a bit restless, and men of course…they do what they like."

"Did you confront him? How did you discover it?"

"He'd purchased gifts for her, and unwisely noted the costs in an accounting ledger for the house. I saw the entries and realized the gifts had never come to me!"

"What did you tell him?"

"Just that he could carry on if he liked, but that he had to choose his bed. And that I would be waiting at home when he understood the depths of his folly."

"Mama!" Gen could actually picture it. Her sweet, gentle, proper mother laying down an ultimatum without raising her voice. "Did he give her up?"

"Within the year, yes. I think he desired the novelty, the apparent freedom. But there's not much freedom in an affair. Only another bond."

Gen sighed. "I don't think this is the same situation."

"I know, dear. But you're not alone in your pain. Other women have suffered it too. And their sympathies will be with you, even if they never so much as glance your way."

She was reassuring Genevieve that she'd not be punished socially for kicking Cameron out. Again. Gen wasn't sure she believed it, but it was nice to have her mama's support at least. Then she yawned.

"I need to rest more, as absurd as that sounds."

"The doctor recommended you eat a little when you wake, and I do insist on following orders. But then, yes, you may sleep."

Gen smiled at last, enjoying being a child again, even for a brief while. "Yes, Mama."

After a long night of restless dreams, Gen awoke to summer sunshine through the windows as Kincaid was pulling the drapes aside.

"Good morning, ma'am," the maid said cheerfully.

Gen doubted it, but she resolved to make it as good as she was capable of doing. Therefore she spent a lot of time in her study, writing to members of the board, looking over accounts of the Society, and reading more about the projects she hoped to emulate. She might not be able to save her own marriage, but she could save other people's lives. And that was worth it, was it not?

Her aching heart didn't agree, but Gen ruthlessly ignored it.

Soon after, the next post arrived, and Gen saw a letter addressed to her in what she recognized as Valentin's hand. She opened it, already guessing at the content. Indeed, he inquired again, with apologies for any presumption, about whether she wished to pursue the sale of Greyslake's pines.

She'd been uncertain before, hoping to save the landscape of her childhood home, and then succumbing to Cameron's promises to help her raise the funds. But now he'd never sign the papers for the property sale, and he'd surely not give a moment's thought to funding the project in another way.

No, if she was going to do this, her options were once again painfully few. She took a clean sheet of stationery from her desk and dipped her pen in the inkwell.

"Dear Mr Brodeur," she muttered, beginning to write. Yes, she did wish to pursue the matter, and she would like to do so as soon as was convenient. If Valentin would alert her when he was next in London, Genevieve would arrange to meet him to discuss the details, including the final price and the date of delivery.

She sealed the letter and addressed it, feeling as if she were regaining a tiny measure of control over her life.

A few days later, Sabine returned from a visit to the country, and came to call. "How are you, my dear? I heard you took very ill. I trust you're recovered?"

"Yes, but Sabine, there is so much to tell you."

"Marvelous," the older lady cried, settling on a chaise. "I am your willing audience."

So Gen told her friend nearly everything that had happened from the events at Thorngrove to the discovery of the letter from Cameron's mistress. The only parts she kept secret were those to do with Cameron's being the Black Mask and his spying.

Through it all, Sabine reacted as if at the theater, gasping and clutching her hands at all the correct moments. At the end, she declared, "It is a wonder you didn't swoon a dozen times before you did. I should have been a wreck."

"A wreck quite admirably describes my state at the moment."

Sabine's expression grew clouded. "If only Deverall was as affected."

"You've heard something?" Gen hated that she craved any news of him.

"He's not been hard to spot in town. There's not a gaming hell he hasn't been in this past week. He's been seen at boxing matches, horse races, and in the worst parts of the city. I wondered at the rumors, but it makes sense after what you told me."

"Surely it's exaggerated?" Gen asked faintly.

"My dear, do you really want to know the details?"

God help her, she did.

So Sabine told her.

♊

THIS TIME, ALL THE RUMORS were true. Over the past week, Cameron had made sure to behave horribly, and in as public a manner as possible. He gambled, he drank, he flirted with anything wearing a skirt. He told anyone who asked that he'd done his duty and now his life was his own again. He made damn sure everyone knew that he was not thinking of his prim little wife.

He thought of Gen *constantly*. No matter how much he drank or gambled, or how much he wanted to get ensnared by the charms of some woman, he couldn't stop from wanting, needing to get back to Gen.

He worried about her health, even though he arranged to get any news of the household from Ainsworth—Quinn stopped by daily for a report. Genevieve was apparently over the worst of her collapse, but Cameron still felt stricken that his stupid mistake had caused it. Not to mention also getting banished once again.

And Gen was unlikely to forgive him within three years now. Possibly a decade. Or never.

"Isn't this what you planned in the beginning?" Quinn had asked the first night back in the rented rooms. "Living apart makes your work far easier."

Yes, but it made his *life* far more miserable. He told Quinn to shut his damn mouth, and turned to brooding.

Not a pastime he usually indulged in, but now he found himself with nothing but lonely hours and an obsession with a woman who hated him, the perfect combination for brooding.

Quinn, God bless him, stayed nearby but silent. The perfect valet. Cameron took a lot for granted, and he needed to be careful lest he lose the one reliable person in his life. He sighed. At this point, he shouldn't be surprised that the only confidant he had was a disreputable servant who was literally being paid for discretion.

Sick of his own thoughts, Cameron went out, night after night after night. Partly to forget why he was alone —though he invariably despised his drinking companions—and partly to make it clear to the world that he cared about nothing. And certainly not Genevieve.

If there was the slightest chance someone like Mireille knew what he was, he didn't want Gen to be a target simply because Cameron cared about her. Far better to make it appear that he had no cares, and no way to be weakened by a romantic connection.

If only his body understood the plan. Every time he woke up, he reached for Gen, who wasn't there. He ached with the need to be close to her again, not just for release but for the sheer joy he got in having her in his arms, feeling her skin next to his and her hair tickling him while she slept.

God damn it.

He was supposed to be an agent. Cold hearted, relentless. Committed to the assignment. Not a lovelorn youth with stars in his eyes.

He ended up in his rooms one night, nursing a bottle of truly foul rum. Quinn tried to take it from him but Cameron wouldn't give it up, saying he needed to finish it.

"Very well, sir. I'll retire and leave you to your abject, stupid misery. Extra strong coffee in the morning." And then Cameron was alone, staring into candle flames, wishing he could wake up somewhere else.

His wish was not granted, because he woke up in the same rooms as before. But this time the candles had drowned in their own wax, and he had a pounding headache.

"Quinn!" he yelled, then groaned at the sound of his own voice. "Quinn?" he asked, more quietly.

The valet appeared, accompanied by the blessed aroma of coffee. He stooped to where Cameron half lay on the carpet. "Drink this."

Cameron took the little cup, which contained not coffee but some vile concoction. Unfortunately, he'd already swallowed it by the time he realized the mistake.

"Bloody hell, are you trying to poison me?"

"You're doing a fine job of that yourself, my lord. Here. Coffee to get the taste out."

The coffee was thick and bitter, but familiar. Cameron dragged himself from the floor to the settee. "Is it tomorrow?"

"It's Thursday, if that's what you mean. Here are some letters to prove it." He offered a tray stacked with half a dozen folded missives.

Cam took them, sorted through them, and encountered one that was distinctly odd, the handwriting unskilled, and Quinn's name on the front. "I think this is yours."

Quinn took the letter, saw the handwriting on the outside, and went still. Then his face transformed into a hesitant, happy smile.

"That wasn't posted from Worcestershire, by any chance?"

"It was," Quinn replied, tucking the letter away in his

coat pocket.

"You're not going to read it?"

"Of course I am. Later." The valet smiled as though anticipating the reveal of a treasure, and for all Cam knew, perhaps that was exactly what it was.

"You can read it now."

"I prefer to wait, my lord. Anyway, there's work to be done." Quinn's eyes sharpened to their usual focus. "You ought to clean up. I'll shave you. You look…well, you look terrible."

After Cameron chanced a look in the mirror, he agreed. Sallow cheeks covered in stubble, bloodshot eyes, hair a fright. "Did I look this bad last night?" he asked.

"Last night's over and done with," Quinn noted practically. "Let's begin anew, shall we?"

A while later, Cameron looked far more presentable, though he still felt like he wanted to die. Quinn's awful medicine had settled his roiling stomach, but his headache remained.

Then a knock came at the door.

"Dear Lord. Turn whoever it is away, Quinn."

"Yes, sir."

But Quinn instead returned with a lady in his wake. Cameron's heart soared for one instant before he saw that the lady was not Gen. This one was smaller, with spectacles perched on her nose. But she was a lady, and she was here in a stranger's rooms, which was not a very ladylike thing to do.

"I think there's been a mistake," he said with a glance at Quinn.

"No indeed, Gemini. I'm Pandora." The woman smiled at him as she removed her large bonnet, revealing blonde curls.

Pandora. The codebreaker that Chattan had mentioned. The brilliant mathematician who was somehow linked to the Zodiac was this blonde bluestocking? Cam squinted at her. "Bit early for work, isn't it?"

She pushed the spectacles up, surveying him with a measured expression. "It's three in the afternoon, my lord."

Oh. Well, it had been a *lot* of rum. "What can I do for you?"

"It's more what I can do for you. I've gone through the papers." She held out the stack of notes from Mireille.

Cameron grew more alert as his brain snapped to attention. He moved to the table, nearly stumbling along the way. "Have a seat."

She followed with obvious hesitation. "Are you quite well?"

His headache felt like he was living inside an ever-gonging church bell. He shouldn't have drunk as much as he had for the past…week?

"I'm perfectly well. Tell me what you found."

"It's not in code," she announced, sitting down and spreading the papers before her. "I've tried every type of cipher method I know of. I also considered the cut out cipher, where only certain words on the page are relevant. But there's no single design that would fit all these pages, or even more than one page." She held up a solid black paper with several random, word-sized holes cut into it. She placed it over the top page of notes. "I made this key up as a test, and you can see it aligns with the exposed words to create the message: "Persuade King Fight Germany Next Year." She chattered away happily, obviously as enthusiastic about her field as she was competent. Cam did his best to follow along.

Pandora was saying, "But if I put the same key over any *other* page, it's just gibberish, and often no words appear or the text isn't aligned. I tried multiple keys—nothing works. Now it is possible that it is a key code, but only one page is relevant. And all the others are extraneous, distractions to make you focus on the whole rather than the part. But…"

"But what?"

"It doesn't fit the situation you described to Aries. If ninety-nine out of a hundred pages are dummies, what's the benefit in hiding them? A distraction like that only works if it's noticed."

"So what's your conclusion?"

She shrugged. "That whatever it is, it's not in code."

"So what meaning can it have? Why would a spy hide these papers in books? They must have some hidden meaning."

"Your guess is as good as mine," Pandora said. "One thing I've learned about breaking codes is this—everything must fit without changing the rules. You work with what's in front of you, not what you expect to be in front of you. If you try to make facts fit a preconceived notion, you'll lead yourself directly into a trap."

"A trap."

"Figuratively speaking. Have you considered that this is exactly what it seems to be?"

But her words gave him a new idea. "Thank you very much for working on this, but I'm afraid I have to go."

He stood up and nearly fell over.

"You need to *sleep*, my lord."

"I need to finish what I started," he retorted. "And that means not wallowing in misery and instead getting back to work!"

She stared at him, wide-eyed. Cameron winced. He was such a mess he was explaining intimate details to a stranger. Worse, a stranger associated with the Zodiac.

"Apologies. Don't need to mention this to Aries," he added quietly.

"Accepted. I'll leave the papers with you," Pandora replied. "If there is more to decode, tell Aries. I hope you're able to get to the end of whatever you're doing."

Cameron reread the papers after she'd gone, and the new idea grew in his mind. But he did also take her advice, and slept until nine at night.

Then he woke up, feeling like himself again. He dressed in his Black Mask outfit and told Quinn that he was going to return to Mireille's townhouse once again.

"Is that necessary? You went through it three nights in a row after we got back. And there is always a Disreputable watching the place, should she return."

"Now I know where to look."

Cameron headed to Mireille's home. All seemed as usual. A housekeeper prowled the environs during the day, but retired to her small apartment on the ground floor when she was done with her duties.

A maid was seen occasionally, either in the house or running errands. The Disreputables said she was a quiet sort, kept her head down, and never made a fuss.

Cam was by now very familiar with the house. He snuck in and moved silently through the rooms to the study where Mireille kept her correspondence and other items of use. Cam had already gone through the bedroom and the other rooms on the previous nights, and found nothing.

But he was no longer interested in Mireille's flat. Pandora had mentioned misdirection. Wasn't that what the agent's flat was? A temptingly abandoned space, supposedly containing the answers to what he was looking for.

Mireille was too smart to leave something behind in her flat while she went to Thorngrove. She had a better hiding place—one in plain sight, if you thought to look for it.

He looked up at the ceiling.

The house must have an *attic*. Mireille's rented rooms had no direct access, but she seized the opportunity and added the space to her realm. He left her flat by the main door, and then took the stairs on the landing up, where they indeed terminated in a small half door. He reached for the knob. Locked.

Out came the lock picks. Working as silently as possible, he got the mechanism to give way. Easing the door open, he hunched over and made his way into the dark space beyond.

The attic was filled with old crates and furniture covered in dusty cloths. There was a bolted door at the back of the house, high above the alley, where one of the Disreputables was on watch even now.

Cam made his way slowly toward that end. He had no gun with him, only a small knife. He kept the knife close, his nerves on edge.

However, it was too dark to see beyond a few feet. Cam reached the door. It was hinged on the top to open, designed to allow things to be lifted directly into the space from the alley. He propped it open to give a little light, then looked at the crowded attic.

Someone was living here. That was the first conclusion. Cam noticed an overturned crate put into use as a table, a lantern on top, and a small pallet on the floor set up as a crude bed.

A glint of green caught his eye, and he bent down to pick up an emerald bracelet. Mireille's jewelry. She was living here in secret, and must have been here since fleeing Thorngrove.

He remembered the Disreputables' reports of the quiet

maid. Mireille, no doubt, dressed in servant's clothing and wearing a bonnet to conceal her features. She bypassed the comfort of her own rooms to hide in the attic, invisible but close to her things if she needed them.

He searched the space, and after a half hour, found a stack of papers hidden away in the corner of the attic by the propped-open door. Papers remarkably like the ones he took from Mireille's room at Thorngrove.

Papers in hand, Cam turned to head back down the stairs to find the Disreputables and issue some new orders.

Then a dark shape rushed toward him, hitting him hard in the stomach.

He grunted, stumbling back toward the open door. The papers fluttered into a storm of white all around him.

Cam shook himself, standing up to fight.

He gripped his knife and slashed at the figure, hearing a woman's intake of breath as she narrowly avoided a wound.

Mireille, home again.

She held a pistol and aimed it at him. The close quarters let Cam reach out and strike her arm, knocking the gun away.

But Mireille was fast too, and kicked him hard in the chest, making him stumble back to avoid losing his balance.

The figure struck him again before he could regain his footing. The force of it pushed him off balance, too far off for him to recover. His foot slid, and then he was falling, falling, falling. He flailed, trying to turn in the air like a cat, thinking frantically that all he needed was to go back in time once—

A crash, a horrible crunch too close to his ears. A moment of shock and silence, then pain. Pain like he'd never felt before. Pure, exquisite lancing pain up and down his body, like lightning darting around, a demon plaguing him for fun. He heard a thin sound, far away, and understood it was him trying to call out, and failing.

Darkness closed over him.

♊

GENEVIEVE LOOKED FORWARD TO SABINE'S frequent visits, mostly because she was avoiding going out more than she had to, and Sabine was her only source of gossip.

On this afternoon, Sabine was especially radiant in cool white linen accented with soft pink trim, which made her silver hair and clear complexion somehow more lovely. It must have been the glow of ripe, juicy gossip on her cheeks.

"Have you *heard*," Sabine said in place of a greeting.

"I can't imagine I have," Gen replied, pouring tea.

"It's the most exciting thing in months! Tragic, of course. But what drama! The theaters will be reenacting his exploits for years."

"Who? What happened?"

"The Black Mask plummeted to his death last night."

Gen's grip on her teacup slipped, and it fell to the floor. She didn't even hear the crash. "What?"

"He was in midrobbery, on the roof of a house I hear, when…" Sabine's hand soared and then arrowed toward the floor, where she noticed the fallen dish. "My dear! Your cup!"

Gen stood up, wobbly. "It is true? He's dead?"

"Well, that's the mystery. He was seen falling, but before the Charleys could come pick up the body, what do

you think? It was gone. Just a pool of blood on the cob-
bles. They say the shadows of London took him back, and
he'll get a burial worthy of the most notorious underworld
figures. I daresay it's all nonsense, but what a story. My
darling, you're white as a sheet."

Gen felt her heart flutter weakly. "Sabine, I don't feel
at all well. Go and tell someone I must lie down?"

Her friend did just that, and a quarter of an hour later,
Gen was in her bed upstairs, having been taken there by
Sabine and Kincaid on either side of her. Sabine fussed
over her and apologized for the too-exciting gossip.

She refused to allow anyone to send for a doctor, saying she only needed rest. Sabine promised to call on her
as soon as possible, though she had to leave the city again
for a few days. After she left, Kincaid pulled the drapes so
the room was dark as night, telling Gen to sleep.

Sleep was the last thing she intended to do. Gen waited for another ten minutes. Then she slipped down the
back stairs to the driveway, intending to walk to the street
and hail a hack.

But the moment she stepped out, an urgent voice
called, "My lady!"

She whirled, only to see Quinn standing there. She
rushed to him. "What's happening?"

"Come with me," he said, grabbing her arm. "I've got
a ride waiting. Hurry."

She never needed less urging. She remembered nothing of the ride, or what she asked or what Quinn said.
Only the tight knot of tension growing in her chest.

He ushered her into a building and up a flight of stairs.
"Through there." He pointed to the door at the end of the
hall.

Gen walked down it with trepidation, not knowing
what she hoped or feared to find. There was a dim light

glowing from within, and she pushed the door open.

Cameron lay on the bed, eyes closed, his body still.

A wail escaped her lips, and then she was leaning over him, her hands flitting helplessly, fearful to touch the many bandages covering his upper body, or the bruised flesh on what few parts of him were visible.

"Oh, sweet mercy. Cameron, don't be dead. Please, I can't have you be dead. I can't live without you."

She reached for his hands, sobbing when the flesh she touched was cold and clammy. "Oh, God, no." Only after a long minute did she see his chest rise and fall.

She rubbed his fingers, willing more life back into him. "Cameron, please."

"He lost a lot of blood." Quinn's voice came from behind her. "There are broken bones. Ribs. Perhaps worse. He hit his head hard. We don't know the extent of the damage. I'd have fetched you sooner but there was too much to do…"

Gen fixated on Cameron's closed eyes. "I'm here," she told him. "I won't leave."

She climbed into the bed, intent on warming Cameron with her own heat.

Quinn didn't blink. "I'll get a kettle on" was all he said.

She had no sense of time. Her world was limited to the bed and the dim room and the sound of Cameron's breathing. She curled close to him, talking of anything that came into her head, and held his hands as gently as possible. And wished for him to wake up.

For a valet, Quinn was a good nursemaid. He always seemed to be at the ready with medicine or something to drink or a book for Gen to pass the time. Both of them tried to get Cameron to accept water or broth. The process was nearly impossible.

But for the most part, Gen was alone with Cameron and her own scattered thoughts.

Some hours later, a knock sounded on the door. "Yes?" Gen called.

"The doctor is here," Quinn called.

Gen sat up in bed, intending to look presentable before inviting anyone in. But the door swung open and a narrow-faced, dark-haired man stepped through.

"I'm Dr Cutter," he announced, showing no trace of interest in her state of *dishabille*. "Apologies for the intrusion, but I have no time to waste."

He set a medical bag on the table and opened it. "You're his wife?"

Gen scrambled out of the bed, and found her robe. "Yes. I'm…" She paused, unsure if this man was treating the Black Mask or Gemini or Lord Deverall. "I'm his wife."

"Good. It helps to have extra hands to change the bandages."

He worked briskly, but with obvious skill. No movement was wasted. Nor did he spare many words apart from curt orders for her to lift a sheet, wet a cloth, turn Cameron over, whatever needed to be done.

From time to time, Cam moaned, but never spoke.

When Dr Cutter was done, Cameron lay in the bed, freshly bandaged, breathing regularly, but with his eyes still closed.

Cutter washed his hands in a bowl of fresh, warm water, and Gen took a moment to watch him. He was wiry but not thin, and not particularly tall. He moved with controlled energy, intent on what he was looking at, rather than how he looked. He pushed his hair back from his forehead, the strands just long enough to threaten to turn into curls. She could detect Jewish ancestry in his complexion and features. She was also certain that he wasn't the sort of doctor to mince words.

"Tell me if he'll live," she said.

"He will."

Tension rushed out of Gen. "You're sure?"

"As sure as I can be. Mind, he's been very badly injured. A blow to the head. Two cracked ribs. Right arm broken in a compound fracture. But he's not in a coma. He's just severely depleted. I trust you and his man, Quinn, are following the regime of feeding him as much liquid as he'll take?"

"Yes." Water, wine, broth. Gen had spent hours trying to get precious drops of liquid between Cameron's dry lips.

"Good. The wounds are all healing well, with no sign of festering. No swelling of the head. He's extraordinarily lucky."

"He was risking his life," she muttered.

"Not a thing anyone else needs to know, ma'am. His injuries are not inconsistent with a bad carriage accident, and if anyone asks, that is the story I'd suggest."

So he knew at least something of Cameron's secrets. Perhaps that wasn't surprising—Gen was starting to understand there was a whole world out there of which she knew nothing. A world in which spies had doctors, and someone made dying thieves vanish before the law could catch up.

"I'll be around again tomorrow," the doctor said. "Have Quinn send word should there be any change before then—good or bad."

She nodded. After Dr Cutter left, she tried to feed Cameron some more liquid, moistening his lips with a wine-dipped finger. "Drink a little," she whispered. "For me. Please."

She got a few spoonfuls down, relying on his reflex to get him to swallow. Then she crawled right back into the bed, needing to be close to him. She dozed, dreaming of rooftops and black cats.

"Gen?"

She heard the voice, and woke up fully, finding herself gazing into Cameron's eyes.

"You're here," he breathed.

"Yes. Yes!" She sat up.

"Don't go. Gen, I love you."

Her heart ached. "I'm not going anywhere. Not till you recover."

Cameron's hands flexed, and she took them in her own. All the lies, all the trouble faded for a little while. Her rage dissolved in the wake of her concern for him. It would return—she knew that and welcomed it—but for now, all she wanted was for Cameron to be alive.

"How did you get here?" he asked, his voice growing in strength.

"Quinn came to the house to get me. He's gone above and beyond."

"Sometimes I think he's the only person I can trust."

"You can trust me," she said, shoving aside the fact that she'd driven him away from their own home.

"I'm glad you came." Cameron closed his eyes again. "God, my head hurts."

"There's something for that, I think." Gen got out of bed and quested among the several bottles, then gave up and called for Quinn.

When the man walked in and saw Cameron awake, he sighed in relief. "Thank the Lord. Now I don't need to find new employment."

"Not rid of me yet, Quinn," Cameron responded with a ghost of a smile.

Gen pointed to the medicine. "Which of these is for his headache?"

"None, ma'am. There's a tisane to brew up. I'll be back in a jiffy." He left, considerably more cheerful.

Over the next few days, Cameron made rapid strides toward recovery. He could hardly walk, but he stayed awake longer each day, he could move his arms and legs, and he was alert and cogent.

Dr Cutter, who visited more than once, said Cameron must have a personal angel…or devil…on his side. "But it will be weeks before you'll be anything close to normal. Expect to sleep much more than usual, and you'll have pain while the bones knit. Don't dare move that arm more than necessary, or you'll risk the bone setting crooked."

"I sleep sitting up," Cameron grumbled. "The damn arm gets more coddling than all the rest of me."

Cutter glanced at Gen, and she caught the tiniest flash of humor. "I doubt that's the case, sir. You seem very well coddled, full stop."

It was true. Gen had not left Cameron's side. When she understood what had happened, she had sent word to the house, and to her family and Sabine, that she was with Cameron and there was no need to worry for her. She refrained from mentioning his "accident." It would only cause consternation—and possibly lead Sabine to think of the strange coincidence with Gen's reaction to the Black Mask's fall, and now Cameron's injuries.

One evening, Quinn entered the room. Cameron was sitting up in bed, and Gen sat in a chair, reading aloud from Bocaccio, because it was Cam's favorite.

The valet bore a number of letters, and handed them to Cameron. Something in his look—distinctly furtive—made Gen leap up and seize the letters. Cameron was in no position to stop her, and Quinn exited the room, having foreseen a storm.

Gen saw the item that the valet was concerned about.

"Ah. Another letter from your mistress. She didn't come here when she heard of your state, did she?"

"Please give that to me. And she didn't come because I never told her, because she's not my mistress."

"So you still deny it?"

"Gen. Sweet, beautiful, wonderful Gen. I've never kept a mistress. Not before I married you, not after."

"What do you call it when you give money to a woman who's not your wife?"

"The money helps her raise her child."

"You mean *your* child."

He sighed in frustration. "He's not mine. For Christ's sake, you think I'd…"

"Why pay for a child who isn't yours? And don't you dare tell me it's out of the goodness of your heart."

"That's what *you* do, Gen. You joined a whole Society for it."

"Not one specific child, for years and years!"

He stared at her for a seemingly endless time, then said, "You want to hear the truth, Gen? Then sit down and don't interrupt me."

His expression—that rare expression that hinted of all the secrets Cameron kept so tightly bound under his mask —had her sinking onto a chair.

"I'm listening," she said. Either Cameron would finally confirm all the stories he'd denied for years…or it would be something much worse.

"The night you saw the woman in my study was the first time I'd ever heard of or met Amelia."

Amelia. He used the woman's Christian name without hesitation.

"She was absolutely intent on getting into our house

that evening," Cameron went on. "She tried the servants' entrance first, but was turned away multiple times, despite offering money to the footmen and then the housekeeper and then even Ainsworth himself to let her in. They all refused, but one of them accepted a note she wrote, which she insisted be given to the lady of the house."

"Me?" Gen asked, feeling lost.

"You, the recently married Lady Cameron. But the woman at the door addressed it to Genevieve Wendover." Her maiden name.

"I never saw a note."

"That's because Ainsworth directed the footman to give it to me. I was in a different room than you were during the party. I got the note and read it, only understanding that some stranger was insisting on talking to you. Well, I wasn't about to let that happen. I went to my study to write a reply, expecting that the woman was hanging at the back entrance. But she'd slipped around to the side of the house and saw me through the window of the study and started pounding on the French doors leading outside.

"I didn't want her to make a scene, or to give her more attention, so I opened the door and let her in, telling her to keep her voice down. She kept going on about speaking to Lady Genevieve, and I told her you were now my wife, and that no stranger would speak to you without speaking to me first.

"When she heard I was the head of the house, she changed her tactics. She said she would bring ruin down on the family of Wendover, unless she got justice for what had been done to her."

"Justice?"

"For what your brother did."

Gen was bewildered. "My brother? Roger? He wasn't even in England!"

"He'd just left. And she was pregnant with Roger's child."

"What?"

"He'd taken up with Amelia as he'd taken up with any number of women before. But this woman was different because she wasn't the usual London slammerkin he could use and then discard when he got bored. She was gentry."

"Roger would never do such a thing."

"Gen, you don't know the half of the things your brother did. He made himself a reputation among certain circles…but he managed to hide that reputation from his family and most of society. His behavior got swept into the shadows again and again.

"He'd got her pregnant, and she was well-born, so he couldn't just pay her off. And in fact, he couldn't pay her off anyway, since he'd been caught cheating at cards."

"What?" Gen had known her brother enjoyed the gaming tables a little too well, but she'd never heard that he was a card cheat.

"There were a few rumors before then," Cameron said, "but it couldn't be proven, and no gentleman would ever accuse a man of cheating without incontrovertible evidence. Then one night, Roger was caught with a queen up his sleeve, and that was it. Thrown out of the club that very night, and fled to the Continent on the next tide."

"Oh, dear." Gen remembered receiving a letter from Roger, postmarked from Paris. He'd blithely announced a sudden desire to see the sights of the Continent, but of course never revealed why he'd left England so abruptly. The full import of Roger's behavior started to filter through to her. "A man doesn't recover from that."

"No," Cameron said firmly. "And if it had been revealed a few months earlier, it would have harmed you beyond recovery as well."

Gen swallowed, finding her throat dry. Cameron never would have been able to marry Gen if Roger's cheating was known beforehand. And her younger sister would never have found a suitor. It would have been crisis after crisis, all stemming from her brother's intemperance.

She realized at last what Cameron had done for Gen and her family, keeping the secret himself and not allowing any hint of it to spread into society.

"He's unlikely to show his face in England again," Cam said then. "Meanwhile, the woman he'd ruined was left to fend for herself. Her family disowned her the moment they learned of her pregnancy, and she had no skills to pay her way in London, other than prostitution. She wanted to avoid that.

"Amelia, as I said, wasn't like the other women Roger dallied with. She was higher class, and she knew how to strike back at Roger in ways his other conquests couldn't. She was smart enough to seek out family, and just ruthless enough to threaten the one thing she knows the *ton* care about. Our names."

"So she demanded money from you to keep it quiet?"

"She didn't demand," Cameron clarified, his tone more gentle, now the worst was over. "She begged for help, and that's the help I was able and willing to provide. I never meant it to go beyond that, but as it happened, we…well, began a correspondence. Entirely platonic," he added. "She needed advice on a lot of matters, and I was the only person who knew her situation, especially at the beginning. She wrote to me, I wrote back. Occasionally, I saw her in person, but only occasionally. Through the letters, we became friends. I know how odd that sounds."

It was far from the oddest thing Cameron revealed to Gen, but she sensed that he was in some ways more nervous about explaining his relationship with this woman than he'd been about explaining his life as a secret agent of the government. Gen wasn't likely to be jealous of the government.

"What's her name? Her full name."

He paused for a moment, then said, "Miss Amelia Metcalfe."

Gen blinked in confusion, and faint recollection. "I know that name."

"The Somerstone Metcalfes," he supplied.

"But she died!" Gen said, suddenly remembering the story—only a little bit of *on dit*, but the sort of thing that stuck in one's mind: the unexpected death of a vital young woman, and a very pretty one at that.

"That was the story the family gave, to hide their shame at Amelia's condition from the world. They'd intended to marry her off to a wealthy man with a title, and instead she was ruined by a penniless card cheat. As far as I know, she's dead to her family, and her family is dead to her."

"And you supported her ever since."

He nodded once. "I paid her that night to keep her quiet, and I paid her regularly later on for…well, many reasons. It's been expensive and it's been lonely, but I thought it was for the best."

"You chose to live apart from me for three years just to keep that secret?"

"I didn't want you to suffer from the scandal if it got out."

"I suffered anyway, Cameron. I suffered from the imaginary scandal you created."

"No one blamed you, Gen. When there was talk, it was all about me."

"Not all of it. You think you know all of what got

said? You haven't been to enough afternoon teas. A lady can eviscerate someone over a cup of darjeeling if she uses the right phrase."

"I'm sorry, Gen. I never meant for it to go so far. You walked in, and you saw her, and I had no time to think of a story. And I thought that you thinking of her as my mistress would be less damaging to you than the truth. I never anticipated that you'd…" He trailed off.

"Be so prideful that I'd never let you explain later?" Gen supplied. His words changed the color of her memories from furious reds to calmer tones. The woman's tense expression, her intense unhappiness. The way she'd been holding her gown's hem—meant to show the disheveled state of her clothing, not to hitch her skirt up for any sexual transaction. "I have always been excellent at jumping to conclusions, haven't I? You must have wanted to get away from me."

"No, it was more that I told myself that it was better to be apart. That I'd be able to work as a spy more easily. And you'd be safer. But I honestly never thought it would be years. As time went on, it seemed harder to approach you, not easier. I wanted to, more than once. But the few times I saw you in public, at a party, or wherever, you always looked so…complete. A perfect lady, in no need of a devil-take-it-all husband."

"Complete? It was all I could do not to fall apart. I threw myself into charity work because it took me away from my own misery."

"You hid it very well, my lady."

"I wish I hadn't."

"I'm sorry," he said, looking utterly drained.

Gen knew he was. Everything he said had the unmistakable ring of truth. She was sorry too. For lost years. For her own refusal to speak to him again. For believing the worst, even if he encouraged that belief as an attempt to protect her and her family's reputation.

And then, without warning, she thought of the child who'd been raised in the shadow of this scandal. She asked, "The boy Peter. He's my nephew?"

"Yes."

"He lives with that woman here in the city?"

"He lives with his mother, yes. He's well cared for."

"It doesn't seem right."

"Nothing about this situation is right. But it's what happened." He exhaled, looking angrily at his bandages. "And now I'm going to fail again. I can't be a proper husband because I was trying to be proper spy, and I can't even do that anymore. I'm in no position to get the rest of the papers. I can barely walk from one end of the room to the other."

"Rest of the papers?" Gen asked.

Cameron explained that the notes were evidently not in code, and that he suspected Mireille had more in her townhouse, perhaps from more than one expatriate in London.

"Can't another agent take on the role?"

"Of the Black Mask? I doubt it. Physical training, plus familiarity with the house, plus knowing what to look for…it's too late to hand the operation off to someone new."

"So what happens now?"

"I don't know. Mireille gets away, I suppose. God damn. I still don't truly know her goals, and now I never will."

"There's someone who might be able to step in," Gen said slowly. "Someone who knows what to look for."

"Who?"

"Me."

♊

"ABSOLUTELY NOT." CAMERON LEANED FORWARD, as if he was going to get up and bar the door. "It's out of the question. It's absurd you even suggested it."

"It seems quite logical to me. I know what sort of papers to look for, and I'm not half-bandaged up."

"Gen, it's madness. I'd never let you walk into a lion's den, and this is the same thing."

"Would Mireille physically harm me?"

"She's an enemy agent. She tried to kill me. She wouldn't hesitate to kill you."

Gen felt a distinct chill down her spine, but said, "There would be no reason she has to know that I'm there to find the papers. She knows the Black Mask stole her notes—she doesn't know the Black Mask is *you*."

He paused, obviously thinking it over. "Even so, what possible legitimate reason would you have to be in her house?"

"I could ask for a donation. I asked nearly everyone at Thorngrove. Mireille even said she might consider it."

"Did she? Wait, forget I asked. You can't do it."

Gen noticed the slight weakening in his stance and pounced. "Just listen. I'll call upon her and ask for a donation. She'll invite me in. It'd be terribly rude not to. A few minutes after—"

"Forgive me," Quinn said from the doorway. He carried a tray holding something that smelled delicious. "But as bold of a plan as that is, what's the point if Mireille isn't receiving? She's been in disguise as a maid—she won't invite you in as herself."

"That's a good point," Cameron said with obvious relief.

Gen wasn't done. "Perhaps I could sneak into the house and just…poke around."

"He prefers to call it reconnaissance," Quinn noted as he placed the tray down. There were two dishes on it, and Gen realized she was starving.

"Reconnaissance was exactly what I was doing when I was pushed," Cameron explained, a bitter look on his face. "Many nights of reconnaissance, scouring every inch of the house, and nothing to show for it but a broken body."

"You'll heal," Gen said, putting her hand on his.

"But not soon enough. She'll get the papers out of the country before anyone catches her."

"Not all assignments end in success," Quinn said.

Cameron clearly wasn't soothed by that observation. "Mine do."

"What's for dinner?" Gen asked, hoping to change the subject.

Quinn revealed two plates. "Beef bourguignon."

"You're a chef as well as a valet?" Gen asked. She hadn't thought about where all their meals were coming from, but she realized belatedly that of course Cameron would never hire more servants than he had to—not when he was actually working as a spy.

"Lord no," Quinn said. "This is fresh from the neighbor's kitchen. We've had a long arrangement. They cook for two extra mouths, and his lordship pays a modest fee for the convenience. And I can stay out of the kitchen."

He left them to eat in privacy. The stress of the last few days had woken her appetite, and she eventually had to stop from licking the plate clean of the savory brown sauce the meat had been served with.

Cameron also ate, though with more difficulty. He refused to let her help him, instead raising the fork awkwardly to his mouth as he strained against the bandages.

Gen cleared the dishes, and sat on the bed next to him. "I'm sorry there's no solution."

He shrugged, still clearly frustrated. "As Quinn said, not all assignments are successful. My superiors might not be happy, but they'll understand. At least I'm alive."

She reached over to touch his face, making him look at her. "I'm very glad you're alive, you know."

The corner of his mouth twitched. "If I could, I'd flip you over and show you just how glad *I* am to be alive now."

Gen laughed, and shifted to curl up next to him, lying carefully to not hurt his chest or his arm. "Later, love. Concentrate on getting back on your feet. Not getting your wife on her back."

"I love you, Gen," he said then. "Waking up to your face was…" He paused, as if choosing his words. "It was more than I thought I ever deserved. Especially after I treated you the way I did."

"I understand why you thought you had to."

"It was sweet of you to offer to take on the Black Mask's, er, mask. But God willing, you'll never have a reason to actually do it. Mireille is beyond capture now."

Gen could sense his turmoil. He had so few venues where his actions were valued, so his work as a spy was especially important for him to excel at. "You might get another chance."

"Anything is possible." His fingers twined with hers. "But right now all that matters is us."

She smiled, leaning over to kiss him. But she knew that as gallant as he was trying to be, the failure gnawed at him.

Over those days, Gen remained close to Cameron. She went out occasionally, and let it be known that Lord Deverall had been in a rather nasty carriage accident which would keep him off his feet for a while.

At the house, she collected the piled up letters for her and Cameron, and brought them back to his rented rooms. That afternoon, they sorted through them and replied as needed, sipping coffee. It was all surprisingly domestic.

Valentin had written once more. She read the letter, which told her that he was in London now, and he would be happy to meet to discuss the sale of the pines. And now Gen was once again changing her mind.

Genevieve owed Valentin an answer however, and she resolved to give it in person. The secretary had gone out of his way to offer to help her after all. So she penned a quick reply, saying she'd call on him early this evening. Gen was going to attend Lady Charing's musicale, so a brief stop beforehand would work out well.

She dressed in the pink evening gown she'd brought back from the house—Quinn proved to be a competent lady's maid in a pinch.

Cameron's eyes widened when he saw her walk back into the room where he was lying on the couch. "You're not wearing that dress, are you? How am I supposed to remain here when I know you're floating around wearing next to nothing? It's not advisable. You'll be unescorted…"

"Cameron, you seem to have forgotten the three years I lived without the dubious benefit of your protection. I can take care of myself. And I don't need your approval to wear anything. Why do you have such strong feelings about this dress, but no other?"

"It's the dress you were wearing when I first saw you again."

His simple answer, along with the look in his eyes, took her breath away.

Quinn entered, bearing a letter. "Evening post, my lady."

Gen took the offered note, seeing Sabine's gracious handwriting on the outside. She opened it and read the brief contents. "Oh, dear."

"What?" Cameron asked.

"My friend Lady Stanfield received some bad news. Her niece passed away quite unexpectedly. I must go see her as soon as possible."

"Tomorrow morning?"

"No. This isn't a social call. Sabine needs a friend. I will go tonight, before the musicale. It won't matter a bit if I'm late for that."

She'd already arranged to meet Valentin before the musicale, but she could simply call on him a bit earlier than they'd agreed. He'd mentioned he'd be at the London house all day.

Gen left Cameron's rooms with the strict admonishment that he do nothing but rest. She would return that evening after the musicale was over.

She did not remember to pack up the letters she'd left on the small table, and when Quinn tidied up after her, he did not think to look at whose letters he was moving to the desk.

Hurrying into a hired hack, Gen ran through the list of things she had to do this evening. Speak to Valentin about her decision regarding the pines. Stop at Sabine's home to see how she was getting on after the unexpected news, and then to the musicale.

She arrived at the address Valentin gave her just as the sun was setting. It was almost an hour before her stated appointment, but she walked up the steps and knocked loudly.

After a moment, Valentin opened the door, looking surprised and not entirely pleased to see her. "My lady. You're earlier than I expected."

"Yes, I'm afraid so. My evening plans got rather muddled, but this is the time I have. If you're finishing something, I could wait in the parlor?"

He nodded after a fractional pause. "Yes, certainly. Please follow me."

He showed her to a small parlor, apologizing for the state of the room, which was rather disheveled, in a scholarly way. Shelves lined one wall, filled with bound books, papers, and notebooks. A fireplace stood opposite that, and on the far wall was a closed pocket door that led to another room.

"I'll try to be quick, my lady."

He left her alone, and she perused the books, finding that nearly all of them were in French.

After a few moments, she became aware of men's voices in the room just beyond. The rise and fall suggested a fraught topic, and both voices sounded familiar. One was Valentin, of course, but the other…who was it? She tried to place it, and only came up with a feeling of irritation.

Then, from the front of the house came a loud knock. Valentin must have excused himself to answer it, because the conversation stopped and a door slammed. Gen put down the French tome on agriculture she'd been flipping through. She'd made a mistake in coming early. Perhaps she ought to leave.

The pocket door slid open, and an obviously foxed Lord Newsham leaned in. "Who's here? Can't have a damned private meeting if there's...oh, Lady Deverall. Didn't expect to see *you*."

"Nor I you," Genevieve replied uneasily, staring at the man's red nose and florid face. What was Lord Newsham doing in this house at all, and how many drinks had he downed since he got here?

He walked into the parlor, heading straight for Gen. His gaze dipped to her neckline, and he grinned. "Lovely to see you, of course. In any shir...shircom...circumstance."

"Indeed, my lord. But I didn't wish to bother you, so I'll wait here and you can finish whatever business you have with Mr Brodeur."

His expression soured. "Damn annoying business too. Beneath me, and he knows it, but what choice have I got?"

Gen stepped back, out of range of his brandy-laced breath. "It's not for me to say, I'm sure."

"Why not, my lovely Lady Devil...Deverall. You're in the same boat, aren't you?" Then he laughed, as if he'd made a great joke. "Boat! There's some naval humor for you."

Gen had no idea what he was talking about. He was so drunk he wasn't in command of his words or his actions. "My lord, perhaps you'd like to return to the study..."

"So I can haggle prices like a grubby tradesman? I need another drink." He looked around, but saw nothing that might supply him.

"Haggle?" Gen echoed before she thought better of it. Oh, she should stay out of the man's business.

But Newsham was feeling talkative. "The damn lumber, yes. I say he ought to cough up more since it's a seller's market, and he just smiles and says that wouldn't it be a shame if news got out I was selling to the French Navy."

"Excuse me?" Surely she'd misheard.

"Boats for Boney," Newsham said, the words jumbling together. "Couple of bad harvests, and there go my profits. What else to do?"

"But you can't… It's illegal…"

"Fine words from you, my lady, but don't play holier-than-thou when you're selling your timber too."

"I'm not selling to the French! Mr Brodeur said he'd found a Scottish buyer."

Newsham snorted. "And you believed it? Brodeur told me you'd agreed to sell all those big pines. He's salivating over the transhac…transaction because they need masts like nothing else. And he found you, an easy touch who believed he just wanted to help you and your silly charity. Damn fool women. I guess they'll believe anything."

"Do not insult me," Gen snapped.

The drunken lord narrowed his eyes. "I'll do what I damn well please. You act as if you're better than everyone, a saint in the slums, whining about food and clean water when those grubby little peasants live by crime. And then you think that you can stroll about as Viscountess Deverall. Where's your damn husband now? Why can't he keep a female in line? That cad…"

Newsham moved closer, trapping Gen into a corner. "Get away from me," she warned. If she screamed, would Valentin hear her downstairs?

"Don't give me an order. You need a lesson in manners. Those slums took the lady out of you."

He reached out, grabbing for Gen's shoulder. She stepped sideways, but she had no more room to move.

"Move back or I'll scream!"

"Good, you can sc—"

Gen squeezed her eyes shut in anticipation of a blow.

But then she heard a thump, and a grunt. She opened her eyes to see Newsham sagging into a heap in front of her. Valentin stood behind him, the fireplace poker in his hand.

"What an ass," Valentin said, contempt in his voice.

Gen stared in shock at the man by her feet. "Mercy, did you kill him?"

"Sadly, no. He's merely unconscious, and will remain so for a while." Valentin looked at her. "I trust he didn't harm you in any way?"

Gen shook her head, panic making her thoughts muddy. If Newsham knew he was selling to the French Navy, that meant Valentin was an agent of Napoleon! She had to get out of here as quickly as possible. "I'm not hurt. But I am rather…shaken. I think I ought to go home."

"My dear Lady Deverall, I'm sure you do. Unfortunately, it's quite out of the question."

Gen blinked, not comprehending him. "I must leave. And in any case, I had decided not to go through with the deal. I love my pines too much. And I have another way to raise the funds, without needing to sell to the Fr…"

"The French Navy," he finished. "He told you. Newsham couldn't keep his mouth shut, but then, he is not exactly a genius."

"You work for Napoleon," Gen whispered. "Does Lucien know?"

"Certainly not. And I can't risk you telling him. So, you cannot leave." The formerly gentle secretary now looked at her with utterly cold eyes, and he raised the poker once more. "Now, my lady. You'll come to the desk and sign the contract so I can get those pines."

"I won't."

"Then I'll kill you."

"You'll kill me anyway. I know what you are."

Valentin sighed. "Very well."

The poker started to come down, and Gen flung her arms upward to ward off the blow.

A new voice spoke. "Step away from her. Or I swear I'll shoot you in the head."

Gen and Valentin both looked to the doorway where Cameron stood, gun in hand.

♊

CAMERON KEPT THE GUN TRAINED on Valentin, but looked to Genevieve, who had a stunned expression on her face.

"Cameron! What are you doing here? How did you…"

"I saw the note on your desk. The one with Valentin inviting you here to conduct some business that's flatly illegal for you to conduct." He was playing the righteous husband to the hilt, saying to Valentin, "She's married. She has no legal standing to enter into a business deal involving property. Her property belongs to me."

"There will be no deal," Gen said hastily. "It was a mistake—I came to tell him that I wasn't going to agree anyway. Come, Cameron. Let's leave."

Cam moved to Gen, who gripped his free hand like a lifeline.

"Did he touch you?" Cameron muttered with a glance at the torn fabric at her neckline.

"Valentin? No. That was Newsham."

"Newsham was here?"

"He's still here," Gen nodded her head meaningfully toward the corner.

Cameron looked, and saw a lumpy form that he first mistook for a pile of sacking, until he saw Newsham's face.

Why was Newsham lying in a heap in the corner of the room?

"He's there because he was stupid enough to reveal the truth to Lady Deverall," Valentin explained just as if Cameron asked out loud.

"He's a French agent," Gen whispered. "It turns out he's secretly working for Napoleon. He's using his time in England to buy materials on behalf of the French Navy. That's what he wanted the Greyslake pines for."

Cameron stared at the secretary, several pieces falling into place. Unfortunately, he was in no shape to take anyone, even the seemingly frail Valentin, in a fight.

He kept the gun on the other man. "I'm leaving, with my wife. Take a step and I will shoot."

Without warning, a force shoved Cameron from behind, and he pitched forward. Gen's hand was torn from his grip as she screamed in alarm.

Someone came at him as he fell. A booted foot jammed into his back. Fists. He lost his grip on the gun, and he heard the metallic clank of it hitting the floor… somewhere.

He crashed into the floor as well, pain radiating through his broken body. He let out a groan.

"Apologies, my lord," a feminine voice announced. "I seem to keep running into you."

Mireille Lambert stood above him, dressed in men's clothing, wearing sturdy boots. She held a pistol in her hand.

She pointed it at Cameron. "Do get up and sit in a proper chair, my lord. You look as if you need to."

Valentin looked annoyed that someone else usurped his position, but he allowed Mireille to take charge, staring uneasily at Cam and Gen.

Cameron crawled off the floor and sat in the nearest

chair, not having much choice in the matter. He glanced at the clock, then at Gen, trying to warn her not to take any initiative.

Her wide eyes betrayed her level of fear, but she kept quiet, pressed against the wall where she'd backed up.

"What are you doing here?" Cameron asked Mireille. "I thought you would have been long gone."

"Not quite. Ever since I returned to London from Thorngrove, I've been near you. I knew my own house was under surveillance, hence my disguise as a simple housemaid. It worked perfectly until you returned yourself, and figured out my attic hideout. No one besides the Black Mask could have taken my papers, regardless of the tales of jewels everyone talks about. And, I happened to know that you are the Black Mask."

Cam shifted in the chair. He'd recovered his breath, but he didn't want to alert her or Valentin to any move. "Did you know before I arrived at Thorngrove?" he asked the woman.

She shook her head. "I had no notion until you broke into my room that one night. Even then I couldn't be sure —after all, it was plausible that a thief would take a gamble on the Bonaparte home. They flashed a lot of wealth around from the moment they stepped on English soil. It was a fine mark."

"What gave me away?"

"The scar on your arm. I was suspicious of a mistaken robbery simply because I also had something worth stealing…and I noticed that the Black Mask was of exactly the same height and build as Lord Deverall. It's a point not many others would ever have a chance to notice, because you've always taken care to not rob houses you were staying at. But at Thorngrove, you had no choice. But I happened to feel the scar on your arm, in the darkness. Later,

I saw a similar scar on your arm when you brought your wife back from the storm, remember? You'd given her your jacket and your shirt sleeves were rolled up. You only revealed it for a moment, and only because the circumstances were so unusual. But it was the confirmation I needed."

Cam let out a sigh, as if utterly defeated. "I underestimated you."

"Don't be upset," she said. "I dare say not many people were ever given so many clues to your identity. And don't forget that I was observing you very closely, my lord. I was extremely aware of your…qualities, so that when the Black Mask stood before me, I couldn't help but match what I knew of your appearance to my unexpected guest. I still wish you would have stayed longer."

"Be glad he didn't." Gen's words cut through the room, startling Mireille. She went on, her voice more heated. "I don't understand how you can be so duplicitous. You helped me after the storm. You gave me tea. You brought that robe. You gave me medicine. Was that all just…tricks?"

Mireille's eyes opened, and she looked a little wounded. "Just because I have loyalty to a different cause doesn't mean I'm devoid of compassion. Political differences are one thing, but we are all still human creatures, are we not? Part of God's creation. You. Me. Your street urchins. The complex Lord Deverall. Even my emperor."

Gen took a deep breath, her expression softening. "Yes. You're right. Forgive me."

Mireille bowed her head, gracious in victory. "Of course."

Cameron didn't quite understand Gen's acquiescence, at least until Mireille looked away. He saw the flash of anger in his wife's eyes, and understood that she was far from forgiving Mireille. But she'd certainly made the spy think her less of a threat.

My god, that's my wife. He was so proud of her. But he still needed to know exactly what the spies intended to do with them. "So you're both spies for Napoleon. Working together."

"No." Mireille glanced toward Valentin. "I knew what he was, and I asked him for aid with my effort. He refused, though he did say he'd stay out of my way."

"Your assignment was singularly petty." Valentin scowled at Mireille as he spoke. "And threatened the more extensive, important work I was doing. I wanted you out of there as soon as possible."

"What *was* your assignment?" Cameron asked Mireille. "How did stealing Alexandrine's book figure into it?"

"My darling man, stealing her book was my sole object."

Valentin huffed in exasperation. "Sad, but true."

Cam blinked, trying to make sense of the notion. "You infiltrated Lucien Bonaparte's guarded estate, in which he and his whole family are prisoners, to steal a *book*?"

"I'm the one holding the gun, my lord. What reason do I have to lie?" She tossed the leather satchel she'd been carrying to the floor. "Have a look, my lord. Carefully. I should hate to shoot you, but I will."

Under Mireille's watchful eye, Cameron carefully examined the papers.

"These are the same notes. Almost," he added. "I remember a slightly different arrangement. The phrasing…. You recopied it all?"

"Yes. After you stole most of what I'd written, I had to disappear and steal the same information over again. It was quite vexing. Hiding on the estate, creeping about like a mouse after dark. Not at all my usual style."

"You remained at Thorngrove after we left?" Cameron asked.

"For a little while. I had no choice. I needed the information. I packed and was driven away in a carriage, but got out at the village of Grimley and snuck back onto the estate."

"All without being seen?"

"Valentin aided me at that point. He supplied me with a hiding place and food. And every night, I snuck down to Alexandrine's study and copied out her notes, which were copious, as you might imagine."

"At the orders of Napoleon."

"The emperor himself," she said proudly. "He achieved his success not just through brilliance on the battlefield but also by capturing the imaginations of millions of French people. He knows the power of a single idea, and in the new empire he is building, all ideas will come through him, or at his behest."

Genevieve said, "And he hates the notion that the second wife of his estranged brother might inspire the French public with her own story."

Mireille shrugged. "You may think it a small thing—a woman's book. And taken alone, it is small. Inconsequential. But as you point out, she is not just any woman. She is the wife of Lucien Bonaparte, the one man who has refused the emperor's love and gifts and honors, and still lives. No, she cannot be permitted to publish her work."

"You can't stop her from publishing it in England," Gen objected in a puzzled voice. "You learned all her research, but she still has the knowledge too."

"True," said Mireille. "But she is working slowly. And I will bring my notes to someone who will use them to work very quickly—the emperor's support will ensure it.

And the book will come out before Alexandrine can complete hers. No one cares about second place."

"You'll break her heart. And enrage Lucien. That's what Napoleon cares about? Hurting his own family?"

"He is the emperor," Mireille said sharply. "It is not my place to question his reasons."

"And your compatriot here works for the emperor as well," Cam said.

"I work for Monsieur Lucien," Valentin snapped.

"You work for him, but your loyalty is not so ironclad." Mireille turned to Cameron, saying, "Valentin became an agent for Napoleon years ago, after he was Lucien's secretary. It was an ideal position—he could report so many little tidbits to the emperor, not to mention carry out tasks only a man outside France could accomplish."

"And your task in England was to find a way to get supplies for the French Navy."

Valentin nodded. "As Lucien's secretary, I had access to people no one else did. Most particularly, impoverished British aristocracy with little understanding of trade, and often little scruple. For instance, Newsham knew that selling timber was illegal and treasonous, but he needed money, and he was quite willing to talk with me."

"And Genevieve?" Cameron asked.

"Far more innocent than Newsham," Valentin explained. "She once confided a need to finance her charity work, and happened to mention the attributes of her home —the unusually tall, old pines. I paid someone living near Greyslake to confirm that those trees were exactly what France needed for masts. Once I knew that, I worked to nudge her to selling them. But she had no idea why I wanted them, or the ultimate destination."

"I thought you wanted to help me," Gen said, sounding disappointed in him.

Valentin gave her a strange smile. "I did. The transaction would have helped both sides. I had no qualms about aiding you—you would have used the money for a noble purpose."

"But you would have used the lumber as masts to build ships of war."

"Also a noble cause," he said.

Mireille added dryly, "Isn't it marvelous that we're all so noble and true? It must be a great comfort to those we're forced to kill."

She raised the pistol and aimed directly at Genevieve.

♊

AT THAT MOMENT, EVERYONE HEARD a faint yell from the streets, and then a window shattered, the glass flying inward as a brick sailed in.

Gen ducked instinctively, falling onto her hands and knees, unknowingly removing herself from the pistol's range.

"Fire!" someone yelled below. "Everyone out! There's a fire!"

"There's no fire," Valentin said contemptuously. "As if we'd fall for such an obvious ploy."

Gen's nose twitched as a hint of smoke stung her nostrils. "I…I don't think it's a ploy."

Cameron turned his head toward the window. "It's not coming from out there, though…."

Gen pointed to the back door, where a thin grey veil of smoke was curling up from the gap by the floor. "Where does that lead?"

"The kitchens," Valentin said, now sounding uncertain.

Mireille inhaled as well, and her eyes widened. She reached for the papers, her highly flammable treasure.

Cameron stood and rushed toward her, but she angled the pistol directly toward him. "No, indeed, my thieving lord. These papers are mine."

At the sight of the French spy threatening her already injured husband, Gen saw red. She launched herself directly at Mireille, with no plan in mind other than to knock the woman off her feet.

Mireille emitted a short scream as Gen collided with her.

"The gun!" Cameron yelled from where he stood.

Gen reached for Mireille's arm, grabbing wildly at whatever she could grasp. Something fell with a clunk.

Mireille cursed Gen in the worst terms as she wrenched herself free. She didn't try to recover the pistol, but instead lunged for the papers, scrambling away from Gen.

Gen looked for the pistol, intending to stop Mireille.

But the pistol had not simply fallen. It had been knocked several feet away, and Cameron and Valentin were both struggling for it.

Gen stood helplessly, terrified that Valentin would seize the weapon first. Cameron was normally the stronger, faster man, but he was severely hampered by his previous wounds.

But even though Cameron's bones were broken, his will was not.

The two men scrambled for the gun, wrestling as each worked to outmaneuver the other. Cameron grunted in pain when Valentin struck his bandaged rib cage. He seemed about to fall back, but then feinted and pushed hard at his opponent with his good arm.

Valentin swung to the side to avoid being shoved to the ground. Cameron let him go, reaching for the gun that Valentin just stepped away from.

Seeing that, Valentin ran for the door. He'd just jerked it open when Cameron ordered him to stop. He'd retrieved the gun.

Valentin looked back, but didn't stop. Cameron pulled the trigger. A shot rang out, and Valentin gave a grunt of surprise and pain. But he didn't fall yet. He ran forward, and disappeared into the smoke-filled darkness beyond.

Gen looked back at Mireille, but saw only an open window, with a hook and a rope lodged into the sill. The female French agent was gone, as was the small leather satchel.

"Gen!" Cameron called. "Where are you?"

In surprise, she noticed that within the few seconds since, the room was now full of a thick haze.

"Cameron?"

"We need to get out of here. Follow my voice. Come quickly."

She moved toward him, taking his arm. "Mireille went out the window!"

"Never mind her. Come." He walked toward the main door.

"Wait! Lord Newsham!" Gen remembered the unconscious lord in the corner.

"Bloody hell." He changed direction, finding Newsham still unconscious in the corner.

Cameron slapped him hard, once, twice. "Wake up!"

"Huh? What's happening?" Newsham asked, rubbing the back of his head.

"Fire!" Gen said urgently, dragging him up by one arm.

Cameron took the other, stumbling with the unexpected exertion. "Get moving, man. The house is burning."

Bending low, Gen and Cameron assisted the groggy lord out to the landing and down the stairs. Gen could scarcely see, and she was no longer sure if she was conscious or in a nightmare.

"Put your wrap in front of your mouth," Cameron

ordered hoarsely. "Breathe through it. It may help."

It helped, but the smoke and heat were increasing by the second. Newsham stumbled and fell, causing Cameron to lose his footing as he tripped over a body lying halfway down the staircase. Valentin's body. Cameron's single shot had found its mark after all.

Gen gasped when she saw Cameron slipping on the stairs, grabbing him the moment before he fell.

"Is someone still in there? Hurry!" a familiar voice howled through the smoke.

Gen took a deep breath through the silk wrap then screamed, "We're here!"

Seconds later, shadowy figures emerged from the billowing smoke, storming up the staircase, grabbing them all and pulling them from the house.

"Over here," a someone urged her, taking her by the arm. Gen inhaled and coughed out smoke, her lungs and throat stinging. But the air in the street was fresh, and she took several more gulping breaths.

"Cameron," she gasped. "Where's Cameron?"

Someone offered her a cup of water, and she drank it without a care for where it came from or whether it was clean.

"Cameron," she repeated.

"The men are there," her companion said, pointing.

Gen saw Cameron sitting on the street leaning up against a fence. Quinn was nearby, speaking rapidly to a few of the people milling in the street, perhaps the same people who'd come in to rescue them.

She stood and stumbled over. "Cameron."

He gave a sigh of relief on seeing her awake and alert. "Gen."

She half fell beside him. "You saved Newsham's life."

He looked over at the miserable lord, who'd been

dragged to the same spot. "For what it's worth. He was willing to work with the enemy."

"So was I, evidently."

"Not the same thing at all, Gen. The moment you understood the truth, you did the right thing."

"I suppose it doesn't matter, since Valentin died. But Mireille got away. I'm sorry."

He pulled her close to him, not caring that the gaping onlookers could see. He kissed her hair. "Don't be sorry for anything. You're here. I'm here. It's over."

♊

AFTER SEEING GENEVIEVE WAS SAFELY back home and put to bed, and giving firm instructions that anyone who woke her would not just be sacked, but also beheaded, Cameron had one more task to complete.

Through nearly empty, rain-soaked streets, he made his way to the offices of the Zodiac. He was greeted as always by Miss Chattan, who ushered him in to Julian's inner office.

They could both tell the assignment was over. It was clear in Cameron's bearing and expression, all tension gone, just exhaustion left.

"Report?" Julian asked as Chattan sat at a small desk and dipped a pen in ink to record his words.

Cameron told them everything. He told them about the strange, petty task Mireille was determined to complete, which Julian considered a waste of an excellent agent's time (he respected his enemies even if he didn't like them). Cam told them about his late discovery of the presence of a second spy—the unassuming secretary who was actually buying naval supplies. He finished with the altercation earlier that evening. At last he said, "And in the end, I got the spy I didn't know about, but couldn't catch the one I was chasing for weeks."

"On the whole, I'd say you got the right one," Julian

said. "Brodeur's assignment would have had an impact on future battles at sea. Mireille's is a mere family squabble."

Chattan agreed. "I'd rather the emperor gets a book than a ship."

Julian said that Lord Newsham would be suitably punished. As a lord, he probably wouldn't stand trial for attempted treason, but there were other ways to make him pay for his poor decisions.

"Overall, I'd say it was a successful assignment," Julian decided. "We'll arrange for another agent to act as the Black Mask a few times while you, Lord Deverall, are in some very public places with dozens of witnesses of impeccable moral character. That should take care of any potential difficulty stemming from Mireille Lambert's knowledge of your identity."

Cam was not so sanguine. "She'll doubtless report the information, and someone might start tracing links among the Black Mask's victims. That could lead them to the Zodiac."

"I'm not sure that's true," Chattan said slowly. "Mireille knows who the Black Mask is. She doesn't know anything about him also being Gemini, or anything about the Zodiac itself. She discovered one secret, and she likely thinks that's the only secret."

Julian nodded, clearly reassured by Chattan's argument. "However, she does know that Lord Deverall worked as a spy in at least some way, and we must assume she'll pass that information along."

"So I'm neutralized as well," Cameron said.

"Yes, the risk of you going on another assignment is far too great. We have to protect the Zodiac. This is the end of your tenure as the Black Mask, and as Gemini. I'm sorry."

"I'm not," Cameron said bluntly. "I've been carrying

around a little too much personality, if you understand me. I'll be pleased to leave a few names behind. I can still serve the country later on, but I'll do it in the open, in the House of Lords."

Julian nodded, pleased. "The Zodiac does like to have friends in high places."

"I think you've got friends in the very highest places."

Chattan put a finger to her lips. "Hush now, Gemini. Some secrets need to stay secret."

"Not Gemini. Just Deverall now."

"You sound comfortable with that."

Cameron nodded. "I am."

He went home again at last.

His path led him directly to Gen's room. He disrobed and climbed into the bed next to her, drawing her into his arms. She gave a sleepy murmur and nestled into him. A moment later, his eyes slid shut.

When Cameron finally awoke, it was bright and dazzling daytime. Gen was up and dressed and gone from the bedroom. Her scent lingered on the pillow, and he smiled, thinking of what he'd do to her once he was fully healed and they were both in bed and awake again.

That morning, he reveled in doing extremely Lord Devil-Take-It-All sorts of things, like driving Quinn out of his mind by waffling over his choice of outfit, then having an extremely late and leisurely and large breakfast—which was in all honesty a lunch—while reading several newspapers to catch up on news he cared not one whit about. It was rather glorious.

The sunlight drew him out to the back garden of the house. Cameron inhaled. When was the last time he'd been in his own garden? Not for years.

He called for a maid to bring him the books off his nightstand, and proceeded to sit in the garden, reading simply because he wanted to. It was the most indulgent thing he'd done in months. He resolved to do it a lot more.

Perhaps Gen would want to go to the bookshop with him. Strolling inside with the intention of finding her and asking, he found a parcel lying on the hall table. He picked it up, curious.

He ripped open the parcel to find a folded note and a somewhat lumpy paper package, wrapped with little evident care.

The note was written in bold, familiar handwriting. He'd stared at Mireille's notes too much to ever forget her particular style.

The note read:

M le Masque: Though you may not believe me, I do not plan to share what I have learned about your identity. Let us call it honor among thieves. I am sure you know who to contact to sell the enclosed items for a fair price. Please use the money to further your wife's good works.

Under the envelope, wrapped in rather dirty tissue paper, was the fabulous emerald necklace and bracelet that Mireille had often worn at Thorngrove.

Cameron picked the necklace up and examined the center stone. His background as the Black Mask usually let him identify real jewels from fake with ease. And these were real. He should show Gen the emeralds. She'd be delighted to know that her project had international support.

Cameron summoned a maid. "Where's Lady Deverall?" he asked.

"Oh, she's gone out. Said she had a call to make near

Trace Street."

His pleasant state of lazy satisfaction vanished, replaced with a sense of danger. "Trace Street?" He stood up. "I'm going out as well."

"Do you expect to be back for dinner, my lord?"

"Couldn't say." In fact, if there was a confrontation between Genevieve and Amelia, it was possible no one would be coming back at all.

Ⅱ

GENEVIEVE RAISED THE KNOCKER ON the door of the address she'd found after snooping in Cameron's desk while he was out. This was probably a foolish idea. She imagined that the tightness in her stomach was rather like the feeling sacrificial maidens got when they were sent to a dragon's lair.

But it was not a dragon who answered the door.

People had called Genevieve beautiful, and they were sincere, and Gen knew she was pretty enough. But Miss Amelia Metcalfe had a beauty of an altogether different order. It was the beauty of a muse, or a saint—something far away and fragile. Her features were symmetrical and refined, with high cheekbones and a slender nose, and a high, clear forehead. Starlight blonde hair floated about her face, despite attempts to tuck it away into a practical, matronly bun. Her skin was all roses and cream, the sort of complexion that young ladies coated their skin with lotions and ointments and mysterious creams in a desperate hope to attain. And then the woman's eyes met hers—eyes of slate blue with a tinge of violet at the edges, like a late evening sky turning misty.

This was a woman who could inspire painters and poets with the slightest smile. This was a woman who should have dominated her coming out Season and become an original such as only happened once in a generation. This was a woman who should have had her pick of husbands from a collection of men stunned by her beauty.

But this woman had met Roger Wendover, and now had none of those things.

Gen cleared her throat. "Miss Metcalfe? Amelia Metcalfe?"

The woman looked at her with caution. "Yes."

"I am Lady Deverall, but I was born Genevieve Wendover. Roger is my brother."

Amelia's mist-colored eyes hardened instantly. "What do you want?"

"May I come in?" This was not a conversation suitable for the streets.

Amelia reluctantly stood aside, allowing Gen to enter the house.

It was cool in the foyer, the shades all being drawn against the hot sun. The house was very modest, but well-maintained. The walls looked as if they'd been plastered recently, and the looking glass hanging on the wall was shiny and bright.

The lady led her farther in, indicating a chair in the small parlor. "Please have a seat," she invited with little enthusiasm.

Gen sat. "Miss Metcalfe, I'm not sure how to begin. I expect that this will not be easy. Your life over the past three years cannot have been easy."

"No, but what's made it easier is your husband's quarterly payments. I suppose you know about that," Amelia said stiffly.

"I do. My brother ought to have supported you, but he proved a failure. I am very grateful that Lord Deverall has helped you."

The other lady now looked uncertain. "You are?"

"Yes. And I'm sorry that I was unaware of your plight. Until recently, I was kept in the dark."

"He never told you?"

"My husband? No. He thought it better to keep it to himself."

"And your brother?"

Gen shook her head. Roger had never been one to admit his faults, something Gen was realizing had been a trait of his from childhood. "He was good at hiding that side of his life from his family."

"But you know now. What's changed?"

"Cameron…my husband has told me everything."

"Without Lord Deverall's friendship, I would have died," Amelia said abruptly, her reticence melting. "I don't mean the money, though obviously I needed that too. I mean his friendship. His advice. Just knowing that there was a single person in London who knew my name and my predicament and still reached out a hand to help me. My own family wouldn't do that."

Gen bit her lip, ashamed she'd ever thought of Amelia as some nefarious creature.

"There was never anything between us, you know," Amelia said then. "Another man might have taken advantage of me—paying my way and thinking that gave him any privilege he desired. But Lord Deverall was a true gentleman, and a true friend."

"I am sorry that you had so few friends at a time when you needed as many as you could get."

Amelia looked at her for a long moment, then said, "Would you like to stay to tea? I have no guests expected today." She gave a sad little laugh.

"I should like that very much."

Not long after, the women were seated at Amelia's little parlor table, enjoying tea and some simple cakes

Amelia baked that morning.

"I do not intend to leech off his good nature indefinite-ly," Amelia said, as if warding off an inquiry, though Gen had not mentioned it. "I've worked to provide an income for myself. It's not much, yet, but I've made more this year than last. People find my skills quite useful."

"What is your profession?"

"I'm a scrivener," she said, gesturing to a desk in the corner. "Most people in this neighborhood can't read or write beyond a rudimentary level, so I read out the letters they receive, or write down what they dictate to me. Sometimes there's other work, and…"

"Yes?"

She blushed in admitting, "I've written some stories that magazines pay to print."

"Fiction?"

"Gothic tales, mostly. Stories of innocent women ter-rorized and threatened by dark forces…though I ensure my heroines always find their way to happiness." Amelia lifted her chin up, obviously proud that she'd never con-signed her creations to the sort of banal suffering she'd endured. "As Gratia Fitzwilliam, I've had some success."

"You're Gratia Fitzwilliam? I've read your work!" Gen said excitedly.

"You have?"

"Yes! I just finished The Castle on the Cliff! It was gripping."

"Oh, I'm pleased you liked it."

"I loved it. Why limit yourself to stories in papers? You can become a novelist, and have books published. You might become the next Mrs Radcliffe!"

"Oh, I don't have time to write a whole novel. I need to supply my publisher with a new story every month, which is already a task. And I've my son to care for, and my other work, and the house to run."

"That reminds me. I should like to discuss Peter."

At this, Amelia spine stiffened. "You shan't take him from me! I'm his mother."

"And I'm his aunt," Gen said. "He is family, and I have a duty to provide for him."

"Your husband does that."

"He offers money, yes. But is this where you truly want him to grow up?" The narrow streets, the fog-plagued air...an already sickly boy would not thrive in the city.

"What other choice do I have?"

"You could come live at my estate in the north, Greyslake. There's a big house that sits empty far too often. There's a lake, and fresh air and green trees and plenty of space for a boy to play. There's a front room that would do well as a study for you."

"I could never accept. And I would not be welcome in such a place."

"Greyslake is mine to do what I wish with. And I say you would be quite welcome."

"An unwed mother?"

"Or a recently widowed cousin... Why not write a new story for yourself?"

Amelia shook her head. "You call it a family home. What about when Roger comes back? You don't think he'll stay abroad forever, do you?"

"He won't come back to society, nor to any place I call home. I'll see to that." Gen would write him a letter, telling him she knew all, and that he'd not be forgiven without serious penance on his part—and she doubted Roger repented of a single thing he'd done.

Before Amelia could reply, a loud knock sounded. Both ladies started, not expecting the interruption.

"Excuse me," Amelia murmured. She left the room, though Gen could hear when she opened the door.

"My lord Deverall!" the cry came.

Oh, dear, Gen thought.

"Is my wife here?" His voice sounded low and urgent.

"Yes, my lord," Amelia said. "Won't you come in? Her ladyship is in the parlor."

"That's what I was afraid of," Cameron replied as he entered the room.

Gen shook her head at him. "What did you think, that I was going to storm over here and make Miss Metcalfe's day unpleasant?"

"In fact, we have just poured tea," Amelia said. "Would you care for a cup, my lord?"

"Er. Yes. I will, Miss Metcalfe." Cameron sat at the empty chair and accepted a cup from Amelia. The exchange brought home to Genevieve that although the two had corresponded for years, they'd rarely ever met in person.

"So," Cameron said after drinking a sip or two. "What have I missed?"

"Oh, not much. It's virtually settled, in fact," Gen announced with a pleased smile. "Cousin Amelia and young Peter are going to stay at Greyslake."

"*Cousin* Amelia?" Cameron asked.

"Yes. We're still working out the details of our family relationship, but we have some time before we need to have it all settled. It will provide her with the solitude to write her novels, and be a good, healthy place for Peter to grow up. She can hire tutors from town, or send Peter to school when he's of age."

"Well…good." Cameron looked only slightly stunned.

"You don't object?" Amelia asked softly.

"Certainly not. First, I have no objections, and second,

even if I did, Genevieve would trample them. I think Greyslake will be a good home for you…cousin."

Amelia smiled. "It's very odd how things work out. I thought Roger was the ruin of me. And he was my ruin, but certainly not my end."

* * * *

The next few days were a flurry of activity. Genevieve was pleased beyond measure to be back at home, not surrounded by spies, and therefore able to work without distraction. She spent hours in her study, writing letters to Society members, responding to inquiries about her new idea for a sanitation project, and recording an influx of donations. The numbers in the ledger were growing to a very reassuring amount, mostly thanks to Mireille Lambert's unexpected offering.

The maid entered, and held out the little tray with the calling card.

"A visitor, ma'am. Shall I tell him you are not at home?"

Gen read the name on the card. *Ashley Allander*. She'd never been introduced to him, though the name was slightly familiar. Curious, she said, "Show him in."

The man who entered moments later was sure to be remembered. An attitude of careless charm radiated from his eyes, and his smile made her stomach flutter.

"Lady Deverall," he said, bowing slightly. "It is very good of you to see me."

"Good afternoon, Mr Allander."

"I know we've never been formally introduced, but this is more in the nature of business, rather than a social call, so I hope you can forgive me." He looked very confident that he'd be forgiven. Gen suspected that was how he lived his life.

"What business is that?" she asked, not offering forgiveness immediately.

"I refer to your endeavor to aid the street children of London by housing them and providing clean water for their needs. I am here to deliver a donation to your cause," Mr Allander replied.

"Oh, you wish to donate?" she asked hopefully.

"Well, no. That is, yes I would, but this donation is not mine. I'm merely an agent."

"On whose behalf? Or is it anonymous?"

He nodded. "To the public, yes. They might not be impressed by a former prostitute's generosity."

She blinked, sure she misheard. "Excuse me?"

"Before she left the country, Miss Regina Fox had heard of your efforts."

Genevieve felt a mild shock on hearing the name of the Lady in Gold, a woman who figured in so many scandalous and strange stories that she sounded more like a myth than an actual person.

And then she saw the amount Miss Fox had instructed her bank to withdraw, and felt a larger shock.

"Since you don't move in the same circles"—he coughed meaningfully—"she asked me to pass her gift on to you, with this letter." He handed it to her.

"I wish she had not done so," Gen began to say, looking from the letter to him.

Allander's expression tightened, and she hurried on, "I mean, I wish I might have thanked her in person. This is an incredibly generous contribution. And Miss Fox must have some...unique...insights into the plight of many of the young girls we hope to aid. I should have liked to meet her, however unconventional such a meeting might be."

He relaxed, and even looked a little wistful. "Yes, I think you and Reggie would have been friends."

Reggie. "You know her well."

"Very well." He did not elaborate, and she did not pry. Gen realized that simply by using that particular name aloud, Mr Allander allowed her to glimpse the depth of his friendship with Miss Fox. Well, it was none of Gen's business in any case.

So she just said, "I would be obliged if in a few days I could send you a reply to forward to her, as I do not know where she is now."

"I'd be delighted," he said.

"And you mentioned you also wished to donate?" Gen pressed.

"You're persistent, aren't you, my lady?" He reached into a pocket and produced a banknote of a large denomination. "Nothing close to Miss Fox's pledge, but I hope it will help."

"I'll write you a receipt," Gen said happily, taking the banknote from him.

It was at that moment Cameron walked in. He stopped for a moment, taking in the scene of Genevieve alone in a room with a man she'd never had a formal introduction to, the money between them. Not unlike what she'd seen when she walked into Cameron's study three years ago.

Allander said, "Don't worry, my lord, it's not what it looks like."

Cameron responded, "It looks like you're offering a donation to my wife's charity efforts."

"Oh, well, then it's exactly what it looks like." Allander's smile was sly.

Gen's cheeks were burning as she thought of how badly this new encounter might have gone. "Your receipt, Mr Allander." She handed the paper to him.

He stood and accepted it with the same sly smile. "Thank you, my lady. I look forward to the letter you'll be sending to me in a few days."

Cameron's eyebrow did go up at that.

"So you may forward Miss Fox my thanks," Gen said hastily.

Allander left, giving Cameron a slightly mocking bow before he sailed through the door.

"So," Cameron said, turning to face her. "I find you in a room with a man whose past is more scandalous than nearly anyone else still walking around London."

"Is it?" she asked with interest.

"Allander? Absolutely. He's a deplorable rake, who's been called out by half a dozen men for the crime of seducing their wives."

"Oh."

"Not to mention being the longtime paramour of the city's most celebrated courtesan."

"Miss Fox, yes," said Gen. "He did imply a…close friendship."

"That's one word for it."

"You didn't think I was up to any sort of wickedness, did you?"

Cameron laughed. "You are not a wicked woman, sweet Gen." He leaned in closer, dropping his voice. "Though sometimes you show a wicked streak, such as when you're wearing nothing but a black silk blindfold."

Gen felt fire in her veins, but she whispered back, "Perhaps you'll be the one wearing it tonight."

His arms slipped around her, and his lips were on her throat. "Tell me more."

♊

Late Autumn 1811

CAMERON LOOKED OUT OF HIS window at the still-new vista. A green lawn swept down to a lake, the surface smooth as pewter on this still, cloudy morning. Around the edge of the water, a few trees glowed orange and red, but the majority remained green, for they were lofty, elegant pines, currently wearing scraps of morning mist like veils.

The scene was peaceful, and Cameron took a deep breath, enjoying the complete lack of any excitement. Yes, Greyslake was well worth keeping.

As he stood there, he caught sight of two figures crossing the lawn. Gen wore a dark green gown, and Cousin Amelia wore rose. But both wore pelisses cut from the same sturdy brown wool, and despite their very different features, there was something sisterly about them.

Gen's true sister Gloria would be coming for a visit soon, along with her parents.

Of Roger, no one had heard a thing ever since the family arranged to send him one hundred pounds, with a note that until he made amends for his many transgressions, it would be the last money he'd ever see from them.

Though Cameron knew that Gen and her family held out hope that he'd see the error of his ways, he bet that Roger was gone for good.

His growling stomach reminded him that breakfast

waited below. He walked down the stone stairs, marveling at the solidity of Greyslake. The oldest part of the house had once been a castle, and it bore its age with grace. Thick carpets muffled the sound, but he could imagine knights and ladies still moving through the halls.

Downstairs, the aroma of coffee drew him to the long room where breakfast was served on the sideboard.

Then his parents walked in. They were visiting until the beginning of the Season, at which point they had to return to London. Cameron smiled at his mother, who greeted him with a cheerful good morning.

One of the best things about his new life was the restored affection between him and the people he cared about. His mother still knew nothing of the truth behind Cameron's old behavior, but she was ecstatic that her son was now an attentive husband, expectant father, and proper viscount.

They'd just finished eating when they heard the voices of Gen and Amelia down the hall.

"Oh, excuse me," Edith said. "There was something I needed to ask Genevieve before I forget." She hurried off.

Cameron's father looked amused. "Like a flock of birds when they all get together. I shouldn't wonder if your mother isn't up to something. Planning a party or some event."

"Let them," Cameron replied, complacent. He stood up. "Care to sit outside? I don't know how many more days we'll have before the mornings grow too cold."

On the slate veranda, the two men sat facing the lake. The air was crisp, but not biting.

"Well, my boy," Lionel said. "What's on your mind?"

"I am very glad to be home," Cameron responded, which was as true as anything else.

His father chuckled. "It is a good home, isn't it? This

is a beautiful place. And this view—the lake, the pines. Magnificent. It would have been a crime to sell it."

The great trees towered over the near landscape, their branches spreading wide, shadowing a large part of the visible lawn.

"Genevieve is happy to be home too," he told his father. "She says it feels peaceful."

"You're both in need of a little peace, I'd imagine."

Cameron wasn't sure how much his father knew, so he thought it best to confess all. "This isn't just a rest, you know. I mean, it is for Gen. We'll stay here until she has the child. I don't want her traveling. But for me…I won't be Gemini any longer. Too much happened, and there's too much risk of my real identity being connected to the Zodiac. I'm sorry."

"You did what needed to be done. Your service with the Zodiac was honorable, and you should never apologize for it."

"But I could have done more…"

"You have other duties. Your wife needs you. Your family needs you. Aries is well aware of that. There are twelve signs in the Zodiac, but the people who bear those signs change. The Zodiac was designed that way, and the Astronomer doesn't need anyone who can't fully commit to the Zodiac. You did your part. Now you have a new role, here at Greyslake."

"Just as well, since Bainbridge House already has a marquess," Cameron said, looking at his father. "And you're not leaving anytime soon."

"God willing, I'll meet not just my first grandchild, but several more! However, I want to enjoy the life I have left. That means you, Cameron, must take on more of the responsibilities of the title. You'll get to know the running of the estate, and what I'm working on in the House of

Lords. You'll be well prepared when my time comes to leave this earth."

"Not for years."

His father nodded. "That is my intention. I have much to teach my grandson as well, when he arrives."

"You're awfully certain it will be a boy. I heard you prognosticating to the neighbors the other day."

"I had a dream," his father said confidently. "And if it's a boy, he'll have a playmate in his cousin Peter."

"I hope so. The boy's been much healthier since Amelia brought him here."

"Such a shame her husband passed away so soon after their marriage. Lost at sea! Tragic."

"She'll endure."

"I imagine she will. Lovely lady. She reminds me of someone…can't think who."

Cameron skipped quickly to the next subject. "Do you think you'll be able to bring the London Water New Sanitation Act before Parliament when the session starts?" Gen had talked endlessly about her new pet project.

"I will certainly do my best. The companies that supply water to the city won't like it. They claim that the Thames water is clean enough."

"It's not. It must be filtered before it goes to households. And the companies must not draw water from the river past the point of…"

"Enough, my boy. I'm convinced, remember. You and your persuasive wife took care of that."

"I took care of what?"

Cameron looked over his shoulder to see Gen standing there.

"We were talking about the water bill for Parliament," he explained as both men stood up.

Lionel added, "I was warning Cameron that it might

take a while to succeed. There will be resistance."

"Then we shall work harder to bring the politicians around," Gen said. "They'll fall in line once the people make their wishes clear."

The older man chuckled. "Listen to her, Cameron. She's going to be your finest councillor." He bowed his head. "Now, if you'll excuse me, I've got to find out what mischief Edith is up to."

"In the front parlor," Gen advised him as he walked to the door.

Cameron waited a moment, then reached for Gen's hand. "He's right, you know. You're the best thing about me."

Gen looked down at their entwined fingers. "You know, I was never quite sure why you chose me. Many women know how to host a party and what the right thing to say is…"

"Gen, I wanted you because I liked that you had a different outlook. That you cared about things beyond your own little sphere. I wanted a wife who I could talk to about whatever matters came up, someone who reads the newspapers and understands what we're facing. Yes, I courted a few others, and they were perfectly pleasant. They were exactly the sort of lady they'd been brought up to be. Nothing wrong with them. But they weren't you. They didn't make me excited to see them. You did. I can't explain it."

"You were excited to see me?" she asked shyly.

"Every time." He leaned over to lay a kiss on her lips.

Gen sighed, leaning into him. "I hope we'll still feel this way in fifty years."

"I'm game if you are."

She smiled at him. "You're on, my lord."

ABOUT THE AUTHOR

Elizabeth Cole is a romance writer with a penchant for history. Her stories draw upon her deep affection for the British Isles, action movies, medieval fantasies, and even science fiction. She now lives in a small house in a big city with a cat, a snake, and a rather charming gentleman. When not writing, she is usually curled in a corner reading...or watching costume dramas or things that explode. And yes, she believes in love at first sight.